BY ROSALIND LAUER

A Simple Winter

A Simple Spring

A
Simple Spring

BALLANTINE BOOKS TRADE PAPERBACKS

NEW YORK

A
Simple Spring

A SEASONS OF
LANCASTER NOVEL

Rosalind Lauer

A Ballantine Books Trade Paperback Original

Copyright © 2012 by Rosalind Lauer
Excerpt from *A Simple Autumn* copyright © 2012 by Rosalind Lauer

Published in the United States by Ballantine Books, an imprint of
The Random House Publishing Group, a division of
Random House, Inc., New York.

BALLANTINE and colophon are registered trademarks of Random House, Inc.

All scripture taken from *The Zondervan KJV Study Bible.* Copyright 2002 by
Zondervan. Used by permission of Zondervan Publishing House.

This book contains an excerpt from the forthcoming book *A Simple Autumn* by
Rosalind Lauer. This excerpt has been set for this edition only and may not reflect
the final content of the forthcoming edition.

Library of Congress Cataloging-in-Publication Data

Lauer, Rosalind.
A simple spring : a seasons of Lancaster novel / Rosalind Lauer.
p.   cm.
ISBN 978-0-345-52673-1 (pbk.) — ISBN 978-0-345-52674-8 (eBook)
1. Amish women—Fiction.   2. Musical ability—Fiction.   3. Lancaster
County (Pa.)—Fiction.   4. Christian fiction.   5. Love stories.   I. Title.
PS3612.A94276S54 2012
813'.6—dc22
2012000456

Printed in the United States of America on acid-free paper

www.ballantinebooks.com

2 4 6 8 9 7 5 3 1

First Edition

Book design by Karin Batten

In memory of my grandmother,
Frances Witker Lauer,
who followed the song in her heart,
attending college in an era when few women
dared to leave the kitchen.
Her fondness for the English language, her passion for travel,
and her love for her family live on today,
along with the recipe for the best tart green apple pie
I've ever tasted.

PART ONE

Follow the Sun

"It is a good thing to give thanks unto the Lord, and to sing praises unto thy name, O Most High; to shew forth thy lovingkindness in the morning, And thy faithfulness every night."

—PSALM 92:1–2

*O*h, send the sunshine down my way. . . ." Sadie King sang the bright song to the green juniper bushes and the chickens and little Sam and Katie and anyone else who wanted to listen on this glorious morning.

All around her on the King family farm, plants and animals were coming alive, blossoming and sprouting green leaves and pushing up strong shoots through the earth. Birdsong filled the air around them, along with the scents of honeysuckle and warm grass. The sweetness mixed with the sharp smell of the fields, where her brothers had turned manure in to the warming soil to make it fertile for more things to grow.

Signs of spring surrounded her and she poured her joy into the melody that flowed from her heart. God was renewing the farm, breathing life into everything.

Including her.

Sadie was in *rumspringa,* and her new life included an Englisher boy named Frank Marconi and the wonderful good bounty of music he had shown her. Music outside the Amish community wasn't just used to praise God. There was jazz and rock and roll, music to dance to, folk music, and songs to sing along to. The English had songs to make you sad and songs that made you feel like you were soaring between puffy clouds.

Like "Blossom," the song she was singing this morning as she steered her youngest siblings toward the chicken coop.

"Stay out here, Katie. You can start feeding them." Sadie removed the heavy lid from the seed bucket and grabbed a small handful.

Two-year-old Katie giggled as she tossed feed onto the ground, attracting the flapping hens. "Eat now! Eat!" she ordered, enjoying this almost as much as the chickens.

"Why do we gather eggs twice a day?" Sam asked as he shooed a handful of hens from the coop. At the age of five, Sam was full of questions.

"If we let the eggs sit for too long, the chickens might hop onto them and break them," Sadie explained as she reached to the hook inside the coop for a pair of leather gloves. "Besides, we want our eggs to be fresh as can be."

Most of the chickens had fled the coop, but as usual cranky Lumpig perched on the edge of a nesting box. Her beady eyes dared anyone to come close.

"She always stays inside." Sam put his pail down, frowning. "Why is she so mean?"

"She's just keeping watch over her little treasures. Aren't you, Lumpig?" Sadie held up her handful of feed for the hen to see, then tossed it out the doorway, onto the ground outside the coop. "Skit-skat."

Immediately Lumpig hopped from the nest, flapping her wings and scurrying to her breakfast.

"How do you do that?" Sam asked.

"Just distract her with the feed."

"Can I do the eggs today?"

"That's fine, but mind you're quick about it. Lumpig will be back to guard her eggs again." Sadie reached for the broom. "You do that, and I'll sweep up." As she started to sweep old hay and manure from the corners of the small hut, she launched into a song that made her think of Frank.

"Daydreaming and I'm thinking of you. . . ." When their band was choosing music to learn, Frank always wanted songs that Sadie could belt out, songs that allowed her to hold the notes a long time. "Bluesy songs," he called them.

"Look at my heart," she sang, caressing each note with her voice.

Sam worked just fine while she sang; he never minded her music, though one day he noted that she knew a lot of songs. And why did he not hear Sadie's songs at Sunday church?

"Because . . . ," Sadie had stammered, not sure how to explain the hundreds and thousands of songs to be learned and enjoyed in the world beyond their Amish faith. "Because they're not in the *Ausbund*," she had told him.

Sam seemed satisfied with her answer, but it shifted Sadie's thoughts to the Ausbund, a book published over four hundred years ago. There was no music printed in the book, only words, but the melodies had been passed down over generations. Was that the reason why music seemed to be part of her very soul? Even as a little baby she had been brought by her mamm and dat to Sunday services, where *Vorsingers* led the congregation in song. Over time, the German songs were carved into each person's heart.

Amish songs were very different from music in the Englisher world. Sung without an organ or piano accompanying it, an Amish song was slow and haunting. Sometimes it took more than fifteen minutes just to do three stanzas. Most of the songs in the Ausbund had been written by Anabaptists while they were prisoners in the dungeons of Passau Castle so very long ago, back in the 1500s. Amish songs were the music of her childhood, part of her heritage. Sadie believed they had unlocked the voice inside her and opened the door to her curiosity about music.

All music.

She had met Frank because of music. They both worked at the Halfway Hotel, Sadie as a housekeeper and Frank on the maintenance staff. One day Frank had heard her singing as she pushed her cleaning cart down the hotel corridor. She'd been singing a popular hymn that teens might do in youth groups. She couldn't remember what exactly, but she did remember how he came tromping down the corridor with a rake in his hand.

With his dark hair that stood up straight from his head and the little triangle of a beard on his chin, Frank had frightened her at first. He was just a bit taller than her, but his shoulders were broad and he reminded her of an angry bull as he stomped toward her. Oh, he'd scared her.

"Is that you singing?" he demanded, leaning the rake over one shoulder. "What's a church girl like you doing with a voice like that?"

She pressed a hand to her mouth. She had already stopped singing.

"What's the matter?" He squinted, studying her. "Are you shy?"

"I . . . I thought you were mad."

"I'll only be mad if you let a voice like that go to waste. Do you do any singing professionally? Choir? Band? The shower?"

She laughed aloud, and that eased things between them. Although Sadie wasn't comfortable talking while she was supposed to be working for her boss, Mr. Decker, she agreed to meet Frank after work. They went across the street to the pizza place, and Frank bought two slices of cheese pizza, one for each of them to eat while they chatted.

The whole thing still made Sadie's heart race when she recalled how she had gone on her first date with an Englisher, just like that. They had talked and laughed, and before they parted she agreed to sing for him—just one verse of "Silent Night" in the parking lot.

Oh, the courage she'd had that night! And foolishness, too. Dates with strangers in town and performances in dark parking lots were not the sort of activities Amish girls engaged in. Even Amish girls in rumspringa, their "running around" time as teenagers.

But Sadie knew she was no ordinary Amish girl. It wasn't about *Hochmut,* or pride. She wasn't proud of the fact that she was different. But there was something driving her from inside, something in her heart, and she believed it was Gott pushing her to use the gift that He'd given her—her voice. All good things came from the Lord in heaven, and she was grateful to have music in her heart.

Soon after she met Frank, he brought his friend Red to meet her after work. And a few days later, the three of them, along with a girl named Tara, were "hanging out" in Red's garage, making music. Real music! Red had a drum set and a deep voice, thick as molasses. Tara played bass guitar, which Sadie was convinced was music from the belly of the earth. And Frank's fingers danced over his guitar, finding melodies or strumming to make a field of sound that surrounded Sadie's voice, broader and bolder than any field she had ever worked.

The band had been rehearsing at least once a week ever since, and they'd even taken some trips in Frank's van to Philadelphia to perform some songs at clubs. These clubs allowed groups to come up to the microphone and give it a try. "Open mike night," Frank called it. So far Sadie enjoyed performing with her band, but she hated having to sneak away from home to do it. She had never lied about what she was doing—not exactly—but she suspected that their bishop would not approve if he ever found out.

Phew! It made her heart heavy to worry about such things . . . especially on such a beautiful spring day. And she had much to look forward to today. After she finished her chores here, she would scooter into Halfway and work a shift at the hotel, cleaning rooms and pushing the big, growling electric vacuum over the rugs. She wasn't sure if Frank was working tonight, but the band would surely be practicing at Red's house in the evening, and that was the part of her day that truly warmed her heart.

She pushed the load of dirty hay into the compost heap. It would make good fertilizer for the vegetable garden.

Having finished with the feed, Katie squatted down with a stick in hand, scratching in the dirt. Katie loved her crayons and was always drawing something.

Sadie and Sam made quick work of putting fresh straw in the henhouse.

"Can I carry the eggs?" Sam asked. He was a good boy, always wanting to take on more grown-up jobs on the farm.

She tested the buckets, finding the lighter one. "Ya, you can carry this one. . . ."

As they walked down the lane, little sparrows chirped and jumped in the dense bushes, while a handful of blackbirds soared overhead, heading toward the barns and silos, then circling to the right, down toward the fields and pond.

"Look at those birds, so happy to be flying over God's land," Sadie told the little ones. "Our dat used to take care of them, putting out seed and making sure they had a safe place to live."

"And now he watches them from heaven," Sam said.

Sadie smiled. "Ya." Sometimes, when she was singing, Sadie felt like those birds, gliding on the wave of a breeze. The music could lift her right out of these old sneakers. She couldn't wait for tonight's rehearsal. She was already dressed and ready to leave the farm, with her blue jeans on under her dress, the cuffs rolled up over her knees so no one in the family would notice.

Sam moved the bucket to his other hand and hitched up his straw hat. "Adam's coming."

Sadie raised one hand to shield her eyes from the sun. Ya, Adam was heading this way, moving like a ram with his head lowered. Something was wrong, and Sadie had a feeling it had something to do with her. Now that their oldest brother was the head of the household, they seemed to butt heads often. Although he understood that rumspringa permitted her certain freedoms, he wasn't as generous as Dat had been about letting her make her own choices and mistakes.

Although Sadie adored the small freedoms of rumspringa, she did her best to respect Adam and the church leaders. She had taken on the henhouse chore this morning because she wanted to stay out of the way of her brothers and the visiting men, who were bustling around the farm in the excitement of change. After months of preparation, pouring cement for stanchions and erecting a new milking barn, they were expecting the arrival of milking equipment today. It would be powered by a generator, so they would be following the rules of the Ordnung, but once it was all set up, what an easy task milking would be! Adam said that there would be hoses with clamps that you hooked onto the cow's teats. Hook it up and it milks the cow, one, two, three! Just like that! Sadie was glad that milking would be easier, though in her mind any amount of time spent milking cows was too much. She didn't mind hard work, but sometimes she felt overwhelmed when chores filled every minute of the day with no time to escape to Frank and her music.

As Adam came down the lane, a straw hat covering most of his dark hair, she wondered what his chin would look like with a marriage beard. Although Adam and Remy wouldn't be published until the fall, there was no doubt in Sadie's mind that her brother would marry come wedding season. And that was wonderful good. Adam seemed to have a lighter heart since his soon-to-be wife, Remy McCallister, had come along.

When Adam reached them, they were just passing the Doddy house where their grandmother had lived alone in the years since their doddy had passed away.

"We got the eggs." Sam held up the smaller bucket with authority.

"We got eggs!" Katie repeated, still holding on to her drawing stick.

"*Gut.* You and Katie take your bucket to Mary. She'll show you how to clean them."

"I know how to do that," Sam said.

"Then go," Adam said. "Ask Mary to prepare a cooler with lunch for Sadie and Susie."

Sadie gripped her own pail tighter, shaking her head as the little ones turned toward the house. "What's wrong? Is Susie sick?" Their sister Susie suffered from glutaric aciduria, a disease that might have killed her if it weren't for the help of their doctor.

"She's fine, but she has an appointment with Dr. Trueherz today." Adam tipped his hat back, his body rigid. At times like this, Sadie could see responsibility sitting heavy on her brother's shoulders. "You know I usually take her, but I have to be here when the milking machines arrive. You need to take her to see the doctor."

Sadie blinked. "All the way in Paradise?" By horse and buggy, the trip would take an hour each way. "That will take the rest of the morning and part of the afternoon, too."

"Ya. We'll handle the rest of your chores here," Adam said.

"What about the hotel? I'm due there by eleven."

"Call Mr. Decker from the phone shanty. Tell him you can't make it today, or that you'll be late."

"Why can't someone else take her?" Sadie's throat grew tight as the prospect of her wonderful day began to slip away. "Why can't you ask Mary? Or Remy? I'll scooter over to Uncle Nate's and see if she can come immediately." Adam's girl, Remy, an Englisher, had moved in with their uncle Nate and aunt Betsy when the bishop advised her that she needed to live Plain if she was serious about joining the Amish community.

Stepping closer, Adam put his hands on his hips, his tall frame suddenly blocking the sun. "You are to do as you're told and don't ask so many questions."

"But it's not fair when I have a job to do, and—"

"Don't question my decision," he growled.

"What's all this chatter about?" Mammi Nell appeared at the white fence by the Doddy house.

Sadie's breath caught in her throat, and Adam turned to their grandmother, dropping his hands to his sides.

"I could hear you from the vegetable garden, cawing like two angry jays." Their grandmother stepped through the gate, her eyes stern behind her spectacles. "What's the matter?"

"Susie needs someone to take her for a checkup," Adam explained. "Jonah, Gabe, and I are tied up with the new equipment that should be here any minute. Nate and his sons are on their way, and Mary and Remy have their hands full preparing lunch for all the men who've come to help out."

Sadie frowned, wishing Adam had explained all that to her instead of just trying to order her around. Still, she hated to miss work . . . as well as band practice.

"And you are supposed to be at your job?" Mammi Nell asked Sadie, who nodded. Creases formed around the older woman's mouth as she mulled it over. "And this is what the two of you are snapping about on this beautiful morning?"

Sadie and Adam both looked down at the ground.

"Adam, you are the head of this family now, but sometimes a parent forgets what it's like to be a young person."

Sadie couldn't resist a peek as he lifted his face. Adam had left home when he was eighteen, and only the deaths of their parents had brought him back. Sadie knew that he regretted leaving, but he didn't speak of his adventures in the world.

"Do you remember your own rumspringa?" their grandmother asked him.

His brown eyes were warm with regret beneath the brim of his straw hat. "I do, Mammi."

"Don't forget it. And Sadie, your brother Adam is a good man, and a family must follow the man at the head of the table. You must listen to Adam and try to help." Sunlight flashed on Mammi's glasses as she looked from Sadie to Adam. "Now, the two of you can work this out in peace, ya? If Sadie cannot get out of work at the hotel, maybe you'll find a driver to take you to Dr. Trueherz's clinic. It's too late to hire anyone, but you might try a friend. Maybe Lucy Kraybill or Nancy Briggs. If that doesn't work, I'll take Susie myself."

Sadie's eyes went wide at the thought of her grandmother driving a buggy to Paradise. Although she was moved by Mammi's offer of help and glad to have her grandmother on her side, she worried about the older woman driving an open buggy for nearly thirty miles. With local farmers working their fields, there was much traffic on the roads these days, and Mammi got tired easily.

"The appointment is at ten," Adam said hesitantly, and Sadie sensed that he shared her concern about their grandmother's driving. "But Sadie can go to the phone shanty and see if she can contact someone to drive."

"Gut." Mammi wiped crumbs of soil from her gloves. "You work it out, and don't let me hear angry voices again." She turned toward the garden to go back to her weeding.

"I'll ride my scooter to the phone shanty. I'll try to find a driver," Sadie said as she and Adam headed toward the farmhouse. Once she was out of sight of the house she could stop and try her cell phone, but she usually didn't get a strong signal out here in "the boondocks," as Frank called it.

"You can try. But if you can't find anyone, this is your responsibility, Sadie. I don't want the chore passed on to Mammi."

Sadie bit back an angry answer. She wanted to point out that her brother could have explained the circumstances better, that he could have told her Mary and Remy were busy. She also would have agreed that Mammi wasn't fit to make this trip. But she kept mum. It wouldn't be right to argue. Adam was in charge.

She was glad when he turned off toward the milking barn. "Mind you get Susie there on time," he said before pulling his hat down and striding away.

Oh, how she wished it was proper to speak her mind. She had a few things she would tell brother Adam. Why did he wait until the last minute to tell her that Susie needed a ride to the doctor's today?

Her oldest brother had become mean and bossy, so different from Dat. Their dat had believed in letting all living things fulfill their potential. It was one of the reasons that Levi King had turned this farm into a sort of sanctuary for birds and frogs and all of God's creatures. Dat would not have been so critical of Sadie. This wouldn't be happening if Mamm and Dat were here.

But Gott had chosen to take them.

And so Adam was the head of their family now, which made things difficult for Sadie. Here she was, eighteen years old, and still being treated like a young girl who'd just as soon skip through the meadow as she would take care of the livestock. Sadie was a hard worker, but Adam didn't see that. He didn't see her baking or cleaning or mucking the barn. The only time Adam seemed to notice her was when she was going against Amish ways by heading into town on her own or singing along with her iPod, a device not allowed by the Amish but tolerated as one of the Englisher things teenagers explored in rumspringa.

Rumspringa allowed Sadie a bit of freedom here and there, but it was not the wild time the Englisher people talked about. Amish youth were still expected to follow the Ordnung, the system of unwritten rules that had been upheld by their families and brethren over many years. The Ordnung was to be strictly adhered to, especially by baptized members. Under the Ordnung, there was a rule for every part of your day, from the clothes you wore to the way a farmer plowed his field.

All of her life Sadie had followed these rules. They were part of her nature now, and most of the time Sadie loved her life here in Lancaster County. From planting to harvest, from sunrise to sunset, days on the farm were chock-full of work and rich with love and laughter. For all her fun with the band and her music, Sadie was always happy to come home at the end of the day and drop off to sleep in the big room upstairs that she shared with her younger sisters.

She was in a pickle. Though her heart told her to cherish and follow her music, she didn't fully understand the Lord Gott's plan for her. There wasn't really a place for a girl singer in the Amish community, and yet she wanted to abide by the rules of the Ordnung and still allow her gift to grow.

It was as if she were trying to capture night and day in a single jar.

And Adam didn't have the first clue about her problem.

Her jaw was still set with resentment as she toed off her sneakers on the screened porch, ignoring the clatter of the kitchen, where one breakfast shift was finishing. She swung the pail of eggs through the kitchen doorway, nearly mowing down her younger brother Simon, who was about to leave for school.

His eyes were wide as quarters as he held his lunch cooler

against him. "What's the matter, Sadie? You look grumpy as Lumpig."

Sadie sucked a breath in through her teeth and shook her head. "Never mind." She put the pail of eggs on the counter with a thump that brought a stern look from her older sister, Mary. "You'll understand when you get older."

"Older folk always say that to me, but I don't think so." Simon took his straw hat from a peg on the wall. "I don't think I'll ever understand."

"A wise boy," Jonah said, pressing his own hat to his chest. Twenty-three-year-old Jonah was only a year younger than Adam, but very different, with a quiet manner and a true knack for farming. "And you're probably right, Simon. I don't think we'll ever understand the goings-on in a woman's head."

Simon hid a grin behind the brim of his hat, and Sadie couldn't help but crack a smile. Such a tender heart, their Simon. It was always good to see merriment in his eyes.

"Off with you now, or you'll be late for school," Mary said, shooing Simon out the door. "I reckon Ruthie and Leah are already halfway down the lane."

"But I'm a fast runner. Don't forget, I run with the horses."

"Let's see how fast," Jonah said, stepping out the door behind Simon.

"Good thing they're gone," Sadie said, sorting through the eggs. "Simon is so attached to Adam, I didn't want to say anything in front of those young ears, but Adam is picking on me again. We got into it right in front of the Doddy house, and Mammi was none too happy about it."

Mary let out a breath as she nodded toward the egg pail. "There's a crack on that one. Quarreling with Adam or not, you've got to take it easy with the eggs. Next time take your anger out in the cowshed. Manure doesn't break."

"It's only two that cracked," Sadie said as she gently transferred the eggs. "I'll cook them now. Scrambled or fried?"

"Scrambled, and I'll add them to the sausage casserole. That'll help me stretch it out. Simon and Ruthie had big appetites this morning. They must be having a growing spurt." Mary turned the flame up under the coffee. "And what were you and Adam going round about this fine spring morning?"

Sadie's lips hardened. "What don't we fight about? He made it my chore to take Susie to see Dr. Trueherz, and I don't mind that one bit, but if I go I'm going to be late for my job at the hotel. And Adam doesn't care at all."

"Oh, Sadie." Mary glanced up from the stove, her hazel eyes heavy with sympathy. "Why is it so hard for you to follow Adam's rules and decisions? He's the head of the household now, and the weight of it all is heavy on his shoulders. You know he doesn't want to argue with you."

"I know that." Sadie felt her spirits sag. She never wanted to cause trouble, but somehow, when she tried to reason with Adam, she always managed to step right into it. "But he could have told me about Susie's appointment earlier in the week. I could have talked to my boss at the hotel."

Mary just nodded. "That's all water under the bridge. What worries me is you and Adam. Storm clouds darken the sky overhead whenever you two speak."

Sadie snickered at the notion of black clouds following Adam and her. "You're right. We're always butting heads, and I don't know what to do about it."

"We'll pray to the Heavenly Father for peace in our house. I know you don't mean to stir the pot, but mind you keep quiet when Adam gives an order. I shouldn't have to tell you that Adam's decisions are more important than your boss at the hotel."

Sadie nodded. This she knew, but she was always juggling so

many things—her music and her chores, her job at the hotel and her English boyfriend—sometimes her sense of order wasn't so clear.

"Now, open that jar of peaches while I get the biscuits before they burn. In a few weeks we'll have fresh cherries and strawberries. Summer fruits."

"Did you know the honeysuckle is blooming?" Sadie said. "Spring is my favorite season."

"Because of the honeysuckle?"

"Because of the new life everywhere. Remember how Dat used to get so excited when the birds came back?"

"Back from their winter vacation down south, he used to say." Mary's face glowed with the memory.

Their dat had taught them to respect all of God's creatures, and though he'd been gone for more than a year now, Sadie still felt Gott's peace when she worked their farm—the peace their father had opened their eyes to.

Sadie missed her parents, but she was grateful for all they had taught her. If Dat had shown them peace, Mamm had helped Sadie delight in song. Was Sadie the only one who remembered the sweet lullabies Mamm had sung for them when they were babies, with her voice as fresh and smooth as a spring wind?

"Tell me why the stars do shine," she sang as she broke the seal on the peaches.

Without looking up, Mary joined in. "Tell me why the ivy twines. Tell me why the sky's so blue. And I will tell you just why I love you."

If Sadie closed her eyes she could almost hear Mamm's voice chiming in. Mamm had taught her how music could make the most boring chore pass quickly, and they had spent many an hour in this very kitchen singing together.

"Because God made the stars to shine," the sisters sang together.

As she put the peaches on the table, Sadie's eyes combed the mouthwatering breakfast Mary had prepared for this second shift of the day, after the children under fifteen had eaten and headed out to school. Sausage-and-egg casserole. Biscuits. Peppers and peaches from the pantry.

Sadie felt a sudden swell of tenderness for the older sister who had stepped in to care for their household after Mamm had died. Mary took care of everyone in so many ways, always guided by a calm that kept peace in their home. But come wedding season, Mary would be starting a home with her beau, Five, on the Beilers' farm.

"Sadie?" The song had ended and Mary stood staring at her, oven mitts on her hands. "What's the matter?"

"Oh, Mary, what will we do without you around here?"

Mary patted her shoulder with the puffy mitt. "I'm not going far. And we know it's all part of the Heavenly Father's plan for me to leave this house. Remy's going to be moving in, and you're a mighty good cook yourself, when you don't get too lost in all your singing."

Lost in her singing . . . lately Sadie had spent so much time with her music, practicing with the band or singing in the barn. Funny, but it was far easier to imagine herself singing on a stage in front of people than cooking up an entire breakfast like this.

And that thought tugged on her conscience as she went to the porch to call the others for breakfast. Here on the farm, work was proper and good. Her faith gave meaning to every sunrise, every blooming violet. And the close bond of family showed her that she belonged here.

Not singing to strangers in the big city.

TWO

I love riding in cars," Susie said a few hours later as they rolled past green fields of short cornstalks beginning to find their way to the sun.

"And in this weather, I like the charm of an open buggy. Isn't it funny how the grass is always greener on the other side?" Nancy Briggs, their friend and the mayor of Halfway, had agreed to give them a ride, telling them she had some business to take care of in the neighboring town.

"We're on our way to Paradise," Nancy teased as she passed a horse and buggy that had slowed at the side of the road. "I just love saying that."

Sadie laughed, and Susie clapped her hands together in joy. "We're headed for Paradise!"

As soon as Nancy had pulled up at the farm, Susie had enthusiastically requested the front seat, the windows open, and the radio on. Nancy had warned that Sadie might get blown around in the backseat, but she was willing to give it a try.

With the air teasing at the strings of her prayer *Kapp* and the music of the radio swirling around her, Sadie was very comfortable in the backseat of Nancy's Jeep. Her spirit was lifting again, now that Nancy had come to their rescue. She would make it to work and band rehearsal, and going to the doctor with Susie was a lot more fun than weeding the garden or scrubbing the floors. Besides, it was time Sadie learned more about Susie's condition since Mary would be leaving them in the fall.

The doctor's office was in a small white building that looked like it used to be a house. Although Dr. Trueherz treated many Amish folk, he wasn't Plain himself, and the building had electricity. Sadie noticed the electric pole as they pulled up. She climbed out of the Jeep and patted the cell phone tucked into her jeans pocket under her dress. Maybe there was cell service here. While Susie was being examined, she could pass the time talking with Frank.

"I'll plan to head back here in an hour or so," Nancy said through the open window. "But you can call me if you finish up early."

Susie led the way inside to a small waiting room filled with a sofa and chairs, where a handful of people were waiting. A hole had been cut into one of the walls, and a woman in her fifties worked at the little desk area there.

"Well, if it isn't Smiley King," the woman said, one brow arched over her gray eyes.

Sadie couldn't help but smile herself. Smiley was a good description for fourteen-year-old Susie, who always managed to look on the bright side of things.

"It's *Susie* King." Susie leaned on the counter, grinning. "But you know that, Mrs. Trueherz. You always remember me."

"How could I forget you, Smiley? I was just saying we needed a bright star like you to liven things up around here. And who did you bring along today, Smiley?"

"This is my sister Sadie."

"I've been here before," Sadie said. "Once when I had strep throat."

"And once was enough for you, right?" the woman teased.

"I'm thankful to have been blessed with a good throat since then," Sadie said.

"You can have a seat if you like, Sadie. Your sister will be examined, then you can both meet with the doctor. And in the meantime, I'll get you the family report to fill out." The woman pulled a file from her stack. "The doctor will see you in a few minutes, Smiley. While you're hanging around here, let's make sure I know where to find you. Still living in Halfway?"

"Yes, ma'am."

"And this is still your date of birth?" She slid the form over to Susie, who nodded.

"Well, I'm glad that hasn't changed," Celeste Trueherz said dryly.

Susie pressed a hand to her mouth to muffle a giggle. "Mrs. Trueherz, my date of birth is never going to change."

"I know, but I just have to be sure," the older woman said. "Dr. Trueherz has a slew of questions for you, but I'll let him do the hard part. Have a seat."

As soon as she sat beside her sister, Sadie remembered the calls she needed to make. "I'm going to step outside and call the hotel, just to say I might be late."

Around the side of the gravel parking lot was a little patio with a wooden picnic table near a neatly trimmed hedge. Sadie was glad for the bit of privacy behind the green bushes, as she had to hike up her skirt to fish the cell phone from her pocket. She called the hotel, but Lorraine, who worked the front desk, said Mr. Decker was in a meeting. Pacing along the patio, Sadie explained that she was at the doctor's with her sister, and that she would be late for her shift. "But I'm definitely coming in," she said. "I'll be there as soon as I can."

"I'll tell him that," Lorraine said, sounding bored.

Next she called Frank, just to be reassured that the second half of her day was going to work out better.

"Hey, how's it going?" he asked.

"Good, except I'm going to be late for work," she said. When she started to explain what had happened, Frank cut her off.

"I can't talk now. I'm on the road, driving to work. But we're on for practice tonight, right?"

She smiled, imagining the beautiful sounds that would fill Red's garage that night. "I'm looking forward to it."

"You just hurry and hustle yourself to work. I've got a new song for you. Can't wait to hear you sing it."

"Okay," she said, smiling at the bushes. Her heart felt full as she closed her cell phone and turned back toward the parking lot.

"Sadie?" Someone was calling her.

She moved toward the voice, and found Mrs. Trueherz coming around the house. The young man beside her seemed familiar. He was tall, maybe six feet, with a broad mouth that wanted to smile and eyes as blue as a summer sky.

"Oh, there you are," said the older woman. "I thought you escaped."

"I was just getting some fresh air."

"It is beautiful out here. Not a cloud in the sky." The woman reached up and clapped a hand on the young man's shoulder. "This is Mike. He's our son, and he's helping out with some of the bookkeeping."

Sadie's eyes went wide as her gaze combed the towering young man. Surely her tongue would twist in knots to talk to such an attractive man.

"Oh, don't worry, sweetie, he doesn't bite," Celeste added, sensing Sadie's hesitation. "And don't let the baby face fool you. He's twenty-two. And very responsible. Two years in the Peace Corps."

"Mom, please," Mike interrupted, tucking his clipboard under one arm. "You don't have to give her the whole family history."

Sadie felt a flicker of recognition. "You work with the fire department, ya?"

"The Fire and Rescue Squad. I'm a volunteer."

She nodded. He had been one of the medical attendants who had cared for Remy when she had gotten sick at the marketplace.

"Mike is training to be a doctor . . . down the road," Celeste explained. "Someday he'll take over his father's practice here. But for now, he goes to the community college and helps out with paperwork."

"Which is a long way of asking, do you mind if I go over some of these forms with you?" Mike asked.

The shyness Sadie usually felt around Englisher men melted away under Mike's smile. There was honesty in his eyes, and her mamm had always said that eyes were the mirror of the soul. "Sure," she said, surprising herself. "I can talk with you."

Celeste Trueherz went back inside and Mike turned to the picnic table. "Do you mind if we talk out here? I've got a touch of spring fever."

"I do love springtime," she said, sinking onto the sun-warmed wood of the picnic bench. "It makes me smile to see everything around me come back to life."

"Then I guess you've got a lot to smile about this time of year." He sat right across from her, face-to-face. So very close.

Looking up at him shyly, she realized that Mike Trueherz was as beautiful as any spring flower she'd ever seen. Those blue eyes reminded her of summer afternoons spent staring into the sky with her sisters. And when he smiled, his teeth were white as snow. His sandy brown hair wasn't long like an Amish boy's, but it was combed across the top of his head, short and natural. Not like Frank's *verhuddelt* spikes that shot straight up.

"Since Susie is a minor, we need consent to treat her. That's what this form is about." He showed her where to sign. She wrote her name, and he flipped to another page. "Okay. This is a family tree your parents put together with my father." He slid the clipboard around so that she could see the paper.

At the top were her parents, Esther and Levi King. And dropping down from their names were thirteen boxes, one for each child.

"Thirteen? But we only have eleven," she said.

Mike pointed to two of the boxes. "These two were children who died soon after birth . . . David and Deborah."

"Oh, ya, that's right. I forgot about them."

"Which is understandable, since you weren't even born when they passed. That all happened before my dad was working here in Lancaster County. But from your parents' descriptions of their symptoms, there's a good chance they suffered from glutaric aciduria, as well."

Her fingers worried a pin on her apron. "Mamm loved those babies. She said she could never understand why Gott had to take them so young, but she knew they were happy with Him in heaven."

"It must have been a heartbreak." When she met his gaze this time, some of the glitter had faded from his eyes. Instead, she saw sympathy. True understanding.

"Do you have a question about this family tree?" she asked.

"I do. We noticed that a few of you are of age to start families of your own. Adam, Jonah, and Mary, in particular. Have any of them married or had kids?"

"Not yet. But I think we'll be seeing some changes, come wedding season."

"Got your celery planted?" he asked with a grin.

She laughed softly. An abundance of celery in an Amish family's garden was said to be a sign of an upcoming wedding, because much celery was needed for the wedding dinner. "So you know about the Amish custom?"

He nodded. "You don't grow up in Lancaster County without learning a thing or two about the Amish community."

"But why do you care if someone marries?" she asked.

"It's really a concern about when you or your siblings have children of your own. We want to make sure everyone in your family is educated about glutaric aciduria type I. When you have a baby, it should be tested when it's born." He squinted at her, then looked down at the table. "Am I making sense? The thing is, this disorder can be passed down through the genes."

Jeans? She glanced down and saw that one leg of her jeans had come unrolled. "Oops." She shifted her legs, trying to cover up the denim with her dress.

Mike glanced down at her legs, then straightened. "Not that kind of jeans. We're talking genetics here. When you have babies of your own, if your husband has the same disease in his family, you could pass it on to your children."

She felt her cheeks grow warm. To be talking with this Englisher about having babies . . . this was not something she was ready for. She dropped her eyes to the ground and noticed his leather moccasins, so different from the fancy sneakers English boys favored, or the functional boots worn by Amish on the farm. What kind of a boy wore moccasins? Mike Trueherz was certainly different.

"Not to scare you or any of your siblings," he said. "This disorder is treatable if we find the baby who's at risk in the first few days after birth."

"That was when your dat came to us," she said, remembering. "Your father made a house call to our farm shortly after the twins— Susie and Leah—were born."

Mike nodded. "Dad calls them barn calls. We had just moved here that year."

"And Susie needed his help. She was sick already." Sadie pressed her palms flat onto the warm wood of the table. "Your father saved our Susie's life."

"By the grace of God."

She glanced over at the parking lot where one car and two buggies sat. The hitching rail was under a tall overhang so that the horses had shade in the hot weather. "Your father treats many Plain folk, ya?"

"He does. Before he came along, very little attention was given to diseases that struck the Amish community. Glutaric aciduria. Bartter syndrome. Maple syrup urine disease."

"Your dat knows about all the things that strike Plain folk."

"Research was his first passion. He started by treating people with GA when Amish patients came into Philadelphia, but often it was too late. That's why Dad moved our family out here. He wanted to help Amish kids before their health issues got out of control."

"And he is here, helping people every day. I think your father is a wonderful good man."

"He is. His work is everything to him." His voice had changed, as if he suddenly had a heavy heart.

Sadie didn't know what was wrong, but she had so enjoyed talking with Mike. She wanted to spend a little more time with him. "So you moved to Paradise about fourteen years ago? Do you live in this house?" She nodded toward the office.

"We did, when we first moved here." He looked up at the rooftop of the small house. "That was a tough move. I was eight years old and I had a ton of friends back in Philly. Not to mention baseball and basketball teams. I was not happy to be here in farm country. And I still love the city. Visiting Philadelphia is great. I'll be going to school there in the fall, transferring to Temple." He sighed. "I can't wait."

"I'll tell you a secret." Sadie leaned closer across the table. "I love the city, too. I have an Englisher friend who drives me into Philly."

"No way." He cocked his head, as if seeing her from a different angle. "So what do you do in town?"

"Have you ever heard of Mad River?"

He rubbed his jaw, thinking. "Can't say that I have."

"It's a club. My band performed there last Saturday at open mike night, and the manager wants us to come back. I'm the lead singer."

"Really? You have an Amish band?"

A little laugh escaped Sadie's throat, and she put a hand to her mouth. "The band is Englisher, except for me. But I don't dress Amish when I perform, except for my kapp. You should come see us sometime."

With a dramatic flourish, Mike smacked his forehead. "What's an Amish girl like you doing in a club in the city?"

Sadie laughed again. "It's my rumspringa, of course." She knew that was a weak excuse. In her congregation, rumspringa was intended as a time to find an Amish mate. No one ever intended young people to go wild, though sometimes it happened.

"Of course," Mike said. "Some kids get cell phones, and I've seen guys trick out their buggies. But to be singing in a club?" He gaped, his arms spread wide. "How did you learn the songs? Or are you performing songs from the Ausbund?"

This time they both laughed. And Sadie pressed a hand to her mouth until it all subsided.

"Oh, Mike . . ." She wiped tears from her eyes. "You are so funny. But you can't tell anyone in Halfway. Or Paradise."

"I'll keep it all on the down-low, songbird."

Songbird. The word reminded Sadie of her father. Dat had loved the song of birds on a spring morning.

Mike put his hand over his heart. "Your secret's safe with me. But really, how do you learn the songs?"

"My friend Frank gave me an iPod. He puts songs he wants me to learn on it. Then I make him add some others that I love. I just learn the singing part from listening. That's not so hard."

"And what kind of music do you do?" Mike seemed genuinely interested.

"Blues and pop. That's what Frank calls it."

"Ho!" came a shout from the parking lot.

Sadie and Mike both turned just in time to see a buggy enter, swinging wildly as it turned. The driver, an Amish man in a green shirt, dark pants, and suspenders, had his hat on at an odd angle. He managed the reins with one hand, while he bent gingerly over the other hand, bandaged in his lap.

Instantly, Mike was on his feet. "Excuse me," he said, then took off running toward the injured Amish man.

Sadie hurried alongside him, waiting as Mike spoke quickly to the man and helped him down to the ground.

"Easy, now," Mike said to the man, who was ghostly pale and slick with sweat.

Sadie winced when she saw that the white rag covering his hand was soaked in blood. "What happened?" Mike asked.

Speaking in Pennsylvania Dutch, he said there was an accident with a saw. His hand got mangled.

"His name is Jacob Esher," she said, quickly translating for Mike, who supported the man by his good arm.

"Do you speak English?" Mike spoke firmly. "You need to hold this hand as high as you can to slow the bleeding."

"Ya, ya." Jacob raised his hand. "I speak English. I just got confused a moment."

"You're probably in shock," Mike said. "And you drove yourself here?"

Jacob explained how busy the farm was, with planting season here.

"Let's get you in to see the doctor." Mike was already leading the man into the building.

"I'll tie up the horse," she called after them.

"Ya. Gut," the injured man said.

Sadie secured the horse to the hitching post, then hurried inside to see if she could help with anything else.

The waiting room was abuzz, with the three other patients looking on in a mixture of curiosity and alarm. Mike was wrapping gauze around the wounded hand and holding it up above Jacob's head.

Celeste Trueherz came out from behind the counter. Her joking demeanor had given way to genuine concern and authority. "We're not really set up for emergency care," she told the man as she tapped two pills into a little cup. "The doctor might send you to the hospital."

"But I don't have money for the hospital," Jacob said, speaking English now. "And Doc Trueherz sewed up my friend Caleb's hand last year. Good as new."

"We'll see what the doctor has to say." Mrs. Trueherz handed him the pill cup, along with some water. "I'm giving you Tylenol to help with the pain."

He nodded and tossed back the cup of pills with his free hand.

Sadie had been so captivated watching that she didn't see her sister emerge from the hall.

"Dr. Trueherz says we'll have to wait if you want to meet with him because he has . . ." Susie's eyes went wide as she noticed the man with the bloody hand. ". . . an emergency."

"Let's get Jacob into exam room one," Celeste said, and Susie stepped closer to her sister as Mike helped the man to his feet and guided him down the hall.

"That poor man." Susie pressed a hand to her chest. "My heart is flapping like a butterfly."

"Excitement like that I could do without." Celeste returned to her chair at the counter.

"Will he be all right?" Sadie asked.

"We'll make sure he gets the care he needs." There was kindness in the older woman's voice. "I know it's frightening to see that much blood, but the doctor can handle it." She pulled a pencil from the cup on the desk. "Do you girls want to wait, or are you heading out?"

"I must get to work," Sadie said. Though she hated to leave without saying good-bye to Mike Trueherz.

Susie touched her arm gently. "We can go. My checkup went wonderful good. Dr. Trueherz says things are under control. My diet is working, and he likes the pink in my cheeks."

"That's good news." Sadie was warmed by her sister's positive attitude. Susie always saw the sunny side of things. As they made the appointment for Susie's next checkup, she realized Mike would no longer be helping out here the next time Susie came. By November he would be through with community college and living in Philadelphia.

As the girls stepped outside to call Nancy, Sadie thought what a strange day it had been.

She had made a new friend, but somehow she had lost him already. A friend found and lost in a single morning.

THREE

Mike Trueherz always felt his stomach wrench at the sight of blood. He wished that he could slip out the back door and go for a run, or see a movie, or shoot some hoops with friends. He wished that the part-time job with his father involved mowing someone's lawn or preparing someone's taxes. Even taxes would be better than this—trying to repair a man's dismembered fingers.

"My son tells me you brought the fingers in a jar," his father said to the patient, whose mangled fingers were soaking in Dreft baby detergent to clean out the wound. "Do you want them reattached?"

"Can you do that?" Jacob's face brightened.

"I can't do it here." Mike's dad adjusted his spectacles, though his blue eyes never left Jacob. "But you have a chance if I send you over to the hospital. They have a lot of success with surgeries like that."

Go to the hospital, man, Mike thought. *Save your fingers.*

Jacob shook his head. "I can't go to the hospital. I don't have money to pay for a fancy hospital bill. Can't you just sew them up here?"

"I don't have the technology and know-how to reattach." The doctor took Jacob's wrist and lifted his fingers from the soap they were soaking in. "The bones in these two digits were crushed on the end. If I sew them up, I'll have to cut them back to the knuckle. That's the best I can do."

Mike's head kept ping-ponging back and forth between his father and Jacob, hoping that the patient would come to his senses and get a ride to the hospital.

"But you can sew them up and get me out of here?" the patient asked.

"I can. But I'll have to trim the bone back, and you need to realize that I can't replace what's lost. You'll never have nails on those two fingers again."

"So two less nails to trim," Jacob said. "Do it, Doc."

"As long as you're sure. Will you be able to manage your work with a few less digits?"

"I reckon. Since the Good Lord decided to take away a few of my fingers, I don't have a choice. I'll get by."

Gently, Henry Trueherz lowered the hand back into the soap. "You just keep soaking. I'll get my tools and some medicine to numb your hand. You won't feel anything during the procedure." He looked up at his son. "Is Amy still working with Nella Mae?"

Mike looked to the door, wishing he could flee. "I think so."

His father rubbed his jaw. "I'll need her help with this procedure."

Thank you, Lord! Mike had no desire to assist with a case like this, and in fact he wasn't a licensed nurse like Amy Owen. With any luck Amy would take his place in this room and he could go chat with a patient or wipe down an exam room.

"I'll go find Amy," the doc said. "But in the meantime, you can get the surgical supplies ready. I'll need forceps, bone snips, and a suture driver. Oh, and don't forget a stack of gauze."

"Got it." Mike's voice sounded a lot more confident than he felt.

As Mike pulled on sterile latex gloves and spread out a sterile towel, he asked Jacob a few questions, trying to distract him with conversation. It was clear that the guy was in constant pain, but once he got an injection of local anesthetic, that would subside. Mike laid the sterile tools out on the towel, along with a stack of gauze. Then he went around the exam table to speak with Jacob, face-to-face.

"You okay?" he asked.

Jacob gritted his teeth, but nodded.

"Are you scared?"

"Some. I don't know that I can take any more pain."

Mike put a hand on Jacob's good arm. "It's going to get better. Any minute, the doctor will be in here with Amy—she's the nurse—and they'll inject you with a painkiller. Your fingers will go totally numb."

"Yeah?" Jacob let out a breath. Although there was still anguish in his eyes, the fear seemed to have faded. "That'd be good."

"It'll be better soon." Mike squeezed Jacob's arm, silently praying for the Lord to guide his father's hands during the procedure and help Jacob heal quickly. Probably the greatest health concern for a wound like this, besides the obvious loss of manual dexterity, was the risk of infection.

"Oh, and one more thing," Mike added. "Most important. You'll need to keep your injured fingers cleaned and bandaged for a while. We'll give you sterile gauze and tape, and you'll need to come back for follow-up. But if you remember just one thing, it's this: Keep your hand clean and covered. Got it?"

Jacob bit his lower lip. "Clean and covered."

"Right. You don't want a staph infection. If you get an infection, it could kill you, so don't forget."

"Clean and covered," Jacob repeated.

"Good." The door opened, and Mike stepped away as his father returned with Amy, the nurse who assisted him weekdays in the clinic.

"Let's see how those fingers are cleaning up," the doc said, checking the hand again. "I think we're ready. I see Mike's got us all set up here. Amy, let's get a syringe prepared for Jacob." He went to the sink to wash up.

"Will do," she said.

Mike took that as his cue to leave. He had his hand on the doorknob when his father said: "Feel free to stay and observe, son."

Mike felt the burden of expectation. His father wanted him to stay, but he couldn't stomach it. "That's okay. I'll make myself useful elsewhere."

The door to the other exam room was open and he poked his head in. Amy hadn't had time to clean up, so he went in, tore the paper from the exam table, and tossed it into the trash. For good measure, he wiped the table down with antiseptic, rolled out new paper, and clamped it down onto the table. Mike wasn't afraid of work. After high school he'd taken the advice of his pastor and spent two years with the Peace Corps. Assigned to a rural village in Jamaica, he'd worked to bring health care and hygiene awareness to the people there.

Sometimes the faces of the people he'd worked with in Jamaica were vivid in his mind.

There was Algernon, a nine-year-old boy who had worked the beach at the property line of a major resort, selling beaded necklaces. He'd befriended a few children of Mrs. Fitzroy, a woman struggling to make ends meet after her husband was mistakenly killed in a drug raid. He'd visited scores of children receiving care in the local hospital, kids whose parents could not afford to give up a day's work to make the trip to see their children. And then there were the local kids who stopped by his bungalow every day, hoping for some papers to color on or a taste of a warm Fanta soda. Oliver, Rodell, Vonnie, Leonda . . .

Every mission came with its share of frustration, but when he'd left Jamaica Mike had been exhilarated by the opportunity to touch countless lives . . . and the blessings those people had brought him. He had been able to embrace the goals his parents had engrained in him: to help, serve, and love.

But not long after he'd arrived back in Paradise, he'd realized that his gifts were far different from his father's. Mike could rally people to take care of their personal health, but he was not equipped to work in the trenches, suturing wounds or diagnosing diseases. He had learned that he was a people person, but he didn't have the stuff to be a surgeon.

Or a country doctor, like his dad.

Every day, that was becoming more and more clear to Mike. It was his parents who couldn't let go of the dream of their son attending medical school and taking over his father's practice.

He left the door of the exam room open and returned to the reception office, a tiny cubby filled with file cabinets and his mom's desk.

"You didn't want to watch the procedure?" His mother didn't even look up from the calendar she was filling in.

"I took a pass. As time goes on, I've got less and less of a stomach for that kind of thing."

"No kidding." She lifted her eyes, suddenly focusing on him. "How are you going to take over the practice when you can't handle a simple surgical emergency?"

He leaned against a tall file cabinet and gestured toward the back hall. "That is no simple emergency, Mom. I wish Dad would send cases like that on to the hospital. That guy's fingers could have been saved. Someday, a patient might take legal action against him for doing a quick fix when the hospital could've done a more thorough job."

"No, honey." She shook her head. "Your dad's patients are not going to sue him. These people appreciate his earnest care and his availability. Didn't you hear Jacob? He can't afford the two or three thousand dollars that a hospital visit would cost him. And your father is the most dedicated health care professional I've ever met. Dedicated to a fault." She spun her chair toward him and tilted her head. "What's this really about?"

He bent down to peer out the pass-through. The waiting room was empty for the scheduled lunch break. "I'm not surgeon material. Two years in the Peace Corps showed me that I'm really good at working with people. That's where my talents lie."

"Doctors work with people every day." She clicked her pen open and shut. "Are you getting cold feet about going into medicine?"

Mike tried to breathe against the crushing weight of pressure in his chest, pressure to fulfill his parents' dream. "I'm just saying that I can't stomach surgical work like that. If I joined the practice someday, and that's assuming I could even get into med school, I would have to send cases like Jacob's on to the hospital."

"I hear what you're saying." His mother tapped her pen against one knee. "Your brother Drew was disappointed on that front. I think he would have been a great doctor, but a few hundred med school admission departments didn't agree with me."

"It's cutthroat competitive, Mom," he said, trying to prepare her for the inevitable.

"But don't count yourself out, son. You'll get credit for serving in the Peace Corps, and it takes a special college student to give up two years of his life. And think about it; you're going to get a degree from Temple University. Your father and I are both proud of you, Mike. You need to trust in God that everything will work out."

"I hope so." He crossed his arms, uncomfortable with the conversation. Mike had spent the last year and a half trying to escape the fact that he was miserable living and working here. Each week he ticked off the days until he could escape to the city. He wanted desperately to get away from Lancaster County. Unlike his father, the local healer, he didn't really belong here. Everything about the city had more appeal to him, even the Episcopal church he attended with his gran.

His mom turned away at the sound of the outside door opening—another patient—and Mike realized that his father and Amy had worked through the short lunch break. As the Amish woman checked her daughter in with Celeste, Mike recalled Sadie King, the most unusual Amish girl he had ever met.

Now, there was another person who didn't belong in Lancaster County. He grinned at the thought of Sadie King singing onstage in a dark, smoky club. She'd really thrown him when she'd shared that secret confession. He wondered if Sadie was overdoing the rebellion thing, maybe compensating for missing her parents, who'd been killed a year and a half ago.

Maybe. But most likely she was a kindred soul, someone who just didn't belong here.

That saying—bloom where you're planted? Life didn't always work out that way.

FOUR

*O*kay, here's proof that I am such a city slicker," Remy McCallister said as she and Mary headed down the sunny lane toward the road. "I never knew you needed to weed a wild strawberry patch."

"Sure you do. Otherwise it'll get choked out, just like any other plant. If you don't clear out the weeds, they soak up all the good things from the soil, and take all the sunshine and water. And pretty soon, you have no strawberries left at all."

The two young women carried empty pails, which Mary had promised would be stuffed with weeds by the time they were through. It was the perfect time for some outdoor activity, with the little ones napping, the men installing equipment in the new milking barn, the other children off at school or in town for Susie's appointment with the doctor.

As the oldest female in the King household, Mary was the expert on everything from baking shoofly pie to getting windows sparkling clean to caring for the little ones, Sam and Katie. Every day Mary coordinated the preparation of three meals for eleven people—twelve, when Remy was eating with the family—and she seemed to manage it all with ease and good humor. Today, for example, Remy had helped Mary prepare lunch for the family as well as for the neighbors and friends who had come over to help Adam, Jonah, and Gabe install the new milking machines in the barn. Without blinking an eye, Mary had fed a small village of people. In the morning she'd packed coolers for all the children going to school, as well as for Susie and Sadie, for their trip into town. Then she'd stretched things out to produce enough sandwiches and split pea soup for a dozen people.

Remy hoped that at least a few of Mary's fine housekeeping skills would rub off on her. Come October, after Mary wed Five and moved in with the Beiler family, Remy would be the woman responsible for keeping the family fed and in clean clothes. It was a thrill for a girl like Remy who had always longed for a big family. A thrill, but also a huge challenge.

Being Amish wasn't part of Remy's heritage, as it was with the members of the King family. Remy smiled, thinking how Adam still teased that she was an "Englisher," though she now dressed Plain and wore a prayer kapp over her bun. Over the winter Remy had come here to Lancaster County in pursuit of a story for her newspaper. In the process of her investigation, she had fallen in love with Adam King and had come to embrace the Plain way of life. She had been meeting with Preacher Dave and planned to attend classes to prepare for baptism into the faith. The training would last through the summer until baptism in October, but with so much to learn—including the very specific Pennsylvania Dutch language—Remy was glad for the time.

The important thing was that she was on the right path. God

had led her to Adam and his loving family and this tightly interwoven community.

Walking down the lane, Remy turned her face toward the sun and breathed in honeysuckle-scented air, thinking of a song she'd learned at the singings.

Come, gracious Spirit, heav'nly Dove, with light and comfort from above. . . .

She had been searching for a home, and in her quest she had found light and comfort, her God and the love of her life here in Lancaster County.

"Here we go." Mary directed Remy to an embankment by the side of the main road. "These rounded leaves are the strawberries. The tall ones that look like little cornstalks?" She wrapped one gloved hand around a weed and yanked it out. "These are the weeds. Best to pull closest to the ground."

"Got it." Remy put her gloves on and set her jaw. "Let 'er rip." She dug into the tangled vines and tore out weeds with both fists. They went into the bucket, and she reached in again.

"You're mighty good at weeding," Mary said. "Are you sure you haven't done this before, city slicker?"

They both laughed, and Mary turned her head away from a meandering bumblebee. "Oh, go away, bee!"

"Buzz off," Remy joked, grabbing another handful of weeds. The sound of a car on the road drew Remy's eyes away from the berry patch, and she squinted as the black sedan slowed and the male passenger turned to stare at Mary and her.

Mary watched with pursed lips as the car rolled past. "Is that the car? The one that followed you and Adam?"

"I don't know." Remy frowned as she recalled the dark vehicle that had followed them back from the Yoders' barn after last Sunday's singing. Adam had pulled over to the side of the road and tried to wave it on, but the driver had hung back behind the buggy, its bright lights blinding them for a few miles. "It was dark, and for a while we couldn't see anything but the car's headlights. When the car finally passed us, we saw that it was a sedan in a dark color. Blue or black."

"I keep hoping it was just a visitor who was lost and was afraid to pass," Mary said as the dark car dipped down the hill and out of sight. "We're seeing more and more tourists these days, with the good spring weather."

Remy nodded. She had been hoping the same.

"Oh, well." Remy reached into the briar patch and plucked another handful of weeds. They were chatting about the excitement over the new milking machines when they heard a rumble on the road again.

Although Mary kept working, Remy stepped back from the berry patch, her hands on her hips as the same black car came gunning over the hill. This time she stared right at the driver, almost daring him to stop or say something through the open car windows.

And then, to her dismay, the car slowed as it approached.

"Look, Mary. He's coming here." Fear shimmered down her spine as the vehicle rocked over a bump in the road then seemed to roll to a stop.

Mary straightened and moved beside Remy. "Maybe he's lost. Folks are always coming down here, needing directions."

The man behind the wheel wore sunglasses that masked his face. Remy also noticed a searchlight attached to the side of the car, near the side-view mirror, which she recognized as a tool used by some police officers. Was it a cop?

No . . . there were no markings on the car, and the driver was dressed casually in a green polo shirt. Remy clenched the bucket, her knuckles white as the car slowed. The man stared at them, as if soaking up the details of their appearance. Then the car rolled on past, leaving Remy staring at the dust swirling behind it.

"Just someone who's lost, I think," Mary said as she bent back to the strawberry patch.

Remy had a feeling there was more to it. Many a stranger barreled down this deserted country road raising dust behind their car, but most didn't give her a feeling of insecurity. She suspected that this was the man who had followed Adam and her in the buggy. What did he want from them?

As she bent down to tug on a weed, the hairs at the back of her neck still tingled. Someone was watching. Who was he?

An hour or so later, golden sunlight still bathed sections of the garden as Remy lifted a heavy watering can.

"More water for this one," Mammi Nell advised. The creases around her eyes were pronounced as she watched Remy pour water into one of the many potted celery plants growing in the garden behind the Doddy house. "Just a little more. Celery plants drink lots of water," the older woman said.

So far Remy had toted four buckets of water out here from the kitchen of the house, and it looked like they would need a few more for their thirsty celery plants. Although watering the garden sounded like an easy task, it turned out to be far more time-consuming when there weren't handy faucets and hoses everywhere.

Nell moved behind Remy, inspecting each plant as Remy watered. At one point, she didn't like the damaged outer stalk of one of the plants, and she found a sharp tool to trim the bad area off.

"I didn't know you could do that," Remy said.

"Oh, ya." Nell nodded. "It will grow back."

File that away as gardening tip number two hundred and twelve, Remy thought. She had learned much about cooking and gardening already, but every day some new bit of information came her way. Some days she felt like she needed a crash course on all things Amish, but most of the time it was a delight to be expanding her knowledge with practical skills. She felt sure that if her mother were still alive, she too would have enjoyed learning about the Amish way of life.

"So." Nell plucked a dried leaf from a plant. "I hear you're starting *die Gemee,* the classes with the ministers, soon. Getting ready for baptism."

"Yes, Mammi." Remy nodded, feeling a bit awkward about calling Nell King "Grandma." In her heart, she felt that she was already a part of the King family, but nothing was official. She and Adam couldn't marry until she was baptized in the faith.

"And then, the wedding."

"In November. So many huge events are coming my way this fall. I don't know which one I'm more excited about."

"They are two very big decisions." Nell spoke slowly, deliberately, and Remy focused on her every word. "I reckon you know that they are both forever. There is no divorce in the Amish church. And if you leave the faith . . ." She frowned, shaking her head. "You will be shunned. Adam might be shunned, too. It's not like other religions where you can turn away on Sunday, then come back on Tuesday."

"I understand that, and I'm very committed. I love Adam, and . . . and I'm thrilled to be his girl. I'm still learning about the Amish faith, but I'm equally committed on that front, Mammi. I believe God brought me here to live with you and your wonderful grandchildren. I think . . ." For a moment, the knot of emotion in

Remy's throat made her pause. How could she tell Mammi Nell how much it meant to her to have found a home here? How could she describe the attraction to this man who could make her pulse race with the brush of his hand? How his vow to lead this family inspired her? How his secret sense of humor and tenderness warmed her? *Keep it simple,* she thought, adding, "I think God's love has brought me here."

The stern approval in Nell's dark eyes was magnified by her spectacles. "You will be a gut wife for our Adam," Nell said, placing a hand on Remy's shoulder.

Coming from Nell, those words meant so much. Remy felt as though she might melt to the floor right then and there—melt into a puddle of sheer relief and joy. But instead she bolstered herself, said *"Denki,"* and watered the next plant.

As she worked side by side with the older woman, Remy realized Nell must have been in a similar position many years ago. "Can I ask you a personal question? How was it for you, when you were first married and came to live here on the farm?"

"So many years ago." Nell sprinkled fertilizer on one of the plants. "I was younger than you, for sure. The first few months, I do remember I missed my mamm. But every time I got to feeling sad, my Alvin would do something nice. Read his Bible to me at night or walk with me down to the pond to show me how to scare off the geese. And so many times I burnt the eggs. I don't know why, but I couldn't get it right. One day I was so frustrated I was about to cry, and my Alvin, he just scooped the egg on a plate and sat down at the table. 'I'm getting to like them that way,' he told me. He loved to laugh. Adam's father had that in him, too. Always smiling, with peace in his heart."

Remy smiled. "I wish I could have met them."

Nell shrugged. "But Gott our Father took them off to heaven. I miss them both. Levi's wife, Esther, too. Ach, but when you get to be my age, you see many go when it's Gott's plan for them. Still, the heart aches. We can't help that."

Remy nodded, thinking of her mother. She still missed her, but the ache of loss had eased over the years. "Did you grow up far from here?"

"No, no. I was in an Amish settlement nearby, closer to Paradise. I met my Alvin at a youth gathering at my cousin's farm. Alvin was visiting from Halfway, and though he was a quiet young man, he caught my eye." Wrinkles creased the older woman's face as she frowned. "Though I must say, it's hard courting a fella who lives so many miles away."

Remy had heard that sometimes Amish youth mingled with teens from other communities. "Were your parents upset when you moved away?"

Before Nell could answer they were interrupted by the sounds of sneakers pounding dirt, and laughter beyond the garden. Although it was only April, the leafy foliage around the garden made it difficult to see out to the lane, but Remy could make out the twins, Susie and Leah, and eleven-year-old Ruthie, who seemed to be racing one another on the lane. Remy noted that Susie was back from her doctor's appointment. The girls chatted as they approached.

"Can I see the letter?" Ruthie asked.

"Mind your manners," Susie answered. "Nancy said it was my job to deliver it straight to Remy."

"I just wanted to see it. I wasn't going to open it." Ruthie puffed, her breath uneven as she clambered up to the garden gate and peeked into the shaded arbor. "Mammi? Is Remy there? We have something for her, and it's very important."

"It's only a letter," Leah said, smoothing down her dress. "You'd think no one ever got mail before."

"But it's the first letter Remy has ever gotten here," Susie said, hands on her hips.

"She's here," Mammi called. *"Kumm."*

Remy tipped the watering can as the girls scurried into the garden. "Easy, there. My own express delivery service."

"Here you go!" Susie handed her the envelope. "Nancy Briggs said it was delivered to her house just this morning."

"And it's from your father!" Ruthie said, her head bobbing. "A letter from your father! Aren't you so very happy to hear from him?"

"You haven't seen him for months now," Leah pointed out. "Do you miss him?"

"He must miss you," Susie insisted.

"Well, if he missed me that much you'd think he would have written before this." Glancing over at the three girls, their adorable faces lined up under their white prayer kapps, Remy tapped the envelope in her hand. "So many questions. I guess you want to know what the letter says."

Ruthie's brows rose. "We've always wondered how you could leave your dat behind, but—" She glanced over at Mammi Nell, as if afraid of reproach. "Mary told us to leave it alone. Curiosity is a dangerous thing."

"It can be at times," Remy agreed, though she wondered if the girls' fascination with her father had something to do with their own loss. The least she could do is let them enjoy vicariously what little relationship she had left with her father. "Okay. What is it you want to know?"

The twins looked at each other, their faces beaming with interest.

"We're all aching to know what's in the letter, of course," Ruthie said.

"I appreciate your honesty." Remy handed the envelope to Ruthie. "Why don't you read it out loud?" she suggested. "I have no secrets to keep from the family." It was true; in the months since she had fallen in love with Adam, she had shared her past and opened her heart to him, and he had reciprocated with details of his own loving concern for the children he'd committed himself to.

"I don't believe it!" Ruthie clasped the letter to her chest with pursed lips while the twins egged her on. As she unfolded the paper, Leah exclaimed over the fact that he'd had it printed up, all professional.

"Don't be too impressed. He had his secretary do it on a computer," Remy explained.

Ruthie took a deep breath and began reading. "'Dear Remy: I've been worried sick about you since you left. As I write this I'm thinking of those cults that brainwash kids and take them captive. I have half a mind to drive out there and rescue you.'" Ruthie paused. "What's a cult?"

Remy struggled for a definition. "He's talking about a group of people who force others to do things their way." The accusation that the Amish would have captured or recruited her was laughable; no one here had proselytized or pressured her at all. Instead, she had been drawn here by love. Her life in Philadelphia had been so drab. Thinking back to those days, she recalled the sting of loneliness that had shadowed her daily routine. She didn't miss the long days in the sterile office or the long nights spent searching for the comfort of sleep. Here in Halfway, whether helping out down the road at Nate and Betsy King's farm, or here with Adam and the family, her days were busy and her heart was so very full.

"Are we a cult?" Leah asked.

"No, we are not," Remy said firmly.

Mammi Nell lifted a hand to stop discussion. "We live separate from the rest of the world. We are not guided by what Englishers think of us, good or bad."

Remy nodded, heeding the older woman's advice. "Does the letter say anything else, Ruthie?"

"Oh, there's plenty more." She squinted, reading on. "'Loretta is sick with worry about you.'" Ruthie sighed dramatically. "Who is Loretta?"

"My stepmother."

"Do you miss her?" Susie asked sweetly.

"Not at all. To be honest, when I lived in Philadelphia, Loretta didn't seem comfortable when I visited their house. I wasn't invited there for holidays or family dinners. We saw very little of each other."

"But she's worried about you," Leah pointed out.

"Loretta probably hasn't even noticed that I've been gone. Chances are, my father is just trying to make up a story that will persuade me to come home." Remy wondered if she should be educating these young girls in the insidious ways of the Englisher world. She glanced over to Mammi, who had taken a seat on the bench. She didn't seem to have an opinion one way or another.

"'It's time you end this nonsense and come home,'" Ruthie read, her voice far more gentle than Herb's must have been when he dictated the letter to his assistant. "'Your condo and job are waiting for you, as well as the car.'"

The condo and the car . . . They had been weighing on Remy's mind, but certainly not as a lure calling her back to the city. The responsibilities of her old life had to be settled before she could fully engage her new life here. Herb was right about that; she had a few things to sort out.

"'Come back now if you want a place to live. Enough with playing country girl. Stop the shen . . . shen . . .'"

Leah looked over her sister's shoulder. "The word is shenanigans."

Ruthie looked up. "What's that?"

"It means silliness," Remy explained.

"It sounds like a silly word. Shenanigans." Susie's fingertips danced over the leaves of a plant. "It makes you smile when you say it."

Though it didn't take much to make Susie smile, Remy thought.

Ruthie lowered the letter. "Will you go back, Remy? Are you going back to your father?"

"Oh, Remy, I don't want you to go." Susie stepped into her arms and hugged her.

"Honey, I'm not moving back to Philadelphia." Remy put the watering can down and rubbed Susie's shoulders.

"But a daughter must obey her father, ya?" Leah asked.

"That's not always true, at least not with the Englishers." Remy hesitated, wringing her hands. She hadn't told them much about her father, mostly because she didn't want to dwell on her own disappointment in his moral fiber. "I know that obedience to your parents is very important, and I've always been respectful of Herb—my father. But . . . how can I explain it? He doesn't really act as a father should."

"We understand," Leah said. "Every father isn't as good and kind as our dat was."

"That's true." The girl's words warmed Remy's heart; how lovely that Leah remembered her own father that way. "Herb is very different from your dat. He wants me to leave you and this life I've chosen, but in this case, he doesn't know what's best for me. I'm a grown woman now, and I know my heart."

Remy pressed a hand to her heart as the right words seemed to find her, and suddenly she had the answer to Mammi's penetrating gaze and the girls' multitude of questions. "I've already made my promise to this family. I want to be baptized here. This is where I belong."

FIVE

*S*adie's shift at the hotel was almost over, and it had been uneventful.

There hadn't been much work left to do when she had arrived, half an hour late after the appointment with the doctor. The hotel guest rooms had already been cleaned, the hallways vacuumed. She had busied herself cleaning the windows in the lobby to a sparkling shine, though this had annoyed Lorraine at the front desk.

"The smell of that cleaner gives me a headache," Lorraine had said, waving a hand to push the bad air away. "Can't you work somewhere else?"

"Sorry." Sadie had tried to keep the spray closer to the windows. "It's just that the sun is shining outside, and I thought that clean windows would bring a bit of that sunshine inside to cheer up the place." She had been listening to a song about country roads on her iPod, and the images of sunshine and mountains had lifted her spirits again.

But Lorraine had not been impressed. She'd just perched at the desk like a mouse watching for cheese to drop, saying, "I think I'm allergic to ammonia."

From there Sadie had gone out to clean the windows in the little breezeway that attached the office to the downstairs guest rooms. That job had taken longer than she'd expected because of the many fingerprints from children.

Now she was preparing to mop the tile floor in the breakfast area, and the love song on her iPod about a beau who was so far away made her think of Mike going off to Philadelphia.

Silly for her to think that. She barely knew him.

But the lyrics tugged at her heart as she rolled the bucket out of the maintenance room. The singer burst into a glow when she sang about seeing the boy's face at her door. Now wouldn't that be a wonderful sight, to open the door and see Mike Trueherz standing there, the light of his good soul shining through his sky-blue eyes and friendly smile.

She was just stowing the chairs on the tables when the hotel owner appeared.

"Hey, Sadie. How's it going?" Jeff Decker had always been a kind and fair employer.

"Everything is good." She smiled as she lifted a chair onto the table. "How are you, Mr. Decker?"

His lips pressed together. "Not so good. I'm afraid I have some bad news. Business has been a little slow, the bad economy and all. I'm afraid I'm going to have to let you go, at least for the time being."

Sadie felt the blood drain from her face. "You mean . . . I'm fired?" The words were tight in her dry throat. This couldn't be! She was a good worker.

"It was a tough choice, Sadie, but you have to admit, you've been unreliable lately."

"If it's about today, I'm sorry, I was—"

"Today was just one example. You've canceled on me a few times, leaving me in a tight spot. A few weeks ago I had to step in and clean a few rooms myself. I need a cleaning crew that I can rely on."

Sadie's shoulders fell as she realized it was true. She had canceled a few times when Frank wanted to have more time for the band to practice, and there had been some nights when she'd left early with Frank, either to go into the city to clubs or to rehearse in Red's garage with the band. At the time, it hadn't seemed like a problem.

But now . . . now she realized that she had brought this on herself through her own bad choices. How could she have been so irresponsible?

"I'm so very sorry, Mr. Decker." She pressed her hands onto the edge of the table to keep herself steady. "I know how important it is to keep your hotel clean. The customers like it so much, and I've always done my best to keep it spic-and-span. But I haven't been reliable these past few months. I see that now, and I'm so sorry."

"It happens." He shrugged. "But right now I need to scale back, and you're the weakest link. This will be your last shift. Lorraine will have your final paycheck for you by the time you finish up."

Shame flamed within, warming her cheeks as she apologized again. "Please, Mr. Decker, is there anything I can do to keep my job?"

"Not right now, but I'll think about bringing you back next month, if things pick up with summer tourists. You've always been a good worker when you were here, and I'll remember that. You take care now, okay?" He gave her a friendly smile, then headed to the back office.

Humiliated, Sadie got down on the floor and scrubbed with extra strength. She was a hard worker. This couldn't be! Besides her disappointment at losing the job, she would also be losing her only way out of the house. Her job at the hotel had made it easy for her to see Frank and go to band practice every few days.

But now that was all over.

She had made a terrible mistake, and it would cost her the music she loved and the only boyfriend she'd ever had.

As she scrubbed, Sadie tried to work through the embarrassment that burned inside her. How would she tell her family? Adam would have questions; he would want to know why she'd missed work. Oh, there was trouble ahead, and it was all her fault. She had always tried to be a better person than this, but she had failed Mr. Decker.

As she scrubbed the grout between the tiles, she tried to focus on her music and let her heart be light. There was a reason for everything on God's earth, she knew that. But in her heart she worried that the reason here might be to punish her for being irresponsible.

She had scrubbed her way over to the open French doors when a pair of low work boots appeared out on the patio.

"Hey, church girl." Frank called her that, even though he had only ever seen her wearing jeans and a T-shirt. She liked dressing in Englisher clothes, though she left her prayer kapp on at all times. As a little girl she had been told that the kapp helped send her prayers directly to God, and she wasn't able to part with her connection to God in heaven. "What's shakin'?" he asked.

Fighting back tears, she rose to her knees and looked up at him. "Oh, Frank, it's horrible. I've been fired."

"What? What happened?"

Looking around to make sure Mr. Decker wasn't nearby, she quickly told Frank about their conversation. "I feel sick about it," she said. "And I don't look forward to telling my family. When they hear this, they're going to know about the bad things I've done."

"You haven't done anything bad," Frank insisted. "And why do you have to tell your family at all? If they don't hear about it from Decker, and they probably won't, you can keep coming in to town on your scooter, but instead of going to work you can go to Red's garage . . . or to Philadelphia with me. How about that for a plan?"

"And lie to my family? I couldn't do that."

"No need to lie," he said. "You just don't tell them you were fired."

Sickened by shame and the fumes of ammonia, Sadie wiped her brow with her wrist and thought about Frank's idea. She would not lie to her family, but then she wouldn't have to do that if they thought she was heading off to work. His plan might work . . . but was it too far from the truth?

"Trust me," Frank said, "this is going to work out. I know you feel bad now, but down the road you'll look back on this day and wish it had happened earlier. With the extra rehearsal time we can get in, we'll definitely get some summer gigs—paying gigs. With you fronting the band, we're going to make ten times as much as either of us made slaving away for Decker."

"This is not slave work." She shook her head as she went over the grout with a hand brush. "I never minded working here."

"Yeah? Well, how about getting paid for singing your heart out, church girl? You loved those concerts we saw, right?"

"Ya," she admitted reluctantly. Although she'd been to two concerts with Frank and Red, Sadie still found it hard to imagine that people made money for their music. But that was another world—Frank's Englisher world—and he didn't understand how she now ached to correct the way she'd wronged Mr. Decker.

Frank checked his watch. "We're off in thirty minutes. Soon as you're done, meet me at the van. Red and Tara are going to be psyched to hear about your new availability. Chin up, church girl. This is going to be awesome."

Two hours later, Sadie was lost in another world. Tonight, the music was really coming together, and each song was taking Sadie off to a different place.

Behind her, Red swooshed a brush over his shiny golden cymbals or thunked a steady beat on his drums, giving her a place to land after she soared over each note. Tara's bass gave each song deep, warm rumbles, like the churning of earth under the plough in spring. And Frank's guitar wailed in the empty spaces or plunked away sweetly like a brook trickling over stones in the distance.

"But God bless the child that's got his own," the music spilled from her heart, "that's got his own." With her eyes pressed shut, she swayed to the music as the song swung to an end.

"Woo-yeah!" Frank clapped his hands together. "That was awesome. Is this not one of the best rehearsals we've ever had? Yes!"

Sadie opened her eyes to the animated faces of her fellow band members.

"Yeah, that was smooth," Tara Grace said. She cradled the large electric bass as she perched on one of the big amps.

"Sadie, I love the way you just pour it out when you get in the zone," Frank said. "It's like you go off and visit the melody of the song in a land far, far away."

"Yeah," Red's low voice rumbled. "It's like some weird, energized trance comes over you," he said, shaping an imaginary ball with his hands. "Really cool."

Sadie hugged herself, basking in their praise. "I love that song," she admitted. She didn't always agree with the songs Frank picked, but "God Bless the Child" was one that everyone in the band could climb into, like a boat carrying them together down a winding river. That was how it felt when a song worked; as if they were all traveling, one boat, but four very separate passengers.

Sadie always enjoyed the voyage.

"You know what?" Frank rubbed the hairs on his chin, squinting at his bandmates. "We sound really good tonight. I say we get some of this recorded. I'm going to get my video camera." He slipped his guitar off and went out the side door of the garage.

While Tara pecked out a low murmur, Sadie went to thank Red for the tunes he had downloaded onto her iPod. Sadie bought new songs with money from her job, but Red was always happy to download any music from his CD collection.

"I love the James Taylor songs," she said. "He's a wonderful good singer, but best of all, his songs talk about things I know. Colors and growing seeds. Rivers and mountains and roads. Sunshine and the moon." *And longing and love,* she thought, though she didn't dare say it aloud. That would be too embarrassing to mention to an Englisher boy.

"Cool." Red tucked his drumsticks under one arm, his long, flame-colored hair falling over his eyes as he looked up at her. "Yeah, JT knows how to put a song together. His phrasing is great, and he can play the guitar like nobody else on the planet. So which song did you like the best?"

"'Blossom,'" she said. "I want to sing that song. Do you think we could try it sometime?"

"We can't do James Taylor," Frank said from across the garage, where he was setting a camera on a little stand. "Our style is nothing like his. It would fail, man."

"You never know." Red stood up from his stool and stretched his drumsticks over his head. He was a tall, skinny boy, all bones in his T-shirts and baggy jeans. "You can't be sure till you try it."

"We are not playing 'Blossom,'" Frank snapped.

"Just chill, Frank," Tara said. "You're not the boss of this band."

Frank grumbled as he bent over and squinted into the little

camera on the stand. "Okay, this is going to be great. This shot will get all of us. Perfect."

"What exactly are we recording for?" Red asked. "Is this our first music video, because I didn't get the choreography memo."

"It's just a trial, okay? Something to send out to promoters or clubs so they can get a taste of us."

"But I can't do it." Sadie lifted a hand to one cheek, worry piercing her chest.

"Sure you can," Frank said. "You're doing great. Just keep going the way you are."

"Not that. I'm not afraid. I can't let my picture be taken. The rules of our church forbid it. The Bible says we are not to let ourselves become graven images."

"Oh, yeah." Frank straightened, rubbing the patch of hair on his chin. "I forgot about that." He bent toward the camera again, then went over and turned off the overhead fluorescents so that the light of a single lamp on one of the amps cast a shadowy golden glow through the room. "How's that?" Frank asked. "This way people will see only your silhouette. Not enough that anyone would ever be able to identify you."

"I don't know." Sadie glanced over at Tara, who shrugged. No one cared but Sadie. "Are you sure no one will see me?"

"Positive," Frank said. "Here. Have a look if you want. I like the dark profile. It's sort of mysterious that way. Who is that mystery singer? People will want to know."

She bent over and took a peek at the tiny screen on the back of the camera. Frank was right; she could see the shape of Tara sitting on the amp, but the image was fuzzy. She resembled a sack of potatoes more than a girl.

"I guess that will be okay," Sadie said, though it still worried her a bit. To have her picture out there, to even be here after getting fired from the hotel . . . She was dipping into the Englisher world more and more. If Adam and the church brethren found out, she would be in trouble. They might even ask her to repent for breaking the rules.

But they were not going to find out. And for now, Frank and the band brought comfort to her lonely heart by helping her make beautiful music.

She stepped back into her spot by the microphone and the rehearsal continued. Once again, she went to that special place when she closed her eyes, soaring high like a bird in the sky.

When the rehearsal ended, Frank loaded his guitar into the back of the van and gave Sadie a ride home. This was their routine on rehearsal nights. Frank would pull up to the embankment on the main road, just out of sight of the farmhouse. There he would turn off the engine, and they would talk a bit more about the rehearsal or songs or the weather.

Tonight, as Sadie wondered if she should try to find another job in Halfway, Frank couldn't stop talking about the "gigs" he was trying to set up for the band in Philly. He frowned down at the screen of his cell phone, annoyed that he had missed a call during the ride.

"That was my cousin Heather." Frank winced, showing his teeth. When he did that, he reminded Sadie of illustrations of the devil she'd seen in children's Bible storybooks, especially with his pointy chin with that patch of hair on it. "She's got an in with this club owner in Philly. I think we're going to get our first real gig out of it."

"That's nice of her."

"Nice? It would be an amazing break for us. Big-time, baby! We're going to get your voice out there." He pointed out the open van window.

She glanced over the dark landscape. "Out in the cornfield? I already sing to the sprouts. So far they haven't sung back."

"Funny girl." Frank shook his head as he texted someone. "You know what I'm saying. I'm going to make you a star."

Sadie rolled her eyes. She loved singing, but she didn't share Frank's desire to perform in a bar. Sure, she loved making beautiful music, and she believed the Heavenly Father meant for her to "make a joyful noise" and share her gift. But performing in taverns? That was not her dream. She knew the ministers would never approve of it, and to be honest, the few times she had done karaoke in the city with Frank, she had been uncomfortable with the looks of the place. The lights were always dim, the rooms were dank and cluttered with tables, and they all served alcohol. She had worried that she could get in trouble with the police since she was only eighteen.

"Nah, it's cool," Frank reassured her at the time. "See those rug rats over there eating with their parents? If the place serves food, and you stay away from booze, you're fine."

As she'd gotten to know Frank, Sadie had learned that he had a story to explain everything. Sometimes his stories amused her; other times his habit for stretching the truth annoyed her.

Frank grinned down at his BlackBerry. "My cousin thinks she can get us a spot in May. We just might get a regular gig by summer." Frank's eyes lit with hope at the prospect of a gig, but for Sadie it meant a shiver of guilt and uneasiness.

"I can't do a regular gig," she said. "Already it's hard to slip away from the farm for rehearsals." If she started doing it every night, surely Adam would question her.

"But now that your job at the hotel is done, you've got nights free."

Sadie bit her lips together. "It's not a good thing that I lost my job. It was my fault, you know."

"Hey, I know it sucks that you got axed, but there's a silver lining in that cloud."

Sadie folded her arms. For a while during rehearsal the music had carried her away from her problems, but Frank's reminder of her lost job now made her sink into shame again.

"Church girl . . . relax. You've got nothing to be embarrassed about. I've lost more jobs than I can count, and I can't even count that well. Wow, maybe that's why I lost all those jobs."

The cold feeling began to drain. "You're joking, I know that. You're trying to make me feel better."

"And is it working?"

"A little." She cracked a smile.

"Good. You know, you're beautiful when you smile. I know girls who would kill for those cheekbones."

She pressed the backs of her hands to her cheeks. "I hope not."

"Aw, church girl. What's it going to take for you to be comfortable with me?" He cupped one of her ears, his dark eyes glistening in the shadows. "When can we get closer?"

"Get closer?" Sadie squinted at him. He was pretty close already. More words twisted like a pretzel. "You know, you Englishers can be very confusing with all your expressions," she said.

"We're confusing? I'm talking to a girl who can rip a tune like Billie Holiday but won't let me peek under her bonnet."

Sadie tugged the string of her kapp. In the months that they had been dating, he had always been so curious to see her hair, but it wasn't something Sadie would consider right now.

"Do you know the saying 'Curiosity killed the cat'?"

"Well, I am one persistent cat, but you've probably figured that out already." He grinned, his teeth gleaming in the lights from the dashboard. "How long have we known each other, Sadie? Since November? That's five months and I'm still kissing you good-bye on the forehead like an old grandpa. You won't let me drive down the lane to take you all the way home. What gives?"

"How many times have I explained it, Frank?" Sadie shook her head in dismay. Why didn't he see how it was for her? "The Amish way of courtship is so very different from the way you Englishers do things. Courtship takes time."

He tilted his head, cocking one eye. "Five months isn't enough? How about six?"

She grinned, giving his shoulder a teasing shove. "I'll tell you when the time comes."

"Typical female. I'm convinced that you girls have some secret rule book that guys can't read." He looked out through the windshield. "So I guess I'm still not allowed to drive down that lane and take you all the way home."

She nodded. An Amish boy would have understood this. "Not yet." She opened the door and got out of the van. Frank met her at the rear of the vehicle, where he helped her get her scooter and dress from the back.

"Call me," he said, making the funny little gesture with his thumb and pinky finger sticking out.

"I will." She had charged her cell phone at the hotel, but in the future she would need to figure out a way to keep it charged. Ach! Such a problem not to have her job anymore.

"We're set to go to Philly this Saturday," he reminded her. "Open mike night. Take good care of those pipes."

"You and your expressions." She shook her head as she got on her scooter and rolled toward the lane.

As she steered carefully, trying to avoid the ruts, she thought once again about her courtship with Frank. She kept waiting for love to come over her. How she longed for the simplest brush of his fingertips or squeeze of his hand on her arm to stir her heart.

Sadie wanted to fall in love. A big love—true love—would cure the loneliness she felt in her heart, the ache that reminded her she was different from most Amish girls. Like an exotic seed that somehow blew onto the farm and blossomed despite all odds, she didn't quite fit in among the pansies and petunias and wild buttercups. Even in a family of eleven kids, Sadie felt a loneliness that squeezed her heart.

A big love would ease that. She knew her parents had shared a deep, solid love for each other, and she'd noticed the look in Mary's eyes when she saw her beau. And the way Remy smiled at Adam at the dinner table. So far, she hadn't dared speak of it with anyone, but she was eighteen now, old enough to ask about it.

She would ask Remy about it, she decided. Remy would understand.

When exactly did the big love come over a girl? When Sadie turned sixteen she had attended every youth gathering, singings and bonfires and volleyball games, always on the lookout for a wonderful good Amish fellow. She had accepted rides home from a few of them, but none caught her fancy. Ruben Zook liked to laugh, but he was a terrible prankster, and when Amos Lapp stared at her with that grin, all she could think of was a large dog who wanted a pat on the head. She had even drawn out a few of the quieter boys who kept to themselves. How she'd prayed to find the seeds of love, the spark in a fellow's eyes, the heart-racing feeling she'd heard about.

Oh, but it had never happened. The only excitement she'd known was the thrill of having a secret boyfriend, and even that was wearing thin now.

Dear Lord, please let it happen soon, she prayed, looking to the stars sparkling in the heavens above. *Please, let it happen for me, too.*

SIX

As usual the long kitchen table was the hub of activity, but this time instead of eating, nearly everyone in the family was trying their hand at dipping eggs into cups of water turned red or sapphire or crimson with food coloring. Sadie could hardly believe that tomorrow was Easter Sunday, but then her favorite season always moved by quick as a rabbit. Uncle Nate, Aunt Betsy, and their family had come over to visit and found the Kings dying eggs. It was a tradition Mamm had allowed, as long as the children remembered the real meaning of Easter.

Seated at the table covered in newspaper, Sadie listened as her cousin Rachel compared the emerging egg colors to the light of a setting sun or the yellow of a daffodil or the blue of a winter sky. Rachel King saw the world through an artist's eye, a gift that had always set her apart from most Amish girls. Sadie felt sure that she and Rachel would have been good friends if they hadn't already been cousins first.

"I think I'll make a green egg next," Rachel said. She had pale blond hair and blue eyes that always seemed to sparkle with humor. "So tomorrow for breakfast Sam can have green eggs and ham."

"I know that story," Sam said.

"Um-hmm." Rachel dipped an egg into the forest-green dye. "But how will you ever find green ham? Do you have a green pig out in the pen?"

"We don't have any pigs at all," Sam replied, and Sadie had to suppress a smile.

Although the Easter tradition didn't hold its usual excitement for Sadie, she had to hold back amusement as she watched Katie dabble in coloring eggs for the first time.

"Look at that!" Ruthie nodded to their baby sister, who was lifting a hard-cooked egg from the cup of dye. "Katie dropped her red egg into the blue dye, and now it's purple!"

"Purple is *gut*," Katie said, her eyes bright with wonder.

"It's wonderful gut, Katie." Sadie guided the toddler's wobbly hand to lower the colored egg onto the newspaper for drying.

"So red and blue make purple." Simon dipped an egg in a cup of orange by hand, ignoring the dye that had already soaked into his fingertips.

"I wanted to use crayons," Sam said dolefully. "But Mary says if I press too hard, the egg will crack."

"Mary's right, but I can show you a trick for dying eggs with crayons." Rachel bent her head close to Sam's and handed him a white crayon from his box. Ever the artist, Rachel possessed far more patience than Sadie.

Sam smiled up at Rachel, warmed by the attention. It struck Sadie that he had lost their mamm's love at so young an age. Sam was only three and Katie not even a year old when their parents had been killed. Though Sadie missed her parents every day, she offered her sorrow up to the Heavenly Father, and over the weeks and months she had been blessed by his healing grace. But Katie and Sam had been so young to lose their parents; too young to understand how to turn to Gott.

Heaviness overcame her like a cape of sadness, and Sadie got up from the table in a fit of restlessness. Was she getting too old for coloring eggs? Or was it the heat of guilt that kept her from feeling at home with her own family?

Two weeks had passed since Sadie had lost her job, and she still hadn't told anyone in her family. No one had noticed anything unusual, since she had left the farm three or four times a week, as if she was working a shift at the Halfway Hotel.

Frank was happy to have more rehearsal time, and Sadie noticed how the band was coming together. They sounded wonderful good. As Tara had said, "We rock!"

But Sadie's joy in the music was slightly spoiled by guilt. She didn't like sneaking around.

And now, the Easter preparations that she usually enjoyed seemed to be happening miles away. The laughter, the talk of horse auctions and vegetable gardens and recipes, the glee of the children dying eggs, the smell of chocolate chip cake in the oven . . . this was the quilt of her life. This was her own family, ya? So why this feeling that her future was outside this farmhouse, somewhere down that road?

The kitchen had grown warm, and suddenly Sadie found the room airless, her face hot. Circling around Uncle Nate and Adam, she went out through the porch and breathed in soft, fresh air. Out on the wide swath of grass in front of the house Jonah and Gabe were having a volleyball match with cousins Ben and Abe. She headed in that direction, content to sit on the grass in the shade of the tall, swaying beech trees. Normally she would have joined in the volleyball, as games were a favorite activity of hers, but today, she held back.

Near the house a quilt had been hung out to dry, and Sadie

fixed her eyes on the beautiful colors as it flapped in the gentle breeze. It was a Sunshine and Shadow quilt, a vivid diamond surrounded by lines of color alternating from bright to dark. Rose to black, blue to orange, brown to lime green.

Darkness and light. Sunshine and shadow.

The old quilt reminded Sadie of her two worlds: the shadowed music she lost herself in at night with the band, and the sunshine that bathed this farm, the home of her birth.

I've got one foot in each world, she thought, pulling at a sprig of grass. *I'm straddling the paddock fence.*

A movement close by caught her attention, and she looked over to see her brother Jonah coming toward her.

"Was ist los?" He sat down beside her, tipping his straw hat back to make eye contact. "When I see you pass up a volleyball game, I know something is wrong. What is it?"

His dark eyes were so earnest, Sadie wanted to share her thoughts, starting with the fact that she'd lost her job and explaining the irresistible attraction of making music with the band. She knew Jonah wouldn't be mad at her, but he would have to tell Adam, and that would make for a sticky mess. "A girl can't sit and enjoy a beautiful day?" she asked, trying to make her voice light.

The low growl from his throat told her he wasn't convinced. He pulled his hat off and rubbed the back of one hand over his damp forehead. "Is it about the baptism classes starting after Easter?"

"Baptism?" She hadn't been thinking of that at all, but now that Jonah had mentioned it, the decision seemed to be charging toward her like a team of horses.

Baptism . . .

She wasn't ready, but now that she was eighteen people would be expecting it, wouldn't they?

She stared down at the grass, wondering how she could have

forgotten that the classes would be starting soon. Everyone would be watching her on that Sunday, watching and hoping that she would join the classes with the bishop, declaring that she was ready to be a part of their church. A baptized member.

"I know it's a big decision." Jonah let his hat flop onto the grass. "When I was facing it, I felt kind of trapped. Everyone just expected me to get baptized. The quiet one, that's what they called me, ya?"

"They still do," she teased. "But right now you're gabbing enough to shed the nickname."

He swiped at a cloud of gnats with one big hand. "Anyway, most folk thought I would go without a ripple of doubt. But it wasn't an easy thing for me. I got all worked up with questions about our church and other churches, too. I rode my horse off every other Sunday, visiting other churches."

"Ya?" Sadie wound a string of grass around one finger. It was hard to imagine calm, steady Jonah worked up over anything. "I remember you being gone, but I didn't know where you went off to."

"I didn't tell anyone, but Dat knew. Somehow he guessed what I was doing."

"Was he upset with you?"

Jonah stared off toward the cow barn. "Not our dat. He told me it was good to learn everything you can about something. That Gott gave us a brain in our head so that we could gain knowledge. That was all he said. He never pushed, but I came around on my own."

Sadie thought of Jonah visiting other churches. She knew a bit about the Mennonites, but truly none of that interested her. She didn't want to go off and find another faith. She had been raised Amish, and she had always wanted to be baptized in the Anabaptist tradition, just like everyone else in her family. Faith wasn't her problem. Her love of music was the thing that was pulling her away from this life she had always loved.

How she wished she could have both—her music and her Amish life. Right now they both seemed equally important, like night and day, earth and air.

"The thing is, I don't think I'm ready to be baptized," Sadie said, regret heavy in her heart. "I wish I could do it. You know I want to ease everyone's mind, and I surely can't imagine spending the rest of my days anywhere but here."

"Then what's holding you back?" Jonah's brown eyes studied her thoughtfully. "Is it the English boyfriend you've been sneaking off to see?"

Sadie shook her head; although she liked Frank, he wasn't standing in the way of her decision.

"Then what is it, Sadie?" Jonah cocked his head to one side, eager to hear her answer.

How she wanted to tell him, to let her sorrows and worries spill from her. There wasn't a better person to talk to than strong, patient Jonah. But she couldn't put her feelings for music into words, at least not words that made sense. "I can't explain it to you, Jonah, but I know in my heart that nothing will ever take me too far away from our family. Don't you worry about me. I want to be baptized in the faith. Just not yet."

"Okay, then." He gave a nod and reached for his hat. "If you ever want to talk about it, you know I'm a good listener."

"A wonderful good listener," she agreed.

"They call me the quiet one for a reason." He swatted his hat against her knees playfully, then got to his feet. "Kumm. I need you on my team in volleyball."

After two rounds of volleyball, the players were about to switch teams when Ruthie marched out from the kitchen, her skirt flapping behind her. "The cake's done. Mary says anyone who wants a piece had better get it now. It's going fast!"

Ben tossed the ball to his brother. "You pick the team. I'm going for cake."

"I'm going, too," Abe said, dropping the ball to the ground.

"Game's over," Gabe announced, kicking the ball straight up, then boosting it again with his knee.

Leah and Jonah were already crossing the lawn, heading toward the house. That left only Sadie and Rachel, who was tugging on Sadie's elbow.

"Quick now, cousin," Rachel said, grabbing her arm. "Before they come back and make us play five more rounds, let's find a quiet place to talk."

Sadie couldn't help but grin at the amusement on Rachel's heart-shaped face. "We can hide by the woodshed."

"The woodshed is good." Rachel's sky-blue eyes were lit with mirth. "No one will find us till the first frost of autumn."

Both girls laughed as they linked arms and passed through a patch of wild clover. With so much of her time spent in Halfway, Sadie didn't get to see her cousin often these days. There was only church, every other Sunday. Sadie didn't realize how much she'd missed her until now. "I needed a good laugh," Sadie said.

"I have plenty of laughs to give if you come around more often," Rachel said. "Why is it you never visit on off Sundays anymore?"

"You know where I've been going," Sadie said, glancing back at the door of the house to make sure none of the little ones had followed. Rachel was one of the few people she had confided in after Frank had so boldly begun courting her.

"The Englisher boy." They had reached the woodpile, and Rachel sat on the giant stump used for splitting wood. "You do like to push the rules. Has he won your heart yet?"

Sadie wished she could say that was true . . . or did she really? Did she want the Big Love so badly that she would really like to lose her heart to an Englisher boy? When she had first met Frank, there was a certain attraction in breaking the rules. Maybe she had wanted to rebel. But she'd gotten past that now. "These days it's not Frank winning my heart as much as all the things he's done for me. I told you about the band, ya?"

As Rachel nodded encouragingly, Sadie sat beside her on the fat stump and told her everything . . . about the band, about getting fired from her job, about sneaking to rehearsal, about the wonderful way she felt when she was singing with the group of talented musicians.

"So it's the singing that's become important to you," Rachel said.

"It's always been a part of my life. Mamm always sang us lullabies."

Rachel's eyes narrowed. "And your mamm had a beautiful voice, too. I used to love sitting near her in church."

"I'll never forget Mamm's sweet voice."

Rachel gave her hand a gentle squeeze. "And you miss her."

"I do. She always told me that Gott had blessed me with a special gift. I keep wondering if Gott means me to do something with that gift."

"You know I've been feeling the same way, but not about music."

"About your art," Sadie said, thinking of how her cousin had created lovely landscapes and paintings of Amish scenes since she was a little girl. One Christmas Rachel had received a set of watercolors as a gift, and a true talent had blossomed from those small plates of color. So far, the bishop hadn't raised any objections, though Rachel had been warned not to illustrate Plain folk. It was all right to show a hat on a table or a quilt hanging on a clothesline, but Rachel was not to reproduce images of the Amish.

"My painting. I've been staying up late every night working on watercolors. Last week I slept right through the morning milking. At first Mamm thought I was sick, but when she found out what I was doing, she gave me quite a tongue-lashing."

Sadie could imagine Aunt Betsy giving her daughter a good talking-to. Betsy was a kind woman, but she kept a close watch on her children.

"Aren't you a little old for a scolding? You're eighteen now," Sadie pointed out.

"All the more reason that I should be responsible, Mamm says." Rachel's pretty pink lips curled down in a frown. "She says I'll have to give up my painting once I start the classes for baptism." Her eyes were round as quarters. "I don't know if I can do the classes if I have to give up my painting."

"I'm in the same boat." Sadie clutched her cousin's wrist. "I'm not ready to join the church if I have to give up something that is this important to me."

Rachel's blue eyes were unwavering. "So what are we going to do?"

"I don't know." Sadie wiped her moist palms on the skirt of her dress. "But I do know that if we don't start those classes, there's going to be a lot of disappointment around here."

The next day, Sadie put her worries aside as she helped Mary prepare the meal for Easter supper. After a morning of baking, with Mary making shoofly pie and Sadie mixing and kneading bread dough, they worked in tandem glazing a ham that Uncle Nate had brought yesterday. They baked stuffing, as well as potatoes au gratin spiced with winter onions from the garden. From the storehouse, there would be canned green beans, corn, and apple butter for the bread.

And, of course, as they worked, the kitchen was filled with song.

"What should we sing next?" Mary asked as she grated a block of cheddar cheese for the potatoes.

"Let's do Dat's favorite," Sadie said. The small ache inside reminded her how much she missed their parents, despite this sunny April day. Sometimes when Mary moved about the kitchen, pulling a tray from the oven or bringing a dish to the sink, Sadie was reminded of their mamm.

"That's a wonderful good choice," Mary said. "Whenever I see a group of sparrows fluttering in the bushes I think of Dat."

Sadie nodded as she began the song "His Eye Is on the Sparrow." Although she knew the words by heart, each time she sang it she saw something new in the lyrics. Today the third verse fit her mood:

"Let not your heart be troubled," His tender word I hear,
   And resting on His goodness, I lose my doubts and fears;
   Though by the path He leadeth, but one step I may see;
   His eye is on the sparrow, and I know He watches me. . . .

The song reminded her that she could trust in the Lord for the right path, and He would surely ease her doubts and fears. It was useless to worry about her decision not to get baptized. She had prayed about it and it felt like the right choice for now, and the Lord was watching over her.

As they sang their way to a delicious Easter meal, Sadie thought about the rhythm of their days on the farm. From the early rise for milking to the quiet of night when they said their prayers and slid under a quilt, all the King children pitched in to care for the animals and cultivate the gardens and fields that would feed them all. Even as she and Mary tended to their supper, she knew Simon and Gabe were in the barn, caring for the horses. Jonah and Adam would be doing quiet work on account of the day of rest, minding the cows or horses or matters that couldn't wait. For the others there were chickens to feed, the henhouse to clean, and simple tasks of sweeping and making beds.

Looking out the window, she saw Leah and Katie walking down the lane to the Doddy house garden to fetch radishes for supper. How little Katie loved digging in the dirt and coming up with the prize of a radish! Over in the corral, Simon was training his horse Shadow, while Ruthie reached a fistful of seed up to the birdhouse the family had built last month.

"Would you look at that?" Mary paused beside her, peering out the window. "The mercury hit the seventies. I say we clean up the picnic tables and have dinner outside."

"That'll be nice, for as long as the sun stays with us," Sadie agreed. Five, Remy, and Mammi Nell would be joining them, making the supper a true family meal.

Hoping the warm spell was here to stay, Sadie stepped outside with a broom to start sweeping off the tables. Susie, Sam, and Ruthie were there to pitch in as well. They helped tie down the vinyl tablecloths and tote plates and utensils outside.

Before long they were sitting down to a fine meal under a heavenly blue sky. Adam sat in a folding chair at the head of the table as everyone grew silent for the prayer.

"Here's a reminder to the little ones." Adam lifted his chin to look down the table at Katie and Sam. "I know you enjoyed coloring eggs yesterday, but don't forget the meaning of Easter, the resurrection of Jesus."

"Amen," Sam said aloud, and there was a bit of laughter. Gabe clapped a hand on the back of Sam's neck and gave him a friendly jostle, while the rest of the family settled again.

Then heads bowed for the silent prayer.

Sadie closed her eyes, thanking Gott for the blessing of this good meal. She thanked Him for her family, for the gift of music, and asked for guidance in the coming days. The baptism question still ached like a splinter in her finger, and she hoped no one would mention it at dinner and probe the wound again.

Once the eating and conversation started, she realized there was no reason to worry. It seemed that Adam and Mary had planned to use the meal to make an announcement, telling the family of their plan to have a double wedding in November.

"I knew it!" Ruthie exclaimed, her amber eyes lit with delight. "I knew something was up, with all those celery seedlings planted in the Doddy-house garden."

Sadie smiled as she passed the bowl of string beans. It was really no secret. With the tragic deaths of Esther and Levi King more than a year ago, Mary and Five had quietly decided not to marry in last year's wedding season. And anyone could see the love shining between Remy and Adam.

"I keep hearing about the wedding celery," Remy said. "I know it's a tradition, but how much celery can a person eat?"

Everyone laughed.

"You're talking about hundreds of people," Mary said. "Since it's a double wedding, there will be more than usual. Maybe four hundred or more."

"And besides going into a lot of the dishes, celery is always on the tables at weddings," Ruthie explained. "It sits in a jar of water like flowers, only you can eat it."

"An edible centerpiece," Remy said. "Well, that's a very practical idea."

"We'll need to invite family and friends from near and far,"

Mary said. "All of Five's family, and your friends too, Remy. Do you think your father will come?"

Remy cocked her head to one side, her lips twisted in a frown. "I don't know, but I'd like to invite him and my stepmother. And my friends from college."

"Can I come to the wedding?" Sam asked. "I think Katie is too young, but I can behave good and proper."

"Everyone in our family is welcome," Mary assured him. "But don't be talking about it with anyone outside the family. With wedding season still months away, it makes me a bit nervous to speak about the details."

"Don't you worry about people hearing the news," Five said. "The bishop is so eager to see the oldest Kings married, he won't mind the word slipping out."

Sadie shifted on the picnic bench, thinking how much things would be changing around here. Mary would be off to live with Five, and Remy would be moving in. Like a mother to the little ones, she'd be. Already she had gained the confidence of the younger King children. It would be an easy change for them, a very good thing for Sam and Katie to have a good woman to take care of them when Mary left.

She glanced across the table at Jonah. How did he feel, with things shifting? Jonah was by no means too old for courting. But despite his regular attendance at singings and youth gatherings, he didn't have a girl. Sadie wasn't the only one who hadn't found the Big Love. At least she wouldn't be the only lonely heart around here.

"I knew something was going on when I caught Mary sewing a white dress," Susie said.

"But you couldn't have been so surprised," Mary said. "Five and I have been courting for a long time now."

"Ya, a hundred years at least," Five teased.

"What about your dress?" Leah asked Remy. "Have you started sewing it?"

"Oh." Remy's green eyes grew round. "I have to sew a dress? By hand?"

"You can use a sewing machine," Mammi Nell said. "With a pedal for the feet." To demonstrate, she made a waving motion with one hand.

Remy's surprise turned to fear. "The machine. Yes, I've tried that. I don't think it likes me."

"We can help you, Susie and I," Leah offered.

"We know how to sew right well. We'll do it for you," Susie agreed. "The machine likes us."

"Denki," Remy said. "I'm so grateful, and I'll help you in any way that I can. I want to learn everything, but some things take longer than others to master."

"I'm sure you'll get the machine to like you one of these days," Adam told Remy, his face softened with a small smile. His dark eyes glimmered with such love for her that Sadie felt a knot form in her throat.

The Big Love.

Watching them now, Sadie suddenly realized that she and Frank didn't have an attachment like this. They weren't even close.

"But this news is a family matter until the fall," Adam told everyone. "Nothing will be official until we're published in church shortly before the wedding."

"But you can't wait until that time to start getting ready," Mammi warned. "There are countless things to be done for the big day. There will be nuts to crack, corn to husk, furniture to be moved, floors and walls to be scrubbed. You'll need to borrow dishes and tables for the wedding dinner."

"So we're going to cater it ourselves," Remy said, nodding.

"That's how we do it," Adam said. "You don't have to serve on the wedding day."

"But the bride and groom pitch in with cleanup the day after the wedding," Mary said. "And Five is a very good worker, so I think he'll have it all done in a snap."

"Whoa, Mary!" Five's blue eyes sparked with humor. "Just because they call me Five doesn't mean I can do the work of five men."

"Of course you can." She waved him off. "That's why your father doesn't want you to leave the farm."

"Oh, he wants me to leave, all right. He just doesn't have any way to get rid of me. There's no land left to be doled out when we get married."

"Is that so?" Jonah asked. "Then what's your plan?"

"We'll be making a home over the carriage house," Five said. "At least for the first year or so. My dat's talking about building another house on the farm, but that would be down the road."

Sadie knew that Five's father had set the older Beiler sons up with parcels of land, but many Amish farmers had no more left to give without cutting the farm too small. It was a problem for some Amish men when they married and started their own families.

"So, Mary, it looks like we're stuck living on top of the old buggies," Five said, a mischievous smile lifting the corners of his lips.

"That's fine by me, as long as we're together." Mary tucked her chin, as if to hide her face from the family, but Sadie could see the radiant love in her eyes.

Oh, how she ached to know true love like theirs.

But maybe she knew it wasn't ever going to happen with Frank. She hadn't wanted to admit it, but there it was . . . a cold, hard truth.

Perhaps her heart had been hardened by the past year or so . . . the tragedy of her parents' deaths. The pain of finding that they'd been killed by someone just down the road, a neighbor, a friend.

She took a drink of water, grateful to hide her conflicted emotions in the deep cup. When she looked down the narrow barrel of the cup, she tried to see herself falling in love with a nice Amish boy.

Who could it be?

Ruben Zook glared at her, a devilish look in his eyes.

No, no, that would not do.

And then there was Amos Lapp, only that silly grin belonged more on Daisy the cow.

Was there no young man in the world who could spark the light of love in her heart?

She stared into the bottom of the cup, eager for an answer.

And the face that floated into her mind nearly made her choke on her sip of water.

Mike Trueherz.

SEVEN

*M*ike stared down at the dissected cat, its skin and flesh neatly pulled back to display its innards. Heart, liver, intestines . . . he could identify them all, but a perverse desire to flunk this test made him pause.

Failing Bio 101 at the community college definitely wouldn't bode well for med school. Maybe that would be a way out. Maybe then he could . . .

No. Stupid plan. It was already April, and he was just six weeks away from being done with community college; he'd only be sabotaging himself if he screwed things up now.

He filled in the correct answers on the captioned test form and moved on to the next specimen: a frog pinned down to the paraffin, paralyzed then meticulously carved so that students could see its beating heart.

It seemed criminal to use a living thing that way—even if students did need to learn anatomy.

He turned away, but when he found himself facing two other

students with lab tests in hand, he moved again. The last thing he needed was for someone to accuse him of cheating on an exam. Mike knew the answers; he just didn't want to be here.

Maybe the smell of formaldehyde in the airless room was getting to him. Going to a counter to fill out the rest of the exam, he longed for the smells of Jamaica, the sweet aroma of star apple fruit, or the mango tree that used to grow right outside his little hut. So many afternoons he'd come home from the clinic to find his porch full of kids from the village, some who didn't have the means to attend school, others who had finished for the day and just enjoyed spending time with Mike. Oh, and there was the tire swing beside the porch, too. Sometimes Mike had felt as if he'd been supervising a playground, but that was fine with him. He'd enjoyed chatting with the kids each day, getting them to draw pictures with his supply of crayons, and even getting some of them started on the basics of the alphabet and building words. He'd loved coming home to see them on the porch—Algernon and Vonnie and Oliver. Their bright eyes were the best welcome in the world. In Jamaica, he'd been able to really make a difference, getting families to pursue medical care, getting children into school.

But here . . . he felt like a paper-pusher and a fraud.

Gritting his teeth, he quickly reviewed the test one last time before turning it in. After this, he was free for the weekend, and his Honda was already packed for his escape. He was heading to Philly, where he'd hook up with old friends, let his gran take him out to dinner, and sleep in the top story of her historic townhouse, a home that had been in the family long before Mike was born. Since he'd returned from Jamaica, his weekend trips to Philadelphia had kept him sane. He was surprised that his parents hadn't gotten suspicious about their son always flying the coop, but the upside was that he got to spend time with Katherine Trueherz, his father's mother.

It was Getaway Friday, and Mike was already gone.

WELCOME TO PHILADELPHIA,
CITY OF BROTHERLY LOVE

Whenever Mike passed that sign he breathed a sigh of relief. Some people were dying to get out of the city, but he enjoyed the faster pace, the lights and noise and endless activity. Normally he drove straight to Gran's house and dropped off his stuff, but tonight he was headed to a reunion of sorts, a get-together with two of the other Peace Corps volunteers he had trained with. His friend Daryl Taveras had scored three tickets to the Phillies game and Mike didn't want to arrive late to their meeting place.

The coffee shop wasn't crowded. Mike spotted his friends at a small table under one of the orange drop lights along the glass wall. "Austin! Daryl!"

Daryl rose and threw his arms out. He was a short but solid African American man with a wide smile that lit up his face. "Mikey! I haven't seen you since last weekend!" He pulled Mike into a bear hug.

"Wait a minute. I'm the prodigal son." Austin Dorsett, who had just moved to Philly from Maryland, pushed in beside them and made it a group hug.

Mike laughed. He could always count on these guys for a few laughs. "Austin! I haven't seen you since Jamaica."

"Yah, mon." Austin clapped Mike on the back. Although he was well into his twenties, the freckles that stood out against his fair complexion made him look like a kid. With his blond hair and blue eyes, Austin had always stood out when they were traveling together in Jamaica. "And I brought you a souvenir." He reached into a backpack on a chair and took out an oblong sphere.

Mike squinted. "Mango? Really?"

Austin shrugged. "For old times' sake." He tossed the mango to

Mike. "Got it at Safeway. Every time we talk on the phone, you wax sentimental about the islands."

"Product of Costa Rica," Mike said, reading the label.

"Hey, it's the thought that counts," Austin said, rubbing one hand over his bristly blond hair.

"Do I have time to grab a drink before we go?" Mike asked, pointing a thumb toward the counter.

"Go for it. It's still more than an hour till game time. I figure we should hang here awhile, keep out of that hot sun."

Mike ordered an iced coffee, and the three young men sat around the small table, where the guys had a game of checkers going.

"Don't let me interrupt your big game," Mike said.

Daryl was already scooping the checkers into a box. "That's okay. I'm so far ahead of Austin, he doesn't have a chance."

"Not true. I employ the 'come from behind' strategy."

"Yeah? Well, I'm glad the Phillies don't have you coaching," Daryl said with a wry expression. "I like my team to win, if you know what I'm sayin'."

They chatted about old times, recounting anecdotes of their assignments. While Mike and Austin had been assigned to different locations in Jamaica, Daryl had gone to the Dominican Republic, where he had used his horticultural degree to assist residents in planting trees.

Listening to Daryl talk about his new job with the city parks department, Mike felt right at home with his old friends. He wondered if they too felt that their time in the Peace Corps was the highlight of their lives. It had been a time of discovery and adventure for all of them. For Mike, it was a period in his life when he had been the best person he thought he could ever be. Sometimes it felt like his life had peaked in Jamaica, and it had been racing downhill ever since.

"So I'm looking forward to having you guys around here twenty-four/seven," Daryl said. "One at Temple and one mooching off a girlfriend."

"Really?" Mike turned to Austin, who had propped his sunglasses on his head, two dark disks sinking in his thick blond hair. "You've got a girlfriend? Does she know what you're really like?"

Austin grinned. "No, and please don't tell her, or she'll send me back to Maryland." He added that he would move in with Daryl while he looked for a teaching position. Job opportunities were tight all over, but he had a lead at a charter school, where his two years of teaching in Jamaica would be a valuable asset.

"And how about you?" Austin asked. "Are you the head of the ER at Philly General yet?"

"That would be the ten-year plan. Sort of." Mike let his gaze drop to the paper cup in his hand, his spirits sinking at the thought of the work ahead of him.

"What's the matter?" Daryl gave him a bump on the shoulder. "You look like they just canceled *Grey's Anatomy.*"

Mike shook his head. "Just a bad day at work. I'll get over it."

"This is not the Mike we know and love." Austin squinted at him. "What's up?"

"What?" Mike shrugged. "I can't have a bad day?" But even as he said it, he knew he was trying to contain a tempest that had been swirling inside him for a while now. He put his coffee on the table and snorted. "Actually, I've been having a string of bad days. For the past year and a half."

Daryl and Austin laughed, but Mike kept his deadpan expression.

"You're serious?" Daryl asked.

"Yah, mon." Mike rubbed his eyes and groaned. "I don't know exactly what's bringing me down, but I know I've got to break the routine. September can't come soon enough. I'm going to see if I can get a summer job here so I can move out of the house as soon as my finals at the community college are done. Really, if I see another cornfield, I'm going to self-destruct."

"You really hate it there, don't you?" Daryl nodded, concern flashing in his dark eyes. "Then it's good to have a plan to get out."

Mike turned the coffee cup in his hand. "Do you ever miss the Caribbean?"

"Sometimes." Austin ran one fingertip over the lines of the checkerboard printed into the tabletop. "Our lives were a lot simpler then. No girlfriends or taxes or career anxiety. But that was then, this is now."

"Yeah. We're different people now than we were back then, and believe me, that's a good thing." Daryl straightened, hands on his knees. "Do you remember how naïve I was when I set off for the Dominican Republic? I thought I was going to go into that village and hand out trees and sage advice on how to plant them. When I got there and people wouldn't even talk to me about trees, I was floored. They'd talk to me about the weather and their children, but I couldn't sell them on the importance of trees. I remember sitting in my bungalow, thinking that I'd be spending two years doing a whole lot of nothing. But I learned. I got into the pace of the village and I learned how to talk to people. Life lesson number one for me: You can't force a person to embrace your cause." He raked his dark hair back and grinned. "No matter how charming you are."

"But I felt like I made a difference there," Mike said. "Since I've come back, nothing here seems to matter as much. I'm not changing anyone's life for the better."

"So get out and change somebody's life," Austin said.

"You need to get out of your comfort zone, bro." Daryl clamped a hand on his shoulder. "St. Mark's Men on a Mission awaits you." Daryl had been after him to join the charitable organization at their church. "We've got a truck going around tomorrow, collecting furniture. You could be on the crew."

"I'm talking about how my life is void of meaning, and you want me to move furniture. Do you think that would really help?" Mike asked.

"I know it." Daryl rose and plunked a red Phillies cap on his head. "You need to get beyond yourself, take care of someone else's problems for a change. Now pick yourself up so we can get to the stadium on time. We got tickets on the first-base line; got to see my man Ryan Howard close-up."

As they headed out to Daryl's car, Mike realized his friends were right. He'd been self-absorbed, focused on his own issues and worries. It would feel good to get out and do something for someone else. Time to break out of his boring, safe bubble.

EIGHT

*I*t was a worship day, and everyone was busy preparing to attend the service down the road when Sadie peeked into the new milking barn in search of Adam. She desperately wanted a word with her oldest brother before today's services. Why had she waited until the last minute? She'd had more than two weeks to talk to him and give him a hint of warning about her decision. Two weeks! But every time she'd had the chance, she'd chickened out, knowing that Adam wouldn't want to hear what she had decided. Now here it was, the first Sunday in May, and soon everyone at church would know her decision.

Sadie didn't see Adam in the new structure, but she paused, awed by the gentle click and whoosh of the new milking machines. It used to be that everyone in the family helped with the milking. Even the littlest ones could help sweep up or lay out fresh hay. But since the machines had arrived, Sadie really wasn't needed in the milking barn anymore.

She moved down the aisle to where her brother Gabe was bent under Daisy, cleaning her teats in preparation.

"How are the cows liking the machines?" she asked.

"Don't know." He gave her a deadpan look. "They haven't said anything to me."

"Everybody knows you're the one the cows like the most." She moved to Daisy's head and patted her neck. Holsteins were big cows, but gentle if you treated them right. "What do you think?"

"I think it's saving us a lot of time. By hand it used to take half an hour to trim a cow like Daisy. Now she's done in three minutes."

"Three minutes? That's good. Now you'll have more time to muck out the pens," she teased.

"That's your specialty, isn't it?" He straightened, his mouth curved in half a grin as Simon came over lugging a vat. Attached were many hoses, which the boy held looped over one arm.

"Want to see how, Sadie?" Simon asked, his face aglow with interest. "It's easy as pie."

"Sure," she said. Though Jonah had already given her a lesson, she didn't want to spoil Simon's excitement.

"Mind you don't let the end of the hoses touch the ground," Gabe reminded him. Together they showed Sadie how the hoses attached to Daisy's teats. Then there was one switch to turn, and the machine began to make that gentle sound again: click and whoosh, click and whoosh.

Sadie smiled, thinking that it could be the rhythm of a song. For a moment both her brothers stood beside her and the three of them watched, just staring in wonder as Daisy got milked without anyone needing to sit under her.

"It's pretty wonderful," Sadie said.

"Now Simon and I can handle the milking on our own," Gabe replied.

"It takes no time at all." Only nine years old, Simon was barely up to Gabriel's shoulders, but he looked every inch a little man as he tipped his straw hat back and surveyed the barn. Sadie felt a surge of love for him. He'd suffered deeply when their parents were killed. As the only person to witness the crime, Simon had shut down, unable to speak for months after the tragedy. And then he had been haunted by terrifying dreams that sent him walking through the house in the middle of the night.

"It's given Jonah and Adam a chance to take care of other things. Like the fence on the back field that's always giving us trouble." With Daisy done, Gabe shut off the machine and hung the hoses over a nearby rail. "And good fences make for good sleep. I'm sick of getting out of bed in the middle of the night because one of the cows got loose."

"I think the new machines are wonderful good." Sadie paused. "Have you seen Adam this morning?" she asked, lifting the vat of steaming milk. She was used to pitching in. As Mamm used to say, many hands made light work.

"Saw him in the pasture earlier, but I'm sure he'll be at breakfast," Gabe said.

Simon scooted under the next cow to clean its teats for milking. "I saw him go into the new washroom. I think he's washing up extra clean for the preaching service."

Gabe rolled his eyes. "He wants to smell sweet for Remy."

"There's nothing wrong with a bit of extra washing," Sadie said as she toted the container to the back of the barn. "I'm going to see if I can find him."

She stepped out into the spring morning and let her eyes comb the horizon of sloping hills, a patchwork of fields, the pond with its marsh grass and trees, the other barn and outbuildings and the main house. She saw the twins returning from the henhouse with Sam and Katie, and she knew Ruthie was in the kitchen helping Mary prepare a quick breakfast.

No sign of Adam anywhere.

She had hoped for a moment alone with him before they

headed off to the service, but as the time for breakfast approached, it was clear she'd missed her chance to speak with him about her decision.

Behind the milking barn was an ancient beech tree, her favorite hiding place during hide-and-seek when they were little. She stood between the jutting roots of that old tree and leaned against it. The morning sun was a burst of lemon rising in the spring sky, and despite the familiar surface of the tree's bark, Sadie felt like she was about to fall into very strange territory. Today was the day to say yes to baptism, and no amount of searching could produce that single word in Sadie's heart.

She wasn't ready.

Would Adam be upset with her?

She was afraid that he would be. Although he wasn't her father, he had taken on Mamm and Dat's place after their passing. Adam felt responsible for her, and she understood that he wanted her to follow their faith and join the church. For sure, Mamm and Dat would have wanted it too, if God had not taken them on that dark winter day.

But this was Sadie's decision to make, even if it would disappoint Adam.

Although Adam was careful with his words, Sadie felt his disapproval like a rain cloud hovering over her head. His scolding dark eyes followed her when she headed down the lane after dishes were done on Saturday or Sunday nights. Her job at the hotel always caused him concern, even when she offered to turn the money she made there over to the family account. Adam told her to keep her wages. He said that she had earned the money, but his words had bristled with scorn. Sometimes she thought of him as an angry bear, just watching and growling, but Adam wasn't the only bear eyeing her. The bishop and Preacher Dave kept a careful eye on the youth in their congregation. Young people in rumspringa had a lot of freedom, but if you went too far, the bishop wouldn't hesitate to pay you a visit and give you a talking-to, whether you were baptized or not.

After breakfast the girls grabbed their bonnets and the family filed out the door to the preaching service. Jonah took Mammi Nell in a buggy with his horse Jigsaw, but the rest of the family walked, as this week's service was being held at the Zooks', owners of the neighboring farm who shared the phone shanty with the Kings.

Just after they turned off the lane, Sadie spotted the line of buggies on the main road, all of them on their way to the service. Here and there groups of folk went on foot. Truly, the sight of the people and buggies heading off to worship the Heavenly Father always moved her.

All to the glory of Gott.

And even with all the confusion stewing in her heart, Sadie believed that Gott would understand if she did not choose baptism this year.

Up ahead a carriage slowed, and a young man jumped out—Sadie's cousin Ben.

"It's Uncle Nate's carriage." Ruthie lifted her skirt and scurried ahead. "I want to see Remy before church."

Sadie picked up her step to follow her younger sister.

Up ahead Cousin Abe emerged from the carriage, followed by Remy. Though she wore a prayer kapp, her hair was a bright orange that belonged to no woman born Amish.

"Remy!" Ruthie reached out and took her hand. "Walk with us! Today is such a big day for you and—" She lifted Remy's hand, as if something were curious about it. "So soft! Your skin is smooth like whipped cream."

"Not like our hands." Sadie rubbed her own hands together. "Calloused and thick from years of farmwork."

"But I'm trying to toughen up," Remy said, flexing one arm. "You know I had blisters a few weeks back from mucking the stables." Her green eyes darted to someone beyond Sadie, and Sadie turned to see her brother Adam walking by with Simon and Gabe.

"Good morning," Adam said, his dark eyes on Remy.

It's a good thing Remy McCallister came along, Sadie thought. God must have brought her around to put a little light back in Adam's heart.

"Guten Morgen," Remy responded, her face lighting up with love as she watched the group of young men pass. "A beautiful morning, isn't it?"

"Ya, and a special one for you, today being your first class with the preacher," Mary said as she approached carrying a shoofly pie, one of her specialties, to be served at the community meal after the service.

"Or did you forget?" Ruthie asked.

Remy pressed a hand to her heart. "Are you kidding me? I've had butterflies in my stomach since I woke up this morning."

"Are you scared you're making the wrong decision?" Sadie asked. All night, she'd tossed and turned as if sleeping on a bed of thistle and worry.

"Oh, no, not that. I'm just a bit nervous about the lesson being in German, and sometimes the bishop seems so stern. I'd never want to be disrespectful, but my German isn't so gut and what if I say the wrong thing?"

The girls laughed softly, though they sympathized with Remy's dilemma.

"Here's the most important thing," Ruthie said gently. "*Ya* means yes. *Net* is not. And *nein* or *nay* is no."

"Thanks for the primer, kiddo, but I'm leaving it up to the Big Guy to get me through the language barrier."

"The Big Guy?" Mary turned to Remy. "Who's that?"

"God, of course. He's the only one who could make sense of a kooky Englisher like me seeking to join your community. And though I joke about my nerves and fears, I do feel like God has been leading me here, beckoning me to join this congregation. It's the end of a bumpy road for me, and I'm so happy to see home in sight."

"It's a wonderful good day," Mary said, lifting her face to the sunshine, then turning to catch Sadie's eye. "How about you, Sadie? Will you be starting the classes, too?"

"She doesn't want to be asked," Ruthie said, shaking her head at Mary. "I know that because I've asked her a hundred times."

"I'm not sure yet," Sadie said quickly, hoping to turn the conversation away from herself.

"It is a big decision," Mary said, "but if you ever want to talk about it, I—"

"Make him stop!" Just then Susie came running back down the road, squealing.

She was being pursued by Simon, whose mouth was open wide in a gleeful grin. "Say hello to Froggy," he said, raising his cupped hands.

"Simon has a frog, and it's going to hop on me!" Susie ducked behind Remy for cover. "Make him go away!"

"Mind your manners and your church clothes, both of you."

"A frog can't hurt you," said Leah. "At least, not the ones around here. But they do have poisonous ones in South America. A poison dart frog . . ."

As Leah rambled on about the frog world, Sadie breathed a sigh of relief at the distraction. She stared at the rolling green pastures and wished that she shared Remy's certainty about baptism. It seemed that the older she got, the less certain she was becoming about things. But her personal road was not as straight as Remy's. Bishop

Samuel had said time and again that baptism was a promise to follow the *Regel und Ordnung,* the rules and order, for the rest of your life. A promise not to depart from the Ordnung through life or death. Sadie wanted to commit to God and do the right thing, but when she thought of baptism worry pressed heavily upon her, a huge stone on her chest. What if she found that she could not follow the Ordnung? Then she would be shunned. Such a humiliation for her heart and her family. She didn't think she could bear it. Better to wait and choose baptism when both her heart and soul were in it.

A sad love song circled in Sadie's mind, and she thought of Frank. He was one big reason why she couldn't get baptized yet. Frank had discovered her gift for music, and she was grateful for the way he had taken her under his wing, inviting her into the band and taking her to Philadelphia.

The city . . . there was another thing she loved that didn't match with joining the faith. Philadelphia was full of bright colored lights and so many people. Such different people! People with rings in their noses or shaved heads. Some even had hair standing up in a line along the center of their heads like a bristle brush! Some had skin as brown as coffee. Others had golden skin and eyes that pinched at the edges. Every time Sadie visited the city she was fascinated by the variety of people God created. God had so many recipes! Sometimes she tired of the same old clothes and hairstyles that were traditional in her community.

And then there was her music, another big reason. The biggest one. She stifled a yawn, thinking of the dimly lit club where she had sung onstage last night. Frank had worked it out so that their band could do a few songs, like a real show. Sadie's nerves had trilled as she'd stepped up in front of the lights, opened her mouth, and found that special place where she could escape in the song. It was a satisfying feeling, sweet and biting, like lemonade on a parched tongue or squishing your toes into the mud of the pond on a hot summer day. Singing onstage was thrilling and tender, brash and quiet all at once. She loved it.

If Sadie started the baptism classes today, she would need to give up her singing and her weekend trips to Philadelphia. Just as other Amish teens had to sell off their cars or give away English clothes and iPods, she would have to abandon her blue jeans and Frank and the band. Although there would always be the slow, soulful songs during preaching service, she would have to say good-bye to the music of her heart forever.

Sadie was not ready to do that.

When they arrived at the Zooks' farm, there was much quiet commotion. Young men parked the buggies. Horses had to be un-hitched and put out in the paddock, as the families would be here for a good four hours at least, with the service and the meal after-ward. Women brought baked goods into the house, or gathered their little ones and told them to mind, or stood around with their friends for a bit of conversation before the service began.

Sadie moved out of the way of incoming buggies, but she didn't have the heart to go into the house with Mary and her sisters. In-stead, she lingered by a pile of stacked hay bales, watching solemnly as Remy and another girl—Elizabeth Mast—accompanied Bishop Samuel into the workshop beside the barn for their first lesson. And there went her cousin Abe . . . and David Fisher, too. Such a big moment, but barely noticed by others in the congregation.

As a buggy pulled past she noticed Adam watching Remy go in, and just when she thought he didn't see her, he turned his head and met her eyes.

Why did she feel the burning in her face? As if she had done something ever so wrong?

Adam would have to understand that she could not do it. She

was sorry to disappoint her family, especially Adam, but she could not make the promise yet.

"Sadie?"

The girl's voice came from the other side of the hay bale. Sadie leaned forward and peeked over. Her cousin Rachel stood there, tearing at a long strand of hay as if it was very important to split it into tiny pieces.

"You're not going?" Rachel asked. She didn't have to spell it out; she was clearly in the same pickle as Sadie.

"I can't do it," Sadie told her. "And you?"

Rachel picked at the dry straw. "No. I thought I might feel differently when this morning came, but for some reason I can't make my feet move in that direction."

"I've been thinking the same thing." It was some consolation knowing she wasn't alone. "Maybe next year," Sadie said.

"Ya." Rachel's voice was heavy with a mixture of disappointment and concern.

Sadie bit back disappointment. "It's the right choice for now," she said, trying to convince Rachel and herself. "I've heard that the ministers keep asking the people in the class if they're ready."

"They do. Last year Abe got turned away after a few classes, when the bishop saw he wasn't getting rid of the speakers in his buggy." She turned her head toward the barn where the candidates had followed the minister inside. "I reckon that's why he passed the buggy on to Ben last week."

"So Abe is ready." Sadie pinched her fingers, still torn over the decision. Baptism would put an end to the pursuit of some of the things they loved—Sadie's music, Rachel's painting. But joining the church would seal their places with their community, their family, their homes. "Next year," Sadie said. "There's always next year."

NINE

A breeze kept things cool, but the sun, lingering over the green trees and buildings at the edge of the church lawn, warmed Mike's skin. On the lawn of St. Mark's Episcopal Church, the volleyball soared over the net and Mike jumped up to punch it back with both hands. It darted over the net and hit the ground between two people.

"Good job, Mikey." Daryl stepped over and bumped fists with him. "Let's win this match and wrap it up. My stomach is rumbling for an early supper."

Gran was waiting for Mike, somewhere over by the church hall. Mike glanced over at the picnic tables and held tight to his new resolve not to get those Sunday blues. He always stayed for activities after church, but today felt different. Today marked his new attitude. Renewal had ignited in his heart like a flame snapping to life, and for now his restless spirit had been quieted. Repositioning himself on the volleyball field, he thanked God for getting a message to him.

It was uncanny, but today's sermon seemed to be handpicked for Mike. The minister had read from Second Corinthians, where Paul wrote: "Therefore we do not lose heart. Though outwardly we are wasting away, yet inwardly we are being renewed day by day."

Day by day . . . that was how Mike was going to take it now. No more looking back to the sunny days of the past or dreading the future. The time to live was now.

Yesterday, something had sparked inside Mike while he was out with the church group on their pickup run. Most of the stops involved a few friendly words and a lot of heavy lifting, with people giving away sofas and chairs, desks and dining room sets. Daryl had explained that at the end of the day, they would drop the furniture at the church's thrift shop, which was also run by church volunteers. At first Mike hung back and watched as one of the other men spoke with the "clients" as the leader of their group. Then Daryl suggested that Mike step up on the next run, and he gave Mike some quick instructions, explaining that they wanted to leave people with a good feeling about St. Mark's, and they had to get a signature releasing the valuables for their records.

The small Tudor home in the suburbs was well hidden by the trees and ivy that had been left to grow over the years. "Invasive ivy. A horticulturist's nightmare," Daryl muttered as they pulled up in the van.

While the men opened up the truck, Mike went up the front path and rang the bell. The door was promptly answered by a woman in her late fifties. Although she was nicely dressed in jeans, a blouse, and a yellow scarf, her hands were smudged with grime. She held a wad of paper towels to her forehead.

"Good afternoon, ma'am." As Mike pushed back the sleeves of his sweatshirt, he noticed blood blossoming through the paper towels. "We're from St. Mark's Thrift Shop, and—are you all right?"

"I know, this is quite a greeting." She frowned, glancing up toward the wound. "I was rooting around in a closet and the shelf above me fell right out on my head."

He winced. "Ouch. So you're not okay. Do you think you need stitches? Want me to take a look?"

"It's not that bad. Just bleeding. See?" She lifted the wad of paper, and he saw that it wasn't a deep cut, though he could already see some bruising.

"That must have hurt," he said sympathetically.

Her lips rippled as she steeled herself. "Mostly, it wounded my pride," she said. "And it made me angry with my father for leaving his closets in such a mess. And now I'm mad at myself for blaming an old man who's lived alone for thirty years." Her voice quavered with the unchartered waters of grief.

She's holding back tears, he thought, feeling awkward. What did you say to calm a woman who reminded you of your mother? He didn't know the answer, though in his experience he'd always found that it helped just to talk.

"This looks like a bad time for you," he said. "I'm not sure of the schedule, but if you want I'll check and see what later dates are open for us to return."

"No, please. It would be more painful for me to reschedule. Come on in." She pushed the storm door open and motioned him in.

Mike followed her through the foyer, past a curving staircase to a wide living room. The place had old charm, but some cobwebs and cracks in the walls, too.

"Everything has to go . . . all the furniture. I emptied the dressers upstairs, but if you come across any other items like clothes or knickknacks, just leave them on the floor, please." She paused at a large, handsome leather chair and collapsed into it. "This is over-whelming."

Although it was awkward, Mike had to ask. "Is your father moving to a smaller place?"

"He died. He had a heart attack and died, just like that." She snapped her fingers.

"I'm sorry."

"He was in his eighties, so I guess I should have expected it. But I didn't. And now I've got a houseful of furniture that won't fit in my condo. And things . . . so many things that he accumulated over his lifetime." She sighed. "So I really appreciate you guys coming with the truck. It all has to go. Everything." She ran her palms over the leather on the arms of the Barcalounger, worn smooth with time and use. "Even this. He lived in this chair."

She hiccuped, pressing her other hand to her mouth, and Mike saw that her eyes were flooded with tears.

"Look, I'll have the guys start upstairs. In the meantime, do you think your father kept a first-aid kit? I'd be happy to help you get that cleaned and bandaged."

"I think there's one in the kitchen." With a weary sigh, she pushed herself out of the chair. "I'll get it."

He returned to the guys waiting in the vestibule. "She says everything has to go. Do you want to start upstairs in the bedrooms?"

"Sure." Daryl slid his gloves on. "Did you get her signature on the release?"

"Not yet." Mike tucked the clipboard under his arm. "She's looking kind of fragile, and I thought I'd talk with her first. Can you give us a few minutes before you clear out the living room?"

Daryl nodded, his eyes sharp with understanding. "You got it."

As Mike swabbed the woman's cut with antiseptic, he introduced himself.

"I'm sorry. I'm Persephone Bailey. My students call me Percy. And I appreciate your kindness, Mike. You have a good bedside manner."

Gently he pressed the bandage on and crumpled up the wrapper. "I should. I've been raised to be a doctor all my life. I'm supposed to follow in my father's footsteps."

"I know how that is. My father was a sociology professor. So what do I do? I teach sociology."

"If you don't mind me asking, how old was your father?"

"Eighty-two. He wasn't teaching anymore, but he was still active." Percy went on to describe how her father volunteered at an art museum in town. He had a passion for antiquities and had visited Egypt, China, Greece, and Peru during the last decade of his life.

"It sounds like he had a wonderful life," Mike said.

"I think he did. I'm just mad that he didn't tell me about his heart condition." She frowned. "Or maybe I'm angry to be left behind. Are your parents alive?" When he nodded, she added, "It's very scary to have both your parents gone."

"If it's any consolation, it sounds like your father certainly dug in and savored the moment."

"Many moments," she said. "And thank you for listening."

From the foyer, the strains of a hymn rose. The guys were singing. Most of them were in the church's a cappella choir, and they liked to sing to pass the time.

"I can have them stop singing if it bothers you," Mike told Percy.

She waved her hand. "They're fine. I don't even know if my father believed in God, but a few hymns might help, right?"

Mike nodded, thinking how devastating it would be for him if his father didn't have faith in the Lord.

Daryl paused in the arched entryway. "Is it okay if we start on the downstairs rooms?"

Percy waved him on. "Please. Oh, and this chair, too." She rose and moved to the back of the leather chair, biting her lips as she gripped the headrest.

"You know, Percy, we don't have to take that chair," Mike said. "I can see that you're attached to it."

Percy closed her eyes. "I can still see him sitting here, grading papers or reading the newspaper. He was not a fan of electronic gadgets."

"Take the chair home," Mike said. "You should keep it."

"I guess I could put it in my study, but . . ." She shook her head. "I have no way of getting it there."

"We'll deliver it for you. We can do that, right?" he asked Daryl, who was lifting an end table.

"I'm sure we can figure something out," Daryl said.

When Percy went to write her home address on the back of a business card, Mike noticed that she taught at Temple University. He told her he was transferring there in the fall, and she seemed glad.

"At least now you know one person there," she said.

Although the guys had ribbed him a little about "giving back the furniture," no one had minded delivering the chair to Percy's apartment—especially after they'd heard Mike's description of her father's attachment to the chair.

Now, standing in the waning sun, watching for the volleyball to come his way, Mike realized that Daryl had been right about volunteering. The experience had renewed his heart.

The game ended, and Mike went to find his grandmother, who had been talking with friends when he last saw her. The picnic was breaking up. It was time to head back to Gran's so that he could pack for his trip back to Lancaster County.

Already Mike felt the shadows of Sunday night creeping over him. When he began to make the trip to Philly nearly every weekend, his parents thought it was out of duty toward his grandmother. And though he did worry about Gran, who at seventy-eight was moving slower and becoming more forgetful, Mike knew he had selfish motives for being here, too.

Back at the townhouse, Gran was sitting on the stoop tending her spring flower boxes when Mike emerged with his duffel bag, ready to go.

Mike paused on the top step. "Your flowers look great, Gran. What are those, pansies?"

"Pansies and daffodils. Though I'm surprised the bulbs survived all that snow we had this year." Katherine Trueherz seemed fragile as a porcelain doll sitting on the steps. Her silver hair was nearly translucent now, and from the way she stooped over, her body seemed to be shrinking.

"Stay for dinner, Mikey," she said, her eyes twinkling in her wizened face. "I'll take you out."

"You always do." Gran didn't do much real cooking anymore, and neither did he. "And believe me, I appreciate it."

"But . . . ?" She glanced up at him, her inquisitive blue eyes reminding him of his own eyes.

"I should be getting home." He moved carefully around her to the bottom of the stairs, dropping his duffel onto the sidewalk.

"You always leave with such a heavy heart," she said sternly. "Though you seem a little bit better today. What is it that turns you into a Crabby Appleton every Sunday evening?"

Mike rubbed his jaw, holding back a grin. "I haven't heard that expression since I was a kid. But I guess I'm guilty as charged. The problem with Sundays is that I dread going back to Paradise. And then it gets compounded because I feel guilty about not wanting to go home."

"You know, you're overanalyzing."

"It's what I do best."

She laughed. "Well, it's good to have a sense of humor about it. And pretty soon you won't have to feel guilty anymore. You'll be going to Temple in September, so no one will expect you back in Lancaster County."

"That's true." He grabbed the broom that she'd propped against the side of the porch and swept the clippings that had fallen to the sidewalk. "Then I can shift to being miserable about studying medicine."

"Oh, poppycock. If you're going to be miserable in the fall, don't plan on coming around here."

He laughed. "You're telling me not to visit you? My own grandma?"

"Not if you're going to be a downer. Really, Mike. If you don't want to study medicine, change your major. It's as simple as that."

"The problem is that my parents are counting on me. They expect me to take over Dad's practice in Paradise. And if you've ever seen how busy his office is, someone has to do it."

"But it doesn't have to be you." She reached under a wavering pansy to pluck a weed. "First of all, have you ever thought that Drew might want to take on the office?"

His brother Andrew was in Afghanistan, working as a medic. "Drew is interested, but he didn't do well in college. He'll never get into med school."

"Never say never. And it's not your job to fulfill your father's dream. Yes, Henry did a noble thing all those years ago when he went out to Lancaster County and took on all those sick children with symptoms no one understood. Honestly, he is a good doctor but he's a terrible businessman, and it's fortunate there's enough family money to support his philanthropy. He did surprise me by raising the funds to build the clinic. But the clinic was his dream, not yours. If he's any kind of father, he won't force you to follow in his footsteps."

"Wow." Mike gripped the cement rail and stared up at her. He had never heard Gran talk so frankly about his father. "I didn't know you had an opinion about the future of the clinic."

"I'm not concerned about the clinic; it's the family baggage that worries me."

"You don't miss much, Gran." All this time, when Mike thought he was bucking up, she must have seen him straining under the weight of his own "family baggage."

"Apparently you haven't heard my part of the family history. If my parents had gotten their way, I would not have married your grandfather."

"Really? But Grandpa Will was a minister. You'd think that would be every parent's dream."

"Not Mr. and Mrs. Theodore Witker. My family was well off, and they were so disappointed that I reached beneath our social circle for a beau. My father was a banker, and he had a habit of reducing everything to its monetary value. Maybe that's why I chose a spouse in such a different profession. Believe me, banking and the Christian ministry are at the opposite ends of the rainbow."

"Did you try to hide it from your parents?"

"Oh, no. That's how naïve I was. I just invited Will to Sunday dinner . . . and what a calamity that was! Will had just returned from a mission in Africa, and he was bubbling with stories of kind villagers and miracles. That did not go over well with Daddy. I think he hoped it was a phase, but then it stuck."

"Wow." Mike scratched the back of his neck, enjoying the mental image of his gran as a defiant socialite. "Gran, I didn't know any of this."

"The skeletons in our closet." She rubbed her hands together with a merry smile. "In time, my folks came to accept Will, but when you think about the pressure to take over your father's practice, remember, I know a thing or two about how it feels to disappoint your parents."

"Do you ever look back and regret the choices you made?" Mike asked.

"Oh, I have always wondered how a girl who liked to make trouble ended up as a minister's wife. But I can't regret a minute of it. Will was a wonderful man. He had a heart of gold. That's probably where your father got his helping instinct." She used the railing to pull herself to her feet. "I'm happy with my choices. But you are another story."

Mike swept the weeds into a dustpan. "How's that, Gran?"

"God has a plan for you, my dear. And you are the only one who can figure out what that is. Don't be bamboozled into pretending your father's dream is yours, too."

"Yes, ma'am." Mike was glad his grandmother saw other potential in him, and it was great to hear her on top of her game. Gran might be slowing, but mentally she was still sharp as a tack.

"Now . . . if you'll tidy up the tools, I'll get washed and you can drive us to dinner."

"Okay," he said, thinking that the once-defiant socialite still knew how to get her way.

TEN

I didn't see Sadie at the singing," Remy said as their buggy pulled away from the remaining group of young people gathered around a bonfire on the Zooks' land. As it was customary for a young Amish man to give his girl a ride home from a singing, Adam sat beside Remy in an open buggy, heading back to Nate and Betsy King's house, where she was staying.

"Sadie's been ducking off in the other direction," Adam said. "No doubt going to town to see her Englisher friends."

From his gruff tone of voice, Remy could tell it was a topic that bothered Adam, who had told her of his disappointment over his sister's choice not to be baptized this year.

She took a deep breath and tipped her head back to take in the field of diamonds scattered over the purple sky. The cool night was upon them, a blanket of privacy, and she was grateful for it.

"Such a beautiful night. I'm glad they held the singing around a bonfire. And I was glad to see that Gabe seemed to be enjoying himself. And Jonah . . . I never know what he's thinking. He's so quiet around the farm, though I noticed he does come out for the singings."

"Jonah's always been a quiet one."

"Do you guys ever talk about personal stuff? Has he ever mentioned a girl he likes?"

Adam smiled, his face warming in the moonlight. "If he did, do you think I'd tell you?"

"If it's not a big secret, of course you would." Remy gave his arm a gentle punch. "And even if it is, I'm your girl, Adam. I'm going to be your wife. You can tell me anything and my lips are sealed. You know that, right?"

His hand dropped from the reins to her thigh. "I know that, Remy. I do trust you."

Oh, the warmth of his touch . . . Remy knew her rational thoughts could evaporate into sheer desire with Adam so close, and she had to prod herself to stay on track. She pressed her hand over his, loving their closeness.

"You were nervous this morning," he said. "How did your first baptism class go?"

"Fine, I think. Preacher Dave was the teacher, so that was good. For some reason I just relate to him. And the language barrier wasn't so bad. He helped me with a few things in English, but I understood a lot of it. I think I'm getting better with Pennsylvania Deutsch."

"Bit by bit."

"It's harder to learn when you weren't raised Amish. Sometimes I still feel like the outsider. After twenty-four years in the English world, I have a lot of catching up to do."

"If you learn the secret to a good pie, many other faults will be overlooked."

"I've been working on that, too," Remy said proudly. "Have you ever had sawdust pie?"

He laughed. "Being a carpenter for so many years, you'd think I'd know it. But, no. Never had it."

"Your aunt Betsy thought it would be a nice surprise. I baked it myself, and there's a slice waiting for you back at the house."

"As long as it doesn't have sawdust . . ."

"No sawdust or wood chips, I promise. But maybe a little coconut." She waggled her eyebrows.

"You know me too well."

"I'm working on it." She swayed to her right, leaning against him. Even that small contact of her shoulder and arm against his solid body made her melt.

He looked down at her, then slipped his arm around her waist and pulled her close. "Sometimes it seems like wedding season will never come. I've always been a patient man, but with this, marrying you, I don't want to be patient anymore."

"I know." Remy pressed her face to his chest, allowing her hand to smooth over the top of his jacket. "I wish we could be married sooner, but I do love the history of the tradition, with weddings taking place after the harvest." By then she would be through with classes and baptized into the church. "I'm going to keep studying German for services. It's so different from the German I learned in school. But I think Sam understands me."

"A five-year-old." He nodded. "That's progress."

She laughed. "Indeed, it is."

He turned to her, his face serious. "Sometimes I wonder, why would a nice Englisher girl want to give up the luxuries of life—a car and electricity, television, and a place to go where they paint your toes? Are you sure about this, Remy? Because there's no going back after you're baptized. This can't be a whim. The consequences of breaking away are severe. I've seen people shunned. It's a terrible thing."

Remy felt the weight of the decision. "I know it's unusual for an outsider to join the faith. But joining the Anabaptist church was not an afterthought for me. I've been searching for years. . . . I'm a Seeker." That was what the bishop had called her, and she liked the sound of it. After all these years of yearning and searching, at last she had found a place to be, a place where she belonged.

At last, she had found a way to God.

"That's gut," Adam said. "Because if you wanted to go back to the city, my heart would be broken."

Remy pressed a fist to her heart. "I love you, too."

He reached for her hand and they wove their fingers together and held fast to each other as Thunder's hooves clip-clopped on the paved road. Remy was sure she felt the pulse in Adam's wrist beating against hers, their two hearts beating as one.

Thank you, dear Lord, for bringing us together.

They rode in comfortable silence for a while. The air had turned cold, and she separated her hand from Adam's and pulled the lap blanket over their knees. She realized they were getting close to Nate and Betsy's place, but she didn't want their private interlude to end. "Can you slow Thunder down a little?"

He spoke to the horse, which slowed to a walk. "That's one of the oldest courting tricks in the book, you know. But if you're cold, move closer. I'll warm you up."

"That must be the second oldest trick in the book," Remy said as she tucked her arm through his and snuggled close.

"Ach, you caught me."

She sighed. "Summer nights are so beautiful here. In Philly, I lived in the air-conditioning." An image of her apartment came to mind, dust motes swirling in the stark daylight. "I need to go back soon. I know we've talked about it before, but it's been weighing on my mind. It's time to tie up loose ends I left behind."

"Can't you take care of things by telephone?" Adam asked.

"I wish. But there's the matter of my car, sitting in Nancy's garage, and my apartment. I need to return my car to Herb. He helped me come up with the money to buy it, so it's rightfully his. And the apartment has to be cleared out so that it can be sold. It's my responsibility. I talked to the bishop about it and he agreed. I have to start leaving my English ways behind."

"What's your plan?"

"I just ended my cell phone contract, so that's done. My car has been safe in Nancy's garage, but I need to drive it back to Philadelphia. Maybe I'll use it to haul my furniture to Goodwill or to Herb's house. Whatever I have to do to clear the place out."

"Most Amish don't have so many things to give away before they get baptized. That will be some work. When do you plan to do this?"

"Soon. And I'd like to take Sadie with me. She likes the city, and two sets of hands are quicker than one."

Adam rubbed his chin, considering. "I don't know about that. She might want to buy your car from you."

Remy laughed. "Maybe so. But she's a hard worker, and I could use her help."

"I don't know." Adam's voice was thick with concern. "Sadie already has one foot in the Englisher world. Even Bishop Samuel has commented on her many trips to the city."

"But she's in rumspringa. She's finding her way."

He grunted. "She's finding the wrong way, if you want to know the truth. Many youth get the wildness out of their system during rumspringa. The drinking and dating. But Sadie is *unzufriede* with the Amish ways, and that's far worse than simple bad behavior."

"*Unzufriede?*" It wasn't a word Remy was familiar with.

"It means she is not so satisfied with being Amish. I see it in her because I was once there myself." That flicker of regret was still evident in his voice when he talked about his own falling away from the Amish.

When Remy had first met Adam, he'd been returning to Halfway from a three-year absence, burdened with grief and remorse. She knew he still felt guilty for not being here when his parents were killed, but he was doing his best to put the past behind him and deal with the family concerns of the present.

And lately Sadie seemed to be the foremost concern on his mind.

Remy squeezed his arm. "You're really worried about her, aren't you?"

"She's looking beyond our ways to the rest of the world."

"I thought that was part of the decision-making process. To taste the Englisher world before choosing to get baptized."

"Mmm, not so much. Sadie is meant to become Amish. It's expected of every Amish child since the moment of their birth. An Amish girl is to remain Amish, and that means she must choose baptism. If she is looking the other way, it's up to everyone in the community to turn her head back in this direction. Sadie belongs here, with her family. Her baptism is the thing that will seal her place in the Amish community."

Only Sadie didn't choose baptism . . . at least, not for this year.

Remy was about to say something reassuring, but bit back her words as the realization settled over her like the blue pitch night. Remy held tight to him as they turned down the lane to Nate and Betsy's, the open carriage jiggling over the rutted gravel road. Tipping her face to the sky above, she wondered what the Lord had in store for Sadie.

When Sadie didn't show up for the first class, Remy had been disappointed, but for selfish reasons. It would have been reassuring to commit to the faith in the same group as Sadie, whom Remy thought of as a younger sister.

But now, hearing Adam's concern, she realized that Sadie's decision that morning could have major ripple effects. There was a real chance of losing Sadie to the English world. For the first time, she saw the risk clearly, and she understood the weight of Adam's concern. This was no simple matter. If Sadie couldn't be lured back to the community, she would be lost forever.

ELEVEN

·

The future was as long and vast as the dark road ahead, but for once, Mike wasn't worried about it. With the radio playing and cool country air blowing through the car, Mike felt as if he were soaring, the wheels hovering over the road as he returned home. Gone was the dread that usually weighed him down on his trips west to Lancaster. Gran had given him his freedom back, and the awesome feeling he hadn't felt since he'd been in Jamaica now blossomed in his heart.

He kept his eyes on the road, though in these parts the lack of lights made it impossible to see beyond his headlights. He was grateful for the red triangles on the backs of Amish carriages, making them far more visible in the dark. He had just passed through the town of Halfway and figured he was twenty minutes or so from home when his headlights flashed on a woman riding a scooter in the road ahead.

It was dangerous, especially after dark. No helmet and just one slim reflector on the back of the scooter.

As he slowed the car, he saw that her hair was tucked into a white prayer kapp, but she wore jeans and a dark shirt. As if she were half Amish, half English.

He didn't want to spook the girl, so he gave her plenty of space as he crept past her. Still, he couldn't resist a look as his window came up beside her.

Sadie? Was he imagining it or . . . no, it was her. Susie King's sister.

He hit the gas, pulling ahead a bit so that he could give her time to stop. Then he threw the car in park, put his emergency flashers on, and stepped out.

"Sadie," he called, straining to see in the darkness. "Sadie, it's me. Mike Trueherz. From the doctor's office?"

The white of her kapp shone under the moon as she scootered up to him and put her sneakered foot down, stopping a few paces away. "Mike! What are you doing here?"

Mike folded his arms across his chest. "Me? How about you, riding a scooter on a pitch black country road?"

She shrugged. "I usually get a ride home, but my friend had to go to his cousin's house."

"And he let you travel alone in the dark? That's no friend at all." The words were harsh, but they were out before Mike realized he was sounding like his father.

"I had band practice and I didn't want to miss it." Sadie's eyes were round as quarters, her skin creamy smooth in the moonlight.

She was a beautiful girl, though Mike had a feeling she didn't have a sense of that yet. When he'd gone over the King family tree, he had noted that she was eighteen. She was no longer a kid, but she hadn't really crossed into the next age. Sadie was a woman-child, and he felt a strong urge to protect her from a world where so many things could go wrong.

"Let me give you a ride home," he said. "Your scooter will fit in my trunk, right?"

She blinked those big, beautiful eyes. "I don't want to trouble you. Our farm is just a few miles ahead."

He could tell that she was demurring because she didn't want to put him out. "Hey, it's no problem. I'm going that direction." He closed the distance between them and clamped a hand on the scooter's handlebars. In the scooter's basket was a small bundle of clothes. "Really. I wouldn't be able to sleep thinking about you alone on this road."

She snorted, pressing a hand to her lips to cover a smile. "You sound like a dat."

"Hey, it never hurts to be careful. A lot of drivers wouldn't pick up the small reflector you have on that thing. Besides, if you go down, you've got no protection."

"I'm a careful scooter rider."

"Yeah, well, I still have a scar on my knee from when I went down on my bicycle, and that was years ago." The scooter didn't fit into his trunk, but he was able to angle it into the backseat, and they were good to go.

He started the engine and the radio blared. "Sorry." He went to turn it off, but Sadie waved his hand away from the dash.

"No, please, can we play the radio? I'll turn it down some."

"That's right. You're the secret music buff. The songbird."

"Yes, and I need to find a good song." She was focused on the radio, pushing buttons. "I don't get to hear new music much."

"Play what you want," Mike said as he pulled onto the empty road.

"I love this song." She sang along, "You really had me going. . . ."

He listened as she went through the song, mimicking the singer's voice to a T. The girl could really belt. Her lustrous voice filled the car, and though she stumbled on some of the lyrics, the lines she hit were clear as a bell. "You're good," Mike said as the song ended. He didn't know much about popular music, but anyone would recognize Sadie's talent.

"That's Rihanna." She rolled the window down more and dangled her right hand out to catch the air. "I love her music. But I don't know all the words yet. Frank doesn't want our band to do her songs. He likes the old ones."

"Frank is the bandleader?"

"Ya. And my friend." She found a new song and bobbed her head in time to the beat. "Can you drive faster? Cars can be so thrilling when the wind blows in."

"No. I don't want to take the chance of running into any more Amish girls out on scooters after dark."

Sadie giggled. "I don't do it all the time, but I'm grateful for the ride."

He could tell she was enjoying her time in the car. Besides fiddling with the radio, she kept playing with the electric window and adjusting her seat.

"This is a very comfortable seat," she said, tilting it back. Her head rolled lazily toward him. "Where were you headed?"

"I'm on my way home. I spent the weekend in Philadelphia."

"Ya?" There was interest in her voice. "I was there Saturday night, at Mad River. We did a couple of songs, and there were real lights on us. It made my heart flutter like a butterfly, but it wasn't a bad feeling at all."

"So you liked performing?"

"It's sort of a secret because no Amish girl has ever gone onstage like that, but I do like it. Singing is a part of me I don't want to let go of."

"Well, you have a beautiful voice."

"It's a blessing from God." When he looked over, she was

smoothing her hand over the armrest in the door, staring out the window. "Do you ever wonder what God intends you to do with the gifts he gave you?"

Mike thought of his ability to draw people out—his people skills. "I've been wondering about that a lot lately. With my personality and skills, I'm fairly sure I'd be a pretty lousy doctor."

She turned to him, squinting. "You think that?"

"I know it. But I just started thinking about how I might use the talents I have."

"You know, I've been thinking the same thing. God gave me this voice. I think He wants me to use it. But the bishop and the other leaders aren't going to agree. There's nothing for me to do with a singing voice in our community. I can't even be a song leader in our church. The song leaders are always men."

"So if you pursue music, it's going to take you away from the Amish community," Mike said. When she nodded, he asked, "Does that scare you?"

"Ya. But right now, I'm trying to do both. Most of the time I do as I'm told on the farm. But at night, when my family thinks I'm working at the hotel, I go to rehearsal. And sometimes, like Saturday, I go perform in the city."

"It's like you're living two separate lives," Mike said, thinking of the way he'd divided himself between Philly and Paradise these past two years. He'd gritted his teeth to get through school and his part-time job at his father's clinic. He had pushed through each week focused on escaping for the weekend.

"That's right. And if I keep them separate, I think I can continue singing and make everyone at home happy, too."

Mike saw the flaw in Sadie's plan; he'd made that mistake himself.

But he was hardly an expert. He was still figuring things out, too.

"I hope it works out for you, songbird. I've been leading a double life myself, but it's coming to an end."

"What's this double life?" she asked.

"You know . . . two lives. I've been torn between my family in the country and my friends in the city." It was an oversimplification, but their ride wasn't long enough to dredge up much more. "But I'm moving to the city in August."

"I think you'll be mighty happy there, Mike."

He took his eyes off the road to catch her shy smile. Her big, round eyes were full of hope. He didn't know how she would reconcile her two worlds, but she still had hope . . . and something else. Sadie King had courage.

"Oh, Mike . . . slow down!"

"What?" He snapped his attention back to the road, but there was nothing but the circle of headlights on the bare asphalt.

"The turnoff to our farm is coming up." She tapped the window. "You can pull over by that beech tree."

"I'll take you up to the house," he said.

"Oh, no, denki. That would set tongues a-wagging."

"When their sister Sadie pulls up in a car with a mystery man." He grinned as he pulled onto the dirt shoulder. "The gossip would fade when they realize it's only the doctor's son."

"You're still an Englisher. That's trouble for me." Sadie popped open the door and went to retrieve her scooter.

Mike met her at the backseat and maneuvered the scooter out of the car. "Well, stay out of trouble, okay?" he teased as he wheeled it over to her.

"I'll do my best. Denki. Thank you for the ride." She smiled up at him, with a sparkle in her eyes that held him cemented in place. Something about Sadie, her brusque honesty or her easy manner . . . something about her made him feel both comfortable and on edge when he was around her.

"You're welcome," he said, adding, "Next time I find you on the side of the road, I'll take you back to town for ice cream." As soon as the words were out of his mouth, he wanted to roll his eyes. *Ice cream? Really?* He sounded like a creepy uncle.

"I'd like that," she said, "as long as you let me blast the radio."

"You got it."

She nodded, then wheeled off into the darkness.

Watching her disappear down the lane, he said a quick prayer that things would work out for her, too. *Please, Lord, guide her with your loving hand.*

TWELVE

A few days later, as Sadie stared out the van's window at passing cars, she realized she was trying to find one that matched the shape and color of Mike's car. A blue Ford Fusion; she had seen that written on the back of the car in silver.

It seemed silly, for what would she do if she spotted Mike driving alongside them on the highway? Wave? Smile? Open the window and shout that she was on her way to a gig in the city?

Well, maybe she would give a shout, and Mike would smile right back at her and holler to ask where the gig was. And then he'd follow right along so he could watch and listen from one of the tables. He'd said she had a beautiful voice, and she could tell he didn't want to say good-bye that night when he'd given her a ride home.

And Sadie had felt the same way . . . but she had a boyfriend already. A small blue car approached, but it had an *H* on it instead of the word *Ford* inside an oval. She sighed and turned away from the window.

Foolish thoughts she was having. Besides, if she did run into Mike, she didn't even know the name of the place where they would be performing tonight. She asked Frank about it.

"Tin Angel," he said as they neared Philadelphia. Many houses clustered along each street now. Sadie felt the rumbling excitement of the city with its traffic and lights and noise.

"I think I'm going to like this place," Sadie said as they circled the block to find a spot to park. "A place with the name Angel in it has to be good."

"Easy, church girl," Frank said as he turned the wheel. "We don't want people to think we're Holy Rollers."

"I like angels," Red said. "Angels are New Age, man. And Jimi Hendrix got rescued by a sweet one."

"Whatever." Frank frowned as he backed the van into a spot. He was a little sour today, so Sadie left him alone and tried to keep her mind on the songs they would be performing. Two sets! That meant five songs, then a break, and then another five songs. It was a wonderful good chance for the band to be heard by the Saturday-night crowd, and Frank was sure it would lead to bigger and better things for them. He was working on how they might start getting paid for performing, which would be fine with Sadie. Now that she didn't work at the hotel, she was getting short on money to pay for her cell phone and new songs for her iPod.

While they were setting up their equipment, a group of girls came over to Frank, very excited to see him. They hugged him and squealed like pigs fighting over food . . . and there were so many of them. Sadie counted nine.

"It's my cousin Heather and her friends," Frank explained just before they went onstage. "They came out to show their support for the band. Isn't that great?"

Sadie didn't feel great about it as she peered at the three tables in front of the band taken up by sparkling girls with very red lips.

They had hugged Frank, but ignored Red, Tara, and her. The girls were here for Frank, not for the band, and the tables were a little too close for comfort. Although none of the clubs they performed in had actual stages, usually the band was allowed a bit more space in a corner or at the back of the room. Here, the flashy girls seemed within arm's reach.

Her bad feeling grew worse when, after Frank thanked everyone for coming out and they started their first song, the girls kept talking and giggling. Sadie closed her eyes and tried to go to that special place where she soared above the earth. But then someone hooted like an owl, and she opened her eyes to see one of the girls on her feet, dancing with Frank.

The girl flung herself to and fro like a porch swing in the wind. At one point Sadie had to step back so that she wouldn't get hit by her, and she almost missed a line of the song. It was all so distracting!

The second song, "Summertime," was slower, and the girls seemed to calm down at last. Sadie found her way to the zone, closing her eyes to let her voice flow from her like a river.

But when she opened her eyes, she noticed some of the girls staring at her with meanness in their eyes. She wiped her sweaty palms on the back pockets of her jeans. This wasn't as wonderful good as she usually felt performing.

Just close your eyes and forget about them, she told herself. And she pushed through the next few songs until the end of the set.

When Frank announced the short break, the girls shrieked and rose to their feet. As soon as he lifted his guitar strap over his head, the girls were on him again, like bees on a hive. Silly girls.

Tara's boyfriend had come to see her, and she went outside with him to smoke a cigarette. Smoking seemed to be one of Tara's favorite things to do.

Sadie turned away to go to the washroom.

"Good job, Sadie," Red said, stretching. "It's different when you've got a loud crowd, right?"

"Ya. Once I almost forgot the words," she admitted.

"You'll get used to it," he said.

She went to the back stall of the ladies' room, sat down on the toilet, and thought about the songs they would do next. Would the girls fall in love with "God Bless the Child" the way Sadie had?

Just then the door creaked and other girls came inside. From the volume and shrill tone of their voices, she realized it was Frank's silly girls. Sadie tried to tune them out, but she wasn't going to budge from this stall while they were there. This would be her little corner of peace.

"And what about that singer?" The words scratched through her little cocoon. "I mean, she's got a voice, but the face needs work."

"Check out her unibrow," someone else said. "It makes me want to pull out my tweezers and start plucking."

Stunned, Sadie pressed the fingertips of one hand to her brow ridge, gently touching the smooth hairs that grew there.

"I know! I know! She's a chimp. You'd need a chain saw to de-forest that thing."

"Well, yeah. Frank said she's a farm girl."

"Elsa the cow and her unibrow."

Someone made mooing sounds, trying to sound like a cow, and the girls laughed.

That's not how a cow sounds. Not at all, Sadie thought as she sank forward, resting her forehead on her arms.

She waited there, curled up in the stall, until the girls finally left.

When she was sure no one remained, she got up and peeked

out of the stall. Empty. Her knees felt shaky as a new colt, but she couldn't fall apart now. She had five more songs to do.

She went to the sink and scrubbed her hands with soap. Then she splashed cold water onto her hot face. She needed to cool down.

Dabbing her face dry with a paper towel, she saw that her skin was still pink from embarrassment. She hoped that would go away soon.

Sadie dared to look at herself in the mirror, to really look at her eyes and the little hairs that formed a line above them. She didn't know what a "you-knee brow" was, but she felt stung by their criticism. She had always been a little surprised by the image of her face in public restrooms. At home, there was only a small shaving mirror, and it was cloudy and too small to see her whole face. But now, in this bright light, her lips looked wider than she ever imagined. Her whole mouth was too big for her face . . . except when she smiled, and then it seemed okay.

Looking at herself now, Sadie felt her face begin to crumple on the verge of tears. Maybe she was not pretty. How was it that she had not seen the problem before? Her furry eyebrows had grown in across the top of her nose. The other girls had skinny little brows, arched like macaroni noodles, while Sadie's grew across her face like one fat caterpillar.

And what about her eyes? They were nice enough, with little flecks of gold in them. "Be happy that you have eyes that see," she told herself, thinking how silly it was to find fault with the blessings that God gave her.

Still . . . she needed to face her reflection in the mirror and see herself as those girls did. Next time, she didn't want to be taken by surprise by their comments.

And her skin? Though it was pale as the paste that grade-school children used, she didn't have any red bumps right now.

As a girl, she had never thought about her looks. Her only thought had been that she wanted to be good and work hard to please her parents and Gott. Her dat used to say she was one of his best workers, even when she was four and collecting eggs or feeding the calves from a big bottle. "That's my Sadie girl," he used to say, patting her on the back, and it had made her feel good, knowing she had done her best, knowing that he loved her.

Sadie didn't remember her mamm talking about any of her daughters' hair or faces, but Mamm had made sure their hair was always twisted back the right way and tucked under their kapps. Mamm had not been one to talk about the look of a person. Instead, she had valued how they spent their time. "Hard work is the yeast that raises the dough," Mamm used to say.

Oh, Mamm and Dat, I miss you. Sadie longed to run to one of her parents, to be held in their arms, comforted and consoled.

But her parents were in heaven with Gott, and Sadie was left alone, with no one to pick up the broken pieces but her.

She lifted her chin and forced a smile. There came the little dimples, the same ones Dat used to have. *Give me strength, Heavenly Father,* she prayed. And with a deep breath, she went out to finish the show.

The hurtful comments from the girls helped Sadie escape to the zone during the second set, and once she found that special place, she dug in and held on tight. She was here for the music. She pushed herself to stand in front of strangers because she felt it was right to share the voice God had given her. And when the music flowed through her, she knew she was truly blessed.

After the performance, the loud girls rushed Frank once again, and Sadie turned away and started packing up. The microphone system belonged to the club, but there were wires to be coiled, amps and drums to be carried out to the van. She worked side by side with Tara and Red, aware of Frank holding his guitar in the center of the group of girls.

"Frank, we need to get out of here," Red reminded him. "There's another band coming in."

"Give me a minute," Frank said.

When Sadie glanced over and saw Frank exchanging numbers with Heather's friends, she felt betrayed. Didn't he see how the girls had hurt her? Maybe not. He hadn't heard their cruel comments in the washroom.

But why was he planning to call these girls, if Sadie was his girlfriend? She was his girlfriend, wasn't she? They hadn't talked about love or anything like that yet, but they had been courting, there was no denying that.

When they finally got Frank out to the van, Sadie asked her question.

"What were you doing, getting phone numbers from all those girls?" she asked. "You made it look like you don't have a girl-friend."

"Sadie, are you jealous?" He cocked his head to one side and peered into her face. "I think you are."

"I asked a question. You know, they're not a very nice group of girls."

"I know, they have issues, but I'm trying to make connections for the band, hon. Those girls loved us tonight, and they're going to get the word out to their friends the next time we have a Philly gig. It's called networking, in the English world. Don't be mad."

"We're packed and ready. Let's roll," Red called.

Sadie climbed into the van. She could forgive Frank for enjoy-ing the girls' attention, but she hoped that she would never see those mean girls again.

In the van on the way back to Lancaster County, Frank asked Sadie why she always wore her prayer kapp. "I know it's part of the Amish thing, but since you ditched the dress for cooler clothes, why not get rid of the bonnet, too?"

"Frank . . ." Tara bristled with annoyance. "Can you just give Sadie a break? You're all over the way she dresses and what songs she listens to. It's a free country, and I'll tell you right now, this band is never going to wear look-alike costumes."

Red grinned. "We could all wear Penn State T-shirts." That was his usual outfit—a navy Penn State T-shirt with an unbuttoned flannel shirt over it.

"I'm just asking a question," Frank said. "What's the deal, Sadie? Bonnet or no bonnet?"

"It's called a prayer kapp," Sadie said. "It says in the Bible that I should cover my head when I pray, and a good woman should be praying most of the time, so I wear it."

"Would something bad happen if you took it off?" Frank asked.

"Probably not, but I like wearing it. When I was a little girl I used to imagine my prayers lifting to God through my kapp. It was comforting." Sadie didn't want to admit that her kapp was still a source of comfort.

"Well, would you try doing a performance without it?" Frank asked. "It would give us a more contemporary look if you got rid of the kapp and cut your hair."

"You want me to cut my hair?" Sadie scowled in the shadowy van. Shivers ran down her spine at the thought of cutting her hair.

"Hold up a second." Red scratched his head. "I too find the scrutiny of Sadie's clothes excessive. If Sadie wants to wear a kapp, so be it."

Tara shook her head. "I agree, but you're such a nerd."

Red continued: "And if you're concerned about marketing the band, Frank, think of the odd juxtaposition that Sadie's wardrobe poses. Bonnet and jeans. Innocent and cool. Old-fashioned and New Age. People like mysteries. What's the real person like? That's what they'll be thinking. They'll want answers. You'll leave them wanting more."

"Let Sadie stick with the kapp," Tara said flatly. "And don't let anyone mess with your hair, Sadie."

Sadie took a breath, reassured by the other girl.

"Okay, okay, I got it." Frank nodded as he stared through the windshield. "Red's right about the intrigue, and it's something that sets our band apart from all the others. In fact, I think we should play it up. How about if we call the band Amish Blues?"

Tara shrugged.

"I'd rather remain nameless," Red said. "But I could live with it."

"How about that, Sadie?" Frank nodded. "The whole band could be named after you."

"I don't think the bishop would like it much," Sadie said.

Frank laughed. "Probably not."

The conversation turned to something else, and Sadie weighed the idea of calling the band Amish Blues. That could be a big problem if the leaders of their congregation ever found out. But how would they hear of it? Men like Bishop Samuel did not go into the city often, and they certainly did not frequent clubs. She let it go, knowing that Frank would probably change his mind before he acted on it.

When they reached Red's house, they carried the drums and other equipment into the garage. Tara headed off to meet her boyfriend in Lancaster, though Sadie was yawning from the late hour. Red was setting up his drums in the garage when Sadie and Frank left for the King farm.

"Here we are." Frank let the van roll to a stop on the side of the main road, just before the lane. He turned off the engine and yawned. "Wow. That trip takes it out of you after a performance."

"Mmm. I'm tired, too." It had stripped away her strength, hearing those girls make fun of the way she looked. Right now she felt drawn to her bed in the big upstairs room of the house. She could almost hear the comforting whisper of her sisters' breathing. How wonderful it would be to slip under the sheet, surrounded by such loving peace. "I'll call you tomorrow."

"Hold up a sec." His fingers closed over one arm, stopping her. "Hang out a minute and talk."

She paused, staring down at his hand on her arm. For the first time she had the sense that he was trying to hold her back, the way a horse was tethered to a post. "Don't do that . . . please."

"I'm sorry. Look, I just wanted to ask you about your kapp. I understand that you want to keep it on for the shows and all that, but what about me? Do you think someday you'll take it off and let your hair down for me?"

Face-to-face with him, so close, she sensed his neediness. Many times she had explained the age-old tradition of Plain folk to Frank. A girl learned at a young age to coil her hair into a bun and keep it pinned back under her kapp. Why was he pressing her this way? He was giving her the rush, which was what the Amish called it when a fella pushed a girl.

"Why do you want this?" she asked.

"I don't know. I guess you're a challenge . . . and kind of a mystery, like Red said."

Her resolve hardened, like a puddle turning to ice. "Because I'm a challenge?"

"You're one of a kind, Lady Sadie, and I know you're into me. What's the harm in letting your hair down for me sometime?" His mouth puckered in a sad expression, but she wasn't sure it was real.

That was the thing she was learning about Frank; he didn't always say what was in his heart.

"You've been wonderful good to me, and singing in the band makes my heart glad."

"But . . . ?" he prodded.

"It's late. And I'm not ready to go to that step, to take my kapp off." She had always imagined that it would be a moment she would share with her husband, removing her kapp and uncoiling the long, golden brown hair that had never been cut. "Why do you keep asking me about that?"

"The mystery, I guess." He turned back toward the windshield and sank down in his seat. "I'm beat. I should head home." He opened his car door, and she quickly followed, going to the back to get her things.

"Good night, Rapunzel," he said as he lowered her scooter to the hard-packed dirt.

Stung, Sadie wondered if Frank knew how his crazy name game could hurt a person. She knew the fairy-tale story of the princess who let her hair down from a tower, but she didn't like being compared to an odd character like that, just because she kept her hair up. Frank needed to learn a thing or two about respect. "Oh, and you're the fair prince come to rescue me?" she quipped, rolling her scooter away. "I don't think so."

"Funny girl." With a smile, he turned back to the car.

As she walked down the lane under the starry sky, she hugged herself, needing comfort and warmth. She wanted to hear Ruthie remind everyone of her upcoming birthday for the umpteenth time. She needed the comfort of Katie's chubby cheeks to kiss and the steady burn of Jonah's dark eyes, wise and calm like their dat's.

The events of the night had set her heart in a spin, and she wasn't sure how she felt about Frank anymore. But she knew Frank was fond of her, no matter what those girls said. Let them call her names and make fun of her you-knee brow. She reminded herself that Jesus Christ suffered a lot worse treatment when he was here on earth. And besides, Sadie had her escape. When she was onstage, she could close her eyes and fall into the music and forget anyone else was out there. When she was floating on a song, no one could hurt her.

THIRTEEN

*M*ike bounded down the stairs of Gran's house, humming a tune that had been on his mind since he'd awakened that fresh May morning. It was the song Sadie had found on the radio last month, the one she liked by Rihanna.

Actually, *loved* was the word she'd used, which sounded like any other teen Mike knew. But Sadie King was definitely unique. She was a girl with one foot in the Amish world, one foot in the English. The dichotomy made her more interesting and down-to-earth than any of the girls Mike knew at church here in Philly or at college in Lancaster. Then again, maybe he related to Sadie because he had spent the last few years trying to make sense of combining these worlds.

When he hit the first floor, Gran wasn't sitting in her favorite chair, reading the paper in the sun, where he found her most mornings.

"Do I smell coffee?" He made his way to the kitchen, where he had promised to make scrambled eggs and toast if Gran got the coffee started.

The rich fragrance of French roast made his mouth water. Black liquid was streaming into the glass coffeepot, but where was Gran? "Where'd you—"

When he turned to the pantry he saw her down on the floor. It looked like she had slid down against the open door, and though her eyes were open there was a dazed, glassy look about her.

"Gran . . ." Mike hurried over and dropped to his knees beside her. "What happened?"

"I was . . ." Her head lolled to the side. "Leg just turned to ssstone."

Her speech was slurred and she kept pressing on her right thigh, saying something about her leg.

"What happened to your leg, Gran?" Mike asked as he stared into her eyes.

"Leg . . . numb."

Mike fished his cell from his pocket. "Gran, I think you're having a stroke. I'm calling 911."

"Ah . . ." The fact that she wasn't telling him not to call underlined the fact that his grandmother was in distress.

Mike stayed next to her, rubbing her arm as he told the dispatcher her symptoms and the address of the house.

"Don't hang up," the woman told him. "Stay on the line. Does she seem to be breathing okay?"

Mike's heart was racing as he answered the woman's questions, grateful for her knowing, patient tone. Just like a doctor. Mike had responded to distress calls like this dozens of times as a volunteer paramedic on the fire and rescue team in Lancaster County, but somehow, when the emergency involved someone you loved, the protocol was erased from your mind.

Within minutes, he could hear the approaching sirens of an ambulance. He thanked the dispatcher, then quickly went to unlock the door and let the paramedics in.

When they rolled the stretcher out the front door, Gran seemed thin and frail, like a wounded bird. Mike locked the house behind them and climbed into the front seat of the rescue vehicle, having been told he wasn't permitted to ride in the back with his grandmother, "Even if you are a paramedic," the driver said, a sympathetic look in his eyes.

A few hours later, Mike hoped that the worst of it was over as he sat at his grandmother's bedside in a patient room at Philadelphia's Doctors Hospital. Gran was asleep for now, which allowed him to think of all the things that could have gone wrong. What if the stroke had happened during the night? Dr. Somers had explained that immediate treatment increased the possibilities for a full recovery. In fact, the medication dripping in through Gran's IV line was only administered if the patient received treatment within three hours of the stroke.

Mike had thanked God, over and over, that he had been visiting Gran when the stroke happened. He was grateful for that, though it made him worry to think that she might have languished alone for hours . . . or even days.

Which made him wonder: How would Gran manage alone after this?

She wouldn't. He rested his head in his hands and tried to swallow back the sorrow that rose inside him. Gran would probably lose her independence. She would probably have to move out of the historic old townhouse. Mike would be visiting her in an assisted care facility.

It was the end of an era.

Footsteps grew louder, and Mike sensed someone lingering in the doorway.

"Mama?"

Mike looked up to see his father enter the room, looking more like a concerned son than an experienced doctor himself.

"Mama, it's your son, Henry." His eyes glistened with tears as he leaned close and took her hand in his. "Can you hear me?"

"She's out," Mike said, rising from the upholstered chair. "I think they might have given her something to help her sleep. How are you doing, Dad?"

"I got away as quickly as I could." Henry Trueherz's mouth puckered, and he released his mother's hand and pressed a fist to his lips. "It's a terrible feeling to be so many miles away, unable to help, and . . ." His voice broke off as a tear streaked down his cheek.

Mike felt his lower jaw drop at the sight of his father losing control. This sort of emotion was not something he'd ever seen his father display.

Letting him grieve in silence for a moment, Mike moved across to the bedside table, grabbed the box of tissues, and handed it to his father. Sometimes small acts were more meaningful than grand gestures.

"I'm sorry, son." Henry said, taking a few tissues from the box and wiping his eyes. "This is all so unexpected."

Mike put a hand on his father's shoulder. "It's hard when it happens to someone you love."

His father sniffed, nodding. "How's she doing?"

"They confirmed that she had a stroke, but the prognosis looks good, especially since she got immediate medical care. This is the drug they're giving her to break up the blood clot. I wrote the name down, since it's a mile long. They call it t-PA for short," Mike continued, passing on the information the doctor had explained to him. "I know the doctor wants to meet with you. I'm sure he'll explain everything all over again."

"I talked with Dr. Somers in his office. It sounds like you've got a good grasp of the situation, son. I can't tell you how relieved I am that you were with her this morning. That's a divine intervention, if ever there was one." He took a deep breath, calming himself. "Do you mind telling me what happened? I know you've probably been over the story countless times, but—"

"No problem." Mike pulled the second upholstered chair closer. "Have a seat, Dad."

He went over the story again, from seeing Gran upstairs in the hallway, where Mike had agreed to make breakfast, to finding her slumped on the kitchen floor thirty minutes later.

"You handled everything well, Mike. Did your training with the Lancaster Rescue Squad come in handy?"

"In some ways." Mike was glad he'd known to call an ambulance, but even now when he closed his eyes he still saw the terrifying image of his grandmother slumped on the floor by the pantry. "It's so different when the emergency involves your own family."

"That clinical detachment is there for a reason, I guess." Henry dropped his head and rubbed the back of his neck. "When it hits home like this, no amount of medical training can erase fear."

Mike was surprised to see that his father's hands were shaking a little. The crisis had brought out a side of Henry Trueherz that Mike had never seen. To see his father cry, to see him so vulnerable, even grateful to Mike for being in the city, anyone would have been moved. Mike's opinion of his father shifted as he felt the first glimmer of real compassion for him.

"I should have seen this coming." Henry straightened, his face pinched with concern as he gazed over at the elderly woman asleep in the bed. "Mom has always been fiercely independent and I've respected that, but in the back of my mind I was afraid something like this would happen. Even all those years ago when we moved out to Paradise, I hated leaving your grandmother alone here in the city. She was more spry back then, got around a lot better. Now . . ." He shook his head as the words trailed off.

Leaning back in the chair, Mike steeled himself to be the strong one here. He had always relied on his father to know the right course of action, but Dad was in no shape to make decisions. His father needed him to be the clear thinker now. "The doctor said she would need therapy," Mike recalled.

"She will, and that will vary depending on the extent of the stroke damage. She might need physical, occupational, or speech therapy. We'll need to hire an aide for her once she's released from the hospital . . . unless she goes to a rehab facility."

"No . . ." The hoarse voice from the bed startled Mike. Gran's eyes were open, and she seemed alert. "No nursing home." Her voice lingered on the *s* sound.

Instantly Mike and his dad were on their feet at Katherine's bedside.

"How are you, Mom?" Henry asked, touching her shoulder.

"I was resting until I heard myself getting the bum's rush." Her words were more pronounced than they had been earlier that morning. "I'm not leaving my home."

"Mom, you might not be able to handle stairs for a while," Henry pointed out. "And even simple tasks like making a sandwich or getting dressed might be difficult. You're going to need to accept some help until you're back on your feet."

"Not at a home," she said vehemently. "Sending me out to pasture like an old horse."

Dr. Trueherz reached up to rub tension from one temple. "Mom, it's not like that."

"I won't be sent off to shrivel up in a corner and play bingo on Wednesdays. I have my garden club and the church and the neighborhood association. I'm the vice president, you know."

Watching Katherine stand up to her son, Mike saw yet another new light cast on Henry, who clearly was frustrated with his mother's demands. "Dad, I know you want Gran to have the best care possible," Mike intervened, "but can't she get that at the townhouse? She has a lot going on in her life, and if she's stuck in a facility, she'll be bored to tears."

"You're darn tooting," Gran said.

"But you can't turn the house into a rehab facility," Henry said, rubbing his chin. "And in-home care is expensive."

"I've got excellent health coverage," Gran said.

"And why can't her house be a place for rehab?" Mike walked around the hospital bed as the idea gelled in his mind. "Making coffee in the kitchen could be occupational therapy. We could put a bed in the den so Gran wouldn't have to go up and down the stairs. She can tend her plants in the back. I'll help her hoist soil and water. With some help she can even host the neighborhood association."

"There you go, Henry." Gran's eyes flashed with quiet strength. "Mike will be my assistant."

"I don't know." Henry's spine stiffened and his lips pursed in that authoritative stance that Mike had always associated with Dad the doctor. "We would have to bring in an aide . . . a physical therapist, too. . . ."

"You can bring in anyone you like, Henry, as long as I can be in my home," Gran said in her characteristically craggy voice. Then, with the decision settled, she closed her eyes and eased down into the pillow.

"What do you think, son? You're not even finished with exams yet."

"I just have a take-home final due next week, then I'm done," Mike said as his mind reeled ahead. This meant he would need to move to Philadelphia sooner than planned; he'd be spending the summer here.

"You'd have to give up your summer at home," his father was saying.

"That's okay, Dad. I can do it. I don't mind."

His father clapped a hand on his back. "It's a wonderful thing you're doing, son. You can see how much it means to your gran. I feel guilty that I can't do more for her myself."

Again, there was a quick glimpse of the vulnerability his father so rarely revealed. Mike was about to respond when Gran cut in.

"I still hear you. Don't talk about me like I've lost my marbles."

Mike and his dad laughed softly, and for the first time in a long time, his father gave him a hug.

FOURTEEN

*S*adie was deep into a dream where she was singing on a sandy beach, curling waves of water sparkling in the sun, just like she'd seen in books, when someone nudged her arm.

"Wake up!" a voice whispered. "It's Ruthie's birthday."

Rolling over, Sadie sighed. "We need you to lead the clapping song," the voice breathed in her ear.

The clapping song . . . it was a birthday tradition their mamm had begun. On the morning of a child's birthday, Mamm had gathered all the kids together to wake the birthday boy or girl with a rousing rendition of the song she had made up.

Sadie opened her eyes to see Leah and Susie leaning over her. Mary and Simon stood behind them, and Katie and Sam were over at Ruthie's bed, watching curiously.

"Ruthie sleeping," Katie said, and Sam pressed a finger to his lips to shush her.

"I sent Simon to get Jonah and Adam," Mary said. Her dark hair was pulled back and coiled into a long braid that hung down her back. "But kumm quick. Out of bed. You're the song leader, Sadie."

Sadie threw back the sheet and popped up to her feet. She didn't mind Mary's bossiness when it came to the birthday tradition—especially for Ruthie, who enjoyed her birthday so! "I'm ready to go," Sadie said, "as soon as those boys get here."

"She awake," Katie pronounced from Ruthie's bedside, and Sadie was sure she saw a hint of a dimple as Ruthie rolled away to face the window. Nowadays the older kids woke before the song could be sung, but it was fun to stay in bed, pretend to be asleep, and savor the attention.

"Here," Adam whispered, ducking into the room with one hand on Simon's shoulder. Gabe and Jonah followed, keeping their heads bent so that they didn't bump them on the dormered ceiling.

"Kumm," Mary ordered as they gathered around Ruthie's bed.

Sadie let her eyes roam over their faces, excited and giddy. The birthday song always brought out a bit of childish glee, even in the most serious person. With a deep breath, she started clapping, then sang:

> Rise and shine
> And give Gott your glory.
> Today is Ruthie's birthday
> And this is her story.
> She was born this very day
> Just twelve years ago.
> We love her so, we hope and pray
> She'll have a smile that lasts all day!

As soon as the song started, a smile lit Ruthie's heart-shaped face. Her amber eyes flew open, and she sat up to face her siblings, soaking up their love.

Of course, the song needed to be repeated a few times for the fun of it, and before long Ruthie was out of bed, clapping along and bobbing her head in time.

"Happy birthday, Ruthie!" Sam called when the singing stopped.

"Denki." She hugged him close, then went down the line and gave everyone a hug. "I'm so glad you remembered."

"How could we forget when you remind us over and again?" Jonah asked, giving her braid a playful tug.

"I like to make the most of my birthday, and I just wanted to be sure you would remember that it was May twenty-second," Ruthie said, bending down to give Katie a hug.

When she came to Sadie, she squeezed her hand. "Gott gave you the voice of an angel. It's a good thing, because someone strong has to lead the birthday song."

"You can count on me to take care of that," Sadie said. The birthday song was a tradition etched deep in her heart, and with ten siblings, there was a birthday cropping up at least every few weeks.

"Oh, but someday you'll go off and start a family of your own," Mary said. "Then Adam will need to lead the song." She scowled up at their oldest brother. "Maybe Sadie can give you some lessons."

"I can sing," Adam insisted.

"In the shower," Gabe added.

Adam waved them off with good humor, but it made Sadie feel a bit wistful, imagining herself leaving her home, leaving someone else to lead the song for Katie and Sam, Simon and Ruthie. Her heart ached at the thought, but she knew it was true. She was eighteen and it was getting to be time to move ahead with her life . . . whatever that meant.

"What kind of cake is Mary making you?" Sadie asked over the clip-clop of the horse's hooves on the road. It was the late afternoon of

Ruthie's birthday, and the two girls were in the small buggy, headed toward the cemetery where their parents had been laid to rest.

"Peanut butter cake with chocolate frosting, and I could smell it baking when we left." In the afternoon sunlight, the long lashes outlining Ruthie's amber eyes seemed incredibly dark. She had the eyes of a woman now, wise eyes, even though her manner and small body were still very girlish. "Thank you for my birthday present. This was just what I wanted."

"I would think the colored pastels from Mary would be more fun than a trip to the cemetery."

"But this is much more grown-up." Ruthie scratched at her forehead then swiped back the downy wisps of hair that always sprang forth. Angel bangs, Mamm used to call them. "You only turn twelve once in your life, and it's time for me to take on some new responsibilities, I think."

"Ya, but not on your birthday." Ruthie's other birthday gifts had been more traditional. A puzzle. A new Monopoly game with Disney characters. And a packet of soaps carved into animals from Remy. "I don't mind at all, and I've been meaning to get out here, but this trip could bring you a touch of sadness."

"But I wanted to help you tidy up. You've been good about going and tending to their graves, and it's time someone else came along." That was Ruthie, caretaker to all. Her wise eyes had a soul to match, though she had just turned twelve. Sadie thought there was something deeper at play here, but she didn't probe. Everyone was healing from the loss of Mamm and Dat in their own ways.

"It shouldn't take us long," Sadie said. "I remembered to bring the weed whacker this time." She gazed beyond the horse's bobbing head to the patchwork of fields and gentle green hills surrounding them. Corn stood in short, neat rows to their left. To the right was a dairy farm where a group of cows sunned themselves, brown heaps in the grass. Small birds swooped, circled, then returned to their leafy tree homes, and here and there wildflowers added dots of color to the roadside. The season was at its peak, soon to give way to summer's long, hot days. "If only springtime could be saved in a jar, the way we put up peaches and plums," Sadie said absently.

"Such a notion." Ruthie smiled. "And then we could open the jar in the cold of winter and have a warm helping of spring."

"My favorite season," Sadie said as they passed the sign to Paradise. It made her think of Mike, the doctor's son. Was he still down the road in Paradise, helping his dat take care of people?

Mike told her he had a double life. Until Mike said the words she had never heard of such a thing, but now she saw doubles in so many of her hopes and dreams. How she loved the country on a warm spring day like this, even as she wanted to be in the crazy noise and excitement of the city. How she loved her family and the patterns of their lives on the farm, but she also felt her spirit come alive when she was singing with the band.

The thought of Mike leaving Lancaster County made her feel a little hollow inside. He wouldn't be coming upon her on the road anymore, giving her a ride, letting her play the radio so very loud. Ever since that day, every time Sadie was scootering down the road she imagined that Mike would come along and drive her back to the ice-cream parlor. But it wasn't the ice cream she was so interested in; she wanted to see Mike again. Though she didn't know him well, Sadie knew she could trust Mike. She wanted to be his friend, which wouldn't be easy, him being an Englisher.

Still, they could be secret friends in their double lives. Englisher and Amish. She smiled at that.

At last they passed farmland that gave way to a scattering of small gravestones. The cemetery. Although more than a dozen cemeteries in Lancaster County were used by the Amish, this one was closest to their farm.

Sadie shifted the reins to guide the horse into the cemetery.

Most of the graves were covered only with grass and a simple stone marker. A large, fancy marker would be considered a foolish waste of money. And what was the point, when the real wealth of spirit and love would be in the world yet to come?

Ruthie turned her head to take it all in. "It looked very different in the snow." She hadn't been here since the day of the funeral.

It had been during a cold spell in February, more than a year ago, when they had buried their parents, Esther and Levi, here. Sadie had heard that the ground was so frozen that the men had to chop with special axes to dig the graves.

A very cold winter that was, for the heart and soul.

But now Mamm and Dat's graves were covered with green grass, as if those two stones belonged there in the corner. It was Gott's will, of course, but Gott's will wasn't always easy to accept. *Like trying to chew and swallow pickled beets when you've got a fever,* Sadie thought. It didn't always go down so easily.

Their buggy drew up to the edge of the cemetery and Sadie stopped the horse.

"Well. Would you look at that?" Sadie said, squinting into the sunlight.

Ruthie shook her head. "What are those brown spots?"

"Dirt." Sadie climbed down from the buggy. "Looks like some critters have been digging."

Ruthie ran ahead, light-footed and curious.

As Sadie drew closer, her heart sank. Her parents' grave sites were mottled with patches of brown. Holes in the dirt.

"Esther King. Levi King." Ruthie read the gravestones quietly. "This is it."

"But the nice bed of green grass is ruined." Sadie stopped a few feet away, hands on her hips. "Who did this?"

The chattering sound overhead drew Sadie's attention to a nearby tree.

"Is this your doing, Mr. Squirrel?" She pointed up to the tree, where a squirrel perched, holding an acorn as it watched them.

"Squirrels!" Ruthie's grim expression softened. "Maybe. But more likely it's moles." She poked at the holes in the ground with the toe of one sneaker. "See how it's caving in? They love to build tunnels."

Sadie laughed at the sight of her sister gently pressing her toes into the ground.

"At least Dat would be glad to know that his grave is home for a little animal," Sadie said. "Let's fetch the seeds and tools from the buggy."

"Good thing we brought along grass seed."

Sadie slipped an arm over her sister's shoulders as they headed back to the buggy. "You'd better give that Mr. Mole a good talking-to before we go," she said affectionately. "Tell him to dig his tunnels on the other side of the fence."

They brought the spade, weed whacker, and grass seed to the graveside and knelt down in the dappled sunlight. With the soil loosened by the digging critters, it was easy to smooth it out and pour on handfuls of seed.

Ruthie took extra care, tamping down the soil gently over the tiny flecks of seed. "There you go. Time to grow where you're planted," she said with a note of contentment.

Sadie wasn't sure whether her sister was talking to the grass seed or to her, but she decided to keep silent. For Sadie, there was something soothing about being here, no matter what the season, and it seemed that Ruthie felt it, too. A certain peace. Maybe it was the quiet here, away from the busy life at the farm, that opened the gate to memories.

Sadie tapped the spade against a rock to get the remaining soil off. The steady beat reminded her of Red playing the drums, and she wondered what Mamm and Dat would think of her singing with the band. Mamm had taught her how to turn her work to joy by singing, and Dat had often asked her for a song as they rode into town on the buggy. "Sing me another one, Sadie girl," he would say. Did they look down from heaven and watch her singing in dark clubs in the city, singing for strangers in her blue jeans and T-shirt?

They wouldn't like that.

Sadie didn't like the bars herself. It wasn't the way she had dreamed of sharing her music with the world. When she closed her eyes and tried to imagine using her gift, she pictured herself singing songs that glorified the Heavenly Father. But it was a fuzzy dream she had, one that didn't make much sense in either the Englisher or Amish world. The song leader at church was always a man and the Amish didn't have much call for music in any other way. And Englishers wouldn't want to hear a girl singing hymns when they could turn on a radio to hear countless songs that were far more exciting.

No, it was a verhuddelt dream of hers, this music from the heart. She kept thinking the Heavenly Father would show her a clear path, a way to use her voice, but maybe that was verhuddelt, too.

Sadie was so caught up in her worries that she lost track of her sister beside her until the silence was broken by a tiny whimper, sad as the cry of a forlorn puppy.

Her head turned to Ruthie, whose bottom lip protruded, her face crumpling in a sob.

"Come here, *Liewe.*" Sadie opened her arms, using the word for "darling," which Mamm used to call them.

Ruthie nearly fell against her, tears streaming down her face. "I miss them so. I surely do. But when I close my eyes, it's getting harder and harder to see their faces, and that's a terrible thing. I don't want to lose them in my mind."

"I know." Sadie hugged her sister, wishing she could squeeze the sorrow right out of her. "Time makes everything fade a bit— the good and the bad, too. But sometimes I see Mamm and Dat in things at home. Every time I see Simon training Shadow or talking to the horses, it reminds me of Dat's easy way with the animals. And Gabe with the cows; he knows just what to do to keep them healthy and happy. The way Mary runs the kitchen, feeding us all, reminds me of Mamm. And when Leah helps the rest of you with reading and writing. And you, Ruthie, I see Mamm's love in your golden eyes when you make folks smile and feel at ease. You've got Mamm's optimism. She always saw the silver lining in the storm clouds."

Ruthie sniffed. "She did. Do you remember that little smile that lit her eyes? Even when she scolded us, you could see the love in her eyes."

"So you *do* remember."

"Some things." She swiped away the tears, leaving a smudge of dirt on her face.

Sadie's heart swelled with sympathy for her sister. *Twelve is such an important year,* she thought. *No longer a child, but far from a woman.* It wouldn't be easy for Ruthie, but Sadie vowed to keep an eye on her little sister, and she knew Remy and Mary would be there for her, too.

"We'll talk about Mamm and Dat anytime you want," Sadie said. "Sometimes talking brings out the memories."

Ruthie nodded. "And can I come back here with you again?"

"Sure. We're going to need to tidy up their graves from time to time."

Wiping her hands together, Ruthie looked down at the simple headstones. "A long time ago I forgave the man who killed them, but I'll never forget our mamm and dat." She squatted down, her skirt bunching around her as she patted down the soil once more. "I'll never forget."

FIFTEEN

*H*ere it is. . . ." Remy turned the key in the lock, pushed the door, and stepped into her apartment. "Exactly as I left it . . . except maybe for a few dust bunnies."

The apartment looked the same, though she remembered the unshakable cold of winter the last time she'd been here. And now it was May, and she'd found a home many miles west of here in Amish country.

Back in February when she'd gone to Lancaster County to investigate a news story, she had gotten snowed in at the King farm for nearly two weeks. When she'd returned here in late February, the apartment had seemed cold and sterile, a dismal place after days of love and laughter with the Kings. Besides that, she had fallen in love with Adam and the Amish way of life, though she'd been convinced that there was no way she and Adam could be together. The last time she was here, her heart was heavy with loss and confusion.

But now it was very different. Remy crossed the parquet floor

and placed her big box of garbage bags on the counter. Sadie followed, gawking at the cathedral ceiling and tall windows.

"It's wonderful good." Sadie's fingers toyed with her kapp
strings as she stepped around the leather sofa to check out the view
from the windows. "So modern . . . like a museum of your own.
And you can even see the real museum from here!"

"Two of them, actually." Remy went to the window and pointed
out the small Rodin Museum across the parkway, as well as the
majestic Philadelphia Museum of Art. "I used to love this view. It
was one of the few things I liked about living here."

"What are you saying?" Sadie held her arms wide, taking in the
expansive room. "This is a wonderful apartment. From here you
can look out over all of Philadelphia! For me, it would be a dream
come true to live in a place like this."

Remy smiled as she perched on one of the stools at the kitchen
counter. This was exactly the reaction Adam had predicted his sister
would have. He worried about her attraction to the English world,
and his concerns were well-founded. But Remy didn't think that
pressure from Adam would sway his sister to commit to the Amish
faith, and so she frequently pointed out to the man she loved that
baptism was a personal decision. Wasn't it a matter between Sadie
and God? She was convinced that they had to trust the Heavenly
Father to guide Sadie's choice.

"You know, Sadie, when I picked it out I thought it was a beautiful apartment. But I was never really happy here, and that can
color how you feel about a place."

"But . . . leather sofas?" Sadie sat down and sighed. "Heavenly."

"But they're cold in the winter," Remy said, remembering the
chill she hadn't been able to shake when the specter of her life
without Adam had hung over her. "And they can be slippery, too."
She sat on the edge of one and pretended to slide right off. She

landed on the floor, her emerald-green Amish dress bunched over her knees.

Sadie laughed. "But sliding is not a problem," she said, slipping down beside Remy. "Because there's this fluffy white rug to land on." She patted the rug curiously. "Is it the hide of a polar bear?"

Remy snorted. "No. It's acrylic. A polar bear, really?"

Both girls laughed.

"Did you think I went hunting in the North Pole?" Remy asked, doubled over with laughter.

"Knowing you, I wouldn't be surprised." Sadie giggled again, then sprang to her feet and swayed to the window dramatically. "Show me the rest of your apartment. I like it very much, though I can't think what you'd do to pass the time here, and it does take a while to get outside with the elevator and those long hallways."

Remy showed her the bedroom, where Sadie announced that she would never be able to sleep with the world waiting there beneath her window. All the cars and museums and people walking around.

In the bathroom, Sadie admired the little flowers in the tiles, the light fixture bright as the sun, and mirrors covering an entire wall. "How could you even think of leaving such a place?"

"It's easy to walk away when you're lonely," Remy said, stepping into the bathroom beside Sadie, who was frowning into the mirror.

Sadie pointed at Remy's face. "How did you do that?"

Facing the mirror, Remy lifted a hand to her face. "What?"

"Your eyebrows? They curve, like a sliver of moon. Mine are like a big furry caterpillar crossing my forehead."

"Oh, yours aren't so bad. Mine are shaped this way because I had laser hair removal."

Sadie pressed the ridge above her eyes, as if trying to wipe her brows off. "How do I get this lay-sir hair thing?"

"It's very expensive," Remy said. "And it's electric. I don't think it would be allowed by the Ordnung."

With a touch of defiance, Sadie put her hands on her hips. "I'm in rumspringa and my you-knee brow is ruining everything."

"Really? I don't think people even notice."

"Plain people don't notice, but the others do." Sadie turned away from the mirror and leaned against the granite counter. "I've heard girls make fun of me when they didn't know I was listening." She touched her brows self-consciously. "Now I'm beginning to wonder if Frank notices, too."

Remy's lower lip jutted out sympathetically. She wanted to tell Sadie that friends who were judging her based strictly on appearance were no friends at all, but she didn't think Sadie would believe her. When you were eighteen, that sort of lesson was something you needed to learn on your own.

"God made you a beautiful girl." Remy touched Sadie's shoulder. "I wish you didn't feel bad about how you look."

Sadie dropped her eyes. "It's just what other people are saying."

"Okay." Remy slid open a drawer in the vanity, fished around amid the plastic cases and tubs of makeup, and found a pair of tweezers. "Maybe I shouldn't do this, but you can have these. It's what most people use to shape their brows. They pluck them."

"Plucking?" Sadie squinted. "Like a chicken."

"Something like that, but instead of taking all the hairs out you want to shape them, sort of like a crescent moon. There's really an art to it, but I can help get you started. Here."

Together they leaned into the mirror, and Remy showed Sadie how to use the pointed edge of the tweezers to grab the hair.

"You want to pull in the direction that the hair grows," Remy said. "And it hurts at first. Ready?"

"Ya."

"Okay, face me." Armed with tweezers, Remy pulled, and Sadie bravely kept mum.

"Like being pecked by a chicken, right between the eyes," Sadie said.

"An apt description. Do you want me to keep going?" When Sadie nodded, Remy honed in on the tiny hairs at the center of Sadie's forehead. Gritting her teeth, she plucked rapidly.

A minute later she had made a smooth space between Sadie's brows.

"Ach!" Sadie blinked back tears. "It's mighty painful!"

"I know, but we have a little space now. No one can say you have a unibrow anymore."

Sadie brushed at it, leaning into the mirror. "It looks good."

"We don't have time to shape now, but you can keep the tweezers. We need to be ready when the truck comes to pick the furniture up this afternoon."

"Denki, Remy."

"You're welcome." Remy was glad to help Sadie feel better about herself, though Adam was going to be upset if he noticed a visible change in his sister. Well . . . she would cross that bridge when she came to it.

"Where do you want me to start?" Sadie asked.

"I guess we should start bagging all the clothes. I just want to be sure that the two dressers are empty when the mission truck gets here."

Sadie ripped open the box of garbage bags and got to work, singing an old song that Remy recognized as Cole Porter's "My Romance."

"I've always loved that song," Remy said as she tucked a bundle of sweaters into a bag. "But it's quite an evolution from 'How Great Thou Art.'"

"Frank has taught me many songs," Sadie said. "I don't like some of them. But that's a good one."

"Sing another one," Remy said as she loaded up another plastic bag, and then moved on to the walk-in closet.

This morning as they had driven into Philly, Remy had worried that she might have trouble parting with her belongings. Although her time here in Philadelphia had been laced with sadness, she was saying good-bye to possessions accumulated over all twenty-four years of her life. But Remy felt good about "recycling" her former life. Maybe a teenaged girl would make good use of her leather jacket and many pairs of jeans. Someone would benefit from the money made on her laptop, which she'd wiped clean of data. And before she had closed up the laptop, she had found a local charity that would come to the apartment and pick up all her furniture. She and Sadie would make a few trips to Goodwill to donate everything else, from her designer suits to her pots and pans—a task that would have taken her days without Sadie's help. She had canceled her credit cards and would transfer her savings to the bank in Halfway. Things were coming together nicely.

The closet was halfway empty and Sadie was singing a song about riding on a railroad when Remy pulled down the box of photos.

"Oh." This was going to be her downfall.

She gathered the skirt of her dress, sat cross-legged on the closet floor, and opened the box, which was nearly overflowing with packs of photos shoved haphazardly inside. There were shots of her summers at camp. High school proms. Halloween parties with her friends.

This was her life: so precious to her, and yet the box of old photos would be meaningless to anyone else. She couldn't throw them away.

I'll give them to Herb, she thought. *I'll make him promise to hold on to these, even if he stashes them up in the attic.*

But as she sifted through the photographs, Remy thought of something that brought her to her feet. She grabbed the box of photos and flew out of the closet, through the bedroom to the living room.

"What's wrong?" Sadie called after her.

And there it was, on the built-in bookshelves: the photo of her mother in an old-fashioned frame of marbled dark green stone set in sculpted wire. Hugging the box and the framed photo, Remy crumpled to the floor. How many hours had she spent staring at this picture of her mom? In the photo her mother's head was cocked to one side, the subtle curve of her lips saying that she was listening but was ready to make light of whatever problem was in the air.

That was how Remy remembered her mom . . . making games of things. She'd been a woman who delighted in catching fireflies, dressing up for tea parties with real china cups, and playing barefoot flashlight-tag on a summer night. Remy had been eight when her mother died, and though the pain of loss had eased over the years, the ache of missing her remained.

"Was ist letz?" Sadie's eyes flooded with concern as she gathered her dress and knelt beside Remy. "What's the matter, Remy?"

"I don't know what to do with this picture of my mother." She showed it to Sadie. "It's really all I have left of her." She sighed. "Oh, Sadie, it makes my heart ache to think of destroying it."

Sadie considered the photograph. "She looks like a nice woman. She must have loved you very much."

Remy nodded. "I guess I could give it to my father, but his wife probably won't be too happy about storing it." How could she describe her relationship with her stepmother to kind, free-spirited Sadie? "My stepmother, Loretta—I don't think she ever liked me too much. When she married Herb, I think she wanted him to make a clean break from the past."

"But that's verhuddelt. You're his daughter."

"It's verhuddelt, all right," Remy said, enjoying the kinder word for crazy. "But I never was able to win Loretta over."

"What will you do with the picture of your mamm?"

"I don't know." Remy ran her finger over the scrollwork of the frame. "I always thought that one day, I'd share this with a daughter."

"That would be a nice thing if it weren't forbidden by the Ordnung."

"Do you think the bishop would make an exception since it isn't a photo of me?" Remy asked. She knew the Amish objected to photos for various reasons, one being that a photo showed a certain level of pride and vanity—traits discouraged by the Amish.

The younger girl shook her head. "I don't think the bishop would allow it."

Holding the photo to her heart, Remy sighed. Sadie was right. Besides, how would it look for a candidate for baptism to ask for exceptions to the rules? Remy didn't want anything to stand between her and her devotion to the faith.

Sadie sat back on her heels, a muted glow in her eyes. "Sometimes I wonder 'bout Katie and Sam, so young when Mamm and Dat were killed. I don't know if they'll remember what our parents looked like, and that's a sad thing."

"It is, but they'll remember the love. I'm sure of that. And everyone will tell them stories about their parents. Stories that will keep your parents' love alive in their hearts."

Sadie gestured to the photo in Remy's arms. "And when you have a daughter of your own, you won't need that photograph. You must tell her stories about your mother's love. That's better than just looking at a photo, ya?"

"You're right." Remy took one last look at the photo, grateful for Sadie's insight. This ink dried on a piece of paper held no power over her. It was the memory of her mother's love that mattered.

Resolute, Remy tucked the photo into the box and closed it. She would ask Herb to store the photographs in a safe place, but she knew she would never look at them again. Instead of looking to the past, she would look to the future, to the moments she would share with Adam and the Kings. And if God blessed Adam and her with a child, she would regale him or her with stories of the grand-mother who loved to laugh. A photo told only part of the story, but her memories, full and rich, would say it all.

SIXTEEN

*S*adie pushed a squishy plastic sack of clothes into the trunk of Remy's car and pressed until it was wedged into the tiny corner by the taillight. White plastic bags filled the trunk, like puffy clumps of snow. Sadie slammed the lid closed, but it bounced back open. She had to slam it three times before it stayed shut.

They had already made one trip to drop off a carload at the Goodwill store, and now the car was ready again, but they would have to wait so that they didn't miss the furniture truck.

So many things! Sadie couldn't imagine when Remy had found the time to wear the dozen or so pairs of pointy-toed shoes with high heels, or the three pairs of boots, none of them fit for working in their barn or even riding out to check the fences.

Truth be told, some of Remy's clothes had caught Sadie's eye, making her heart race with longing. There were smooth jackets with buttery leather, and so many blue jeans. And when Sadie saw the drawer full of T-shirts, she couldn't resist. Right now she had two T-shirts that she had bought with money she'd earned at the hotel, and one of them had a hole under the arm.

"Do you think it would be okay if I kept a few things?" Sadie had asked, holding up a brown T-shirt that said "Hurley" across the chest in fancy letters.

"Well, sure." Remy had looked up from the floor of the closet. "But what do you need them for? Cleaning rags?"

Sadie had pressed a hand to her mouth as she giggled. "I want to wear them."

Remy had seemed a little concerned, her lips pinching a bit, but she had said yes.

Her heart merry with the new little gifts, Sadie had quickly tried to choose the colors that looked best on her. Greens, and browns that matched her amber eyes, and one in ruby red. She also took a simple summer dress with large blue and green blossoms that seemed to be giant smiles, and a simple pair of black leather shoes with a flat heel. Not wanting to take too much time away from their work, she had bundled them up right quick. They sat on the kitchen counter, and Sadie felt a bit like a little girl who'd gotten a dolly for Christmas. Now she wouldn't have to look the same every time Frank saw her. She could wear a different shirt every night, like Heather and the other fancy girls.

A rumble shook the basement garage as a big white truck pulled into the far corner and parked in two empty spots. Was that their truck?

Sadie turned back to lock the car with the plastic nub, the way Remy had shown her. Behind her she heard the truck's doors close, and one boy said something about an echo. A minute later, a deep voice sang out: "La, la, la!"

Amused, she turned as laughter broke out. A handful of young men stood around the truck.

Then, from the far corner of the garage an amazing sound burst forth. They were singing—all the young men together—and their voices blended in harmony.

Harmony!

The beautiful sound lifted her heart. Music like this was a gift from the Heavenly Father. She rubbed her arms to soothe the gooseflesh there.

And the words were so simple. . . .

"God will take care of you." It was like the voice of the Lord Himself, singing a lullaby to a little baby in his arms.

She listened in awe as they approached Remy's car near the elevator, their voices blended into one big, warm sound in the garage.

A few of the young men noticed her and smiled, their hymn drawing to a close.

"That was beautiful!" She clasped her hands to her heart. "How did you learn such a lovely song?"

"We're in a church choir," replied a young man with skin the color of chocolate. He had dark eyes and a very nice smile beneath his baseball cap.

"It must sound wonderful good Sunday morning when you go to church," Sadie said as she walked alongside them to the elevator.

"Hey, Sadie!" One of the young men stepped out of the group. "I thought that was you. I almost didn't recognize you with—well, you look different every time I see you."

She glanced up at the tall man and recognized his sparkling eyes and the smile that made her heart feel light. "Mike? What are you doing here?"

"This is my church group. At least, when I'm in the city. Guys, this is my friend Sadie King." He introduced Sadie to the other young men, though their names went by quickly—Leo, Daryl, Mitch, and Alex.

"You're the group coming to collect furniture, ya?" she asked.

When Mike nodded, she laughed. "Well, it's my friend Remy who's been waiting for you. She's got an apartment full for you."

"Sounds great," one of the other young men said as he pushed the elevator button.

"I can't believe it's you." Mike leaned casually against the concrete wall by the elevator. "I see you everywhere. So I have to ask, what are *you* doing here in Philly?"

"Remy needed help closing up her apartment."

He squinted. "Refresh my memory. Who's Remy?"

"She's going to marry my brother Adam come wedding season."

"But she used to live here?"

"She's an Englisher, joining the faith and learning our ways."

"Wow." Mike's eyes, blue as a summer sky, sparked with interest. "That's unusual, isn't it? I mean, I know a lot of tourists are intrigued by the Amish, but not too many are actually willing to live Plain."

She nodded. "Ya, but our Remy is a very special girl."

"Must be."

The men waited for Sadie to enter the elevator first, then filed in, filling the boxy little space. As the doors slid shut, Sadie looked up at them shyly.

"How about another song?" she suggested.

"She likes us," said the man with brown skin.

"No, Daryl. She likes our singing," Mike corrected.

They began to discuss what song to sing next.

"Should we do 'Rock of Ages'?" someone said.

"Hold on, guys." Mike put his hands up, then gestured toward Sadie. "This young lady has an amazing set of pipes. Why don't we do something together?"

Joy warmed her heart at the prospect of singing with these musicians.

"You pick something, Sadie. I like to think our choir knows just about every hymn out there."

"Do you know 'His Eye Is on the Sparrow'?" she asked.

"Sure," Daryl said. "You set the key. Just start and we'll join in."

Tentatively, she began singing: "Why should I feel discouraged, why should the shadows come . . ."

On the third word there came a low rumble of voices under hers, following her as closely as a plow followed a horse.

Harmonies!

Sadie could have cried out in joy for the beauty of it.

And to feel her voice as a part of it all . . . music as a burning flame of faith that joined their hearts together . . . it was a wonderful feeling as Sadie glided into the refrain.

I sing because I'm happy,
I sing because I'm free,
For His eye is on the sparrow,
And I know He watches me.

They had just started the second verse when the elevator doors opened, and Sadie looked up at Mike questioningly.

But he kept singing, motioning for her to go first, and she stepped in the hall, leading the walking choir of singers to Remy's apartment, where the door was cracked open.

Still singing, Sadie pushed the door open and peeked inside. Remy came out of the bedroom as the group finished the verse.

"Fabulous!" Remy applauded. "Where'd you get the choir?"

"Look who I found in the basement." Sadie couldn't help but smile. "Our movers. And my friend Mike Trueherz is one of them. His dat is Susie's doctor."

"Hi, Mike. Hey, guys. You sound great, but it's a little early for caroling, isn't it?" Remy joked as she motioned them in the door. "Come on in. I'm so grateful that you're doing this."

Daryl appeared to be the leader of the group, and he followed Remy around the apartment, making a list of everything that would be packed into their truck. While they were talking, Mike went to the window while the other boys joked about how many stools each one could carry at a time.

"Check out this view. Awesome."

"Ya, awesome." Sadie turned her head toward Mike. "I didn't know you sang, Mike."

"Just in the a cappella choir. That's when you have singers without any instruments playing along."

"We sing our Sunday hymns a cappella, too," Sadie said. "But Amish songs are very different from yours. They're written in Deutsch, and there's no harmony. The melodies are sort of drawn out, like a piece of taffy."

"I've studied that in music class. Amish songs have been compared to Gregorian chants," Mike said.

Sadie shrugged, not sure what that meant. "Do you have an organ in your church?" she asked.

"We do. I'm Episcopalian, and our church allows lots of instruments. Sometimes the string choir plays. There's a bass and a violin, a guitar. Sometimes there are brass instruments. That's my favorite. The trumpets rock."

"In church?" Sadie couldn't imagine it. "I think I would like that very much."

"You're welcome to come to our church some Sunday and check it out," Mike said.

"Okay, guys. Break time's over," Daryl announced. "Let's get this furniture outta here."

To Sadie's surprise, the young men sang as they worked, just as she did. Mike agreed that it made the work go faster, and she stayed close to them, toting bags downstairs while they carried furniture just so she could listen to hymns so lovely they made her heart beat faster. Unlike the slow songs from the Ausbund that were never sung in harmony, these hymns were bright and exciting—poppies and mums blooming in a field of green! She tried to think of a way that she too could learn such hymns. Frank certainly wouldn't let the band do them. How she wished she could go to choir practice like these guys and learn music there.

"How did you find so many wonderful hymns?" Sadie asked during a break.

"They're there for the singing," Daryl told her. "Some of these songs were written back in the eighth century. Anyone can perform them."

If only that was true, Sadie thought. "I've never heard songs so beautiful. Like prayers touched by an angel."

"What's your favorite?" Mike asked.

"It's hard to choose. But the one you sang that second time in the elevator, 'Be Thou My Vision,' it gave me goose bumps. In fact, you have to sing it again. I want to learn it."

"Wow, girl, you got it bad," Daryl said with a silly scowl.

Sadie decided she liked him. Daryl tried to make a joke of most everything.

"You know we're happy to do the song again," Daryl said. "But if you want to go bonkers with it, we have a CD in the truck. It's the Mennonite Singers, and the harmonies are amazing. You can have it, if you want."

A CD. "Thank you, but I have no way to play it," Sadie said.

Mike pointed to Remy's laptop. "Could we use that? I can download the songs onto your iPod right now, if that's okay."

Remy said she didn't mind, and Mike sat down, his fingers tapping the keys and making Sadie's dreams come true. Within minutes, he had added the song to her playlist. He even gave her the little booklet from the CD so that she could see all the words—the lyrics, they were called.

When the truck was all packed, Sadie went down to the garage with the guys, asking if they could do just one more song together.

"I like your enthusiasm," Daryl said.

"Really," said a shorter boy named Rex. "You should join our church choir. The girls could use a strong voice like yours."

"I would love to do that, Rex, but it would be too far to travel each week," Sadie said. "I live with my family in Halfway. That's Lancaster County."

"Well, you should find yourself a choir out there," he said.

Sadie had to breathe deep to keep hochmut, pride, from pressing on her chest, but she managed the breath and started "Silent Night," which she knew from the singings.

"Sleep in heavenly peace . . ." The music bounced off the concrete walls of the garage, making them sound bigger and louder. A few other residents on the way to their cars stopped to listen, nodding in approval.

In that moment, as Sadie smoothed down her apron and fell into the song, she felt accepted in the Englisher world, despite the differences that usually seemed so obvious to her—her thick eyebrows, her unpainted fingernails, a pale face without makeup, and of course, her dress and kapp. These fellows didn't think she looked like a cow!

All the young men were wonderful kind. There was such an easy feeling here, with boys she'd just met. And why was that? she wondered.

Watching Mike, she realized he was not treating her differently because she was Amish. He accepted her for who she was, and that made her feel strong inside.

"Let's stay in touch," Mike said.

Behind him the men were beginning to climb into the truck, and Sadie felt sad that her time with them was coming to an end. Quickly she exchanged cell phone numbers with Mike, and he promised to call and set something up.

As she waved good-bye to the truck, her heart was light for so many reasons. There was Mike Trueherz wanting to be her friend. And there was this group of very nice guys, Englishers, who had shown her this music—these beautiful harmonies. The day had brought a wonderful joy to her heart.

Back upstairs, Remy was in the hallway talking with a neighbor when Sadie returned to the apartment. She headed toward the big bathroom with the mirror so wide it was like another world you could fall into.

Feeling braver, she cocked her head and smiled at the girl in the mirror. Maybe she wasn't so terrible to look at, but her thick eyebrows clearly marked her as different from the rest of the world. No matter how she dressed, these eyebrows would announce that she was not a part of the big world.

She took the dreaded tweezers from where she'd pinned them into her apron and leaned toward the mirror. *How do you shape an eyebrow?* She wanted to get started, and she certainly couldn't afford to pay the experts Remy had mentioned. *Hmm.* She started by pulling out the little stray hairs between her eyes.

"Sadie? You okay?" Remy called.

"I'm good. In here."

Remy peeked in the open doorway, and sighed. "Back to the torture?"

"I want to get it done. I don't want to stick out anymore." It had hurt to be mocked by Heather and her friends the other night, and though the young men from Mike's church had accepted her as she was, that didn't mean others would be so kind.

"Please, Remy." She held out the tweezers. "Will you help me be pretty, like you?"

"Oh, Sadie, I think you're beautiful as you are," Remy said. "But I do remember wanting to look prettier when I was your age." Remy sighed as she took the tweezers from Sadie's hand. "I don't think your brother would approve of this."

"Adam doesn't really like anything I do these days," Sadie said.

Remy sighed. "I guess it's better to ask for forgiveness than permission."

"Denki. Where do you want to do it?" Sadie asked.

"The light is good in here. Just sit on the counter and relax."

Sadie slid onto the counter and braced her hands on the edge as Remy began to pluck from the tender skin under her brow. The pain brought tears to her eyes, but she ignored them and tried to distract herself by thinking of how much prettier she would look for the band's next club performance.

As Remy worked, it occurred to Sadie that this was a good time to ask the question that had been haunting her. "You don't think Adam will really be cross with you, do you?"

"He might, but it all stems from his worries about you. Under his brusque manner I know he loves me and will forgive me."

"Do you mind if I ask you something personal?" Sadie thought it might be a good time, with Remy concentrating so fiercely on the plucking.

"Something tells me you're going to ask anyway." Remy's voice was firm, but she was smiling.

"When did you know that you loved Adam? I mean, not just the love you have in your heart for everyone, but the special love. The Big Love."

"The kind that makes your pulse race. The adrenaline rush that keeps you up all night, just thinking about him?"

"The Big Love that God gives you so you know that this is the man you want to spend the rest of your life with?"

Remy drew a deep breath and closed her eyes. "It happened during the snowstorm, but it was subtle. It crept up on me when I least expected it. One minute he was sending me home on an icy road. I thought he couldn't stand to be near me. And then, over the next few days . . . I began to realize that my life would feel hollow and incomplete without him. I couldn't help but see how much love Adam had for everyone. He was so good at taking care of the farm, and you and your brothers and sisters. He seems tough and distant sometimes, but when you get past the macho patriarch thing he's the kindest person I know."

Sadie listened carefully. Her brother Adam sounded ever so different when Remy described him. Did Remy truly see such warmth in the brother who sought to keep her on the family farm, the one who was disappointed in her for choosing to stay in her rumspringa one more year? She was glad Remy loved Adam, but it just showed how God had a very different plan for everyone under the sun.

"So you found the Big Love," Sadie said. "And you decided to stay, even though Adam was responsible for his ten brothers and sisters and a dairy farm."

"Are you kidding me?" Remy's green eyes sparkled when she smiled. "That was the bonus! I have always wanted a big family, but eleven! It's better than my wildest daydreams. Being a part of your family is such a blessing for me, and after years of kicking around with no strong family ties, it's so good to have a home."

To hear Remy talk of her love for Adam made Sadie that much more sure that the Big Love had not happened for her yet. She didn't feel so hollow without Frank . . . at least, not now.

She would have to wait and be patient. Patience was a virtue, Mamm used to say, though it never came easily to Sadie.

PART TWO

Listen to Your Heart

"*Every good and perfect gift is from above, coming down from the Father of the heavenly lights, who does not change like shifting shadows.*"

—JAMES 1:17

ALMOST!

Within my reach!
I could have touched!
I might have chanced that way!
Soft sauntered through the village,
Sauntered as soft away!
So unsuspected violets
Within the fields lie low,
Too late for striving fingers
That passed, an hour ago.

—EMILY DICKINSON

SEVENTEEN

June

Although it was evening, the orange sun still hung in the red and lavender sky and heat waves shimmered over the blacktopped roadway as Sadie scootered down the hill, headed toward Halfway. Her dress and apron were stashed in the scooter's basket, but even in her T-shirt and jeans, sweat beaded on her upper lip. If it was this hot the second day in June, it was going to be a scorching summer.

A ribbon of guilt tightened in her chest when she thought of leaving Remy and Mary behind with the laundry and dinner to prepare. Sure, they believed she was going off to her job in the hotel, but with all the work to be done in summer, it was hard to get away from the farm. They had already put up berry jams, but with the garden overflowing with fat cucumbers, early peaches and plums, and asparagus, someone needed to work the roadside stand to sell off the extras.

But even with all her responsibilities, the promise of music tugged at her, and it was a pleasure she couldn't resist.

Her cell phone vibrated in her pocket, and Sadie scraped one foot over the pavement to stop and fish it out. She smiled when she saw the caller ID.

"Mike! You caught me at the right time. I'm just on my way into town."

"On your scooter," he said. "No doubt racing a team of draft horses."

She laughed. "I do like to go fast."

"You're a tough person to reach."

"I know, but I have to leave my phone off at home. The reception is bad, and if I'm not careful it runs out of battery completely." These days she charged her phone during band practice, and Red didn't seem to mind at all.

"How is your grandmother?" Mike had told her about Katherine Trueherz's stroke during one of their many conversations since they'd run into each other in Philly last week.

"She's making real progress, but she's not quite steady enough on her feet to give up the wheelchair yet. The doctor said that part may take some time."

"God bless her. She must be happy to have you there with her."

"It's worked out well. When the physical therapist and the aide are here, I'm off at the bakery, and I usually get home before Stella leaves." Mike had gotten a summer job at a neighborhood bakery, which he was hoping to keep once he went back to school.

"And did you bake something good today?" she teased, enjoying the easy exchange between them.

"Rugelach. It's dough rolled around chocolate and nuts."

"Mmm. Anything with chocolate and nuts must be good."

"I'll have to bring you some when we get together," he said.

Her heart danced at the thought, even though she scolded herself as they ended the call. It was verhuddelt to think of spending time with Mike.

They had been talking this week about meeting each other somewhere, and though Sadie wanted to see him, she knew it would be another black mark against her at home if her family learned she was making a new friend among the Englishers. Not that it was forbidden. Gott wanted His people to abide in faith, hope, and charity toward all mankind. But the brethren wouldn't approve of Sadie expressing such interest in any form of the outside world, when her singing was already attracting a few suspicious looks.

She felt sure the ministers knew nothing of the band, but sometimes she worried that word had leaked out that she'd lost her job at the hotel. Although she believed her sisters had kept her secret, she felt sure Adam knew she was dabbling in the Englisher world. He had seen her scootering off toward town instead of attending singings with the Amish young folk. Did he recognize the restlessness in her heart . . . the same bold spirit that had lured him away from home when he was around her age?

Sometimes worry ached inside her, like a bad hangnail that throbbed at night. The more you prodded the cut, the worse it got, though you couldn't help but twiddle the loose skin. Torn between her family and the call of Gott in her heart, she could see no proper ending that would make everyone happy.

By the time she arrived at Red's house, her mind was crowded with a jumble of thoughts. She parked her scooter by the side door of the garage, which was propped open to catch the breeze. Music streamed out from the open door. Swallowing back a touch of nerves, she smoothed down her T-shirt and wiped the sweat from her brows. She hadn't seen Frank since she and Remy had transformed her eyebrows. What would he think? Would he even notice?

"Hello?" she called, stepping into the open doorway.

Red sat at his drum set, moving his sticks in time with a song playing from his iPod docking station.

Frank was on the old flowered couch, staring at the large cell phone computer in his hand. "Hey, church girl," he called without looking up. "You'll be happy to know I've got a gig lined up for us. A real one."

Sadie paused a few feet away from him and hooked her thumbs into the pockets of her jeans. "Ya? When is that?"

He looked up at her and suddenly the tension fell away from his face. Frank seemed to see her with new eyes. "This weekend." He patted the couch beside him. "Come. Sit. That's a new shirt, right? I like it."

"Thank you," Sadie said, happy to see that light back in his eyes. It reminded her of the way he'd looked at her when he'd first heard her sing. "So . . . this Saturday. That would be exciting."

"Yeah." He didn't look away from her, even for his beloved cell phone. "I'm glad we're rehearsing today. It's been almost a week, and we don't want to get rusty."

"Sure." She leaned back on the couch and his eyes followed her all the way.

"Did you change your hair?" he asked.

Sadie felt a slow smile of satisfaction warm her lips. He had noticed. "Frank . . ." She tugged on one of her kapp strings. "You know my hair and kapp are the same as ever."

He held up his hands and shrugged. "Whatever it is, you look great."

Tara arrived, and Frank and Sadie got to their feet to start setting up their instruments and the microphones. As she worked, Sadie thought it was a wonder what eyebrows could do for a girl. Of course, there had been a bit of trouble when she got home and her sisters had gaped at them. Adam had scowled with disapproval, though he'd kept mum. She had wondered if the plucking had been worth it. All that pain and the tears running down her cheeks. It had left her skin blotchy and red, though that had faded after the first day. But now, seeing the look on Frank's face, Sadie knew it was all worth it.

From the very first number, Frank praised Sadie's part in every song. Odd, how the way she looked had sweetened him. She wasn't singing any differently, but he liked her performance better.

"Awesome, Sadie. I love the way you held back until the bridge," Frank said.

She nodded, not wanting to be proud, though his praise warmed her like sunshine slanting through the clouds.

When they took a break, Frank invited her to sit beside him on the couch again. "We need to talk about our set list for Saturday."

She got a bottle of water from the fridge and sat down, thinking that Frank might be open to her suggestions on some new songs. How she'd love to try some of the wonderful good music that the choir singers had shared with her. In her mind, she could hear the melodic strains of "Be Thou My Vision." That song made her heart soar whenever she heard it on her iPod. How she would love to share that experience with an audience!

"I've been thinking that it would sound good if the band did something with harmonies," Sadie said. "You and Tara could sing." Although Red had a fine, deep voice, she had learned that it was difficult for a person to sing while working the drums.

"That would take some doing," Frank said, "and it sort of shifts the style of music away from what we've been practicing."

"That was another idea of mine . . . to try something new." When Frank bit his lower lip in tension, Sadie turned to Red, who seemed interested. "I was thinking we could do some hymns. They're so beautiful in harmony. Something like 'Amazing Grace' or 'Be Thou My Vision.'"

Frank's face crumpled as if she'd hauled manure into the room. "That's Christian music you're talking about."

"What's wrong with Christian music?" she asked.

"Nothing, it's just boring."

"Actually, Christian hymns are a part of our vast musical heritage," Red pointed out. "Some religious hymns are ancient. Did you know the word comes from the Greek 'hymnos'?"

"Don't start," Frank whined.

Sadie looked to Tara for more support, but the girl was collapsed on a chair, plucking out a melody on her bass. Her spirits sinking, she stared down at the floor. She knew her voice, and she was starting to learn a few things about music, too. Their band could do wonderful good things with a beautiful hymn, but Frank did not want to talk about it.

"I think Sadie is on to something," Red said calmly.

Sadie straightened as hope rose inside her again at Red's support. Frank's moods never seemed to bother Red.

Red tucked a strand of curly hair behind one ear. "Did you know that Van Morrison recorded a version of 'Be Thou My Vision'? If you want, I'll find it for you on YouTube."

"I would like to see that." Red had shown Sadie videos on his computer before, and she'd been surprised to see how it worked like a little television.

"And what about 'Amazing Grace'?" Red added. "Any soloist worth his salt has covered that hymn. In the past decade, it's become a sort of spiritual anthem for our nation."

Sadie nodded, awed by Red's knowledge of music.

"We need songs that entertain people," Frank said, scratching his small beard. "We're playing clubs, not churches."

"But part of entertaining involves pathos. Stirring the soul," Red said. "I say we give it a shot. Sadie here is going to be rocking the hymn."

"It doesn't hurt to try it, Frank." Sadie felt a new strength solidify inside her.

And Frank was coming around. "Maybe 'Amazing Grace.' We all

know that one. But I'm not going to start learning church songs. We're not a God Squad."

Red pointed out that every band member brought a unique motivation to the experience, but Sadie's mind wandered from the conversation as hope swelled at the thought of sharing a song she so loved with Englishers.

When they set up to try it, Red stood up from his stool and looked around the garage.

"Hold on. I'm just looking for that old Wurlitzer. Where'd we stash it, Frank?"

Frank rubbed his chin, considering. "I think it's over by that furniture."

"There it is." Red carried out a small keyboard on its own table.

"It's a little piano," Sadie said.

"Sort of." Red set it beside the couch, plugged it in, then sat down and pressed into the keys. The instrument sounded like a piano in an empty barn with echoes. "I don't think we're going to need much percussion here," Red said, "so I'll give the Wurlitzer a shot."

Sweet notes wavered from Red's little piano, and Sadie dug into the lush melody. "Amazing Grace, how sweet the sound! That saved a wretch like me! I once was lost, but now am found, Was blind, but now I see." When she started the second verse Red and Tara joined with sweet harmonies under her voice, and Sadie closed her eyes to escape into the song.

"When we've been there ten thousand years, bright shining as the sun . . ." Sadie imagined God's presence as a yellow ball of fire rising over the distant dark green hills, a sight she saw most mornings when she set out to begin her chores. How she longed to share the fresh cool dew on the grass, the smell of clover, or the surrounding chorus of birdsong with people who had never known such wonders.

If she could bring these things to their audience, it would help her believe that God had meant this path for her. This was how she was supposed to share the light burning inside her.

When the song ended, Sadie held the microphone to her heart and turned, gaping at the other band members. "Did you hear us?" She laughed. "We sounded good as any group on my iPod."

Red nodded, and Tara flashed an uncharacteristic smile.

"It was good," Frank admitted.

"Good? We nailed it," Red said, his hands poised over the piano keys. "We can keep the jazz and blues in our playlist, but that is our money song."

"Amazing Grace, how sweet the sound! That saved a wretch like me . . ." Sadie was lost in the hymn, barely hearing Tara and Red's harmonies behind her. The tingling sensation at the base of her neck told her that something special was happening here, and she began to see the song as a prayer to Gott, a prayer from the entire band and everyone in the club.

The Saturday-night crowd had been loud and wild while they were setting up in the tavern. Not a very welcoming audience, and they had talked and laughed while the band had performed their first few numbers.

But now, for their closing song, the patrons listened in silence as the band completed the last verse.

"Was blind but now I see."

There was a twang of Frank's guitar and the lingering notes of the little electric piano . . . then silence.

Then a blast of noise as the crowd applauded and shouted and stomped their feet against the wooden floor.

Sadie's eyes opened to see people on their feet. A few young men stepped forward to high-five Frank, and Heather and her friends were jumping up and down as they shouted Frank's name.

Frank bowed and then pointed to the rest of the band.

"Thanks," Red told the audience. "Thanks a lot."

Suddenly Frank grabbed Sadie's microphone. "Thank you! We're Amish Blues, and we hope to see you again soon!"

Oh, not that name! Suddenly Sadie's lovely floating cloud of joy sank down to earth at Frank's announcement, and it brought back the memory of the poster she'd seen in the doorway of the club when they'd arrived that night. The bold advertisement had the words "Amish Blues" with a photo of an Amish girl in a kapp. Well, a profile shot. When she'd looked more closely, she'd seen that it was her—her photo taped up on the wall of a bar!

She had wheeled toward Frank.

"So I made some flyers," he'd said. "It's publicity for the band. You don't have anything to worry about, church girl. See? It doesn't show your face." Frank was always telling her not to worry, but he didn't understand the rules of the Ordnung or the things that were expected of you when you were Amish. He wasn't always fair with her. She listened to him and tried to understand his hopes and dreams—his longing to make their band successful. But he was not mindful of the narrow path she walked so carefully to sing in the band and yet remain true to the things that really mattered to Plain folk. It was getting to be a problem with Frank, and she wasn't sure what to do about it.

The girls at the front tables cheered and squealed again amid dying applause, and suddenly bright flashes of light peppered the crowd.

What was that? Sadie blinked from the bursts of light as she realized they were taking pictures of the band by holding up their cell phones.

Immediately she put a hand up to cover her face, but by then it was too late. Her photograph had already been taken, more than once. Fear and shame burned her face as she turned to Frank for help. . . .

But he had been swallowed up in the group of girls.

"Frank?" she called to him.

He was surrounded by girls. He leaned forward and pulled one into his arms. From here Sadie could see only her bright red fingernails as her hands gripped Frank's back. The girl was hugging him and . . . and kissing him, right here in the middle of the room.

The image stabbed through her.

Isn't he my boyfriend?

Feeling the sting of tears in her eyes, Sadie knew she had to get away. She pushed into the crowd, bouncing off people in the hot club, desperate to get away. *He's not your boyfriend,* she told herself as she finally spotted the glowing red exit sign. Why did she feel so hurt when in her heart she knew that the Big Love had not come for the two of them?

It didn't make sense at all. But lately she had learned that a lot of feelings didn't make sense.

The back door of the club loomed ahead, open to the night. Escape. Taped to the wall beside the restroom signs were two more of the Amish Blues flyers. She paused to rip them both from the wall and crumple them in her hands. They landed in the trash as she stepped into the night air. Her emotions raw, she tugged open the back door of Frank's van, which never locked properly. She folded her arms and sat on the ledge.

Her world was coming apart . . . like an egg that had been cracked right through the middle. Frank was in there kissing another girl, a bunch of strangers had just taken her photograph, and Frank had officially named their band Amish Blues, which seemed to take a piece of her life and put it on display in front of Englishers who didn't understand.

Maybe that was why she felt so devastated, to see Amish traditions she'd grown up with torn without a care. That hurt, too. Whatever the truth, there was no denying the ache in her soul. She bit her lower lip, trying to hold back tears as she stared down at the cobblestone street and two casual leather moccasins came into view. She knew those shoes. Lifting her chin, she locked eyes with him, relieved to see his familiar face and his warm smile.

Mike Trueherz.

EIGHTEEN

*I*t made him feel a little geeky to admit it, but Mike had never been to a club before. Sure, he hung out with his friends all the time. They went out to eat, watched ball games or movies. They played basketball in the park all summer, flag football in the fall. But he'd never had a reason to go into a club before, not until Sadie had mentioned she would be performing tonight. Knowing she would be in the city, he couldn't let the chance to see her slip away.

So he headed out after Gran was asleep. At the door he'd paid a five-dollar cover charge to get into the smoky club, and then he didn't really have a place to sit, so he went to the bar and ordered a beer. Looking around the place, he realized he should have asked Daryl or Austin to come along, because he was sort of out of place on his own here. People came to clubs with their friends. Coming alone was a loser move.

Still, Mike was trying to step out of his comfort zone these days. His friends had challenged him to look beyond his own concerns, and so far he liked the change in perspective he'd experienced.

And when the lights came up on the band and Sadie started singing, Mike knew the trip to the tavern was definitely worth the discomfort. Sadie was amazing, and he suspected that she didn't have a clue about the depth of her talent . . . or her beauty.

Framed by her prayer kapp, her heart-shaped face seemed angelic. With prominent cheekbones, a wide, friendly mouth, and creamy skin that some people paid big bucks for, Sadie's face could have sold magazines if she was to allow her photo to be on a cover. She wasn't just beautiful; something about those amber eyes and that smile sparked interest. And from the way the shadows caught the curves of her body, it was clear that she was more substantial than most of the girls he knew—thin twigs who would be whisked away by a strong wind. Instead, Sadie seemed solid, inside and out.

And her voice—he'd known she possessed a gift. But hearing her perform with these skilled musicians playing behind her had clarified the level of her abilities. Sadie King was an artist. He had no idea how she was going to continue to explore her gift and remain in the Amish community, but that, he figured, was a decision to be faced at the end of her rumspringa.

He'd lost track of her when she disappeared in the crowd, and he was glad to find her out here, glad to find her alone. From their conversations, it had been hard to tell what the deal was between Sadie and the other guy in the band, Frank.

His moccasins were silent on the pavement as he stopped a few feet in front of her. "Hey, songbird. That was an awesome performance!"

As soon as she lifted her face he saw the tears shining in her eyes. *Ooh.* He hated seeing any girl cry, but it was especially difficult to see tough, confident Sadie having a bad moment. Should he ask her about it, or try to distract her?

It dawned on him that maybe the reason for her tears was Frank. *Hmm.* "So . . . I thought it was a great show, but you don't seem so happy about it."

She swiped at one cheek with the back of her hand. "It was a wonderful good show, I think. It's just . . . some of the things with the band . . ." She pressed her lips together, as if clamping down on her emotions.

Mike winced as more tears welled in her eyes. He sank onto the tailgate of the van beside her and put an arm around her shoulders. "It's okay to cry," he said. Yes, it tore at him to see it, but he understood how emotions could run like a wild river that couldn't be dammed up. "Is there anything I can do?"

"I'm just . . . disappointed. My friend Frank turned out to be not such a good friend after all." She sniffed. "Did you see that poster by the door? He put my picture on it, even though I explained so many times that it was wrong."

"I didn't see it, but I know it's something that's not done in the Amish community." Mike frowned. "Maybe he took it down."

"Not Frank. He's probably giving them out at the door right now. And that name . . . I didn't want our group to be named after the Amish. Amish Blues. It makes me feel like we're trying to be something we're not. Ya, I was born and raised Amish, but Frank doesn't understand what that means, how it's about family and customs and faith. About trying to live right by the rules of the Ordnung." She pressed a hand to one cheek. "And would you listen to me talking about breaking rules? I haven't been following the faith so closely myself."

"How's that?" Mike asked.

"You know that performing is not part of Amish life. Folks would think I have hochmut—a bad streak of pride." She shook her head. "I can't imagine what the leaders of our congregation would do if they found out that I was here singing in Englisher clothes. Being around alcohol and smokers. Tara said some of the people in the audience are full of drink."

"Alcohol is a real problem for some people." Mike straightened, letting his arm slip off her shoulders now that Sadie had calmed down. He was glad to have the grace to help her weather the storm in her heart, even if just for the moment.

"I've never had a drop of alcohol," she said, "but I've been in enough clubs to make Bishop Samuel's toes curl."

Mike laughed out loud, and Sadie joined him. It was good to see her smile again. "Well, then, it's probably a good thing your bishop wasn't here to see the show."

"Ya, but did you see all the photographs people were taking in there? If the bishop ever saw one . . . it would be the end of my singing, for sure." She crossed her arms, rubbing her biceps.

"Yeah. I guess it's a good thing the bishop isn't looking for you on YouTube."

She clamped her hands over her ears. "The Internet is such a crazy thing! Do you really think someone would put videos of me on YouTube?"

He shrugged. "We can do a search sometime."

She glanced back toward the door of the club, frowning. "Do you remember how you told me you had a double life, between the city and the country? That's happening to me, too. Sometimes I feel like I'm torn in half." She ran her fingers down the middle of her forehead and over her face, as if drawing a line down the center of her body. "Half of me is an Amish girl on the farm. Half of me is a singer in the city."

"Split right down the middle?" Mike nodded with understanding. "I get it." He knew that devastating feeling.

"Like a baby chick trying to hatch from its shell. The eggshell is splitting in half around me, and I don't know which way to go."

"Sort of a heads-or-tails thing." Mike rubbed his palms on his jeans. "Makes me think of that poster of a little chick walking with a shell on its head."

Sadie frowned. "Something like that. And I still don't know

what I'm to do about it. I keep praying to the Heavenly Father, but so far I don't know His answer. What does He intend for me? In the Bible it says, 'Every good and perfect gift is from above.' God must have given me this voice for a reason, ya? I'm supposed to use it."

He nodded. "That makes sense to me."

"And, to be honest, I like the feeling of freedom. I don't care much for the clubs and all, but I do enjoy sharing music with other people. That part of performing is wonderful good. But sometimes I know this music is just silliness. I should be in classes with the church leaders, preparing to be baptized into the faith." She toyed with a loose string on her prayer kapp. "I don't know what God wants me to do."

"Sometimes the right choice isn't so clear at first. And you know that chick in the shell, it's not a matter of choosing one side or the other. The chick has to shed the shell and stand on its own two feet. The time for the shell is over."

She cocked her head to the side. "'To everything there is a season. . . .'"

"'And a time to every purpose under the heaven,'" he said, finishing the Bible verse for her. In that moment he realized how much alike they were; though they'd been raised in different cultures and worshipped differently, they believed in the same God, and their minds worked in similar ways.

Sadie kneaded her hands together. "Well, I suppose it is time that I hatched, ya?"

Mike liked the way the light of the streetlamp twinkled in her eyes as she stared off into the night. He wished there was more he could do to help her, but the matter was between Sadie and the Lord. "I'm going to pray for you, Sadie."

She turned to him, her eyes growing wide as if she'd just discovered something new. "Denki, Mike. I think it was a very good thing that you came here tonight."

"Yeah, I'm glad you told me about the gig." He looked away from her, not wanting to be caught staring at her sparkling eyes, her wide, pink lips. Did she feel the attraction pulling them together, swirling around them like a dust devil? Mike wanted to ask, but it all seemed too new to give it a name, especially after Sadie had just revealed so much about herself to him.

"I'm glad I got to see you sing," he said, trying to keep things on level ground. "You really brought down the house with that hymn. It must have felt good."

She sucked in a deep breath of night air. "Oh, I had to push for 'Amazing Grace.' Frank didn't want to add a hymn to our playlist, but Tara and Red were on my side. I'm so glad people liked it."

"Liked it? They loved it."

Staring off in the distance, she smiled. "I'm hoping we'll get to do more hymns like that. I love singing with harmonies. And you're the one who showed me the most beautiful harmonies. That day, when you and your friends came to move Remy's things. When you sang in harmony, the music was so wonderful I felt sure God had given me a new set of ears!"

Mike laughed softly. Talking with Sadie didn't give him that tight-shoulder feeling he usually got around girls. He was always self-conscious around girls at school or church, especially when he could feel them watching him. But Sadie didn't have that vibe. Maybe because she was not pretentious; there was something fresh about seeing the world through her eyes.

A new perspective.

And wasn't that what he was supposed to be open to? A new point of view.

Without thinking he took her hand, and she lifted her face to his, her eyes questioning, as if to ask what he was thinking. Something like joy bubbled inside him, and he wanted to tell her how much he enjoyed being with her. . . .

But that seemed too corny.

At a loss for a second, he looked down at her hand. "Look at that. Your hand fits in mine perfectly. It's like finding a piece of a puzzle."

Her lips curved softly. "And that's something I know all about. We always have a puzzle going at the table in our house."

He noticed that she hadn't pulled her hand away. He didn't want to jump to conclusions, but he hoped that meant something. "You know, if you liked the way my friends sang, you'll love hearing a real church choir. And at our church, when they add in piano and drums and guitar and bass . . . it's awesome. The music just hits you, like a wave washing over you."

"It sounds wonderful good."

"You should come to my church one Sunday, check it out."

"I could never do that. It would be too hard to get from home to the church here in Philly. When I come with the band, Frank gives me a ride."

"We can figure that out. I'd be happy to give you a lift. I guess we'd have to leave early Sunday morning. We could have lunch afterward with my grandmother. Now that she's recovering from the stroke, she could really use the company." He paused, scratching his head. "Did I just say that? Wow. A hot date with a guy and his granny."

Sadie laughed, looking up at him shyly. "Sounds like a very exciting hot date," she said. "I don't know how I'd get away, but maybe on a Sunday when there's no church? That's every other weekend."

"Let's do it," Mike said enthusiastically.

She shrugged. "Okay."

Her hand gave his a small squeeze—the tiniest gesture, but it made his pulse race like a jackhammer. It was all good.

NINETEEN

A dazzling reddish-orange dragonfly skittered close, then hovered in the hot, moist air a moment before looping over the water troughs and fence. *So much beauty on God's earth,* Sadie thought as she turned back to her task of shoveling dung from the outdoor pen. Early June and this hot already! But Sadie didn't mind the sweat rolling down her neck and the sun on her back. Sometimes she preferred the good, hard work outside over housework. Out here, no one cared if she sang a tune while she worked, so she belted out the chorus from "Hold Thou My Hand."

As she worked and sang, she thought about how Mike had surprised her in many ways.

In the three days since that gig in Philadelphia, the night that started off so poorly with those mean girls, and losing her boyfriend, Sadie had thought of Mike an awful lot. And was that any wonder, after so many things had changed in a single night?

When he'd first come upon her, crying out on that dark street, she'd known he was kind to listen to her problems. But as their conversation had gone on, something had sparked to life inside her, like a kerosene lamp lit by a match. By the time she had taken a seat in the van to head home that night, hope was a steady flame inside her. It felt right, knowing that things were over between Frank and her. And to think that bad night would end with finding a true friend like Mike. God had put her on a path that was full of surprises. Mamm used to say that when God closed a door, He always opened a window.

"Hold thou my hand, and closer, closer draw me," Sadie sang aloud, so glad God had thrown a window wide open for her. There were still many questions in her heart, but she felt grateful that the Heavenly Father was drawing her closer, like a good shepherd tending his sheep. Mike's advice had made her feel better about the choice that still baffled her heart. She wasn't sure where her singing would lead her, but she knew to trust in Gott.

And Mike was praying for her. It warmed her heart to know he was thinking of her when they weren't together, though they had talked on the phone every day since that night. She usually called him at night after band practice so that she could be sure her phone battery was charged.

Sometimes she lingered with her scooter just outside Red's garage and talked with her face raised to soak up the beautiful stars in God's sky. She knew those same stars glistened over Mike, though he'd told her that it was hard to see all the stars when you were in the city.

She wiped sweat from her brow with the back of a glove as the horses whinnied and stirred—a warning sound. Sadie lifted her head over the butt of her shovel and glanced over the fence. The gray-covered carriage coming down the lane held two men in straw hats. Squinting, she recognized the bishop and one of the preachers, and her high spirits sank like a stone in the pond.

Why were they here?

Probably to talk with Remy about her education for baptism. Or maybe they had matters to discuss with Adam. It was her own guilt that made her worry at the sight of them approaching the house, guilt over her double life. Though she wasn't sinning against God, she knew her activities would be scorned by the church leaders. When she was at home, she was a good Amish girl. She worked hard and helped take care of her family and bowed her head and thanked the Heavenly Father for every meal. But no amount of shoveling muck and scrubbing floors could make up for the places she was going under the cover of darkness. She could say it was all allowed during her rumspringa, but truth be told, she had pressed beyond the limits, venturing far from her family and her faith. And sometimes that made her feel bad inside, like a puckered apple rotting in the grass.

Pushing down the bad feelings, she returned to her work, though she did notice the activity by the house. Remy came out from the kitchen to greet the men—only two men. Perhaps Deacon John Beiler had been too busy harvesting crops to drop everything at the last minute. Serving as a minister in an Amish community was a lifetime commitment, and all the men in the brethren had to work at least one other job. Gabriel unhitched the horses and led them off to the water trough. That meant that the men intended to stay a bit, which made Sadie that much more curious.

Down at the house the screen door slammed and Ruthie emerged. "Sadie!" she called as she ran, the skirt of her turquoise dress flapping against her legs.

"Over here!" Sadie leaned the shovel against the wheelbarrow as nervousness crawled up her back.

"Kumm! Adam told me to fetch you," Ruthie said, her eyes round with alarm. "Bishop Samuel and Preacher Dave have come to see you."

"Me? Do you know what it's about?"

Ruthie climbed the lowest rung of the fence and leaned closer. "That's what I was going to ask you." She looked back at the house, cautiously. "It doesn't look so good. The bishop's forehead is all puckered up, and Preacher Dave keeps pinching his beard."

"Oh, dear heavens." Sadie hurried through the gate. Amish life did not include rushing about very often, but it was never wise to keep church leaders waiting. Sadie bolted down the grassy hill, then paused on the screened-in porch to wipe dust and dirt from her bare feet as she gave her racing heart a chance to calm.

Trying to hide the fact that she was quivering inside, Sadie kept her head down as she entered the kitchen. She passed by a curious Susie and followed the sound of the men's voices into the living room. She had a bad feeling that a meeting with the bishop surely meant she was to be scolded.

And one look at the stern set of the bishop's jaw told her she was right. His lips were pursed so tight he seemed to have trouble budging them open as he tried to sip his glass of lemonade.

Seated in the rocking chair beside the sofa, Preacher Dave noticed her as Remy handed him a drink. "There you are, Sadie. Come in and have a seat now."

"You can sit here," Adam said, rising to give her the blue upholstered chair where Dat used to sit and read *The Budget,* a newspaper for Plain folk. He moved to the sofa beside Bishop Samuel, whose brown forehead creased with tension.

Remy moved behind the sofa, where she waited just behind Adam. "Sadie, would you like a drink?"

"No, denki." Sadie sat on the edge of the blue chair and pressed her bare feet into the floor. *Dear Gott, give me the courage to face these men,* she prayed as their anger seemed to bear down on her. *They are men of Gott. Will they not see that I seek to share your wondrous gifts?*

Bishop Samuel's eyes scalded her from behind his glasses as he unfolded a piece of paper; the flyer with her silhouetted photo advertising Amish Blues. He handed it to Adam, who winced.

Behind Adam, Remy strained to see the source of the tension.

The flyer! Hadn't Sadie told Frank that it was a bad idea?

"What is this?" Adam asked.

"One of our members brought it to us." The bishop's mouth puckered, as if he'd bitten into a lemon. "The young man giving the papers out said the girl in the photograph is named Sadie."

All the air left her body as the terrible truth sank in. They knew what she'd been doing! She dropped her eyes to her lap, wondering how the bishop had come upon the flyer and connected it to her. Not that it mattered now. She was in deep trouble.

Though the church ministers usually looked the other way for youth in rumspringa, they intervened when they thought a young person had gone too far. This was one of those times.

The preacher finished taking a long drink, then put his glass on the table as a slight belch churned through his teeth. Of all the church leaders, Sadie had always thought that Dave Zook was the easiest to talk to, but in this boiling pot of disapproval no one was safe anymore.

"Sadie King." The bishop's eyes reminded her of a bull, anger festering as it planned its charging attack. "Is it true that you are the girl in this picture?"

"It's me," she admitted.

"Did you sit for this picture?" Adam asked.

"I—I didn't want the photo to be taken," she explained, trying to keep the pulsing fear from her voice. "But it was done before I could stop it."

"We have all had photographs taken against our wishes," Preacher Dave said, fanning himself with his straw hat. "Tourists do it from time to time, and we cannot always stop them. Since you're not a baptized member yet, that's not the serious matter here."

"What matters is that you are a part of this." The bishop stabbed a finger fiercely at the flyer. "Making music that's not to the glory of God. Dancing and dressing in fancy clothes. This place listed here, it's a business that profits from alcohol. And to wear a prayer kapp through it all . . . allowing a graven image of yourself to be printed, handed out to strangers. This, *this* goes against the rules of our community."

The bishop's low growl was followed by the sting of silence swelling in the thick, hot air of the room.

Fear rose inside her, a thick knot in her throat as she looked to her brother. Adam's eyes were black and cold, and he seemed distant. Was he restraining himself from voicing disrespect with the bishop and preacher here, or was he angry with her, too? Over the past few months Adam had watched her with disapproval, though he had not forbidden her from taking part in activities outside the Amish community. He must have heard that she was venturing into the city, but did he have any idea that she was singing with the band? Did he know that she had outgrown a romance with one Englisher boy and taken up with another? Oh, that sounded so much worse than it was, even to Sadie.

"We cannot have this." The preacher's beard lifted slightly as he fanned himself. "A sales brochure like this, with one of our own young girls in a photo? Ach. It's a terrible thing."

"I know that." Sadie lowered her head. "I never meant for that photo of me to be taken . . . or for it to get copied." For that part she was sorry, but it wasn't her doing.

"But you have been out singing in the bars, ya?" demanded the bishop.

Sadie dared to look up at the three men, but their faces were stern, their hearts hardened against her. Even her own brother.

Only Remy offered a look of understanding, her green eyes wide as a doe's watching cautiously from the edge of the woods.

"Answer the question, Sadie King. Have you been out in the bars, singing around fancy men and liquor, too?" Bishop Samuel's face was the color of a tomato now. It was as if all the fire of his righteous anger burned inside him.

Sadie wanted to defend herself. She wanted to tell them that she had begged people not to take her photo. That she did not dance in public or drink alcohol. She longed to explain that she knew the Heavenly Father had blessed her with this voice and that she believed He meant for her to make use of it.

But Bishop Samuel would not listen the way Mike listened. The church leaders did not want to hear her explanations. Any more talking right now would be seen as disrespectful. They wanted a simple answer.

"I have done that," she said, staring down at the floor.

A grunt came from the bishop. "And Adam, did you know about this?"

Her brother drew in a breath. "I knew she was going to the city with friends. I wondered, but . . ."

From the corner of her eye Sadie saw the colored flyer move from the table as Adam grabbed it. "I didn't know about this, but I believe Sadie when she says she didn't have a hand in printing it. My sister loves to sing, and she's been blessed with a golden voice. You should hear her sing while she does the dishes."

Surprised by her brother's support, Sadie dared to look up. Remy was smiling and the preacher's eyes had softened, but Bishop Samuel was unmoved. His hands were poised on his thighs, as if he were about to leap out of the chair and pounce on sin itself.

"God does not give us gifts so that we can flaunt them," the bishop snapped. "Certainly not in a bar. We live separate from the world, not in it." He tipped his hat back and scratched his head. "Maybe it's been too long since I preached about the evils of hochmut. We can fall to pride, and not just in our houses or horses. Folks can be proud of their voice or even the color of their eyes. Gifts from God, ya, but we are wrong to take pride in them."

His words made Sadie's heart ache.

Did he think she was proud of her voice? She wasn't a show-off. That wasn't it at all! How could it be that a man of God didn't understand that?

She held still, working to swallow back tears as the two ministers drilled her on proper behavior. They warned her that if she wanted to be baptized into this church, she had a long road of repentance ahead. For now, she would be wise to discuss her choices with her older brother Adam or one of the church leaders.

"And this . . ." The bishop picked up the flyer, then tossed it back onto the table in disgust. "Let's pray that we never again see such heresy."

TWENTY

Remy said good-bye to Dave and Samuel and stood at the door watching as Adam went along to help hitch their horses up. Her heart ached for Sadie, though she understood the mission of the ministers. Folding her arms across her apron, she thought of Sadie and marveled that there could be two very reasonable sides to any issue.

She had hated idly standing by while the ministers grilled Sadie. In many ways it seemed that their measure of discipline far exceeded the crime of Sadie sneaking into the city to do some Saturday-night gigs with her band. How Remy had longed to go to the girl and slip a reassuring arm over her shoulders! In recent weeks she'd felt motherly instincts toward Adam's younger siblings. She seemed to know when Katie was cutting a tooth or when Simon needed someone to check on his progress training Shadow, his beloved horse. Now she felt the keen need to support Sadie with a mother's love, but she did not dare cross the ministers, who were right to worry about Sadie straying from their community.

Just as Remy had found her own sure path to the Amish, Sadie seemed to be finding a road that led away from this community.

More than once while the ministers reproached Sadie, Remy had wanted to interject that she had known about Sadie's activities. Although Remy hadn't been directly involved, she'd been guilty of complicity on some level, as Sadie had confided that she enjoyed going into Philly. Judging from the flyer, her karaoke and open mikes had apparently evolved into some real gigs. Remy would have said something, but she was still acutely aware that she was an outsider easing her way into this Amish community, and as the men had clearly come to speak with Sadie, she hadn't wanted to insinuate herself into the situation.

Passing through the kitchen, she thanked the girls for taking over the chore of lunch preparation. "Look at that platter." Remy eyed a mountain of grilled cheese and tomato sandwiches on the table. "I'm impressed."

"It didn't take long at all when we worked together on it," Susie said brightly. "And we still have plenty of cheese left."

"We're almost finished chopping carrots and radishes, and the soup's heating up," Ruthie said as she carved a carrot carefully into sticks. "As soon as it's done we'll call everyone in."

"Good job," Remy said, patting the two sisters on their shoulders.

In the living room Sadie was still slumped over in the upholstered chair, her face buried in her hands.

Remy touched her back, then went around and knelt on the floor by her feet so that Sadie couldn't help but look her in the eye.

"That was a grueling session. Are you okay?"

Sadie lifted one hand from her face and blinked at Remy. "I'm still breathing, if that's what you're asking. But I've had better days."

"The bishop was really mad," Remy agreed.

"I've never seen Samuel so fired up." Adam appeared at the

kitchen door, his straw hat tipped back on his head. "They're gone, but not without a few words to remind me that it's up to me to make sure Sadie doesn't burn all her bridges behind her."

"That puts a lot of pressure on you," Remy said. "I thought the church leaders recognized that it was up to each person to make his or her own decision about baptism. Isn't that the principle of the Anabaptist faith?"

"That's the idea." Adam paced along the length of the room. "But I don't think a parent is ever really off the hook for a child's behavior. And the choice to be baptized, for a girl born Amish like Sadie, is not as simple as it seems. In our community, baptism isn't just about committing to God. It's about deciding to stay Amish, and it's a decision that every Amish girl or boy is expected to make."

Remy let out a breath. "Okay, so it's a lot of pressure on Sadie, too. I don't understand why the church allows rumspringa when they pretty much demand that a member be baptized."

"It's the Amish way. But for all the wildness of rumspringa youth, Sadie has shown unzufriede—discontent—which is worse. The ministers now see that she's interested in something that might pull her away from the community. They want it stopped."

"I'm not leaving my home," Sadie said. "I'm just trying to follow the music in my heart."

"I know that, but I'm still afraid of what the bishop might do if you continue to sing in that band."

Looking up at him, Remy watched as he rubbed his jaw, deep in thought. Her Adam . . . her husband-to-be. For as long as she'd known him, he'd been troubled about Sadie, worried about her voracious interest in Englishers, concerned over her desire to spend time away from the family and the farm. He'd been cross with Sadie, but today he had revealed his gentle heart, and she loved him all the more for it.

"We know there's no ban if you're not a baptized member,"

Adam said, pacing quietly. "But if you continue with this singing, the punishment might be just as bad as a shunning. Bishop Samuel said they might require you to confess before everyone at a Sunday service. And that wouldn't be pleasant."

"I can't believe they want to punish me this way," Sadie said. "We know kids who've done much wilder things in their rum-springa."

"Really," Remy agreed. "This doesn't seem fair."

"It's not a question of fairness. We have to follow the leaders of our congregation." He sat on the edge of the sofa, facing Sadie. "I know you love this singing, but Bishop Samuel is clearly against it."

"It's too bad Sadie can't do more with the music during church. I'm sure everyone would love to hear her lead some songs."

"No." Adam shook his head. "The song leader is always a man."

Sadie spoke. "And the Anabaptist songs—though I grew up with them, I feel like I've grown beyond them. That day at your apartment, Remy, I heard those beautiful harmonies, and they spoke to my heart. Do you remember those fellas? Mike's friends who sing in the choir?"

"I do." When Remy closed her eyes, she could still hear their powerful voices, clearly praising the Lord. She could understand how Sadie had fallen in love with those hymns.

"There is so much beautiful music in this world, songs that can bring a tear to your eye or warm your heart. Not just fancy music, but music that praises God, too. I want to be a part of that, and I don't think that makes me proud. When I'm singing, I feel my heart opening. . . ." She pressed her hands to her chest and looked at her brother with pleading eyes. "Maybe I don't explain it very well, but music brings me such joy."

"Your words are good enough," Adam said somberly. "When you sing, I see how happy it makes you."

"It reminds me of Mamm," Sadie said, her voice cracking with emotion. "She's the one who got me started."

"I know that." Adam's dark eyes were full of rue. "But when you look ahead to your Amish life, there's no place for it. You heard the bishop. You can't go on with the band and be part of our community."

There was no easy solution.

In the ensuing silence Remy rose, catching sight of the flyer on the table. A year ago, the hazy image on the flyer wouldn't have meant anything to her. Now, looking with new eyes, she could see that it was a problem for this community. "How did the bishop get this flyer?" She turned to Adam. "Do you know?"

"Someone left them at the shops in Halfway. One of our members saw a stack of them on the counter at Ye Olde Tea Shop."

"What on earth . . . ?" Sadie sank in her chair. "I told him not to do it. I knew that flyer would bring us nothing but trouble, and here it is."

Remy sat on the chair across from Sadie. "Have you thought of quitting the band?" she asked gently.

Specks of gold glimmered in Sadie's eyes. "The thought of getting baptized now, and giving up my singing . . ." She shook her head. "That would be like choosing never to feel the sun again. When I think of baptism now, oh, it makes my head hurt."

Remy touched the girl's knee. "You're in a tight corner."

"But I look at you, seeking to be a member of our church, and the choice seems so simple for you." Sadie fixed her amber eyes on Remy. "When you made the choice to get baptized, you didn't struggle so. How did you come to peace with giving up your fancy life forever? Your beautiful apartment and your car . . ."

"My old life didn't hold much meaning for me. It wasn't hard to leave behind." Remy looked up at Adam, a swell of emotion in her throat. "And as for joining the Amish community, I fell in love with an Amish man—an impossible situation. But when I prayed to God, the rest of my life started falling in place. I so wanted to make this place my home, your family my family. I knew there was much to learn about the faith. A whole new language, too. But I work hard every day, and I pray that God will grant me wisdom and knowledge."

Sadie put a hand on hers. "We are in very different places, you and I."

Remy nodded in agreement. When she prayed about being baptized, of promising to obey the rules of the Ordnung, she felt at peace with her choice. Whenever she closed her eyes and imagined her new faith, she saw a steady flame. Faith. She believed that God wanted her to be here, with Adam and his family. And she believed that with all her heart.

"What can I do? I want to please my family. I don't want to anger the bishop and Preacher Dave anymore."

Remy looked into Sadie's amber eyes. "Baptism is not the right choice for you if you look to a future in the Amish community and feel trapped by it. You have to be ready. You have to want it."

Sadie stared pensively, biting her bottom lip.

"Remy is right." Adam's dark eyes held regret. "Sadie, I know I've been pushing you. I know that. It's wrong of me to press you, but I'm responsible for you now, and it's important to me that you do the right thing."

"I know that, Adam. But do you know that baptism is the right thing for me?" Sadie asked, her eyes shiny with tears.

"I want you to remain with this family and in this community," Adam explained. "But I have to trust in God. We know God in heaven has a plan for you. And I believe He means for you to stay Amish, Sadie." He rubbed his jaw, his dark eyes warm with compassion. "I'm sorry. That's not what you wanted to hear."

"I'm sorry, too." Sadie plucked at one of the pins on her apron.

Relief filled Remy as she looked from Adam to Sadie. This was the conversation they needed to have; time for forgiveness and renewal.

"So how can we help you?" Adam asked his younger sister. "How can we ease your heart?"

Sadie shook her head. "You can't. There's no helping me." A tear streaked down her cheek as she stood up. "I'm grateful for you trying, but I can't follow the laws of the Ordnung right now. I can't be baptized." She swiped at her face and ran out into the kitchen.

Adam and Remy got to their feet, surprised by Sadie's sudden action.

"Sadie . . . ," Adam called after her.

A moment later came the sound of the screen door slamming behind her.

Remy stared toward the doorway, wondering what to pray for in this situation. There was no simple answer.

A dark sigh came from Adam as he let his head loll back. Remy put her arms around him and pressed her face to his chest. Showing such affection with the children around and in the light of day wasn't something they normally did, but then this was an extraordinary situation.

"I love you," she said. "And I totally admire the way you handled that. It was so wise of you not to shout at Sadie, though I know you've been angry with her for a long time."

"I figured the bishop put enough fear in her. But only Gott can change Sadie's mind. And right now, it looks like we're losing her," Adam said.

"Oh, please don't say that." Remy couldn't imagine this family without Sadie's cutting humor and her angelic voice, though she sensed that Adam was right.

Since the day Remy had met Adam's siblings, Sadie had stood

out because of her interest in Remy's Englisher life. Sadie, with her cell phone and her jeans barely hidden beneath the skirt of her dress. Her eyes always glowed when she told stories of her exciting adventures in the city, and when she talked of music, that girl positively came alive.

Remy loved her like a sister, and even as she'd always answered Sadie's curious questions about the world beyond the Amish, she was sympathetic to Adam's concerns over the possibility of losing his sister. "She's my responsibility," he'd reminded Remy time and again when they'd spoken of Sadie in private. That was her Adam, always concerned with the care of the large family he'd taken on after his parents' deaths. What a hard lesson, to realize that you can't control the people you love.

"With God's grace, we'll accept the things we can't control," Remy said, strengthened by Adam's arms around her.

"Ya." His voice was rough as he planted a kiss atop her kapp. "We must pray for grace."

"And hope that Sadie finds her way back to us," Remy said quietly. "There's always hope."

TWENTY-ONE

*I*n the four days since the ministers had come to discipline her, Sadie had gone through the motions of daily life with a fevered brow and a cold heart. She'd been hurt by the "intervention," as Remy had called it. Sadie was sure that was just a fancy word for a scolding.

Now, as she scrubbed pots and dishes on this sweaty Sunday evening, the strains of the song she sang with the other girls worked at softening her heart of stone. This was the song they had sung with Mamm every night when they were doing dishes. But as she let herself relax a bit, she felt the pain of the ministers' stunning blow return. Her face grew warm with shame, and her voice grew faint.

"And I will tell you just why I love you . . . ," Ruthie sang, her sweet voice strong and true as she began to dry a dripping pot.

Cousin Rachel was storing the food. Leah was bringing things in from the tables outside. Sadie washed and Ruthie dried. It was a good system, though the kitchen was mighty hot on this June night.

Down the road in the Lapps' barn a singing was going on. The others were there—Mary, Adam, Jonah, and Gabe. But Sadie had no taste for it, knowing that a few tongues had probably been wagging about the trouble she'd stirred. No, it was better to stay home, and she'd been touched that her cousin Rachel had decided to stay too, making up an excuse about having a headache.

"That's everything from outside," Leah said, sliding a tray into the soapy water. "Can I go? I can't wait to start going through that bag of books." Leah always had her nose in a book.

"You got some new ones?" Sadie asked.

"Rachel brought over a big fat bag from Sarah." Rachel's younger sister was a book lover too, and she frequently exchanged bags of books with Leah.

"There's a wonderful good book about ancient Egypt," Leah said. "Did you know they used math to build the pyramids?"

"And here I thought they used muscle to move those stones," Rachel teased.

Leah smiled at her cousin. "That, too. I love reading about olden times. Remy knows a lot of history and such. She promised to teach me things, now that I'm finished with school."

"Are you sad that school is over for you?" Ruthie asked. "I know how you loved it so."

"I'm going to miss it, but Remy says I can keep learning." Leah peered at them cautiously through her glasses. "She's going to talk to Adam about homeschooling me on high school subjects. She thinks I could get a scholarship if I keep on with my studies."

"A scholarship?" Rachel pinched her chin. "I can't see the ministers allowing that."

Leah frowned, then shrugged. "That's what Remy says, and I'm excited about it." She moved toward the living room and stairs. "Can I go?"

Sadie nodded and turned back to her dishes. "That's the first I've heard of more schooling for Leah."

"Me too," Ruthie said.

As Sadie scrubbed at a patch of baked-on beans she worried about Remy, who didn't seem to understand that the Amish ended education at grade eight for a very good reason. Leah's help was needed on the farm, and it was about time she learned more about how to care for the cows and the house. The twins had been coddled a bit, maybe because of Susie's illness. Those girls couldn't even bake a loaf of bread yet.

"What should we sing next?" Rachel asked.

"I think Sadie should tell us what happened with the ministers," Ruthie said, looking up at Sadie as she wiped a plate clean.

"We've got a nosy one here," Rachel said. "Though I don't mind hearing myself."

"And no one else is around." Ruthie was all ears as she put a plate in the cupboard.

"Ach, it was awful." Sadie swiped at her damp forehead with the back of one wrist. "I'm sure you know most of the story."

"Did the bishop make you give up your boyfriend Frank?" Ruthie asked breathlessly.

"Sort of, but not really." Sadie sighed. "If I tell you, you got to promise to keep it a secret, ya?"

Ruthie's head bobbed.

"You know I'm on your side, always," Rachel said.

"The ministers don't want me singing with the band anymore." She explained how they'd gotten ahold of the flyer Frank made. Dim-witted Frank had put them in the shops in Halfway. What was he thinking? Since the bishop and preacher came here, Sadie hadn't gone to a single rehearsal. She hadn't even left the farm, and she'd worked her fingers to the bone, trying to prove herself to Adam and the rest of the family. When Adam asked about her job at the hotel, she had told him that Mr. Decker didn't need her this week. It was a small slice of truth, but Sadie couldn't bear to reveal everything to Adam now, with this dark cloud over her head.

Last night, when everyone was asleep, she had stolen off in the darkness and walked far from the house, out of earshot, to use her cell phone. Out by the pond, with the bullfrogs croaking and cows mooing from the barn, she knew no one in the house would hear her. With frogs croaking from the bulrushes, she had given Frank a stern talking-to about how he needed to respect her family and her community. She told him she wouldn't go to the city with the band anymore. The clubs were Frank's dream, not hers. And she told him that she wouldn't be courting him anymore. Saying the words had lifted a weight from her heart.

"That Frank doesn't sound so nice," Ruthie said as she folded a dish towel.

"He brought music into my life," Sadie said in his defense. "But I'm not sweet on Frank anymore. Not just because of the flyer. We don't agree on much, and I don't like to argue. I had to end it. Which is all for the best, since the ministers would have been even angrier with me if they knew I had an Englisher boyfriend."

"Oh, Sadie, you've surely stepped in the muck this time." Rachel blinked in astonishment. "You pluck your eyebrows and break up with your Englisher boyfriend. Sadie King, I don't even know you anymore."

"Of course you do." Sadie slapped the dish towel over one shoulder and struck a pose with her hands on her hips. "It's me, Sadie, the girl who's always at the center of the storm. Putting eggs in people's boots and tossing up frozen cow patties like Frisbees."

Rachel cocked her head to the side, her blue eyes squinting. "Ya, now I see it's you. Only the girl singing with an Englisher band, that girl I don't know." She shook her head. "If it was me doing that kind of thing, my dat would scold me from here to Saturday."

"Adam has been grouchy all week," Ruthie said. "I think he wants to scold Sadie, but he's not her dat."

Sadie gave her sister a sidelong glance, surprised by her insight. "You hit the nail on the head, Ruthie. But it's a tight spot for Adam. The bishop holds him responsible for us."

"But what can Adam do with an unzufriede Sadie?" Rachel asked. "He can't make you choose to be Amish."

Sadie bit her bottom lip, feeling a pang of guilt for the trouble she was causing Adam. "It's a problem, and I don't know how to fix it."

"But you said it's over with Frank," Rachel said. "That's good. A step in the right direction. Now you're free and clear to date an Amish boy. We should have gone to the singing tonight. Every time I see Amos Lapp, he asks about you."

Sadie shook her head. No, she didn't want to go to the singing, and Amos Lapp was not going to be her beau.

Though there was a young man who'd found his way to her heart. But could she tell her favorite cousin and little sister about him? Rachel would just tease her for finding trouble everywhere, and Ruthie would find it hard to keep Mike a secret.

No, she wasn't ready to tell them about Mike. Her feelings were too new, too delicate to share. Good, funny Mike who made her heart come alive . . . He wanted to date her. "A hot date," he had said. It made her smile to think of the little joke.

Last night, after her call with Frank had ended, she'd phoned Mike.

She could still see the reflection of the moon on the pond, its creamy white edges clarifying and blurring as her story spilled out, along with her shame and regret and fear.

And Mike had understood.

He had understood when she'd told him about the bishop and preacher coming by to warn her. He'd groaned when she'd described the flyer, Frank's carelessness and selfishness . . . Mike had understood how it had unraveled, and he'd been more than sympathetic.

When he promised to call her every day to check up on her, Sadie's heart had warmed. Mike cared about her. "Sadie?" Ruthie called as she wiped down the counter. "A penny for your thoughts?"

Sadie hesitated, drying her hands on a towel. "I was just thinking of the wonderful sliver of moon that was out last night."

The next morning she called Mike from behind the henhouse, waking him up. "It's time to get out of bed, sleepyhead," she teased.

"It's six-something in the morning!"

She laughed. "And you've already missed the sunrise!"

On Tuesday she waited until night to call him, and walked out to stand under the beech trees. The warm breeze clattered through the leaves, making God's own shimmering wind chimes overhead.

"This is a better time for me, songbird," he said. "I'm a night owl at heart, though it was a little hard to hear you with all that croaking in the background the other night."

"The bullfrogs are noisy in summer, but I think it's a happy song. Loud, but good." That made her think of her dat, and she wondered if he would have defended Sadie and her music. She didn't know for sure, but she didn't think so. Dat had wanted his children to grow up and be good Plain folk. Dat had been sad when Adam left the farm, and not just because he missed him. "A boy should grow up to be a good Amish man," she'd heard him say.

She pressed against a tree trunk, feeling the support of the solid beech behind her. Something had changed. It was as if the earth had shifted and adjusted her skirts, and suddenly the grass and trees and sky all fit just a tiny bit better.

"You're kind of quiet on that end," he said. "And your cell phone must be running out of precious battery, unless you managed to make a jailbreak during the day."

"I didn't, but I'm going to visit a neighbor tomorrow to use her outlet. I'm going to call you every day, just like I promised."

"I like a girl who keeps her promises."

His words flickered over her, cool and exciting, like the moonlight dappled by the trees.

"Did you ask Adam about visiting our church?"

"Not yet. I'm waiting for the right moment."

"Good strategic planning," he said.

"But I'm hoping for next Sunday, since there's no church. Can you do that?"

"That'd be great. Just let me know. I can pick you up Friday night and you can spend the weekend here." When Mike had learned of her love for the city, he had expanded the plans.

"Okay." Sadie didn't know how she would work that out with Adam, but she refused to let it shadow the warm glow that filled her heart when she was talking with Mike. "My phone might cut out, but before it dies, tell me about Jamaica, please." Mike had been in the Peace Corps, and she found his stories fascinating. "Tell me about the little boy who sang hymns on the street and climbed trees for fruit that he would sell to you."

"Oliver?" He sighed. "He was a spunky kid. Ten years old and he was making money for his family selling fruit. . . ." Mike had gone on weaving words of this tropical island community in the way that she'd seen her mamm and grandmother work the fabric of a quilt, piecing things together, stitching with needle and thread for a hundred hours until color and images emerged.

Was Mike a gifted storyteller, or was it only that he cared so much about the people in his story that they spoke to her heart? Whatever the answer, she knew that she wanted his stories to go on forever.

The next day Sadie looked up from her gardening and saw her chance to talk to Adam. After a morning spent plowing, Adam and Jonah were bringing the draft horses in, and Sadie knew they could use help currying the hot horses and cooling them down. She tossed her apronful of weeds into the compost heap and hurried over to the edge of the field, the soil of the path warm under her bare feet.

"I've got Buddy," she said, taking the big gray stallion by the lead and heading over to the post fence to tie him up in the shade.

Simon ran over to pitch in, and a moment later Adam and Jonah were headed over to the shade with the other two horses. When Adam tied Cricket right at the next post, Sadie knew this was it. She bit her lips together and got to work on Buddy with a curry-comb as she sorted the facts in her mind. She didn't want to be disrespectful, but she also felt that she shouldn't be treated like a child. She was eighteen years old.

Still, she was asking a lot of Adam.

"So there's no church this Sunday," she said as she muscled the comb into Buddy's back. She could smell the sweet scent of sunscreen that had been sprayed on the horse's head. White-faced horses were likely to get sunburns if they weren't protected.

Adam worked on a knot in Cricket's mane. "That's right, and the week after that it's at Jacob Fisher's."

"So then, this Sunday, I'm going to go into Philadelphia to visit a church."

Adam stopped brushing and wheeled around toward her. "You are, are you?"

"An Episcopalian church. Mike Trueherz, the doctor's son, offered to take me to the church service. He's even worked it out so I can stay with his grandmother." She explained that Doc Trueherz's mamm was recovering from a stroke and needed companionship.

Tipping back his straw hat, Adam scowled. "That's not a good idea. It'd be fine to help out the doc, but the ministers are already concerned over all the unzufriede things you've been doing."

"I know that. But I haven't been with the band all week, and I'm not going to see them this weekend, either. This is about looking at a different faith." *And checking out their music,* she thought, though Adam didn't need to know that just yet.

Her oldest brother shook his head slowly. "Not a good idea."

"But Jonah did it," Sadie piped up. "Back when he was thinking about baptism. Tell him, Jonah."

"I did." Jonah patted his horse's head as he spoke. "I hitched up a buggy and went to a few different churches on in-between Sundays."

Adam put his hands on his hips. "Did you, now?"

Jonah shrugged. "I was curious."

"And Dat thought it was a smart thing to do. That's what Dat told him," Sadie said. "So if Dat thought it was okay for Jonah, he would have allowed me to do it."

Adam let out a grunt and started brushing Cricket again. "All right, Sadie. Have it your way. But I say this is just another path to trouble."

"I'm going to a church." She tried to tamp down the feeling of hope as she got back to work vigorously brushing Buddy. "How much trouble can a person get in at church?"

"A lot, when it's the wrong kind of church with an Englisher fellow. Even if he is the doc's son," Adam said, his voice thick with disapproval. "I'm just warning you, Bishop Samuel won't be thinking it's okay if he gets wind of it."

I'll just hope and pray that he doesn't hear about it, Sadie thought, giving Buddy's mane a brisk rub. At least this time there would be no printed flyers.

TWENTY-TWO

Mike's car topped a hill and the glow of sun in the west blinded him momentarily. He tapped the brakes, dazzled by another amazing sunset, with purple and red clouds peeling from the tantalizing orange in the sky.

He flipped the visor down to block the glare, then caught sight of himself in the mirror. Part of his hair was sticking up, and he finger-combed it down, all the while trying to keep his attention on the road.

You're nervous, Trueherz. Nervous about picking up Sadie. This is like a first date.

A very strange first date, since they would be driving into Philadelphia and spending the weekend at Gran's house. After the spate of trouble Sadie had been in recently with the church leaders, he'd been sort of surprised that this trip was a go. But Sadie had told him that her brother Adam was cool with it, and she was eighteen, after all.

His palms were sweating, and he wiped them on his cargo shorts as he slowed again and turned down the lane toward the King farm. This was a major first, bumping along the gravel drive all the way up to the house. Sadie had told him Amish guys met their girls down at the end of the lane, so he was definitely treading new territory for all concerned here. Although he'd met the Kings through his father's practice, that was different from arriving as an English guy trying to date Sadie. There were definitely some awkward moments ahead.

As he rolled closer to the house, he saw a few people sitting at a picnic table on a grassy lawn at the far side of the house. Finishing dinner, it seemed. Teens and kids were tossing a Frisbee, and he recognized Sadie racing along and leaping to catch it. Everyone was barefoot, and a relaxed atmosphere prevailed. Mike pulled in beside two gray carriages and parked the car.

The panorama of green fields, farm, and Crayola sky that surrounded him could have been the July page of one of those calendars the dry cleaners gave away each year. Lancaster County was a beautiful place. Despite his desire to get away, he could still see that. It was just not the home of his heart.

"Mike! Over here!" a girl's voice called.

He turned and saw Susie aiming the Frisbee at him. "Catch!" She flung it forward, and he ran a few yards up toward the barn to pick it out of the air.

"Don't wear Mike out, now," Sadie said. "He's got to drive us into the city."

"I think I can handle a Frisbee toss." Mike spun around and backhanded the disk to Simon, who caught it with a gap-toothed grin.

"Do you want some ice cream, Mike?" asked Mary. Sadie's oldest sister looked a lot like her brother Adam, with dark hair but smoky hazel eyes where Adam's were dark. "It's homemade."

"And we froze cherries from our own trees," one of the younger girls said. Ruthie, he thought her name was. "It's very delicious."

"Maybe a small bowl," Mike said, looking at Sadie.

"You go ahead." She waved him over toward the picnic table. "I'm just going to get my things."

"Kumm," Mary said, leading the way across the lawn. "We'll get you a bowl of ice cream."

As they approached the outdoor table, Adam rose and extended his hand.

"Mike . . . I know we've met at the office, but have you ever been out to visit us before?" Adam asked.

Mike shook his hand, knowing that this was an English custom. It was a friendly gesture on Adam's part, which made Mike relax a little.

"I was here years ago with my dad. I think Susie was too sick to make the trip, so he made a house call."

"Your father has always taken good care of our Susie. Of all of us," Adam said.

"Here's your ice cream." Ruthie handed up a plastic bowl, her eyebrows wriggling. "I want to see your face when you get a bite of cherry."

"There's chicken left over, too," Mary called from the far end of the long table. "Are you hungry, Mike?"

Mike smiled, appreciating the offer. After all, he was the outsider here.

"I'm good. I had dinner with my parents." Aware that Ruthie was watching attentively, he put a spoonful of ice cream in his mouth and closed his eyes. "Mmm. That is delicious. You get a real burst of flavor."

"I told you," Ruthie said with a satisfied smile.

"How is your father?" Adam asked. "And your mamm? We always see Celeste working in the office."

"They're both fine, but my grandmother suffered a stroke recently."

Adam's eyes narrowed as he tipped back his straw hat. "I'm sorry to hear that."

"She's recuperating at home. We'll be staying at her house in Philly, and I'm really glad she'll be meeting Sadie. My grandmother, Katherine, has been getting impatient with her lack of progress and the caretakers helping her. Gran calls the day nurse 'Mousy' and the night nurse 'Night Mouse,' for their lack of spirit and energy. I think Gran is ready to have some company with backbone and spunk."

"Sister Sadie has plenty of that," Adam said. "One day with Sadie, and your grandmother might be asking for Mousy again." The harsh lines of Adam's face softened as he almost smiled.

Mike breathed a little easier, sensing Adam liked him, though there was no ignoring the strain. No matter how you cut it, Mike wasn't Amish. He took another spoonful of ice cream to fill the awkward silence.

"So you're driving off to Philadelphia," Adam mused. "Going to church on Sunday?"

"Yes. St. Mark's Episcopal Church in Philadelphia. Sadie wanted to hear the music there."

"Ya." Adam stared off in the distance, one thumb tucked under a suspender. "Did she tell you about the scolding she got from the ministers over that band she was in?"

Mike's swallowed a mouthful, but the mashed cherry seemed to stick in his throat. "She did mention that. I was glad to hear things have settled down since then."

"She's not off the hook yet." Adam turned his head to face Mike, his dark eyes penetrating. "They wouldn't approve of this trip, you know. Sadie belongs here with her family. She should be out at the games down the road tonight, playing badminton and getting to know young men from the Old Order. From our congregation. Not that I don't trust you, Mike. But at the end of the day, you're an Englisher. You know what that means."

Mike nodded silently. Yes, he understood that Adam didn't want him to get involved with Sadie.

But it was too late for that.

Sadie was all he ever thought about these days. The air was charged with hope and love whenever she was around. He loved her laugh. He could spend hours talking with her. He even admired her stubborn spirit.

This trip was more than a good deed from an Englisher. This was his chance to spend some time with the girl he'd fallen for that night when he'd spotted her on the road, scootering home after dark. He'd known that her being Amish would be a problem, so he didn't allow himself to daydream about it too much.

But at the end of his day, Sadie was the one he wanted to talk with and share with and laugh with. Sadie was the one.

"Looks like we'll have to walk a few blocks," Mike told Sadie as he circled the block yet again in search of a place to park. Over the years, as the neighborhood had become more and more gentrified, parking had grown tighter, the streets clogged with double-parkers and service vehicles. With Gran's condition, Mike worried about how they would get her to a car when she did start going out again. He would talk to his dad about renovating the garage off the back alley to fit his car. It was yet another piece in the big task of overseeing Katherine Trueherz's care, a responsibility that had fallen on Mike, and he didn't mind one bit. He truly wanted to help Gran, and he also knew that as long as he was managing Gran's care, his parents wouldn't be expecting him to hurry back to Paradise and help out at the clinic.

That took a lot of pressure off his shoulders. Living here was buying him time before he had to face his own family issues.

At last they found a spot on Cypress Street. As they walked through the neighborhood of historic churches and narrow streets of homes dating back to colonial times, Mike realized he was nervous about introducing Sadie to Gran. *Dear God, please let them connect!* He breathed in the cool night air, reminding himself that Gran had been testy since the stroke, but not unreasonable. How could she not love Sadie?

"Will I get to meet your grandmother tonight?"

"Absolutely." Gran would still be awake, even though it was well after nine. "She's a night owl."

"That's good, because I so want to meet her."

And I want you to like her, Mike thought, supporting Sadie as she tripped over the uneven paving stones.

"Mmm . . . what a bumpy lane you have. This neighborhood looks old for the city." She walked slowly, letting her eyes sweep the tree-lined streets. Light pooled in wide arcs around lampposts, and the streets were rutted with cobblestones. "Like a charming old village."

"It's pretty old. This section of Philly was started by William Penn in the late 1600s."

"The man that Pennsylvania is named after?"

"That's the guy." He enjoyed seeing the neighborhood through new eyes. Sadie was so different from any girl he'd ever dated. She lived in the moment, which made everything she did spark with energy.

Mike bounded up Gran's porch and unlocked the door for

Sadie, who held her bundle of clothes close as she entered the vestibule.

She gasped, eyeing the marble-lined walls. "Mike. It's so fancy!"

Closing the door behind them, he looked around the vestibule. "Really? I never thought of it that way. It's always just been my grandparents' place. Great banisters for sliding, and a laundry chute that my brother and I had some fun with when we were kids." Moving past Sadie, he flicked the light switch, and wall sconces lit the way through the parlor.

"Gran? We're here!" He suspected that his grandmother and Helen, the night nurse, were back in the sunroom, where Gran spent most of her time these days. "They're probably in the back, watching television. Hello?" he called again.

"In here!" came Gran's scratchy voice. She sat in her favorite chair, her face illuminated by the flicker of the television set.

"Gran, this is my friend Sadie King." Mike introduced them, and Gran insisted that Sadie call her Katherine.

"You caught me at my guilty pleasure," Gran said. "Reruns on TV Land."

"*Golden Girls* again?" Mike teased.

"It's almost over, but let's turn it off. I've seen this one a hundred times." With her right hand, the good side now, she reached for the remote and pushed the power button. "Come, sit. I'd much rather talk than watch the boob tube. And the Amish don't watch television, isn't that right, Sadie?"

Mike could see that Gran had done some online research.

"It's true," Sadie agreed. "We don't have electricity."

Mike and Sadie crossed to the semicircular sofa that lined the curved walls of the room built in to a turret.

"Where's Helen?" Mike asked.

"She went off to Tahiti to open a surf shop," Gran said dryly.

"Really, Gran. Where is she?"

"Would you believe I fired her?"

Katherine loved to tease. "Gran . . ."

"All right, I sent her home early. I knew you'd be here any minute." Katherine turned to Sadie, assessing. "They have nurses lurking here all day long, and I'm tired of having them underfoot like little mice. I know I need some assistance, but I'm tired of being doted upon. I want my life back."

Mike felt a stab of compassion for his grandmother. Of course she wanted her life back; but it wasn't going to be as easy as firing the home nursing staff. Despite Gran's progress, it would take a while until she was steady on her feet and able to perform all the necessary daily tasks.

"Rehabilitation takes time," Mike said. He and Gran had been through this territory before.

"Well, I may not have too much time left, and I don't want to spend my last days taking orders from mousy nurses."

Mike arched one brow. "Your last days? Do you know something I don't know, Gran?"

"I understand," Sadie offered. "I'm not very good at taking orders, either." She shot a mischievous look at Mike. "If I was more obedient, I wouldn't be here right now."

"Defiance . . ." Katherine's eyes opened wide. "I love it."

She turned on the lamp to her right and pointed to a bookshelf near the arched doorway. "Sadie, can you get me a book from that wall? It's that slender volume in red leather, second-from-the-bottom shelf."

"Sure." Sadie crouched over at the wall of books, letting her fingertips glide over the smooth spines. She seemed small in the high-ceilinged room, her body compact in her denim shorts, T-shirt, and white prayer kapp. "Here it is." She extracted a slender volume bound in red and peered closely at the cover. "Poetry?"

Gran nodded. "Dylan Thomas has a wonderful poem about not giving up. Perfect for old folks like me. It's called, 'Do Not Go Gentle into That Good Night.' Do you know it?"

"I don't think so," Sadie said, handing Gran the book.

"I think I studied it in school," Mike said.

"Well, everyone should have the delight of hearing Dylan Thomas's raging wishes." Gran leafed through the book, then extended it to Mike. "Read for us, Mikey."

How like Gran to run the show, Mike thought as he rose and scanned the lines. "I do remember this," he said, then read the poem aloud. Each stanza repeated a bold warning not to die without giving it a fight, and described how different types of men faced death. Wise men, good men, wild men, and grave men alike tried to resist death, and with each stanza the poet reminded them to "rage against the dying of the light."

"Such strong words." Sadie pressed a hand to her heart, clearly moved. "I can imagine it as a song."

"It *is* lyrical," Katherine agreed. "But I wanted you to read that, Mike. Consider it insight into my current state of mind. I may seem cranky, but this is the good fight I'm waging every day."

"I get it." Mike nodded. "You've certainly been battling it out. Though I'm not so sure I want to encourage you to 'rage, rage.' You're already tough to live with."

Gran pursed her lips. "Smarty-pants."

The three of them laughed softly, which eased Mike's heart. When was the last time he'd seen his grandmother laugh? Not since the stroke. Sadie was going to keep his grandmother on her toes.

Sadie asked for another look at the book, and Katherine told her she was welcome to read it while she was here.

"There are other poets in there, too. You might like some of them."

Sadie thanked her, smoothing a hand over the cover of the book.

Then Katherine sat up straighter and began to sidle to the edge of the chair. "How about a game before bed?"

"Do you have Password?" Sadie's amber eyes opened wide. "Or Scrabble?"

"Let's play Scrabble. Bring me my walker, would you, Mike?" Gran leaned forward and Sadie moved to help her rise from the chair.

"I'll help." Sadie took the walker from Mike and positioned it under Katherine. "You can start setting up the game, Mike."

"Gran, are you sure you can sit at the table that long? I don't think you'll be comfortable."

Katherine clucked her tongue. "I will 'rage against the dying of the light.'"

Mike caught a glimpse of Sadie patiently coaching Katherine up. "I'm surrounded by bossy women," he teased as he turned toward the closet to find the game.

"I heard that," Gran called. "Nothing wrong with my ears, you know."

In no time he had the game set up at the kitchen table, and Sadie helped Gran navigate there, with a short stop at the bathroom. Mike was impressed by Sadie's helping demeanor; she was neither impatient nor embarrassed about Gran's weaknesses, and she listened when Gran described her limitations. Of course, Sadie had spent her childhood dealing with her sister's illness, and the Amish tended to accept people's ailments better than the English. Handicaps were regarded with consideration and affection in the Amish community.

Mike started with the word "keeper," and Sadie promptly got a whopping score by adding "zoo" to the front of the word.

"I think we've got a ringer here, Mike," Gran said. "I'm going to have to put my thinking cap on."

"Looks that way," Mike said casually. He was relieved to see Gran hitting it off with Sadie. One fewer obstacle.

Though there were still many complications and impediments ahead for them. Her family. His parents. The Trueherz medical practice back in Halfway. The scorn of the Amish community.

Frowning, he rearranged the tiles on his placard, looking for a word. He moved the *F* to the beginning and put the *TH* together . . . and suddenly he had the word "faith."

Yeah, baby. Faith was the elixir of life, the blue Jedi light saber, the light at the end of the tunnel. The Bible said that faith was "the substance of things hoped for, the evidence of things not seen."

They would have to hold on to their faith.

TWENTY-THREE

*S*adie felt as if she had stepped into another girl's life.

These shoes weren't used to walking on marble floors. These fingers didn't normally push a button on a tiny box of an oven to microwave popcorn. This heart had never thrilled to the sound of a young man's voice, but now it seemed to skip ahead every time Mike spoke.

Oh, she was walking in some other girl's footsteps, and she was determined never to give up this stranger's shoes, for fear of the blessed happiness ending.

She hugged herself, turning in the lovely bedroom. The edges of the ceiling were trimmed in white like a cake. There were paintings framed in gold, colorful wallpaper with splashes of lavender flowers, and her very own bathroom through that door. She fell back on the big four-poster bed, bouncing on the bedspread with tiny purple flowers. How would she ever sleep with such excitement beating in her chest, beating like a hawk rising into the sky?

After she had helped Mike's grandmother to bed, Mike had led her up the graceful, twisting staircase through this castle of a house with electric lights that looked like white candles coming out of the wall. There were windows with sparkling edges, bouncy carpeting that felt like marshmallows underfoot, and carved wooden banisters that seemed more like sculptures than practical handles to hold on to. Sadie had been surprised to see so many rooms that went unused, but Mike reminded her that his gran used to live up here and offer free board to traveling students and missionaries until the stroke made it impossible for her to do the stairs. Still, all these rooms for one person? "It would take all of an afternoon just to travel from room to room," Sadie had told him.

She rolled over on the bed and opened the thin red book of poetry. Hearing Mike read the poem, she had begun to see how musical a poem could be. The contents promised so many verses, but she let the book fall closed, knowing her mind was too unsettled to read.

Downstairs she heard the gong of a clock—Katherine's grandfather clock—striking twelve times for midnight, and the story of Cinderella came to mind. Was it time for her to run from the ball and return to her life as slave to her cruel, bad sisters?

She laughed at the notion and rose from the bed. No, there was no cruelty in her good, kind family. Only concern, and a little disappointment. They were upset with her because they wanted her to follow the Ordnung. They loved her and wanted her to live nearby forever, a good Amish wife and mother. Of course, that was how her story should end.

But was that the happy ending for her?

She pressed her palms to the cool stone windowsill and looked to the street below where a small car moved down the lane. To be in the city, so close to Mike . . . it hadn't occurred to her before, but now she didn't think she would sleep a wink.

Feeling adventurous, she went to the door and peered into the hall, studying the way the staircase curved up as it rose to the next story. There was a little window seat on this level and she sat down on the velveteen cushion and hugged her knees. The window off to the side seemed to be made of ice diamonds, clear and sparkling in the night. Such beautiful things Katherine's home was made of. It was so different from the Plain life Sadie knew, and yet she found that the smooth marble and glittering glass thrilled her as much as the wildflowers of a spring day. Wasn't a house as beautiful as this Gott's creation, too?

A shuffling sound alerted her, and she turned her head to see Mike coming down the stairs. "Sadie? Hey. Do you need something?"

She shook her head, hugging her knees. "I'm fine. Just enjoying this wonderful good house."

He sat beside her on the window seat, his arm brushing hers. "It is a great house, but I thought you were tired. Don't you go to sleep early so that you can get up with the sunrise?"

He had casually dropped his hand to her knee when he asked the question, and his touch sent shivers running straight to her heart. "Ya, but here I don't have to get up and milk cows."

He laughed. "Right. So I haven't even shown you one of the best parts of the house." He stood up, and she missed the comfort of his body beside hers. "You want to have a look?"

"Sure." She followed him up the curving staircase.

"My brother used to call this the stairway to heaven," Mike called back to her.

"If there are stairs to heaven, I think they must look like this."

Four floors! Mike led her to the tippy-top, where a white door opened to the sky. And suddenly they stood on a patio looking out over rooftops and city lights.

"Look at all the lights," Sadie marveled, taking a breath of cool air.

"City lights. Sometimes they're so bright, they block out the stars and moon. They call it light pollution."

"Even if you can't see the stars, with all these twinkling lights, I could just stand here and watch for hours." She walked to the railing, a fence covered by clear glass so that you could see through to the city view.

"I thought you'd like it. That patch of darkness over there is the Delaware River. On a clear night, it shimmers in the moonlight."

"It is like heaven. And those buildings over there . . . the square of light. Each one is a window with people inside." She sighed in wonder. "So much life in the city. Everywhere I turn, it reminds me of the good people Gott has created."

"That is not the way most people see the city, but I like it." He turned to her. "I like the way you think, songbird."

The sparkle in his blue eyes gave her goose bumps, and she crossed her arms, wanting to hold on to the good feeling. If only she could remember this moment for always—the feeling sweeping her from head to toe, the cool night air, the color of his eyes and the way they looked at her as if she were the most precious flower in Gott's creation.

"Are you cold?" he asked.

She didn't answer; she didn't want to go inside.

But instead he moved behind her and folded his arms around her, pulling her against his warm, solid body.

Sadie gasped at the contact, her senses afire as his arms formed a band across her belly and his head tipped down so that his cheek pressed against hers. The hard wall of his body behind her made her feel loved and supported, and her throat tightened at the sweet feeling of security in his arms.

"Is that better?" he asked.

"Ya." Her voice sounded thin and meek, and that was not how

she was feeling. She covered his arms with hers and held on tight. "Yes, it's warm and cozy."

"You know, I really can't believe you're here. I mean, what are the chances that a guy could get an Amish girl to visit him in the city?"

She laughed. "Slim chances."

"I guess I'm just lucky."

"We're both blessed. My heart is doing flip-flops, just being here in the city and being with you. I feel so new, so alive. Like my life is just beginning now."

"Really? Well, maybe it is. Maybe this is where you're meant to be."

Could it be?

This was all wonderful good. But was this who Sadie really was? She had always thought of herself as an Amish girl from Halfway. Much as she loved the city, Lancaster County was her home.

But this—this beautiful night in a city palace—this was a memory she would cherish for always.

"I think this is just a wonderful fairy tale," Sadie said. "I feel like I stepped into a princess's shoes."

"This is real, Sadie. The real deal." He tightened his grip and swayed gently back and forth.

Back and forth . . .

Emotion blurred the lights in the indigo night as they rocked together and she tamped down all thoughts of the farm and the bishop and baptism. Her troubles could wait while the reality of her feelings for Mike set in.

The Big Love. She was falling for Mike . . . had already fallen in love with him. And the rush of feelings wasn't at all what she'd expected.

How childish she'd been to think that it would chase the loneliness from her heart. Instead, she knew that from now on a new loneliness was going to jab at her whenever she was away from Mike. Real love was going to bring her heartache, she saw that now, and still, she wouldn't have missed these feelings for anything in the world.

"God works in mysterious ways," Mike whispered in her ear. "He's the one who brought us together. And now that I've got you, I'm not going to let you go."

She couldn't help but smile as she swayed in his arms. "Okay, but it's going to look mighty funny when we go downstairs for breakfast with your octopus arms around me."

He stopped swaying and loosened his grip. "Are you calling me an octopus?"

She turned in his arms and pressed a finger to his lips. "I think you should stop complaining about that and kiss me."

"Oh, really?" He pretended to bite her finger and she laughed, pulling it away.

His hands moved to her shoulders, melting the burdens she carried there as his eyes studied her.

Those eyes . . . every time she looked at him she was stunned anew by the light in his blue eyes. Gott's light; that had to be it.

"Really. We're on a rooftop overlooking a sparkling city. My family is many miles away, and the bishop isn't watching. I think it's a good time."

He sighed. "I love a practical girl."

The warmth of his hands moved down her back as he pulled her closer, pulled her into his glittering world of cars and cities and limitless music.

Like a flower opening itself to the sun, Sadie lifted her face for his kiss—a gentle brush of his lips, then a hungrier contact that sizzled down to her toes. Her beating heart roared in her ears, and she was sure he could feel it pulsing through her lips as they kissed and sighed and kissed as if tasting honey for the very first time.

There was a smile on her face as Sadie awoke to the pink light of sunrise at the window.

Kissing under the stars . . . such a lovely night.

She burrowed into the pillow of the princess bed, wanting some time to think and pray.

"Dear Gott in heaven, I didn't know I could ever feel this way." All those times she had prayed for the Big Love, she had thought of it more of a game than a real bond between a woman and a man.

My very first kiss.

She pressed her fingertips to her lips, remembering the kiss. She had never guessed that a simple touch on the lips could stir so many feelings in a person . . . and such a hunger for more.

Stretching under the covers, she closed her eyes and pictured the two of them locked in each other's arms on the rooftop.

Kissing under the stars.

The beauty and wonder of it all would probably fade when she went back to Halfway, but for now the glow still warmed her.

Did this mean Mike was her boyfriend now? Ya, it had to be so. And where was he right now? She knew he had to work at the bakery this morning. With a look at the clock, she kicked off the covers and hurried to get dressed. Maybe she could catch him before he left.

Downstairs she tiptoed past the archway to Katherine's make-shift room and found the older woman still in bed, her breath whispering in and out, gentle as a child. There was a note on the kitchen counter, addressed to "Songbird." She beamed, reading that he was off to work and planned to return by three. Katherine's nurse Stella would arrive by eight-thirty, and Sadie was invited to help herself to anything in the kitchen.

"What do we have here?" She pulled open the refrigerator and found it well stocked with eggs, cheese, veggies, and fruit—everything she would need for a good breakfast. She would shower first, then cook a meal to be ready soon after the nurse arrived.

The morning passed quickly with a breakfast to cook, a kitchen to clean up, and a big house to tidy. Sadie stripped the sheets on Katherine's bed and put them into the electric washing machine. Stella showed her how to add soap, press two buttons, and the machine did everything else on its own. Sadie enjoyed going through the downstairs rooms with a feather duster, a broom, and a pail of soapy water.

"You don't have to do that, Sadie," Katherine insisted. "You're a guest here."

"But I like to stay busy," Sadie said. "Such a beautiful house deserves to be sparkling clean."

While Katherine was reading in the sunroom, Sadie moved into the parlor and noticed a piano for the first time. Big and black as a cow, it sat in an alcove, alone and lonely.

"You want to make music," Sadie said, running her palm over the keyboard cover. "It's all waiting inside you."

"Did you say something?" Katherine called.

Sadie peeked around to the sunroom. "I was talking to your piano. It's telling me it wants to make music."

Katherine squinted, the creases in her forehead sharpening. "Does it?" Her mouth softened. "Yes, it must feel neglected. It's been gathering a lot of dust these past few years."

"Do you play?"

"Not often—and not at all since the stroke."

"Kumm, please." Sadie brought the walker to Katherine. "Will you play for me? Or at least show me how it works?"

"Mike did say you are a gifted musician." Katherine closed her book. "I might play a little something, but I can't really show you how to work it. It's not like a washing machine or a microwave oven. A piano's music is only as good as the fingers dancing over the keys."

As she walked slowly alongside Katherine, Sadie cupped her rough hands together, wondering if these fingers could learn to dance. "I would love to hear a song."

"We'll have to see how my left hand works." As they reached the parlor, Katherine's pale blue eyes slid over to Sadie. "Did my physical therapist put you up to this?"

Sadie laughed. She replaced the piano bench with a hard-backed chair from the dining room, and then helped Katherine settle in.

"I need to warm up." With some effort the older woman pulled herself up, her posture perfect as her hands pressed into the black and white keys. "All right, then, let me try this."

· The song started with a low note, far to the left. The low notes set up a steady beat. And then the melody came, playful and light, like girls skipping in the sun.

Butterfly fingers, Sadie thought, observing attentively. Hands arched. Fingers curled.

Katherine's fingers walked to the right of the keyboard, the notes rising like a kite in the air. At one point her left hand hit some wrong keys, and she grunted, but continued until she finished by hitting many bright notes at the same time.

"Wonderful!" Sadie clapped, beaming in wonder that Katherine could make such a beautiful song.

Katherine tried to hide her smile. "You're an easy sell. That's just a beginner's piece, and my left hand is sluggish."

"But it warms my heart, and I couldn't begin to play it myself. Doesn't it thrill you that you can sit at this big piano and make such music?"

"I never thought of it that way. I was forced to take piano lessons as a child. I had to practice every day before I could play outside, and that made me mad."

How odd to punish a child with music, Sadie thought. "Are you still mad?"

"I worked through it. But it's exhausting now, working my left hand so hard." Katherine was pressing many keys at one time, bringing out tones so lovely they made the hair at the back of Sadie's neck tingle.

"What's that you're playing now?" Sadie asked.

"This? Just chords." When she saw Sadie staring, she elaborated. "A musical chord is a set of notes heard at the same time. You have triads . . . one, two, three. There are extended chords." She struck many keys at the same time. "And major . . . and minor. Many songs have you play chords with the left hand and the melody with the right."

Sadie took a deep breath, trying to take it all in. "I think I would like to play the piano."

"That's because you have music in your heart." Katherine waved a hand in the air. "Pull up another chair, and I'll show you a few things you can try."

Katherine showed her chords, and then had Sadie use her own fingers to strike C major.

The sweet, clear sound filled the room like light at sunrise.

"I love that!" Sadie struck it again, and again.

"And that's just C major," Katherine said with a wry smile. "We've got a ways to go before my nap."

When Mike returned in the afternoon, Sadie was once again testing the sounds of different keys and practicing chords. After a lunch of grilled cheese sandwiches, she had helped Katherine in for a nap, closed the pocket doors of the parlor, and spent hours picking out the melodies of hymns she had learned, adding chords when she could.

"Listen to this—I can do chords," she said excitedly, demonstrating.

Mike sat beside her on the bench, and again she felt a tug of nerves having him so close. "Pretty impressive."

"It's so wonderful to be able to take this music from my head and hear it on a piano, with other notes. A single voice can't do so much."

Mike nodded. "A piano gives you more range, and you're a quick study." He leaned over the keyboard. "You want to see what I've mastered in my twenty-two years? This is called 'Heart and Soul.'"

He made a show of cracking his knuckles, then began with his left hand. Boom-dah-dee-dah . . . The song was a little goofy, but Mike made it even funnier with his silly expressions.

She clapped when he finished.

"Think I'm ready for Carnegie Hall?" he asked, blue eyes twinkling.

"I don't know that place, but I think you're ready to join a circus."

"Ouch!" He played a simple chord. "I've got mad skills on the piano."

She nudged his shoulder with hers. "Sorry, sir. It's a good thing you're getting some mad skills in college."

"Oh, now you're a comedian, too?"

"No, I'm a serious musician. And if you don't mind, I'd like to practice some more chords."

"Okay, okay." He slid off the bench and moved behind her.

A moment later, a tingle traveled down Sadie's spine as his hands covered her shoulders. His fingers pressed into the muscles, soothing and exciting, too.

She had never felt so close to a young man. Mike was her boyfriend, yes, but he was a good friend, too.

With his gentle hands upon her, she played the background chords to a hymn that she'd figured out. From the heart, she sang: "Abide with me, fast falls the eventide; The darkness deepens; Lord with me abide. . . ."

Dinner was a pizza and a crispy green salad with olives and cheese and bread crumbs, all delivered by a nice young man who brought it right to the door.

"I think I could get used to having my dinner dropped off at the door," Sadie said as she lifted a slice of pizza from the box.

"Any night someone else cooks is a good night for me." Gran pointed to the ceiling. "That's one of the reasons I like to fill this place with missionaries and exchange students. I can usually shame them into cooking for me in exchange for the room."

"How did you come to have such a large house?" Sadie asked.

"The easy way. I inherited it from my parents." Katherine rested her fork on the side of her plate and stared off, as if watching the past. "My father was a banker, and we didn't lack for any material things. He owned this house in the city and another one on the shore. My parents set me up to be a proper young lady. Boarding school and a debutante ball . . ." She turned to face Sadie. "And I had to ruin it all for them by marrying a priest."

Sadie swallowed. "That's a bad thing?"

"My parents were very disappointed. My father had hoped I might wed the son of a shipping magnate or a coal baron and help expand the family business. But no, I married a man of God. And poor Will's family . . . they weren't ready for me." She pressed a hand to her chest. "The first time I visited, I asked for a glass of sherry before dinner, and they never kept a drop of liquor in their home."

Some of the details fell away from her, but Sadie found Katherine's story endearing as she shared her embarrassing moment.

"I guess what I'm saying is, I know how it feels to be a fish out of water, Sadie. You walked into a strange place this weekend, very different from your home, but you were open to new things, and you pitched in and cleaned my house. It takes a lot of spunk to do something like that, and you have spunk, dear."

"Thank you." Sadie's throat was thick with emotion as she reached across the table to press her hand over Katherine's. "And thank you for your good hospitality."

"You're very welcome." Gran cleared her throat. "You two should stop back here after church tomorrow and we'll have lunch before you head out."

"Aren't you coming to church with us?" Sadie shot a glance at Mike, who shrugged.

Gran waved with her good hand, her eyes fixed on her plate. "You two just go on your own. I'm not steady on my feet yet, and I don't want all the church ladies doting on me."

"Oh, but I don't mind if you're slow," Sadie said. "We'll leave extra early so that there's plenty of time to get settled in the church."

"Nice of you to offer, but I'm too cranky to deal with church right now."

"Nothing can lift your spirit like church," Sadie said. "Especially if there's wonderful good music, like Mike says." She tapped one finger on the table, nodding knowingly. "You must come, Katherine. If you like, I'll get up early to help you dress and fix your hair. I'm used to getting up with the sun."

"Come on, Gran," Mike chimed in. "If you show your face tomorrow, at least Father Drummond will be off your case for a while."

Gran rolled her eyes, then sighed. "All right. Fine. But if someone even offers me a wheelchair, I'll mow them down with my walker."

⬚

After dinner they played two rounds of Trouble, and then Gran shooed them from the downstairs, telling them she needed extra beauty sleep if she was going to make an appearance at St. Mark's in the morning.

"Do you want to go for ice cream? I think I owe you some, right?"

He remembered! "I thought you forgot about that night when you picked me up on my scooter."

Mike pointed to his head. "Got a mind like a steel trap in here. So, you want to go out?"

Sadie bit her lower lip, hesitating. She didn't want him to think she was too forward, but she couldn't hold back. "Would it be all right if we just went back up to the roof?"

He lifted one hand toward the stairs. "I like the way you think."

Up on the roof, Mike wiped off the two patio chairs and moved them close, so that they were touching. "Have a seat. I'm usually the only person who comes up here. Gran's father used to come up here and smoke cigars, and I think that ruined it for her."

"Such a story your gran has." Sadie settled into the chair. They were just close enough to the edge of the roof to see the scattered lights and dark silhouettes of rooftops. "Sometimes I think I'm the only person in the world trying to walk the steady path through the Ordnung—all the rules and all the things people expect me to do. But then I hear that Katherine had the same problems with her family when she was young, and she wasn't even Amish."

"Everyone has their challenges and struggles." Mike stretched his long legs out in front of him, his hands gripping the chair's armrest. "I feel blessed to have good parents and food and shelter, but you know I've got my issues, too."

"But you got out of Lancaster County . . . and here you are. You're living in Philadelphia, like you wanted. No more double life for you."

"True, but it hasn't solved the issue with my parents. They still expect me to move back and take over the clinic. Just last week, I got a fat packet of brochures for medical schools abroad from my father. He's still stuck on his dream."

"So the problem is just put off until later."

"Basically."

Hearing the edge in his voice, Sadie turned and touched his arm gently. "You're a good son, Mike, and a very good person. And Dr. Trueherz is a very smart man. I know that because he saved our Susie's life, and he's done a good job keeping her healthy. Someday your father will see who you really are."

He turned to her and the flicker of sadness in his blue eyes faded. "I hope you're right." He took her hand and wove his fingers through hers. "Like I said, we all have our hills to climb. You've got the ministers of your church on your back to conform with their rules, but you don't complain."

"Ach! I feel like I talk about it all the time."

"Probably because it's on your mind all the time." He tugged her hand playfully. "I know you love the city and your music. You're the one leading the double life now."

"How do I explain?" Her problems were not as simple and smooth as this velvety summer night. "It's hard. Sometimes I'm not sure what I want myself. Growing up Amish, it's all you know, and it's a good life. I'm a hard worker, and there's something that always pulls me back to my family. There's a lot of love there, and they need me, too. Some of my brothers and sisters were little when our parents were killed, and they need all of us older ones to show them the way."

"You're happy, living Amish?"

"It's a good life we have. But sometimes I feel like I don't completely fit there, because of this . . . this light burning in my soul." She pressed a fist to her chest. "I love singing. That you know. And Gott gave me this voice. I don't want to sound proud, but I can't deny what's in me. And I think that the Heavenly Father gave it to me for a reason. He wants me to use it."

"And you should."

"But that's not allowed by the Amish."

"So you joined Frank's band."

"I thought that would be a way to use my gift, but it doesn't feel completely right. And now that the bishop got ahold of those flyers, I think I'm finished with the band."

"So how will you use your gift?"

Her eyes searched the dark blue city at her feet. How she wished Gott would spell out an answer in the twinkling lights. "That's the question I pray about each and every day."

TWENTY-FOUR

From the moment they entered the jewel box of a building, Sadie loved the music in Mike's church.

A small orchestra played a greeting song as people filed in, and Sadie could only compare it to a spring garden waking up with the morning sun. The violin and cello and guitar mingled like all the plants growing in a friendly tangle of green. The piano popped like the bright bloom of flowers facing the sky. The bass rumbled like bees buzzing over flowers. And the trumpet blast, it was the glorious burst of sunshine that warmed the earth!

Mike had been right; this music was touched by an angel of Gott.

When the music ended, a man in the front of the church asked everyone to stand. Sadie helped Katherine to her feet to the rising sound of voices from behind her. The singers were walking in from the back of the church, their sky-blue robes trailing behind them. Surrounded by song, Sadie tried to still her racing heart and listen to the words of the lovely hymn.

"All that we have and all that we offer comes from a heart both frightened and free. . . ."

As the choir filed onto the stage at the front of the church, she spotted Mike among them wearing a robe that made his eyes seem bluer than ever. Her heart jumped at the sight of him among the choir singers. She recognized his friend Daryl and a few of the other young men who had come to Remy's place to pick up her furniture.

The pastor, Father Drummond, greeted the people and the service began. Katherine pointed Sadie to a book in the back of one pew, and she was able to follow along with the prayers.

A woman in a lovely green dress went to the microphone. Sadie smoothed over the folds of her own dress, the pretty flowered print she had gotten from Remy's Englisher clothes. The flat black shoes were a little loose, but they were comfortable.

"'Ye are the light of the world,'" the woman said, reading from the Bible. "'A city that is set on a hill cannot be hid.'"

The glittering lights of Philadelphia floated through Sadie's mind. Ya, you could not hide the lights of this city.

"'Neither do men light a candle, and put it under a bushel, but on a candlestick; and it giveth light unto all that are in the house. Let your light shine before men, that they may see your good works, and glorify your Father which is in heaven.'"

A new song began, and Sadie felt her heart come alive to the harmonies, the warm bass and bold piano. The violin sighed and mewed like a baby calf—heartbreakingly beautiful—and a cello blended it all together. And when the choir joined in, there was such power in their voices raised to the Almighty. When Sadie closed her eyes, it was as if there was only one strong voice filling the church.

The music warmed her and opened her heart.

This is what redemption feels like. True forgiveness and peace. Gelassenheit.

Though the bishop would not think so. Amish services were in Hoch Deutsch and held in a member's simple house or barn. This was not the sort of place the Amish worshipped in, with fancy colored glass in the windows and a pretty spire outside pointing to heaven. Amish church music wasn't sweetened by stringed instruments or pianos. Under their rules, this would be the wrong place to be on a Sunday . . . but in her heart, Sadie knew it was right. When this music swept over her, all her troubles were washed away.

Music that warmed the soul like this had to be shared. But how could she make anyone back home, Remy or Adam or even the bishop, understand that this was the greatest thing she had ever found? How she would love for them to find it, too.

Father Drummond came back to the microphone and started speaking directly to the members. Ah, the sermon. The sermons at home could be long sometimes, and Sadie often found her mind wandering off.

"What's shining inside of you?" The pastor tapped his chest. "What's your light burning inside?"

The breath seemed trapped inside her as Sadie touched the base of her throat. He was talking to her. Could he see the light inside her? Could he see it inside everyone here?

"Today's reading from Matthew tells us not to hide the light inside us," Father Drummond said. "Matthew uses some basic logic. If you have a flame, you put it in a candle, not under a basket. A flame is intended to light the way. To help people find their way."

She closed her eyes, wanting to hear his words, pure and plain.

"Everyone in this room has a light inside. Do you know what yours is?"

I do.

"What's your gift? Your talent? The piece of you that can turn things around and make something positive in this world?"

I have a voice. Gott blessed me with a voice.

"Some of you know your light. I can tell. And right about now some of you are saying to yourself, 'What on earth is he talking about?' That's okay. At least you're honest. But if you don't know the light inside of you, now is the time to look inward. How do you help people? What can you share with your fellow man? What's the special, unique ingredient inside you that makes you one of a kind?

"That's the light that our Lord wants to let shine."

Back at Katherine's house, they prepared a farewell brunch in the big, sunny kitchen. Mike had picked up pastries from the bakery where he worked. While coffee brewed in a machine, he put oranges in the very loud electric juicer, and Sadie fried some eggs over easy, just the way Katherine liked them.

"I feel like a queen, getting the royal treatment," Katherine said from her seat at the table. "It's going to be a rude awakening for me when I'm back on my feet again, having to do things myself."

"I'm happy to cook for you, anytime," Sadie said.

"Then you're definitely invited back," Katherine said with a slanted smile.

"I don't know if I'll be allowed to come back." Her Amish life was seeping in, bringing her back to reality. "But if I could I would go to your Episcopal church every Sunday. The talk and the prayers and the music made me feel beautiful inside. Like my heart was touched by Gott."

Mike looked up from his coffee, a flicker of understanding in his eyes. "That's the power of God."

Sadie turned her glass of juice on the table. Such a pretty glass; its angles and edges reflected the light, and the juice inside was the rich shade of a sunset. She would miss this house with its lovely things and its charming owner.

"It's been such a wonderful visit," Sadie said. "It's very hard for me to return to Lancaster County."

"I used to hear that every weekend from this one." Katherine gestured to Mike with her good hand.

"Your house is a great hangout spot, Gran."

She gave a grunt. "It can't be my cooking, since we ordered in pizza." Katherine dabbed at her mouth with her napkin, staring at the poetry book Sadie had brought to the table. "Seriously, Sadie, you are welcome anytime . . . and you can take the poetry book with you, if you like."

"I would like to borrow it," Sadie said. Between her piano practice and rooftop chats with Mike, she'd had little time to read.

"Return it next time you visit. That way I know you'll come back and tidy up and play around on the piano. Beyond the occasional visiting student or missionary, most of the upstairs is empty."

"Hey, I'm living up there," Mike reminded her.

"Yes, of course, but you'll be off to the dorms come September."

September . . . It was only June, but Sadie felt that she had reached a crossroads, and there was no telling where she would end up by the end of the summer. She got up from the table, holding the slim leather book in both hands.

"Thank you, Katherine." Sadie put the book next to her bundle of clothes, then went and bent over to give the older woman a kiss on the cheek. Despite her slight paralysis, Katherine seemed so much younger than Sadie's grandmother, though Sadie guessed that they were the same age. Maybe Katherine was just young at heart. "Thank you for everything."

Something in Katherine's blue eyes—a spark of concern, or maybe wisdom—reminded Sadie of her own mamm. "Oh, my pleasure," Katherine said. "Come back and see me soon."

As soon as Mike turned the car into traffic, Sadie lowered the volume on the radio.

He shot her a look. "Everything okay, songbird?"

"I want it lower so we can talk. Did you hear the pastor's sermon today, Mike?"

"I did." He checked his blind spot and changed lanes. "You gotta let your light shine."

Sadie's throat was suddenly thick with emotion. "That was exactly what I was talking to you about last night. The light I feel shining in me. My voice. I want to use it, but I didn't know if that was the right thing, and then, this sermon today . . ."

"It hit you," Mike said.

She nodded. "I wasn't joking before. I did feel blessed. Like I was touched by an angel."

"Maybe you were."

"I've been praying to God for an answer, and now this . . . this minister seemed to speak right to me. I think God answered me."

"The message spoke to you, and your heart was open to it. That's faith in action." He touched her shoulder, his eyes on the road. "Awesome."

Sadie felt as if a heavy weight had been lifted from her shoulders. Now she knew what she had to do. God wanted her to use her voice. He wanted her to let it shine! She just needed to figure out how to do that.

"I feel like something has changed in my heart, deep in my soul." She stared out the window at the colors of the city flying past. Storefronts, signs, trees, and lampposts. Soon they would be on the highway, and the close streets of the city would give way to the suburbs, then the fence posts and fields of Amish country. How would it feel to return with this new heart of hers?

A light to shine . . .

She so wanted to let God's word change her life, but she knew her new faith would be scorned at home by Amish family and friends. Would even her cousin Rachel understand the earth-moving discoveries she had made this weekend?

She drew in a breath, shaking the worries from her mind. One day at a time, as Mamm used to say. "What did you think of Father Drummond's message?"

"It spoke to me too, but in a different way. It made me realize that before school starts I've got to get off my duff and tell my dad to start looking for someone else for the practice. I'm not exactly sure what my gift is, but I'm working on finding it, and all roads lead back to my Peace Corps service in Jamaica. After the initial adjustment there, that job brought out my best qualities. It made me the best person I could be. I need to figure out how that all worked."

She studied the man beside her, fascinated by how his mind worked. So different from the Amish guys she knew, whose talk focused more on the doing than the thinking.

"We've talked so much about the sermon. How about the music?" he asked.

"The music was every bit as wonderful good as . . ." She paused, correcting herself. Some of her words weren't exactly right in the Englisher world. "It was as wonderful as you promised. I do hope to return to St. Mark's."

"I hope you can come back, too. I was psyched about spending the summer in the city, but with you so far away, it's just not going to be the same."

Her heart ached at the thought of the miles that would separate them. Funny, how they had lived in neighboring towns for all their lives but lived in separate communities that rarely crossed paths. And now, now that they realized they fit together like two puzzle pieces, they would be separated by a hundred miles.

TWENTY-FIVE

After dropping Sadie off at the King farm, Mike stopped at home to give his parents an update on Gran's care. He used to dread his visits here, but now, thinking of Sadie in the next town over, he felt the urge to hang here awhile. It felt comforting, knowing she was near.

"You got it bad, Trueherz," he said to himself as he pulled his Ford into the driveway. He found his mother chopping vegetables in the kitchen.

"Hey, there! I got your message that you might be stopping by. I'm just making a salad for dinner. Will you be eating with us? Chicken sausage on the grill."

"I might be persuaded. Gran had some company for the weekend, so I think she might prefer a quiet dinner with Helen. She's the aide who stays through the evening." He stole a slice of radish from the cutting board. "Where's Dad?"

"Out for his walk, but he'll be back soon. So, who was her visitor? I thought we weren't going to have any exchange students in the house until she was further along in her recovery."

"Actually, it was a friend of mine." He paused, wondering how much he should reveal. Mike wasn't a fan of keeping secrets, but he wasn't sure he was ready to talk about Sadie.

His mother stopped chopping and raised her eyes to him. "And . . . ? How about some details, honey?"

"I'm dating Sadie King." He put it right out there, and it sounded pretty good. "You know Dad's patient Susie? Sadie is her older sister."

Celeste was nodding. "Yes, I know the Kings, and I remember Sadie, too. But I'm a little surprised at you. Why didn't you tell me you were dating an Amish girl?"

"I didn't think I needed permission."

"I didn't mean it that way. It's just . . ." She frowned. "There's a cultural divide there."

"I'm aware of that." Man, was he ever. He hadn't planned to fall for Sadie, but it just happened.

"Okay." His mother cocked her head to the side, studying him. "You were never one to be put off by the way someone looked. You've always had the ability to see clear through to a person's soul."

"Thanks, Mom."

She shrugged. "That's probably why the Peace Corps was such a good match for you. Too bad you couldn't make a permanent job out of it."

"Really."

He stole a slice of carrot, and she clucked at him. "Save some for dinner."

Just then the back door opened and Henry Trueherz stepped in. "Mike." He sat on the bench by the door and removed his sneakers. "How's it going with Mom?"

"She's making great progress. It's only been weeks since the stroke and her speech is almost back to normal." Mike recounted the reports he'd gotten that week from Gran's doctor and physical therapist.

As he listened, Mike's father squinted, the creases at the edges of his eyes deepening. His hair was peppered with gray now, something Mike hadn't noticed until recently. "Well, your grandmother is bouncing back faster than any of us expected."

"It's because she's in her own home, Henry." Celeste clamped an opener onto a can of baked beans and started cranking. "It's a good thing you didn't force her into a rehab facility. I told you, Katherine needs her independence."

"Don't we all," Mike said offhandedly.

"Independence is great," Henry said. "But it would have been dangerous to have Mom banging around in that big old house on her own. One fall and she could have seriously injured herself, or worse."

"Well, I'm happy to keep her company," Mike said. "And Gran's been fine about having the nursing staff with her during the day." He didn't mention the many times that Katherine had sent the nurses off for errands, mostly to get them out of her hair for a while.

Henry crossed to the sink and filled a glass with water. "And your mother and I are grateful for the way you've been looking after her. She wouldn't have been able to recover at home without you there to coordinate her care. You've done an excellent job, Mike. For me it just reaffirms that you're cut out for the medical profession." He winked. "You got the service gene from your old man."

"Yeah, well . . ." Mike wanted to say that he was happy to serve, just not as a medical doctor, and not in the Paradise clinic.

"Dinner's ready as soon as you grill the sausages, Henry," Celeste said, removing the long grill tongs from the drawer.

Henry took a swig of water. "I'm on it." He moved toward the fridge, then snapped his fingers. "I almost forgot." He removed his wallet from the back pocket of his shorts and took out a small square of pink paper. "I've been talking with an old friend, Dr. Gary Hill. We met in med school. I'd like you to give him a call."

Mike took the slip of paper reluctantly. "What's this about?"

"Dr. Hill sits on the board at a med school in New England. He said he'd be happy to talk to you about your premed profile. I think he can give you some valuable advice that will give you an advantage over other candidates." Henry ducked into the fridge, then emerged with a covered platter. "It's certainly worth a chat."

"Yeah, okay. Thanks, Dad." Mike folded the paper in half and shoved it into his pocket as he went down the hall to his old room. He needed to get away from his father for a second. Two minutes with him, and Henry was already trying to take control of Mike's life.

The room hadn't changed much, with the old bedspread on the bed and his computer desk in the corner.

He opened the blinds and stared into the late gold of afternoon, frowning at the half-grown hay beyond the fence of his parents' yard. Over the years he'd always hated Jeb Miller's farm, which backed up to their property. The Millers were kind neighbors, generous with produce from their farm stand, but Mike had always hated staring at the flat fields, stinking of manure, buzzing with insects.

Nowheresville.

He raked his hair back and gave a frustrated sigh.

All these years, he'd blamed the surrounding farmland for his own boredom. All these years, he should have been looking inside.

He would call this Dr. Hill, out of respect for his father, but he was going to have to fill his father in on his real plans for the future. Images of the Temple campus and Gran's house and Sadie and his young clients in Jamaica passed through his mind. He was going to tell Dad everything . . . just as soon as he figured out what those plans were.

Now Sadie's daily phone calls were the highlight of his day. Although Mike had always preferred real-life interactions, he was beginning to see the usefulness of a phone for staying in touch with someone who was far away. Of course, she called at odd times of the day, from the chicken coop or the storage shed. Her older brother was watching her carefully after the last spate of trouble, so she had to be discreet. All this week, Mike had kept his phone in his pocket or right beside his bed, not wanting to miss her call.

On Wednesday he was on duty to work on the furniture truck for St. Mark's. When he arrived at the church, two guys had called in sick, so it was only Daryl and him.

"Dude." Daryl high-fived him. "I hope you ate a good breakfast, 'cause we got some heavy lifting ahead of us."

Their first stop was across town in Spring Garden, and Mike asked Daryl to drive because he might have to catch a call on his cell phone.

Daryl pulled the truck out of the church parking lot and shot him a quick look. "So what's this about an emergency phone call? You got a job on the hook or something?"

"It's no emergency. I just want to pick up if Sadie calls."

"Oh, Sadie, the girl sitting with your gran at church this week, right? Didn't I meet her before?"

"On a furniture run. That apartment in the museum district? I think she was totally dressed Amish then."

"Oh, yeah." Daryl nodded. "So you're hanging with an Amish girl?"

"She's a great girl, man."

"No doubt. But are the Amish cool with you? I've never seen any Amish youth checking out St. Mark's before."

"She's in her rumspringa, that time when teenagers get a little more latitude."

"So Mikey, you got to help me wrap my brain around this. I mean, what do you do when you're hanging out with Sadie? The Amish aren't allowed to go to movies or watch TV, right?"

"They don't have televisions, but I don't think it'd be a crime to watch a movie. It actually never came up with us."

"That's cool."

He wanted to tell Daryl how he felt like Sadie's guardian angel in some ways, but he knew that sounded kind of pompous. How could he explain that he felt like he and Sadie were brought together for a reason? He could help her find her way in the Englisher world. His father was right about that part; Mike had inherited the service gene.

Daryl pulled the truck to a stop at a light. "So. What is it you're not telling me about this girl?"

"Nothing. She's curious about music and about the real world, and if she wants an education on it, I'd like to be the one to guide her."

"Come on, Mikey. I saw the way you looked at her that day when we picked up the furniture at that poshy-posh apartment building. And I'm not getting much of that altruistic social-worky vibe, if you know what I'm saying. I'd say you're sweet on Sadie. Are you trying to help her or wanting to be her man?"

Mike sighed. "Pretty much both of those things."

"Okay, that's cool. I was just wondering."

As the truck crept through the city traffic, Mike imagined the sun-drenched hills of home. Ironically, now that he was finally living in Philadelphia, he longed to be back in Lancaster County, where he could at least spend a little time with Sadie, even if it was just a short car ride or a trip for ice cream.

"So isn't that sort of geographically undesirable?" Daryl asked. "You being here and her out in Amish country?"

"Yeah. But actually, I'm heading out there tomorrow. This morning Mario, the owner of the bakery, was asking if someone could drive the truck out to pick up some whoopie pies for a catering gig. Apparently he gets them right from the source—an Amish woman in Strasburg. Which is not far from Halfway. Which means I'll probably get to see her."

"Look at you, all skippy and gaga." Daryl shook his head. "I've never seen you this way. You're all about this girl."

"It's called a relationship."

"More like temporary insanity."

"See, this is the reason you can't stay in a relationship for more than a few weeks. You've got to be all about the girl." Even as Mike said the words, he realized that this was a first for him, too. He'd never really wanted to hook up with anyone for more than a week or two. He'd never really clicked this way with a girl before.

"Whatever."

"Don't worry, Daryl. Someday it'll happen for you, too. And you know what? I'll be right here, saying I told you so."

"All skippy and gaga." Daryl rolled his eyes. "I can't wait."

TWENTY-SIX

A sea of red strawberries stretched before Sadie on the picnic table, and though she and Rachel were fairly swift at cutting off the tops and greenery, Ruthie and Susie were faster at cleaning with the hose and big, round strainers.

"Here's some more," Susie said brightly, pouring another mound of berries onto the table.

Inside the kitchen, Remy, Mary, and Aunt Betsy were already at work on two big batches of strawberry jam. With the berry season coming to a close, it was important to put up the last of the berries while they were fresh. Sadie was glad she didn't have to work in the hot kitchen with the more experienced women; these days the kitchen trapped the heat of the sun as well as the cookstove.

"We need some help here at the table," Rachel called.

"I'll help," Ruthie offered. "I've always wanted to learn to trim berries as fast as Sadie." She picked up a small paring knife. "How do you make such quick work of it?"

"Practice," Sadie said, grabbing clean strawberries with her left hand and topping them off with the knife in her right hand. She made fast work of it, partly from habit but mostly because she wanted the job to be done. Mike was coming to Halfway today—probably not until later in the afternoon, but she wanted to be free of her chores in plenty of time to go meet him in town. She had her cell phone on the picnic bench beside her, hidden under her skirt but close enough to grab it if Mike called.

Ruthie pursed her lips together, focusing on cutting three berries quickly. "How's that?"

"You're thinking too hard," Sadie said, causing Ruthie to frown.

"That's right speedy, Ruthie," Rachel said encouragingly. "You just keep at it and you'll be quick as Sadie in no time." She shot Sadie a look. "Are you feeling okay?"

"Ya." Sadie sucked on a tooth as she continued trimming strawberries. "I didn't mean to snap, Ruthie."

After the fairy-tale weekend with Mike, the past few days on the farm had plodded along, hot and gritty, slow as molasses. At night she tossed and turned in the sticky summer air, and each morning she awoke as grumpy as the bullfrogs who had croaked through the night. It wasn't just that she missed Mike. Being back here on the farm, she saw very little chance to let her light shine. On Adam's orders she'd been ignoring Frank's phone messages. Her time with the band was over. She would have to start all over with her music, and that was near impossible trapped here on the farm.

"It's all right," Ruthie said. "You've been a thousand miles away since you got back from your weekend in the city." She looked over her shoulder to be sure no grown-ups were nearby. "Tell me again about Mike? About how he held your hand while you looked out over the lights of the city?"

Rachel's eyebrows shot up. "You told her these things? She's barely twelve."

"I'm old enough to understand."

"And it's nothing bad," Sadie said, defensively. "I just told her how we talked at night, on the rooftop." When the story spilled out the other night while they were restless in their beds, Sadie had meant to tell her younger sister just a few details. But once she had started, it felt so good to talk about Mike, and their time together, and the wonderful message from God to share her light with the world.

"Those are stories better left untold." Rachel sliced with a vengeance. "At least, out here, where people might hear us."

"But I love hearing the stories," Ruthie said. "Mike sounds like a wonderful good beau."

"An Englisher beau is no beau at all," Rachel said. "At least that's what everyone will tell you. I'm happy for the love in your heart, cousin. But this is going to be another thorn in your side. More trouble down the road for you."

"I know that, but it doesn't change what's in my heart," Sadie said. Of course, the ministers and Adam and even Aunt Betsy and Uncle Nate would be disappointed with her. But it didn't make her love Mike any less.

Love. Yes, she loved him, no matter how much trouble that was going to bring her.

Ruthie looked from Sadie to Rachel. "I think Sadie should be allowed to date Mike. It's not fair that she should have to turn him away just because he's Englisher."

"Not fair, but it's the law," Rachel said sternly. "And there's good reason. When a girl falls for a beau outside the community, he takes her away from her family and friends . . . from all she's ever known."

Sadie wanted to argue that it wasn't true, that she wasn't going anywhere, but she couldn't lie to Ruthie. She didn't want to leave her home, but she couldn't imagine a future without Mike. Where would that leave her?

Ruthie's eyes went round as saucers. "Is that true?" she asked Sadie. "Are you going to leave us and go . . ." She bit her lower lip as her paring knife clattered to the table. "You can't, Sadie. Mary's leaving us in the fall, and you can't go, too! What would we do without you?"

"Rachel is just telling you what's happened to other people," Sadie said. "Lovina Lapp? She married an Englisher fella and moved away, up north, I think. But Rachel's not talking about me." She glared at her cousin, hoping Rachel would calm down with her talk.

"We would miss you terribly. Your morning songs to wake us up. And who would do the cooking and manage the laundry?"

"Remy's learning to do all that," Sadie said. "And you can help. You and Susie and Leah. It's time all the girls get familiar with a woman's chores."

Ruthie stared down at her palms, her fingers dyed red from handling the berries. "And who would lead the birthday song? Leah and Susie are next; their birthday is coming up in August." Her eyes were wistful as she looked up at Sadie. "Oh, promise me you'll be here for the twins' birthday song!"

"Ya, of course."

"Promise me. My heart would break to see Susie and Leah disappointed on their birthdays."

"I promise," Sadie said, her throat gritty with heat and regret. She wished that Rachel hadn't churned up Ruthie's fears for no good reason. Sadie was Amish through and through, and if she was going to fly the coop, she'd had plenty of chances in the past few months with Frank and the band and now Mike.

"Okay, then." Ruthie topped another berry. "Now I'll be able to rest easy again. It's bad enough losing Mary. I can't lose another sister so soon!"

"You'll still see Mary all the time," Rachel pointed out. "She'll just be living down the road at the Beilers' place."

"That's just not the same."

The screen door creaked, and out came Remy and Aunt Betsy, their faces flushed from the heat of the kitchen.

"How's it going out here?" Remy asked, eyeing the mound of clean berries.

Aunt Betsy nearly tripped on the hose, and she told Susie to coil it up neatly. "We're almost ready to put up the second batch. Mary's just watching for the first batch to set up."

"I just can't wait for fresh strawberry jam." Ruthie's dimples appeared when she smiled. "I want to spread it on my toast in the morning. I wish I had some now."

"Good things come to those who wait," Betsy said, touching Ruthie lightly on the shoulder.

"How is the canning going?" Adam called from the path to the barn. "Mammi says she's been smelling sweet berries all morning from the Doddy house."

"Almost finished with the first batch," Remy said, her face warming with a smile when she saw Adam.

"It's been a very good year for strawberries, thank Gott," Aunt Betsy said.

The jangle of her cell phone startled Sadie as she cut through a berry. She dropped the knife and berry as she glanced up to see who else noticed.

And every single person faced her, staring.

Aunt Betsy's brows were raised in curiosity, while a scowl marked Adam's face.

Without wiping her hands, she grabbed her cell phone and winced. It was Frank. With a mixture of disappointment and annoyance, she turned it off and tucked it back under her skirt. She'd been hoping it was Mike, telling her he was coming in earlier. And now, she was in trouble again.

"Is that thing keeping you from your chores, Sadie?" asked Aunt Betsy.

Sadie swallowed, her dry throat straining. "I didn't mean for that to happen. I'm sorry."

"She's been topping berries, quick as the wind," Ruthie said cheerfully.

"Well, I hope so." Betsy pointed to a large pail of berries for Susie to fetch, then headed back into the kitchen.

Adam closed the space between them, standing across the table from Sadie. "It's not a good thing, that phone. I know you're in rumspringa, but it's a bad example you're setting for the little ones, carrying that thing around." He pointed a thumb to Ruthie. "And even the not-so-little ones."

Ruthie hung her head, hurt by Adam's suggestion that she'd been influenced in a negative way, and Sadie felt sickened by the whole situation. Really, did Adam have to make them all feel bad? Over a small little phone?

He held out his hand. "Give me the phone."

"Adam . . ." Sadie gasped. The cell phone was her only tie to Mike right now. She talked to him every day, and if she lost her phone . . . She just couldn't give it up.

"Give it to me." The metallic gleam in his dark eyes frightened her, and she quickly handed it over.

He flipped it open and pressed a few buttons. Of course, he would know how to use it. Adam had been away from the farm for three years during his rumspringa. During that time he must have had a cell phone of his own.

Watching him, she realized he was scrolling through either her text messages or her call list.

Rachel and Ruthie kept cutting berries, but their eyes were on Adam and Remy, who stood beside him. She kept silent, her lips tight with concern.

"Frank? He's the one who just called you." He winced, as if he'd just tasted something terribly sour. "That's who this is about? The bishop told you to end it with the band."

"I'm trying to, but he keeps calling." Despite the sick feeling in her belly, Sadie attempted to keep her voice calm. It wouldn't do to argue or be disrespectful to her older brother, especially in front of all these people. She had to keep peace in her heart.

"All the more reason to get rid of this phone."

"No, please," she begged. "I need the phone right now, Adam. Frank keeps calling me because I never got to finish things off with the band. I know you don't want me talking with them, but I have to let them know. They're relying on me, and it's wrong to just turn away from them. Remember the golden rule: Do to others as you would have them do to you. I wouldn't want a person to cut me off, just like that."

He frowned. "What will it take for you to end it with that band?"

"I need my cell phone back," she said. "And I would have to go into town, to talk to them in person. It's not just Frank. The others—Tara and Red—they're good people. They deserve an explanation."

"They are not your friends, and they need to know that. You need to cut them off, once and for all. Do you understand?"

She nodded.

He put the cell phone on the table, just inches from the red berry stains. "Do it today. And then, after that, we'll talk about you and the cell phone. Is that clear to you, Sadie?"

"Yes." Her pulse raced as she realized she'd answered with the Englisher word. Had he noticed?

She couldn't tell, because he turned and strode off, back to the barn.

"Back to work," Ruthie said in a singsong voice, trying to ease the heaviness in the humid air around them.

Topping berries, Sadie's mind was a million miles away. At least she would have no problem getting into town to see Mike now. But she would have to meet with Frank and the band, too. She had promised Adam, and if she had any hope of regaining his trust, she had to make good on her promise.

"Meet me at Red's place, soon as you can get there," Frank had said when she'd phoned him from her hiding spot beyond the pond. "I've got awesome news!"

As Sadie showered away the grime of her morning chores, she tried to think of how she would give her news to Frank and Red. Frank would argue with her, she knew that, but Red would be more accepting. With his wealth of music information and his talent for instruments and computers, Red had a quiet peace inside, and she hoped that her quitting wouldn't upset him. The thought of leaving the band now made her belly ache with worry.

Maybe the band would find another singer soon, she thought as she scrubbed hard at the berry stains on her hands. Maybe they already had. That was probably the awesome news Frank wanted to give her.

Her heart felt lighter as she pinned her dress in place and smoothed her hair back under her kapp. She would settle things with Frank and the band, and visit with Mike, too. Today would turn out to be a good day, after all.

As she got her scooter from the shed, she left word with Gabe that she would be going off to work at the hotel after her meeting with Frank, so she wouldn't be back for dinner. That way, she would have the evening free to spend with Mike.

The bishop's warning blared in her brain as she glided down the road to the outskirts of Halfway. Behind her, a horse and buggy turned onto the highway, and she felt their eyes upon her. The eyes of the whole community were upon her.

Such heresy, the bishop had said.

And all along, she'd only been trying to let God's light shine from within her, as the Bible said. How could something so pure and good be twisted into evil?

Relief sank in when she rolled past the last Amish farm and turned onto the city street where Red lived. The door to the garage was open, and rock music filled the air. Stepping into the cool shadows, Sadie saw Red at the computer, working on something. His job was on the computer, though she didn't understand what he did exactly. Frank paced in front of the sofa, playing along with the music on his electric guitar.

"Hello!" She shouted above the music.

Red raised a hand to wave, then scooted his chair away from his desk to turn down the volume. "Sadie . . ." He tilted his head and smiled. "Long time no see."

Frank turned and threw his arms open wide. "Sadie! Welcome back, church girl."

She smoothed the skirt of her dress down, not interested in a hug. "I'm not back to stay, Frank. I came to say good-bye."

"Aw, come on! You're not still upset about that flyer going around town."

"Not upset anymore." She had forgiven him, hard though that was. "But it did change everything. I told you, the ministers found out what I was doing. They've told me I have to end it with the band. I have to quit."

"Bummer." Red crossed his thin arms over his chest. "I'm sorry to hear that, Sadie."

"Wait! Wait, wait!" Frank was waving his arms. "Those ministers are going to change their minds when they hear about this. We've been offered a contract. A real contract. The backup band on the Night Shade tour just dropped out, and the tour producer wants us to step in for them. We'll be jumping in on the tail end of their East Coast tour. Six weeks paid, with a tour bus, food allowance . . ."

"A tour?" Sadie frowned. "I can't do that." Even if the ministers permitted it, she wasn't about to leave her home for six weeks. She would miss the entire summer with her family. A summer without her sisters and the little ones. Without Mammi and Remy and the bountiful fruits and vegetables from their garden. And Mike . . . she couldn't be away from him for six weeks. "No, I can't go on a tour."

"Of course you can." Frank pointed a thumb toward the door. "I've got your contract in my van outside. Red and Tara and I have already signed. We've been waiting on you." He unplugged his guitar and took a few steps toward the door. "Let me just get your contract. It helps to see it all laid out in black and white."

"No! Frank, wait," she called after him, but he was on his own track, heedless of her. Same old Frank. "Sometimes he doesn't even hear what I'm saying."

"He tunes everyone out." Red clicked on the computer mouse, then stood up. "But I'm warning you, he's going to put on the pressure for you to join the tour."

"I know that. But you three will have to do it without me."

"Well, that's the thing. . . . There is no band without you. The producer was pretty clear about that. He wants the four of us. Especially the Amish singer. His words, not mine."

"That's not fair," Sadie said, turning to Red. "Can a producer do that?"

Red frowned. "A producer can do anything he wants."

"They saw our video on YouTube and they liked the way we play together," Frank said, pausing at the door. "They want the whole package."

Sadie stood in the familiar garage, worry creeping over her. How could she stop this without crushing Frank's hopes?

"Here it is!" Frank handed her some papers that were stapled together. "Nothing too complicated. You just need to sign on the last page."

"I'm sorry, Frank." She let the papers drop to her side, her heart sinking. Although she didn't share Frank's dream, she didn't want to ruin the tour for them. "I can't go on a tour. The ministers have forbidden me to play with the band at all. I shouldn't even be here now, but I wanted to end things right and proper."

"What? You can't end things." Frank smacked his cheeks dramatically. "You're our lead singer!"

"Not anymore. I told you, the ministers forbid it."

"But they can't tell you how to live, can they? I mean, you don't need them. You won't need anyone if you sign on for this gig."

Sadie frowned. Frank didn't understand.

"Don't look at me that way, bonnet girl. This is for real. If we sign this contract, everything will be taken care of for six weeks. They'll pay for our food and we'll have a place to sleep and we'll get paid. This is a great gig, and it's all because of your awesome voice and your apple-cheeked innocence."

Sadie felt torn in half.

This was exactly what the bishop warned her about. She had gotten involved in worldly things, and now she was caught up with these Englishers. They were counting on her, and she had no choice but to let them down.

To live Amish, she needed to follow the Ordnung.

"I have to go." She shouldn't even be here now.

"But what about the contract?" Frank asked, dogging her as she went out the door.

She grabbed her scooter and handed him the papers. "I'm sorry."

"No, I won't take no for an answer." He refused to take the papers back from her, and she felt her face pucker with anger.

"Don't do this, Frank."

"Sadie, we need you—"

She yanked her scooter toward the driveway. As she passed Frank's van, she tossed the papers on its hood, then pushed off on her scooter.

"Think about it!" Frank called after her.

Heat waves shimmered over the road ahead of her as Sadie put her foot down to stop the scooter. She was far enough from Red's house that Frank wouldn't come after her, though she still wore a cloak of regret for letting the band down.

Their big break had finally arrived, and Sadie was going to mess everything up.

She pulled her scooter to the side of the road and carefully patted the folds of her skirt where she'd pinned her cell phone in. Where was Mike? Had she missed his call?

She was working pins out of her dress to fish out the phone when a cloud of dust came over the hill behind her. A white truck appeared on the road, but she ignored it, looking down at her phone.

A minute later, the rumbling grew closer—too close—and she shot a look behind her. The truck had pulled over.

It had been a while since Remy and Adam had been hounded by that dark car, but caution made her go stiff. No one was in sight on this country road. She had best be careful.

Caution was thick in her throat as she held tight to her cell phone and tried to see beyond the glare on the windshield.

"Sadie?" Mike jumped down from the truck, waving.

Her shoulders sank with relief. "You scared me! What are you doing driving a big truck like that?"

"It belongs to the bakery." He jogged toward her. "Remember? I told you I had to pick up whoopie pies for work."

In all the mayhem of the day, she had forgotten.

"Hey, you," he said, his smile full of light and joy.

Oh, he was a sight to see with his blue eyes and easy grace.

He reached down to hug her, and she closed her eyes and relaxed in his arms. A moment later, he was lifting her off her feet. Her scooter fell on its side, and they both ended up laughing.

"Well, that was a nice hello," she said when her feet were back on the ground.

"What can I say? I missed you."

It had only been four days, but she felt the same way. "I missed you, too." He held a hand up to shield his eyes. "It's crazy hot in this sun. Where do you want to go?"

She recalled the last time he had picked her up while she was scootering down this road. "How about some ice cream? We can head over to Stieger's Ice Cream Parlor."

"That's right, I owe you ice cream." He reached down to pick up her scooter. "This will fit in the truck. If you don't mind riding with some whoopie pies. Actually, they're not assembled yet. I was kind of disappointed."

"You know how they got their name?" She giggled. Her heart felt so light, being with him again. "When someone gives you one, you're so excited you say 'Whoopie!'"

TWENTY-SEVEN

*R*emy usually found the clip-clop of the horse's hooves on the pavement relaxing, but the morning drama between Sadie and Adam had unsettled her, and she could see that the man sitting beside her was still stewing over it as they rode into Halfway.

She turned to Adam. The lines of his face seemed to be hardened by the turmoil inside him. "Do you want to talk about it?"

He stared at the road ahead. "Not really."

"Is it all right if I talk about it?"

"I'd rather you didn't."

"Adam, you're in an impossible position. The ministers expect you to keep Sadie to the rules of the Ordnung, but at the same time you can't control her. It's not your fault that she got involved with the band. We all know how important music is in her life."

"I hate being the heavy," he said slowly. "That's what you call it, isn't it? The heavy. A downer. A bummer."

Remy laughed out loud. "You picked up a few phrases during your rumspringa?"

"Here and there." Under the brim of his hat, his face softened, the tension easing. "I don't like enforcing the law for Sadie, but it's my responsibility."

"I know." An outsider to the Amish, Remy had been seeing these difficult lessons play out in Sadie's situation. Poor Sadie was trying to listen to her heart and please everyone else too, but that was impossible. If Sadie was going to follow her dreams and explore the music she loved, she would not be allowed to join the Amish community.

"Do you think it will be different when we have children of our own?" Remy asked. "Will it be this hard to lay down the law to them?"

"Not at all," Adam said decisively. "Our children will obey their dat."

"And what if we get a wild one like Sadie?"

He groaned. "Don't even say that."

Remy laughed. She enjoyed Adam's wry sense of humor, and she was glad he had asked her to join him for errands in town. Living with Adam's aunt and uncle, she didn't get to see Adam as often as she liked.

Hands still holding the reins, Adam turned around to check traffic behind him. "Go on! Go on!" He waved for the car behind them to pass. "There's plenty of space. I don't know why he doesn't just pass us."

Remy turned around for a look. It was a dark sedan, much like the one that had followed them before. "That can't be the same car."

Adam shrugged. "He should just go around. Or maybe he just wants to complain to his friends about how he's always stuck behind an Amish buggy."

"Maybe."

Adam didn't seem too concerned, but once they reached Halfway she noticed that he zigzagged through the side streets. Still the car trailed behind them.

"He's still following us," Remy said.

"Then I think he is a very bad navigator," Adam said, a twinkle in his dark eyes.

When they turned in to the post office the car rolled past the parking lot, and Remy watched it move off with relief. She couldn't think why someone would want to bother Adam and her, although she had read stories of Englishers harassing Amish people to try to elicit violence.

Tossing off the concern, she climbed down from the buggy and grabbed the two boxes from the back. A customer from one of the markets had ordered custom-made quilts from the Kings, and at last they were completed, boxed, and ready to be mailed.

Their next stop was at the bank, where Adam insisted on taking the buggy to the drive-through window.

"You're kidding me," Remy said. "You're Amish. You're supposed to be patient. No rushing."

Adam worked the reins, prompting Thunder to stop at exactly the right spot. "I like the convenience."

"You're just full of surprises, Adam King."

He touched her knee, sending shivers of sensation through her. "Good. I want to keep you on your toes."

With his receipt in hand, Adam clucked and Thunder pulled forward.

"I wonder how it went when Sadie quit the band today," Adam said.

"That must have been hard for her. I'll bet she's upset about it."

Adam gestured toward the road ahead. "There's the Halfway Hotel, at the end of the block. Sadie's working her shift right now. Maybe we should stop by and cheer her up."

His idea tugged at Remy's heart. Although Adam had to follow the rules of the Ordnung, he wasn't afraid to show compassion to his family. "That's a wonderful good idea."

The young woman behind the desk of the Halfway Hotel had an expression that seemed to be permanently sour and a name tag that read: *Lorraine.*

"Hi." Remy put her palms on the high counter. "We're looking for an employee here . . . Sadie King?"

"Sadie?" The young woman squinted. "She hasn't worked here for a long time."

Remy blinked in surprise. "Are you sure we're talking about the same Sadie King?" With a small pool of surnames, it wasn't unusual to have two people in the same town who had the same name. "Ours is about this tall. Amber eyes and light brown hair?" A door behind the desk opened, and a tall, middle-aged man emerged. "Oh, and she likes to sing."

"Yeah, that's her."

"I don't believe it." Remy glanced up at Adam, who remained silent, though his eyes began to smolder with suspicion.

The man stepped up to the desk. "Is there a problem I can help with?"

"We're looking for my sister, Sadie King," Adam said in a flat voice. "We thought she would be working here tonight."

"No, not anymore. Lorraine is right. I had to let Sadie go a while back. In April, I think. Sometime before Easter. I haven't seen her since then."

Adam touched the brim of his straw hat. "Thank you for your time."

Her spirits sank as Remy followed Adam out the door. "What does this mean?" He was walking so briskly, she had to hurry to keep up with him.

"She's been lying to me. Lying to the whole family." Adam fairly leaped into the buggy.

She climbed in beside him and touched his arm, trying to still him for a moment. "So she's been lying. She said she was going to work, but went somewhere else instead. Probably to practice with her band. It's not the end of the world."

"Don't defend her, Remy. There's nothing good about a lie."

"Lying is a terrible thing, but she made a mistake. We're all human."

He shook his head. "No. There's no room for mistakes when you're breaking the rules. She disobeyed the Ordnung."

"What about forgiveness? Isn't that at the core of Amish life?"

"Not with this. The logic may seem twisted, but that's how it is with the Amish. You may not know all the rules yet, but Sadie does. She knows the rules and she broke them. I don't want to think what the ministers will do when they learn of this."

With a grunt to his horse, he shook the reins and the buggy rolled onto the road once again. Remy struggled to understand the contradictions, then decided to let it go. Sometimes it was best to let these things wash over you without picking at the details; she had learned that from many a discussion with Adam about living Amish.

When he turned the buggy onto Main Street, toward home, Remy noticed the clog of tourist traffic around the more popular attractions like the tea shop, the Amish gift shop, and the ice-cream parlor, where more outdoor tables had been added to accommodate the summer crowds.

As Thunder trotted along, the patrons outside the ice-cream shop caught Remy's attention. There were a few groups of Amish, some younger boys on their scooters. But her gaze stuck on one Amish girl in a dark green dress. She sat at a picnic table, laughing as she licked the sides of an ice-cream cone.

Remy's pulse quickened when she recognized Sadie.

"There she is," she said.

"What?" Adam's head turned toward the ice-cream parlor, where a line snaked through the parking lot. Quite a crowd, but even with all the tourists, it wasn't hard to pick out their Sadie, sitting in the late afternoon sunshine and flirting with Mike Trueherz.

"What on earth?" Adam slowed the horse and directed it into the busy parking lot. His fury was palpable, and though Remy knew he would never resort to violence, she worried that this could blow up into something they would all regret.

But there was no stopping Adam from jumping out of the buggy, no slowing down the perpetual motion of events unfolding so quickly.

Adam stormed over to the tables.

And Sadie looked up from her ice-cream cone, a laugh cut off as she spotted her older brother. All joy drained from her face at the sight of him.

And Mike rose to his feet, as if to protect Sadie.

Adam paused a few feet from Sadie, and when he spoke his voice was so low Remy had to step closer to hear. "Get in the buggy."

Sadie blinked. "What's wrong?" She rose, looking to Mike in concern, then over at the buggy. "Has something happened?"

"Get in the buggy. Now."

She held up her cone, which had begun to drip down one side. "I was just having ice cream with Mike. I already talked to Frank, and I'm finished with the band, so—"

"Finished with your job at the hotel, too," Adam said quietly. "You've been lying to us all along, Sadie. So many lies, I don't know if you have any true words left in you."

"The hotel . . ." Sadie looked wounded as she pressed a hand to her chest. "I'm sorry, but I can explain—"

"Enough. Just get in the buggy now." Adam turned to face Mike. He locked eyes with the young man, the dark bitterness in

Adam's expression a warning. Then he turned and strode back to the open carriage.

Sadie dropped her cone into the trash and pressed a fist to her forehead. "My scooter . . . it's in the bakery truck. . . ."

"I'll get it," Mike said.

In the tense silence, Remy felt the curious stares of customers waiting in line for ice cream. Did Adam seem cruel to them? She knew he was only doing what the patriarch of an Amish family had to do.

Sadie turned a pleading face to Remy. "What can I do?" she whispered desperately.

"Just . . . come. We have to go." Remy motioned her toward the buggy.

Sadie bit her lips together, trying to hold back emotion as she reached for the scooter. Mike squeezed her hand, and despite the absence of words, Remy saw the message that passed between them.

A message of love.

Sniffing back tears, Sadie straightened. Then with quivering dignity, she walked to the buggy.

TWENTY-EIGHT

*T*he ride home was miserable.

Slung low in the backseat of the small buggy, Sadie struggled to breathe with all the fear, guilt, and anger pressing down upon her. The weight of all those bad feelings threatened to crush her, and she had to force herself to take small, shaky breaths, one after the other.

Shame washed over her as she thought about facing Adam once they arrived at home. He would certainly be giving her a scolding now, if she could have heard him in the backseat of the open carriage.

Adam thought she was a liar.

That cut her to the quick, but there was some truth there. She had hidden getting fired from the hotel. So every time she left the farm, pretending to go to work, she'd been living a lie.

But that was her only sin, wasn't it? It wasn't a sin against God to use her voice. To sing with the band. To make friends outside the Amish community.

To fall in love with an Englisher.

She covered her eyes with her hands, feeling so sorry that Adam had found her with Mike. Now Adam thought Mike was just another part of the worldly things Sadie had become involved with. Adam would surely add Mike to the list of things that would be forbidden.

Once they arrived at the farm Adam wasted no time in getting to the heart of the matter. He handed Remy the reins and turned around so that he was facing Sadie, one knee on the seat.

"You've pushed too far this time, Sadie." His face wasn't so red anymore, but his anger hadn't faded. "The bishop and Preacher Dave scolded you once, and yet I find you lying to your family and going off to meet an Englisher."

"Please, don't bring Mike into it. It's not his fault."

He tipped his hat back to wipe his brow. "He's not to be your friend now. The son of the doctor is still an *Aussenseiter,* an outsider. It's time you learn to stick with your own."

Stick with her own? *And how about the woman sitting right beside you?* Sadie wanted to ask. Remy had been an Englisher. Sadie loved her, and she was joining the *Gemeinde.* But it angered Sadie that he could say such a thing. How could he condemn outsiders when he himself was going to marry one?

He held his hand out, palm up. "Give me your phone."

The whoosh of her own heartbeat filled her ears as she handed it over. This couldn't be happening.

"Is that my punishment?" she asked.

"I'm not sure yet." He closed his fist tightly over the silver phone. "I might have to tell Bishop Samuel about this. Until I decide, you are not to leave the farm, except for church and the singing on Sunday. And you will go to the singing. I know you like the music, and it's time you started spending time with young people from the community." He frowned, adding, "You wouldn't be having these problems if you were courting an Amish boy."

"This isn't about courtship," Sadie said, trying to keep the raging heat out of her voice. "I'm looking for something that I can't find here, Adam."

I need to let my light shine.

I have to find a way to share my gift.

She wanted to explain that she was trying to do good things, all for the glory of God, but the hard set of his jaw told her not to speak now.

"If you can't find it here, you're looking for the wrong thing," Adam said, eyeing her sternly. "For tonight, you are to take your supper separate from the family."

She stared at him, her fury mounting. He was treating her like someone who'd been shunned by the community!

Remy climbed out of the buggy, but Sadie remained in the back, arms crossed, as Adam jumped down and started unhitching the horse.

Ooh, she had half a mind to grab the reins and hightail it out of here, running Thunder at full speed until he worked up a good lather. If Adam was going to treat her like a person under the ban, she figured she might as well do something worthy of such punishment.

The reins were wrapped around the stub, tempting her, but she took a deep breath and climbed to the ground. It was best not to act in anger. Mamm had always said that cooler heads prevailed. She needed to think this out once the fire in her belly stopped roaring. Though right now, she was sure the embers would burn for a long time to come.

Although Sadie was banned from the dinner table she wasn't off the hook with chores, and she set to work chopping vegetables, scouring the big pots that had been used to cook up the strawberry jam, and weeding the garden. Work usually helped clear her mind and ease her heart, but not today. Her burdens pressed down on her, like dark clouds gathering overhead.

Tears stung her eyes. She was not even worthy to sit at the family table tonight. At least, that was what Adam thought of her, making her take her supper separate from the family, like a person under the ban.

How had this happened? She had been trying to follow her heart, trying to follow God's word, but Adam and the ministers were sure she was going down a dark path.

And now she was an outcast in her own home.

Squatting in the garden, she struggled with a stubborn weed. When it wouldn't give, she took a spade and stabbed at the soil, stabbed over and over again. Though the stem went slack, the roots clung to the dirt.

The dark centers of two bachelor button flowers burned dark, reminding her of Adam's eyes. How he'd glared at her when he found her with Mike! Her older brother would never trust her again, and that was partly her fault. Oh . . . the lie about her job at the hotel had gotten out of hand. That's what lies did; they grew deep roots like that weed. Roots that burrowed deep and twisted around the healthy plants in the garden.

Her lie had begun to choke the goodness in her life, like a weed.

"Sadie?" The voice penetrated her frenzy. She looked up to Ruthie's curious face.

"I didn't think that was you. It's so quiet in here. Why aren't you singing?"

Sadie didn't have a song left in her right now. "I don't know."

"Are you sick?" Ruthie asked. "Mary told me not to set a place for you at the table."

So Adam had told Mary. Sadie swiped a sleeve across her damp cheek.

"Truth is, I'm not feeling well at all."

"Then you'd better get out of the garden." Ruthie came over and tugged on her arm. "This can all wait till tomorrow." She spoke with gentle authority, reminding Sadie of their mamm.

Sadie stood up. "You're right. I need to go inside."

And hide.

"Take a little rest and you'll feel better," Ruthie said.

Sadie nodded, but before she turned away she noticed that stubborn weed still holding on to the earth, just as misery was clutching her life.

Passing through the kitchen, she kept silent, her head down.

"I've set aside a plate for you," Mary called after her. "Do you want to eat now?"

"Denki, but I'm not really hungry," Sadie said. "I'm going upstairs for a bit."

The afternoon heat still lingered in the quiet of the girls' bedroom. Sadie turned in a circle at the center of the room, wanting to store it in her memory. The deep pink of the walls. The crisp white curtains she had washed herself last laundry day. The six little beds, lined up three on a wall . . . this room had seen her through sweet dreams and nightmares, sadness and warm comfort on winter nights. So cozy with her sisters. "Like peas in a pod," Mamm used to say.

She stumbled to her own bed and fell to her knees. "Oh, dear God, how can I do this? I can't stay here. If I share the music in my heart, I'll be an outsider in my own family." She pressed her face into the familiar bedding and sobbed into the quilt.

Minutes passed, and fresh tears welled in her eyes, but after a time she quieted to listen in on the voices from downstairs in the kitchen. Supper was on the table, and though she couldn't make out their words, the hum of conversation stirred and combined until it rose up to her like a family song.

The low rumble of Jonah's voice . . .

The higher pitch of Simon telling a story.

Mary's steady tone, always reminding.

And Ruthie's chirping lilt, so positive, like a song that ended on a high note.

"I love you all," she whispered, sniffing. "But I can't stay here."

If she stayed here and tried to share the light inside her, she would be forever scorned.

No, she had to go, though it hurt her so.

She dried her tears and reached under the mattress of her bed. The roll of dollars was there—money she had earned working at the hotel. It would have to be enough for now. With the voices of her family tugging at her heart, she started collecting her things on the bed. Her underthings, toothbrush, tweezers, jeans, and the two extra T-shirts she owned. Carefully she folded the dress from Remy and the fancy black shoes. The red book of poems from Katherine. She gathered them into a sheet and stashed them under her bed, far back so that no one would see.

The letter was more difficult than packing her things. Her bottom lip curled in a pucker when she thought of Ruthie and Simon. She would miss them so.

She tucked the letter under her makeshift satchel and lay upon her bed one last time.

She awoke before dawn and dressed quickly. None of the other girls stirred as she made her bed and placed the note on the quilt. Pressing a fist to her mouth, she let her eyes skim over their sleeping forms. Her good sisters. She didn't want to think of how much she'd miss them as she crept out of the house.

The sky was the rich sapphire of coming dawn. The shed door

squeaked as she opened it, but she didn't think anyone would notice with the constant mewing of cows and the grumping of the bullfrogs by the pond. She wheeled her scooter out and nearly knocked into Simon.

"Simon, what are you doing up?" she asked. He had suffered bouts of sleepwalking and night terrors, but it had been a while since he'd roamed the house in one of those spells.

"It's too hot upstairs, and I wasn't tired anymore." He looked down at the scooter. "Where are you going?"

She had already hung her makeshift satchel on the handlebars, though that didn't seem to concern him.

"I need to go into town," she said.

He scratched his head. "Okay."

She stepped onto the scooter, then paused to reach out and hug him.

He hugged her back. "What's that for?"

"Nothing at all. Bye, Simon."

"See you."

Holding her breath, she stepped on the scooter and rolled down the lane. *Heading toward freedom . . . scary freedom,* she thought, her eyes on the rosy glow of light rising beyond the horizon.

As she scootered down the road, she made some plans. After the cemetery, she would ride her scooter to Halfway and find a way to call Frank. One of the Englisher shopkeepers like Nancy Briggs would let her use their phone for a short call. He would be happy to hear her news about the tour. It would be a chance for everyone in the band to be heard on the East Coast—a fitting way to end the summer after all the good music they had made together.

She thought of herself on tour. She didn't favor the same music as Frank, but maybe . . . if she could talk the others into adding more hymns, this tour might be the right place for her to be.

Could that be?

Could the path of so many tears and much sorrow be the way the Heavenly Father wanted her to choose? She didn't know the answer to that. These days she had more questions than answers.

And she would ask Frank for his help getting another cell phone. She had enough money, and she was counting on her daily talks with Mike to get her through this tour.

Her heart ached at the thought of not seeing him for weeks, but she knew he would understand. Mike got her, more than anyone else. He understood about the thing burning inside her, the need to share her light with the world.

The corner of the cemetery caught the early morning sunlight, the grass warm but still damp with dew. This time Sadie had garden tools, but there was no need. The grass had taken root and small green sprigs soaked up the warming sun.

Ruthie would be happy to hear that the neighborhood critters had moved on to make a home elsewhere.

Sadie stood before the graves, suddenly feeling foolish.

Why had she come?

Because she wanted to say good-bye?

No. Mamm and Dat were in heaven above; she knew that. These graves held just the dust of their earthly bodies.

Still, something had tugged her here, like a calf pulled by a rope.

She sat on the grass, cradling the slender red book of poetry Katherine had loaned her. It was comforting to touch the smooth leather of its cover.

"I'm going away for a while," she said aloud. Emotion was a knot in her throat. "Maybe forever."

She didn't blame Adam, but it angered her, the way those men of God placed such a burden on her. They would not be satisfied until she chose baptism.

She opened the poetry book and smoothed back the pages. "This is a poem about a girl who misses something wonderful because she is an hour too late," she said. At least, that was what she thought Emily Dickinson had been writing about. "It's called 'Almost.'" It made her think about the things that God put within everyone's reach, though people missed them. She didn't want to miss something important just because she was too meek or afraid to break a rule.

There was a poem by Robert Frost in the book, which she knew her dat would have liked. "A Minor Bird," it was called. She found it in the book and read it aloud. In the poem, the writer kept shooing a bird away, annoyed by its song. At the end, the man knew he was the one to blame for trying to stop a song.

"'And of course there must be something wrong,'" she read, "'in wanting to silence any song.'"

Her voice would not be silenced. Something about that seemed right; but her choice had been a painful one.

Don't cry for the things you've lost, she told herself. *Think of the good. Good things will come from sharing God's light.*

Oh, how she hoped that was true.

TWENTY-NINE

As Remy rode on a scooter borrowed from Adam's cousin Rachel, she was grateful for the cool summer morning, a festival of green on the roadside. She passed fields where half-grown hay and corn reached up to heaven, and the birdsong was so active, it reminded her of a tropical jungle.

She was glad for her plans to take Leah, Susie, and Ruthie to the market today. Selling quilts and cheese at the market always entailed a social day of conversation with tourists and locals. It would also give her a chance to see Adam this morning and find out how things had settled between Sadie and him.

Mary stood at the kitchen stove, frying bacon. "Good morning! You're here bright and early."

"I always enjoy a day at the market," Remy said, helping herself to the pot of coffee on the stove. "Where are the girls?"

"Still up in bed. Sleepyheads." Mary pulled two strips of bacon from the pan to the platter. "I think everyone had trouble getting to sleep last night."

"Too hot?" Remy asked.

"That, and worries for Sadie. That's how it is in a family. When one person is hurting, everyone feels it."

Sipping her coffee, Remy considered what a lovely gift that was—a family so close that the members empathized with one another. That hadn't been the case in her family with her father, Herb, and her stepmother. And to think she'd been blessed to be invited into this family. The thought gave her goose bumps.

The sound of footsteps popping quickly down the stairs turned her attention to the wide doorway, where Ruthie appeared looking disheveled. She was still wearing her nightgown and her hair was in a braid that hung down the center of her back.

"Good morning, morning glory," Remy teased. "You'd better go back upstairs and get dressed. We're going to have to head off to the market right after breakfast."

"Something terrible has happened!" Ruthie held a small piece of paper up. "I found this note on Sadie's bed."

Her heart sinking, Remy scanned the note.

"And where is Sadie?" Mary asked, slicing a loaf of cinnamon bread.

"She's gone," Remy said. "She wrote that she had to leave."

"What on earth . . . ?" Mary stopped slicing.

"She's run away!" Ruthie's voice cracked with emotion. "Her bed is made, and her fancy clothes are gone. I checked."

"She must have left during the night." Mary frowned, leaning close to Remy to read the note herself. "Probably took her scooter."

"Sadie's gone!" Ruthie pressed her hands to her face as her eyes grew shiny with tears. "We have to go after her. Tell her to come back."

"No, liewe." Mary put her knife down on the cutting board and folded Ruthie into her arms. "No, darling girl. Sadie's eighteen now.

An adult. I want her back as much as you, but we can't force her to stay here."

Remy looked back at the note.

Don't worry about me, because I'm going to a job with pay and a place to stay and food, too. The band is going on tour, and I'll be their singer. I feel ashamed for being fired from my job at the hotel, and I hope this makes up for me not being responsible there.

"She's got a job with the band," Remy said.

"I know she loves to sing," Ruthie lamented, "but I don't think she wanted to go. She was sick with sadness last night."

"Our Sadie always was the bold one," Mary said. "But this is a worry. There'll be real trouble when the bishop hears of it."

Remy looked up. "What kind of trouble?"

Mary shook her head, her face pinched with worry. "Sadie was already warned. If she wants to come back to us and become a baptized member, she'll have to go before the church leaders. They may demand a public confession of her wrongdoings."

Ruthie closed her eyes and sighed. "That would be too much shame for our Sadie to bear."

"No use worrying over it now." Mary put a hand on her younger sister's shoulder. "With the way Sadie's been acting, there's a strong chance she won't be choosing to live Plain."

Tears glistened in Ruthie's eyes, and she swiped them away with one fist.

The heartbreak of losing Sadie was too much to bear, Remy thought as she looked back at the letter, missing Sadie already.

"She says she'll be back in August." Remy turned to Ruthie. "Something about a promise to you?"

Ruthie nodded. "August eighth; it's Susie and Leah's birthday, and Sadie promised me she would be here to lead the birthday clapping song."

"It's a family tradition," Mary said.

"I was here for Sadie's birthday, though I think she had to wake up and help us out with the singing." Remy remembered everyone filing into the girls' room to wake Sadie on the morning of her birthday. She had been touched to see the family gathered round, sleepy but giddy.

"At least we know she's coming back." Ruthie stepped out of Mary's arms, her amber eyes glistening with tears. "That's the silver lining in the cloud."

"It is." Remy touched her shoulder. "Whenever we miss her, we'll remember that she'll be back soon."

Ruthie sniffed. "I'm going up to tell Leah and Susie." She turned and hurried up the stairs.

"And tell them to get ready for the market," Mary called after her. She turned to Remy. "Breakfast is about done. And Adam needs to see that letter. Would you take it to him?"

Remy nodded. "Do you know where he is?"

"In the Doddy house garden with the little ones. They set out to find some ripe tomatoes for breakfast."

Remy stepped out into the sunshine. The weather was promising—sunny and not too humid—but her focus was on the letter that tugged at her heart.

I love you all very much, but I can't stay here. I feel like I'm torn in two, but I have to listen to God, and the voice in my heart tells me to go.

Go with God's blessing, Remy thought, and she realized that was very un-Amish of her. In this faith, anything that led a person away from the community was considered to be wrong. But Remy understood Sadie's quest.

In Sadie's current frame of mind, she was better off away from home, exploring and questioning. Remy had learned a lot from the bishop's classes. The four principles of Amish life—the four *S*'s, she called them: surrender, submission, separation, and simplicity in day-to-day life. It was clear that Sadie was not ready to surrender and submit to the Amish way of life.

For herself, Remy still had a few qualms, though they had eased as she grew more and more accustomed to life here in Lancaster County. When she'd first approached the bishop back in March, he had told her she would have to wait until the fall for baptism, and that time had proven helpful. At first it went against her social conscience to agree to be obedient and submissive to someone else, but in everyday life she had come to see how the social order and the Ordnung were necessary to keep Amish society functional.

And her day-to-day life was chock-full of love, work, and satisfaction. Never one to shy away from work, Remy enjoyed her full days of chores at Nate and Betsy's farm, as well as helping out here. A former city girl in the country, she had a lot to learn. It was a whole new world when the milk on your table didn't come from a carton in the fridge. But whether she was cooking or cleaning or tending to one of the little ones, she felt alive here. Alive and at home.

Ironic that she and Sadie were traveling on such very different paths. And early this morning, Sadie had set off on a journey in the opposite direction, away from home, from farm to city. *Dear God, please keep her safe out there,* she prayed. Sadie was spirited, but kind and genuine. Remy hoped she would find what she was looking for.

As she came upon the Doddy house garden, Katie's chipmunk voice floated about the rows of green. "That one is red! Red, red!" she said, speaking in the unique dialect Remy was learning to understand.

"Who has red tomatoes?" Remy called as she passed through the garden gate.

Katie was pointing to a plant, and her brother Samuel was reaching in to pluck the tomato. Beside them sat a bushel basket half full of shiny red orbs.

"I found the red one!" Katie hurried over and attached herself to Remy, hugging her leg.

"Katie has an eye for a good tomato," Adam said from the rear of the garden, where he held a watering can.

"Good job, Katie." She bent down and hugged the little girl to her, and was rewarded by a smile.

"Tomatoes bad. They taste like dirt," the little girl said, scrunching her face.

Remy smiled. "Then maybe I'll gobble yours all up." She made some chewing noises and tickled Katie's belly.

Katie laughed and touched Remy's cheek. "Tomato on your face," she said.

"And you are a funny bunny," Remy replied, straightening to find Adam again. "But I came to talk to brother Adam. Sam, can you and Katie take this basket back to the house? Mary wants to serve them for breakfast."

"We can do that." Sam picked up the basket and headed toward the gate. "Kumm, Katie."

Watching them go, a five-year-old leading his two-year-old sister, Remy felt a pang of love for them, the children she would be raising with Adam. Her new family.

"Did you have a craving for tomatoes?" Adam asked. He took his straw hat off as he moved close to steal a quick kiss. "Or were you just trying to chase me down?"

"I was most certainly chasing you down." She looked over at him, soaking up the angles of his jaw, the smoky darkness of his eyes and brow. He'd been a hard person to win over, but somehow she'd found the way to his heart and never looked back. "I have some bad news. Sadie is gone."

His dark brows strained. "I've been thinking that might happen."

And I'm ever so sorry for lying to you, Adam. . . .

When Adam read the note, he winced.

"This is what I was afraid of." He frowned, reading over the letter again as if it contained clues. "I didn't want to drive her away, but I couldn't abide the way she was acting. Breaking rules, right and left."

"I know that."

He folded the letter, his dark eyes full of rue. "I'll need to tell the little ones. The truth is the best, but a gentle truth for them."

She nodded. "But there's a hopeful side. Sadie says she's coming back in August," Remy pointed out. "Apparently she made a promise to be here for Leah and Susie's birthday."

Adam shook his head. "I wouldn't count on it. Sadie's proven herself to be mighty unreliable these last few months. And if she's got the will to leave this way, she's probably lost to the community."

"That sounds so final."

"But it's what happens. I've seen young people leave the community before. It's hard to let go, but there's no stopping them."

Remy touched the bud of a straining plant. Tight and small, not yet ready to unfurl. "But she'll always be your sister," she said. "You can't stop caring about her."

"I'll never stop caring, but I can't worry about things that only Gott has power over." He put an arm around her. "Kumm. Let's get breakfast."

As they walked up the lane, Remy thought of how much Sadie had changed in the months since she'd met her. "I'm afraid I nurtured Sadie's desire to leave," she said. Sadie had been so wide-eyed at Remy's apartment, and Remy was the one who had given her the tweezers. Remy had given Sadie a taste of what it was like to be fancy.

Adam pulled her close as they walked side by side. "It's not your fault. Sadie was on this path before any of us met you." He released her as they drew within sight of the farmhouse. "If it's Gott's will, she'll come back to us."

He was right. Change was all around them, in the seasons, in nature, in people's hearts. The peach trees, now thick with leaves, had been covered with vivid pink blossoms only a month ago. *To everything, there is a season. . . .*

PART THREE

So Far Away

"Ye are the light of the world. A city that is set on a hill cannot be hid.
Neither do men light a candle, and put it under a bushel, but on a candlestick;
and it giveth light unto all that are in the house.
Let your light so shine before men, that they may see your good works,
and glorify your Father which is in heaven."

—MATTHEW 5:14–16

THIRTY

In the first week on tour, Sadie quickly learned that freedom had its price.

With her new cell phone using the same old number, she was able to call Mike most any time of day. She loved hearing about funny things that happened at the bakery or about Gran's progress with walking. Once he even had his friends from the choir sing her a song over the phone. They spent many wonderful hours talking, but sometimes she looked at her little silver phone and thought that she didn't like it so much. It was the closest she could get to Mike, and that was very annoying.

She missed her family too, and she hated sitting around on the tour bus. Being on tour wasn't much freedom at all, when you considered that you had to spend most of your time either traveling or sleeping on a bus. It could be cozy, but sometimes, when Mac, the driver, was waving them onto the bus after a show, she felt like one of the cows being prodded into the milking barn.

She missed the rhythm of the days on the farm, from waking up to the old rooster's crowing, to shooing off pesky Lumpig, to breakfast around the big table in the kitchen, to mucking and sweeping and mopping the milking stalls. All those chores that kept her hands busy also gave her a simple feeling of satisfaction.

She missed the Plain life with forthright people who say what they mean. Tara was sulky. Red was kind but awfully quiet. He could go for an hour without speaking a word, much like her brother Jonah. He shared new songs with her and he knew the history of any song you could imagine, but Sadie didn't want to talk about music all the time.

At the end of the first week, she sat on the dark bus feeling very alone. One week on tour, and even with all the people around, loneliness made her ache inside.

The last two shows had been in Massachusetts at clubs with big stages and lights strong as the sun. As dots of light raced past the window, Sadie sat in one of the seats behind the driver and pressed her fingers into chords on the Wurlitzer, Red's portable electric piano, which he'd brought along. Inspired by the book from Katherine, she had written a poem that she was trying to turn into a song. Singing softly, she tried it with a new melody.

Light inside, burning bright,
Like a lantern in the night.
Find its flame,
Follow it home,
And your heart no more will roam.

She practiced a triad on the Wurlitzer, but she didn't have it quite right yet. The first day on the bus, Sadie had told Red about her exciting piano lesson from Katherine, and he had told her she was welcome to use the small piano anytime.

"I'm not really a keyboard man," he'd said, "but I can show you some of the basics."

Since then, she had spent countless hours trying to teach herself how to re-create songs she loved on the organ. Red had told her that was the Suzuki method of learning, to imitate sound and music on an instrument.

The word "Suzuki" reminded Sadie of her sister Susie, whom she worried about, with her metabolic condition. How she missed Susie and Ruthie and Leah. Even Mary, who could be bossy, and Adam, who had been so disappointed with her in the last few weeks—even those two would bring joy to her heart if she could see them right now.

Adam had left her a message on her phone, which she had saved. She played it over again when she wanted to feel like a tree with roots in solid ground.

"I just want to know that you're safe. Are you okay there? Give us a call, Sadie girl."

He'd called her Sadie girl, Dat's nickname for her.

When she called back, no one had answered the phone in the shanty. That had left her disappointed, but what did she expect? Folks didn't usually sit in the small shanty just waiting for a call.

Not wanting to leave a message that the neighbors might hear, she had called Nancy Briggs and asked her to talk to Adam. "Tell him I'm good," she had said.

"Safe and sound?" Nancy had asked.

"Yes, I'm safe." Suddenly she wanted to tell Adam about the neat little bunk she slept in, and how the bus had a toilet room that was also a shower room when you wanted it. She wanted to tell him she was still a good girl, even if she wasn't taking classes with the bishop, as Remy was. She wanted to say that she was trying to find a way to share her light, and she felt like she was on the right road, even if it did have a few bumps.

"Well, you take good care of yourself," Nancy had told her. "Any other message you want me to pass on?"

So many messages . . . but Sadie hadn't been able to put them into so few words. She had simply said, "Just tell my family I miss everyone so very much!" The rest of her news had gone into one of her many letters home.

She tried a few new chords for her song. "Light inside, burning bright—"

"Sadie?" Red appeared above the seat back. His hair was rumpled and he wore one of his usual Penn State shirts, this time with shorts. "I'm glad that you're enjoying the Wurlitzer."

"Yes, it keeps my fingers and my mind busy. I'm writing a song. Do you want to hear it?"

"I've been hearing it for the past hour." He hooked a thumb toward the back of the bus, where beds were built in to the wall in little stalls with curtains over them. "The thing is, I'm sort of trying to sleep, and since you can't turn the volume down on that thing, it's keeping me up."

"Oh, Red, I'm sorry!" She reached for the switch and turned the electric piano off. "I'll be quiet now. I didn't think you could hear everything way back there."

"Thanks," he said.

"Thank you for telling me the truth." She had learned that Englishers didn't always say what they meant; there was a lot of beating around the bush.

"Any major dude with half a heart surely would tell you, my friend," Red said. "That's from a song."

She nodded. "What's a dude?"

He yawned. "I'll explain it in the morning." And he disappeared in the dim, narrow hallway of the bus.

At a small outdoor festival somewhere in Delaware, Sadie imagined herself floating above the stage as she sang. Although she held a microphone and stood in the spotlight, it seemed that it was some- one else's voice that flowed through her, singing of God's amazing grace.

This was the light of God shining through her. The power of the Almighty.

When the song ended and the audience roared with applause, she wanted to cry with joy. God had brought her here for this. On a damp, rainy night in June, God's love had rained down on them all, stirring their hearts.

She wanted to hold on to the moment, but Frank started an- other song—a slow blues tune—and sadly it was over.

After the performance, the lead singer from Night Shade came over to their bus and shook hands with everyone in the band.

"You got some awesome stuff in your set." Duff was a big man with bushy dark hair that tumbled down past his shoulders. "That version of 'Amazing Grace' rocked the house, man. You should do some more hymns like that."

"Yes," Sadie said, unable to contain her smile. "I think that's a very good idea."

"Maybe," Frank said, closing in on Duff for more of a chat.

Sadie moved past them, to the side of the bus where their driver, Mac, had set up a little awning with chairs.

Red sat there, working on his laptop. "Pull up a lawn chair."

With two more shows here, they didn't have to hit the road tonight. "I feel too restless to sit." Sadie looked back toward Duff. "Do you think Frank will consider adding some more hymns to the set list?"

"He might be persuaded to try another," Red said casually.

"'Be Thou My Vision'?" she suggested.

"That would be my choice." He glanced over toward the door,

where Frank slung an arm around Heather. Frank's cousin and her friend had shown up earlier that day.

Seeing Frank with the other girl now, Sadie realized how wrong he had been for her. A very bad match. He was nothing like Mike.

"Frank's a little preoccupied now," Red said, "but when he has a free moment, we'll propose another hymn. I'll support you on that."

She thanked him and sat down in a folding chair. "Too much sitting around. My hands want to work."

"Hence the late-night session on the Wurlitzer."

"I'm sorry about that."

"No worries. There is a lot of sitting around on tour. Too much nervous energy. What do you do at home when you want to relax?"

She touched her chin. "There's not a lot of relaxing time to be had. Sometimes at night we'll play games or work a puzzle. But through the day, our hands are always busy. Out in the fields or in the kitchen. There's cleaning and quilting and milking to be done."

Red looked up from his computer. "Wow. You are the real deal."

"Real Amish? Ya." But even as she said the words, she felt the change inside her. Like a pebble rolling under a shoe, her spirit had shifted and she didn't feel Amish through and through. The Englisher lifestyle that allowed her voice to flow suited her in many ways. If only there were more tasks to fill the hours.

"I wish we had more shows to do. The empty time, it makes me nervous." Sadie thought of her brothers and sisters back home. What were they doing now?

Hmph. At eleven o'clock, they were surely asleep in bed, tucked in under their quilts.

That gave her an idea.

"Do you know where I could buy threads?" she asked Red.

"You mean, like clothes?"

"No. I mean the threads used to sew clothes. And fabric and needles."

"You need to sew something?"

"A quilt. At least I can sew the pieces. It's work that I can do anytime."

"I'll bet we can find a store in town. Maybe a Walmart."

"Walmart?" Sadie smiled. She had been shopping in the big store outside Lancaster only once. Mamm had told her to try on school shoes, but Sadie could have spent hours going through the store with its racks of clothes and bins of chips and even pots of garden plants. "They have threads?"

"If you got cash, they have everything."

"I have my first paycheck." She wasn't quite sure how to turn it into cash. Mr. Decker had always paid her in cash, and she had never done the family banking.

"We'll find a place to cash that, too. If you want, tomorrow morning we'll head into town."

With a pocketful of twenty-dollar bills, Sadie felt a trill of excitement as she stepped into the big store. A woman standing there told her hello, and then Sadie went from one display to another, amazed at all the things she could afford to buy for the first time in her life.

A bin of footballs reminded her of her brothers. They always joked that Jonah had a hook arm because he could hook the ball back and throw it farther than anyone.

A box of drinking glasses would have served the family well. Sixteen for eight dollars, a very good price.

And then she stopped short in front of a rack of men's shirts made of fabric the color of a summer sky . . . the color of Mike's eyes.

Oh, how she would love to buy these wonderful things and share them with the people she loved!

But no one was here to enjoy these things with her.

Loneliness nagged at her again, and she reminded herself of the reason she had come here. She needed quilting supplies.

She found quilting threads in all the colors of the rainbow, as well as scissors and some brightly colored fabric remainders. She rolled past the clothing section and paused. The inexpensive T-shirts would be good for the summer tour, and the shorts were a good price, too. On the way to the registers, she came upon the food section and her mouth watered at the sight of fresh carrots, cheese, and milk. She added some items to her cart, planning a meal. She had been eyeing the bus's small kitchen all week, wondering why everyone ate doughnuts and pizza and burgers all the time when there was a perfectly good place to cook.

Back at the bus, Sadie set to work in the little kitchen area. There was no oven for baking, but there was a stovetop with some pans. Soon the aromas of bacon, eggs, and fresh coffee wafted through the bus, drawing Tara and Frank from their bunks. They sat around the little table with cushioned benches, the four musicians and their driver, and feasted on a fine breakfast.

"Mac asked me to marry him," Sadie told Mike later as they talked on the phone. Sadie had started working on her quilt. She had already cut the fabric into patches, and she was starting her stitching. "But he was just joking. He said he hadn't tasted cooking this good for years." She felt a little glimmer of satisfaction, but at the same time she wondered how these Englishers could manage without knowing how to cook a simple breakfast.

"You are a good cook," Mike agreed.

"I miss baking, but there's no oven. There's a microwave, but it makes everything chewy. Like shoe leather." Rocking the needle, she held the phone to her ear with one shoulder.

"It sounds like you're adapting."

"Yes . . . and no. Singing every day is a wonderful thing. That part makes my heart light. But this is no way to live, traveling with strangers, eating bad foods. I don't think God has called me to tour. Sometimes I wonder what I'm doing here. . . ." Suddenly her voice cracked with emotion. She didn't want to complain. She didn't mean to sound ungrateful, but the words had just slipped out.

"Sadie . . . remember your calling? You want to share your light. You're trying to use your voice for the glory of God. And I think you're doing a great job."

"I don't know. It still doesn't feel right."

"You're a work in progress. We all are."

She pressed her lips together, imagining his clear blue eyes, so thoughtful as he listened to her.

"Remind me, when does the tour hit Philly?"

"July thirtieth. And the last few nights are in New York."

"That's less than five weeks away. And when you come to town, I hope you're planning to stay with Gran and me. She's been asking about you."

"I can't wait to see her again." Sadie pulled the needle through, thinking of the hours she'd spent practicing on the Wurlitzer. She was eager to show Katherine what she'd learned on the keyboard. Funny, but she didn't feel so eager to return to the farm. She missed her brothers and sisters, but not the rules of the Ordnung. No . . . she did not miss Bishop Samuel's scowl.

"Sometimes I wish this was over already. I'm a fish out of the pond here."

"What do you mean? You're the star of the show!"

"Just one star of hundreds in the sky." She closed her eyes, fighting off the tears that wanted to come. She wanted to be with Mike. When she was with him, she was her very best self.

Beyond that, she missed her family. After the tour, she didn't think there was any way of going back without falling to her knees and begging forgiveness from all the church members.

And frightening as it was to think about leaving the Amish ways, she couldn't imagine going back now. God in heaven had made her the way she was; it was up to her to be the Sadie King He had created.

True to her heart.

Even if that meant breaking some rules and walking away from the strict policies of the Ordnung.

THIRTY-ONE

"Really, Henry. I can put myself to bed." Katherine Trueherz put a hand up to stop her son from hoisting her onto the mattress. "Stop it, now," she said firmly.

Mike had to bite back a smile. His mother and father had come from Paradise to visit Gran, but all afternoon Dad had been driving Gran a little bit crazy, doting and checking her medications and trying to help her when she didn't need his assistance. It was kind of fun to see his father, who was accustomed to being the boss, overruled by Gran's velvet fist.

"Now go away, Henry," Gran said. "Go read in the kitchen and let me take a nap."

"Okay, Mom. You just give a call if you need anything."

Mike's dad backed away, then strode through the parlor, motioning for Mike and Celeste to follow.

"Eighty years I put myself to bed," Gran muttered behind them. "You'd think I was a three-year-old."

In the kitchen, Henry poured a glass of milk and let out a thick sigh. "I don't know how you do it, Mike. She's a handful."

"She's different with me. I have fun with her."

"Well." Henry took a sip. "I have to say, I'm seeing you in a new light, and I'm proud. I admire the way you're able to negotiate with your gran. Honestly, I was never able to do that. With me, it seems to be her way or the highway."

"Because you're so much alike," Mike said. "And she's used to playing the parental role with you. You're the last person she wants doting over her."

"You think so?" Dr. Trueherz rubbed the line of his jaw with his knuckles. "That's probably the basic psychology of it. Hmm. Maybe you should specialize in psychiatry."

"Dad." Mike closed his eyes, his palms flat against the kitchen counter. He couldn't put up this ruse anymore. "I'm glad you have so much confidence in me, but I'm not pre-med. Not bio, either. I am interested in psych, but not as a medical doctor. Maybe sociology or social work. My time in Jamaica showed me that I have strong people skills. My science is lacking, but I do well with people."

"But what about the practice?" his father asked. "People rely on our clinic, and we can't—"

"Henry, please." Celeste reached out toward her husband, a plea in her eyes. "We all know how important the practice is. You've saved many a life and brought quality care to people who wouldn't get it otherwise. Everyone in our family knows this."

"Then how can he even think about letting it go?" Henry paced, pressing his hands to either side of his head. "The practice needs a dedicated doctor."

"And we'll find one to take over when the time comes." Celeste stood her ground. "It just won't be our son Mike."

A frown rumpled Henry's face. "This is wrong. It's the opportunity of a lifetime, a chance to help people, and I think that's what you really want to do. Why can't you see that this is the perfect setup for you?"

Because it's not, Mike wanted to say, but he didn't want to appear disrespectful to his father. "Dad, this is hard for me. I've felt this way a long time, but I didn't know how to tell you and I wasn't sure what I really wanted to do. Now I know."

"You don't know anything," Dr. Trueherz said with disdain. "You're a kid. You think you want to travel the world and feed the hungry, but when it comes down to reality, you're going to want a home and a way to help people, and I've got that all in place for you."

"I can't do it, Dad. I'm not med school material, and it's not my thing."

"I can make some calls. We can get you into med school."

"Henry, stop. Please." Celeste's voice was quiet but laden with steel. "Mike is telling us something important, and I think we need to hear him out. Sit down, and let him finish."

"No, thank you." The doctor strode to the door, paused, then turned back to them. "Think long and hard about this, Mike. The offer won't be dangling in front of your nose forever." With a snort of disgust, he turned and left the room, letting the door close hard behind him.

"Arrrrgh!" Mike let his head loll back as he groaned in frustration.

"Well, that went better than I expected," his mother said.

He squinted at her. "How did you expect anything? We've never talked about this."

"You've hinted around enough, and I could see that you weren't completely happy working at the clinic. You tried to make it fit, but it was sort of like a bad shoe. You can wear it, but you'll slog around with blisters."

"How is it you can see that but Dad still thinks I should suck it up and follow his dream?"

She shrugged. "Everyone has different expectations in life. I think you're beginning to figure that out."

"I guess I am." He thought of Sadie, of her family's expectations for her to get baptized and spend the rest of her life in the Amish community. And then the expectations of her bandmates, who expected her to be there to front the band, giving up her personal life and creativity in the process. She was in a similar dilemma, though hers seemed impossibly complicated.

"Will you stay at Temple?" Celeste asked. "I imagine they offer a degree in social work?"

"Sure. I can get a bachelor's in social work. And their MSW program is super competitive, but I might have a leg up with my Peace Corps experience."

"Fantastic." She leaned against the kitchen sink. "And don't worry about your father. He'll come around. He always does."

Mike took a deep breath, glad to have that burden gone from his shoulders. A line from the Bible came to mind.

And the truth shall set you free.

THIRTY-TWO

*B*e sure to hold the reins loose in your hands." Seated beside her in the front seat of the buggy, Simon was a patient teacher.

Remy loosened her grip on the reins and took a breath to calm her jangled nerves. A bead of sweat trickled down her back as she sat up straight, her feet braced gently on the low front board of the open carriage. She was a novice driver, and she was trying to command a novice horse, Simon's beloved Shadow, a piebald mare that didn't have much experience in pulling a buggy. Simon had been reassuring through most of the trip into Halfway, but Remy was acutely aware of the risks of injury if a skittish horse panicked on the road, and all the children in this vehicle were her responsibility.

Behind her, toddler Katie sat between Ruthie and Leah—another thing that rattled her nerves, as the Amish didn't have sturdy safety seats to strap their little ones into. It all seemed too precarious, but Adam had reminded her that the Amish had traveled this way for many generations, and the culture had survived.

Not without an occasional accident, she had reminded him, though she knew she wasn't going to single-handedly convince Amish folk that they needed to strap their toddlers into bulky safety seats the size of a baby bear.

"There's a car waiting behind us," Leah said from behind.

Remy slowed the horse and waved so that the car would pass.

"He's not going around us," Ruthie observed. "Maybe he's just out for a slow country ride."

Or maybe it's the creep who's been following Adam and me. Remy shot a quick look over her shoulder, and quickly saw that it was a different car. This one was black with tinted windows.

"I guess he doesn't want to pass." Remy called for the horse to pick up speed, and the buggy moved along at a faster clip again.

"You see how she listens?" Simon asked. "Shadow's a good horse."

"Your training shows." Remy complimented Simon as she moved the long rein so that it didn't twist around her feet. They had reached the outskirts of town, and there was more traffic coming in the opposite direction. Soon they would be at the market, much to her relief.

The roar of a gunning engine startled her. Her pulse raced as she held the reins securely, turning to look behind her.

The dark car was passing now. Not good on a busy road.

Shadow whinnied as she slowed her. "Stay steady, girl," she called under her breath.

Beside her, Simon was peeking around, his face pale. "What is that car doing? It will scare her."

Remy looked to the side and saw that the car had slowed to match her pace.

"Oh, please . . . ," she murmured, focusing on keeping the horse steady.

A rear window of the car slid down and a man's ruddy face appeared. "Remy? Remy, stop the carriage."

She blinked in astonishment. "Herb? What are you doing here?"

"I've come to talk some sense into you. Stop the horse."

"I will not stop in the middle of the road," she shouted, turning to look ahead for other vehicles. "This is dangerous, Herb!"

"Well, you're a hard person to reach. I came all the way out here, I—"

"Herb, you'd better pass me or drop back before someone gets hurt. Go ahead of me. Pull in to the lot at that red barn on the left."

He looked ahead, frowning. "Fine."

The window closed and the car accelerated, wheels spinning and spewing gravel behind them.

"Careful . . ." Simon gasped, touching Remy's arm as the car shot ahead, cutting in directly in front of Shadow.

Remy pulled back on the reins gently, hoping to avoid contact. Shadow responded well, slowing as the car roared into the distance. "What a good horse," Remy said. The back of her dress was clinging to her with sweat, and Simon clutched her arm in fear.

Of course . . . he was probably remembering the terrible roadside incident that had left his parents dead.

"It's okay," she told him softly. "That was just my verhuddelt father. He doesn't mean to hurt us."

"Are you sure?" Simon loosened his grip. "He's mad at you. Why?"

"That's a long story," Remy said. And to be honest, she wasn't sure she knew the real answer. Herb McCallister was a successful businessman, owner of the *Philadelphia Post* and a shareholder in television stations and major league ball teams. In business he was a god, but as a father . . . well, he had never been there for Remy.

So why was he here now? And having his driver cut them off like a maniac?

"Well, that was exciting and a little bit scary," Ruthie said. "Is that really your father, Remy? Where is his long limo?"

"Probably in the shop," Remy said as she steered the horse into the parking lot of the Zooks' barn where the daily markets were held in the summer. Spotting the dark car in the back of the lot, she guided Shadow that way. She held her breath as the buggy rolled to a stop.

The rear door of the car opened and out stepped her father, looking slightly rumpled in his shirtsleeves.

"Dad!" Remy glared at him. "Are you crazy?"

The children around her watched, aghast.

"Remy, you can't talk to your dat that way," Ruthie whispered.

"Oh, yes, I can, when he nearly ran our buggy off the road." She handed Simon the reins, then jumped to the ground. "What were you thinking?"

"I told Elliot to pursue you aggressively. I didn't know he was going to make it into a Hollywood chase scene."

"That's not a good excuse, or a good apology." She stepped up to him, face-to-face for the first time in months. She felt like she was staring at a stranger, though the creases at the corners of his eyes and the line of his brow were familiar. "What are you doing here, Herb? You have my address, and you've sent just one letter. You refused to see me when I was in town, cleaning out the condo. Loretta told me to leave the car keys under the mat. You wanted nothing to do with me, and yet today you show up and nearly run us off the road?"

"Just because you haven't seen me doesn't mean I haven't kept an eye on you," Herb said. "I've had my guy out here watching, a hired detective." He put his hands into his trouser pockets and straightened, his chest puffed out. "I wanted to make sure you hadn't been kidnapped by this cult."

"No! The Amish don't kidnap. I'm here because I want to be." *Because I found a home. A love. A Heavenly Father.*

"I find that hard to believe. What girl in her right mind would choose to give up the good life—all the things I've given you—for a life of work on a farm?"

Remy put her hands on her hips. "You know I was never afraid of hard work, and I've found something more valuable than any gift money can buy. I've found a family here . . . a wonderful family with children who need me and a good man who loves me."

A man I love with all my heart, she thought, strengthened by the knowledge that she had made the right choice. "I've found a way of life that suits me."

"Well." He rubbed his jaw begrudgingly. "I guess it's good that you're safe. But I really don't want you living way out here. I figured the private investigator would be able to get you back to the city."

She squinted against the sun. "Are you trying to say you miss me?"

"Maybe. I still can't believe you walked out on such a sweet deal. Your condo, your car . . . everything was paid for."

Remy turned to the buggy, where the children were watching, amazed and curious. The sky beyond them was a dazzling blue. The small buildings in this section of Halfway held the quaint, tidy charm of the town, and the hills beyond painted a swath of green over the horizon.

This . . . this was a sweet deal.

How could Herb not see that?

"Remy . . ." Katie squirmed out of Leah's grasp and reached out from the side of the buggy.

"Oh, Katie, don't jump." Remy hurried over and whisked the little girl onto her hip, then turned back to her father. "This is an all-time new low, Herb. You could have hurt these children, or worse. As it was, you spooked our horse, and let me point out that you're lucky she didn't damage your car, the way you menaced us with it."

"I'm sorry, okay?" He stepped closer. "Can I help it if my driver didn't understand what I wanted?"

"Yes, it's your responsibility. That's what you don't get, Herb. Certain things in life are your responsibility and yours alone." *Like being a father,* she wanted to say.

"Fine." He waved dismissively. "If you're fine here, I'll be on my way."

Remy sighed. Although he was petulant and bossy, he was still her father. "Herb, do you want to meet your granddaughter-to-be?"

"What are you talking about? Who, this one?"

Remy stepped closer, little Katie resting on her hip. "This is Katie King. It's her older brother who I'm going to marry."

Bright-eyed Katie gave a greeting in Pennsylvania Deutsch.

"What? Yes, hello." He held a hand out and she grabbed one of his fingers and held on.

"Doesn't she speak English?" he asked.

"A little. It will be her second language."

Herb shook his hand, but Katie held on. "Yes, okay, you can let go now." But she clasped his finger, a hint of a smile on her cherry red lips. Herb huffed out a sigh, then gave his fingers a shake. "Let go. Go. Do you know what that means?"

Katie's grin lit her face, but she held on.

"She reminds me of you at that age. Stubborn and determined to get your way." He waggled his captured finger. "You're going to be just like Remy." His voice was playful, tender.

And Remy wondered where that Herb had been for the past ten years.

Katie laughed, then turned shy, burrowing her face against Remy's shoulder.

Stepping back, Remy turned toward the buggy and summoned the other children, calling, "Kumm." Then, facing her father, she told him it was time to meet the rest of the family.

That night after dinner, Remy sat outside under the stars with Adam and his family. They were missing Sadie, of course, but everyone was beginning to accept that Sadie needed time away for her own personal adventure. Although Remy had heard murmurings from the ever-positive Ruthie, who was convinced that Sadie would make it back for the twins' birthday and resume life as usual on the farm, Remy could tell from the silences of the older siblings that they weren't quite so hopeful.

Gabe built a campfire in the pit on the grassy slope near the house, and the family gathered round, toasting marshmallows for s'mores and singing silly songs. Katie and Sam scampered through the grass, leaping to catch fireflies.

Simon appeared and dropped to the grass beside Adam. "It's too dark to see the Frisbee," he said.

"Did Shadow recover from her scare this morning?" Remy asked the boy.

"Ya. I think I was more afraid than she was." Simon leaned over his knees, his hair glossy in the moonlight. "Remy, why was your dat so mad?"

"My father has trouble holding back his temper," Remy said. "I'm sorry he scared you. He's not a terrible person, but he wasn't good at being a father."

"He's still your father," Simon said.

"Ya. And I'm learning to forgive him every time he hurts me." In the darkness, Adam touched her hand, and she felt a surge of love for the man who sensed when she needed his support. "I wish I had

met your dat," Remy said. "I would like to know what a good father is like."

"Well," Simon said, "I can tell you a very good story about our
dat. He was the one who taught me how to watch over the horses."

"And I have a funny story about Dat when he was plowing a
field and ran into a nest of birds' eggs," Leah said. "He worried so
for those eggs! Like a mother hen."

How wonderful that they remember him, Remy thought.

Under a blanket of twinkling stars, she leaned back on the grass
beside Adam and listened as one by one the stories about Levi King
spilled forth. She could only hope and pray that one day she would
have the chance to witness Adam parenting their children. One day
soon . . .

THIRTY-THREE

As the bus came upon a green sign that read PHILA-
DELPHIA, anticipation swelled inside Sadie.

At last, she would see Mike.

The distant future loomed like a faraway star. But for now, while
the band was in Philly, she would take a break from the bus and stay
at Katherine's house. How she longed to cook for the older woman!
She would tidy up and share the poems she had come to love in the
little red book. And she hoped Katherine would be pleasantly surprised by Sadie's growing skill on the piano.

And tomorrow, she would return to the church that had opened
her heart to this journey. Although music still wrapped around her
and held her in its arms, she was learning that it wasn't just a simple
matter of sharing her talent with the world. It wasn't as simple as
having good intentions. The Englisher world was complicated, and
some days Sadie realized she had just begun to learn about the wide
area of gray that stretched between the clear black-and-white rules
of the Ordnung.

It was almost over, Sadie thought with a heartfelt sigh. She had tried to stop counting the days, but each morning when she woke, the new number appeared in her mind, like a promise. The tour would finish a few days before the twins' birthday, giving her plenty of time to get back to Halfway and keep her promise to Ruthie.

Sometimes it felt like she would never see Halfway again. Every day she was reminded of the many things about her Amish family and the farm that she missed. The quiet breathing of her sisters, close and cozy in their room at night. The mooing of cows in the middle of a hot summer night. The smell of wood smoke and freshly plowed fields and fruit pies cooling on the kitchen counter . . .

Now that August was just days away, they were deep into the growing season, and when she closed her eyes she could see it all. Peaches, plums, and nectarines were hanging heavy in the trees, and the garden was thick with vines of cucumbers and zucchini. There'd be sweet corn, tomatoes, and lettuce. Oh, the sickening sweet deodorizer of the bus couldn't spoil her memory of the smell of a summer garden.

She tucked her needle into a patch and put her quilting away. The others were gathered in the kitchen area, watching something on Red's laptop.

"Sadie, check it out," Red said. "The video of the band has gone viral."

On the screen was their band, standing on a real stage. Someone must have shot it during the tour. Sadie stood in the middle of a spotlight singing "Be Thou My Vision," and this video wasn't shadowy or blurred. You could see the details of her face, the creases in her prayer kapp, as well as the logo on the T-shirt she had gotten from Remy.

"Who did this?" she asked.

"Some fan posted it on YouTube, and look at how many hits it's gotten! This is awesome!" Frank pumped a fist in the air as he moved to the rear of the bus.

Sadie looked on with a mixture of good and bad feelings. Red had shown her YouTube, and explained about viral videos. But she knew what a virus was, and couldn't think how that could be a good thing. Besides, she was not supposed to be photographed—or at least that was what she'd been taught.

How did she really feel about it?

There would be no bishop scolding her. Not even Adam would see this video, because Amish men didn't own computers. So why did she care?

She had been questioning many things lately. Even the prayer kapp that had been pinned to her head from when she was a child. It made her feel secure, and she liked the idea that her prayers went straight from her soul to God. But in her heart, she knew that God would hear her whether she wore the kapp or not.

What if she left it off one day, with her long hair hanging in a braid down her back?

Sadie grinned at the thought of how Frank would go crazy. He would have to change the name of the band.

She rubbed her arms, chilled from the air-conditioning on the bus. Did it matter if she wore a kapp or if her image was out there—inside all those countless computers? People could just click on Amish Blues and find her singing. Well, what was wrong with that? She had been called by God to share her gift, and the viral video was now showing thousands of people a hymn that glorified God.

So it was good to have her graven image out there in the computer wires. She was on the right path here, even if the band wasn't the perfect match for her.

It was right to trust her future to God. . . .

And try not to be sick about the past.

All those years when she was growing up, she had watched Englishers and craved their world. Now that she was here, there was no returning to her Amish life.

And that terrible truth was breaking her heart.

⁂

"Hey, songbird!"

When she spotted Mike backstage, Sadie pushed past the other visitors and leaped into his arms. He staggered backward, holding her so that her feet dangled in the air above the floor.

"It's so good to see you . . . to hug you." She could barely believe she had said such a thing, but with Mike it didn't seem awkward.

"I know." He eased her down to the floor, and she lifted her chin to have a close-up look at him. His blue eyes were a lightning strike to her heart. "It feels like you've been traveling for a year," he said.

"I was getting so sick of holding that silver phone to my ear when I really just wanted to be with you. Did you ever notice that, no matter how much you talk, you only reach a small part of the person on the other phone? It's very disappointing."

"You're right." He took her hand, and she squeezed his fingers. No cell phone could give you a connection this good. "There's nothing like real life," he said. "And by the way, how about those mad skills you've acquired on the electric piano. I know we talked about you taking lessons, but you've hit the ground running. Where did that stuff come from?"

She couldn't help but smile. "I've been practicing, every day. Red let me borrow his Wurlitzer, and he showed me a few little tricks."

Mike talked with Red while Sadie went to the bus to quickly gather her things. Then they were off, strapped into Mike's car and moving through the streets of Philadelphia. Although they had talked at least once a day these past few weeks, conversation flowed easily between them. It was always easy with Mike.

Maybe that was because he was really the only person who knew what she was going through now. He understood the tug-of-war between her Amish past and her future in this other life. After the tour, there were so many good things that Mike was helping her set up. He'd found a review class for the GED, the examination that was equal to having a full high school degree. And a piano teacher who would come to Katherine's house. And church every Sunday, with a chance to sing in the choir. So many wonderful things were waiting down the road for Sadie, after the tour and her visit home.

Her *visit* home . . .

It had taken her most of the time on the tour to realize that she would not be going back to her Amish home to stay. Oh, ya, she missed her brothers and sisters dearly! But she could not deny the journey of her heart, now that she saw her path whenever she closed her eyes and prayed.

Her Amish life was like the beginning chapters of a sweet book. You could read them over and over again, but the story could not go on until you dared to read the rest of the book.

Sadie and Mike talked about how bittersweet the tour had become. Every day brought the clear joy of being able to sing as a job, along with the cloying boredom of living on the bus, eating meals of crackers and soda pop, and putting up with Frank's silly schemes. It would be a relief to finish the tour and bid farewell to Frank.

When they arrived at Katherine's house, it was nearly midnight. Sadie tiptoed through the parlor, trying not to wake her, but the older woman's voice came from the back room.

"Well, get in here already and let me see you."

Sadie peeked around the wall to see Katherine standing with

the help of only a cane now. She straightened, a welcoming light in her eyes. "It's good to see you. I hear you're quite a rock star these days."

"I don't know about that. But I'm happy to have landed here with you again."

"The vagabond life wearing thin?"

"Very thin. I'm grateful to have a real bed to sleep in tonight."

"Good. Well, I need my beauty sleep, but you know your way around the place. Make yourself at home. Oh, and the fridge is stocked with eggs and milk and bacon." Katherine cocked one brow. "That's a hint."

"Ah, good. I'll make a delicious breakfast for all of us before church."

They said good night to Katherine and headed up the stairs. Sadie peeked into the room she'd stayed in, so happy to be here, but there was no stopping now. She followed Mike to the tippy-top and stepped out onto the roof into the warm July night.

Her hands pressed to her chest as she stepped toward the landscape of starry lights. "I've dreamed of this these past weeks. Dreamed of being here with you."

He moved beside her and slid an arm around her waist. "Does that mean I'm a dream come true?"

"Aren't you the funny one?"

"Hey, is that sarcasm I hear?" He turned to face her, his handsome face lit with amusement. "What happened to the sweet, wise Amish girl I used to know?"

"She's right here." She stepped into his arms, reaching up to cling to his broad shoulders. "I've always been right here."

His arms surrounded her, pressing her body to his with a tenderness that took her breath away. This love . . . this was so very right.

She sighed against him as his lips brushed hers, then pressed into a kiss.

With all the fears and doubts that had shadowed her thoughts over the past few weeks, not once did she question that she and Mike belonged together. Mike had told her that in the Englisher world it was not a good thing to marry so young, when they both needed more schooling and jobs to support a family. But in her heart and soul she believed that they would marry sometime in the future.

Oh, to be Mike's wife! Cooking for him and caring for their home, while he solved the problems of the world with his earnest charm. And the babies they would have . . . little ones who would grow up showered by God's love, free to make choices without the weight of tradition on their shoulders.

Sadie couldn't imagine a more wonderful life.

The next morning Sadie found joy in the cracking of fresh eggs and the sizzle of bacon in a fry pan. There were fresh blueberries and Florida oranges that Sadie peeled and sliced into a fruit salad. Mike brewed the coffee and toasted frozen waffles that tasted surprisingly good.

It felt good to sit for a meal with two people she cared for. *My new family,* she thought.

Katherine had so many questions about the tour, and Sadie wanted to know what the doctors were saying about Katherine's progress. It felt like a little family reunion.

As Sadie started to do the dishes, Mike turned the water off and pulled her away from the sink. "The cleanup can wait," he said. "Gran, Sadie has something to show you, out in the parlor."

As Sadie sat down to play "Amazing Grace" for Katherine, joy bubbled in her soul. *Frayliche,* as they said at home. This was what it would be like to perform for her parents, she thought. People who loved her and who were delighted with what she'd learned.

When she finished, Katherine applauded, then gave a hoot that made Sadie laugh.

"Thank you," Sadie said. "Thank you for starting me on the piano. I will always remember my first teacher."

The next morning at church, Sadie was once again mesmerized by the talented musicians who turned prayer into beautiful music. The reading was the story of the Good Samaritan, one of Sadie's favorite Bible stories. She had been taught to help people in need, and she had always helped at quilting frolics or putting up peaches or whatever could be done to raise money for families who had seen hard times.

But today, the story of the man who stopped along the roadside to help an injured traveler reminded her of Mike. Mike was her Good Samaritan. Hadn't he stopped along the road, more than once, to give her a ride?

Mike had always been a fixer. He had traveled to Jamaica and done so many good things. She loved the stories of the young boys who had come to hang out on his front porch—the little soldiers. He had started their friendships by offering soda pops and crayons to draw pictures. Then he had started teaching them how to write and read letters. Before he left the country, he had helped most of those boys enroll in a real school.

Her heart felt light as her gaze wandered to the choir section, where he sat in a blue robe. How she loved him! God's goodness lived in Mike Trueherz. That was his special gift, and he shared it with others every day.

One of the songs, called "Wandering Afar," captured her interest because it reminded her of her own journey.

> Wand'ring afar on the mountain wild,
> Still He is calling, "Come, my child;
> Hasten to Me, I will all forgive;
> Perishing soul, oh, come and live!"

She had been wandering so far from her home, and oh, she felt the need for forgiveness, but not from God in heaven. The people she needed to forgive her were back home in Halfway. Adam. Bishop Samuel. Her sisters, dear Ruthie and Leah and Susie and Mary, who must be missing her help every day. The little ones, who must be wondering where she'd gone. And then Gabe and Simon and Jonah. After losing their parents two winters ago, her siblings didn't deserve to lose a sister.

But she had gone . . . left them all behind.

God had called her to follow her heart, but that didn't make it easy to leave her family behind. Soon she would be returning to Lancaster County, just for the twins' birthday, and she didn't know how they would welcome her . . . or if they would welcome her at all.

THIRTY-FOUR

August third, the last scheduled tour date in Brooklyn, New York, came and went without the tour bus leaving the city. On the last night in Brooklyn, Frank told the band that he had been approached by a club owner in Manhattan who wanted them to perform for the next four nights.

"Four nights in Manhattan," Frank exclaimed. "This is big-time, baby!"

Tara tossed her hair back with a smile, and even Red seemed happy about it. But Sadie was worried.

"I have to be back in Halfway by the morning of August eighth," she said. "Very early in the morning. I won't have time to do a gig the night before."

"Sadie, Sadie, hold on." Frank held his hands up. "You didn't hear me. I said Manhattan. The Big Apple."

"I heard you just fine, Frank. But I promised to be home by then, and it's important."

Frank let out a dramatic sigh. "Okay. How about this? You stay for the gig, and I swear to you, I'll get you home in time. If the bus can't move fast enough, we'll rent a car and leave right after the gig, okay?"

"I don't know." Sadie frowned. "I can't miss it."

"You won't. Cross my heart. If you agree to stay, I'll get you there."

Sadie wanted to refuse him, but then she saw the intense wanting in Tara's eyes and she thought of the story of the Good Samaritan. Right now Sadie was the only one who could help the band make it down this road, and the pressure weighed on her. She wanted to be a helper.

"Whew." Red sighed. "This is huge. Is there a way we can make it work for Sadie?"

"I said I'd drive her home in time." Frank started pacing, his nervous habit.

Sadie closed her eyes, firming her choice. "All right. But—"

"Fantastic!" Frank gave her shoulder a happy shake. "You'll thank me later. This is going to be a great break for us!"

The Manhattan gigs were more noisy and crowded than most. After each performance people streamed backstage, hoping to meet the band and get photos. Sadie was swarmed by people who wanted to talk with her, buy her a drink, or take her photo with their cell phones. Sadie was glad for the band's success, but in the back of her mind was the thought of their last performance, the rush to get back to Halfway, and the worries about facing Adam and her family once again.

At last, the final performance came. Sadie gave it her all, knowing that this might be the last time she ever sang with Red, Tara, and Frank. Closing her eyes, she escaped the earthly world and opened her voice to the heavens. Floating to a place of joy and peace, she thanked God as she sang, thanked Him for teaching her how to open her heart and use this gift.

After the performance the crowd of people backstage made it impossible to find Frank. When Sadie finally spotted him talking with a man and woman, he was jumping with energy again.

"Sadie lady, did you hear that crowd?" he asked her, then quickly introduced her to the two people, Guy Delta—a record producer—and his A and R person, Trina Feldman.

"Guy and Trina were in the audience and they want to talk with us about getting the band into the studio."

Sadie's heart sank. "That's very nice, but can Frank talk to you on his cell later? We need to get driving back to Pennsylvania."

The two businesspeople turned back to Frank, who shrugged.

"Sadie just doesn't get business. She really was raised Amish, so all this talk is totally out of her league."

Her teeth ground together at the insult. She understood what was going on. She simply didn't have the patience for it. "Frank ... we have to go now. You promised."

"Just give me a half hour or so, okay? We can't give up now," Frank insisted.

"I can't spare the time." Desperate, she grabbed his arm, hoping to make him understand. "I have to be home by first light."

"Then you'll have to find another way home." He wrested his arm free.

They argued, with Sadie insisting she must go home in time for a family celebration, and Frank refusing to walk away from the chance of a lifetime—a producer wanting to meet with him. "But you promised ... ," she reminded him. His shrug made her see that promises were not to be taken seriously among the English.

A panic overtook her as she realized Frank was not going to take her home. She was going to miss the birthdays. She stormed out of the club, onto the bus. It took her only two minutes to gather her few possessions into her backpack, and then she wasn't quite sure where to turn next. Trying to think calmly, she remembered someone talking about a train. Remy had taken a train from New York to Philly.

Backpack in hand, she ran to the street and looked around at the gray buildings looming overhead. She knew that trains ran through all of Manhattan and Brooklyn. She had heard them rumbling underground sometimes while walking down the street. How would she find the train that would take her to Philly?

She ducked into a corner store with its lights still blazing and went to the man at the counter. "Can you tell me how to get the train to Philadelphia?"

He scratched his neck. "Philadelphia?" His accent was quick, like a galloping horse. He shook his head.

Sadie's chest burned with disappointment as she turned away.

"You need to take the Amtrak train." A woman around her age stood behind her with a carton of milk and a bottle of soda pop in her hand. "It leaves from Penn Station. Thirty-third Street."

"Oh?" Sadie blinked. "Penn Station. How do I get there?"

"If you're in a hurry, take a cab."

"Thank you." Sadie nodded. "Thank you very much." She wheeled and ran out to the street. Her heart raced as she stood at the curb and waved at the cars moving toward her. She had learned that the yellow cars were the ones you hired for a ride.

Penn Station . . . She said it over and over in her head, so it was no problem saying it to the driver when he pulled up beside her.

Penn Station was hidden under a big building, but she rode the escalator down, and followed the signs for Amtrak, as the woman had instructed. At the ticket office her spirits lifted when the agent told her that a train to Philadelphia was boarding at that very moment. She purchased a ticket, found her way to the right platform, and collapsed into an empty seat on the train.

It was going to work out. She would be back in Philadelphia by one A.M. And after that . . .

She could only think of one way home to Halfway, but she hated to call Mike in the middle of the night. She settled back into the seat and stared out the window to the passing lights. The train was quiet, with most people either asleep or reading. The gentle rocking motion of the train on the tracks relaxed her, and she imagined that everyone on the train was in God's cradle, being rocked so gently.

By the time the train was pulling in to Philadelphia's South Street Station, Sadie had decided to call Mike. He was a helper; he'd said so himself. And right now she needed help.

Inside the station she juggled her bag to her left arm to get to her cell phone. But when she flipped it open, she saw that the battery was blinking. It was running out.

Quickly she pressed Mike's name, but before it could ring, the phone blinked and turned off.

Oh, no! What good was this Englisher technology when it left you stranded so far from home? She wanted to toss her cell phone into a trash can. A sob slipped out of her throat, and tears filled her eyes.

She was going to miss the birthday song.

Her promise would be broken.

THIRTY-FIVE

*T*he buzz of his phone startled Mike awake. He checked the screen, but didn't recognize the number. Who would be calling at one-thirty in the morning?

"Hello?" His voice was low from sleep.

"Mike, it's Sadie."

"Sadie . . ." He swung his feet down and sat on the edge of the bed. "Are you okay?" She didn't sound okay. And why was she calling from this strange number?

"I'm so very sorry to wake you, but I have a problem here. I'm in Philadelphia, at the train station, and I need to get back home before sunrise. If I don't leave soon, I'll miss the birthdays and . . . oh, I promised Ruthie, and now . . ."

"You need a ride?" Mike had already pulled on his sweatpants. "No problem. I'm on my way." He swiped a hand through his hair. If it was a mess, at least it would be uniformly ruffled. "So you're at the South Street station? Are you in a safe spot where people can see you? Under a light, with people around?"

"Yes, I'm fine. Sitting right outside the ticket office, and there's a very nice policeman who's let me borrow his phone. Mine is out of battery."

"Okay, you just stay where you are." Mike opened the tall oak door of Gran's house, stepped out, and locked it behind him. "I'll be there in a flash."

Because of the late hour he was able to find a spot right in front of the nearly empty train station. He jogged into the building, searching for Sadie.

She sat on a wooden bench, under an old-fashioned globe that cast a halo of light around her white prayer kapp. As she spotted him and arose, she resembled an angel. A fierce, earnest angel.

"Come on," he said, taking her hand. "Let's get you where you need to be."

As he stowed her backpack in the backseat, he could see that she was on edge. Tired and a little shaky.

"I'm sorry to wake you up in the middle of the night," she said.

"Hey, I'm glad you called. I want to be your go-to guy."

The breath caught in her throat, and suddenly her amber eyes filled with tears.

Something ground deep inside him. He liked to see himself as a fixer, but some things were beyond his control.

"It was a big mistake, trusting Frank. You know I wanted to help the band, and that's why I agreed to stay. But Frank . . . he let me down. I should have known."

"Hey, how could you know?" She was too kind to see that Frank Marconi was a complete and utter jerk, Mike thought. He had smelled a rat when Frank had pushed to extend the tour, but he had let Sadie make her own decisions. Long ago he had realized that she wanted it that way. She had left her Amish life because she needed her independence, and Mike could respect that. He could give her space and freedom because he loved her.

"And now . . . now I'm going to be late for the birthday song! Just because of my own stupid decisions! I made a promise and . . . I . . ."

"Easy." Mike cradled her and rocked her gently, overcome by the love he felt for the woman in his arms. If he had his way, he would never let her go . . . but right now she had a promise to keep.

"There was nothing stupid about your decision. You are one of the most thoughtful, caring people I know. You're also one of the bravest, to leave your family and the only life you've ever known to explore the wonderful talent that God blessed you with. That took a lot of guts."

"I don't feel very brave now." She sniffed. "I'm afraid to face my own family."

He had sensed that. Sadie carried a lot of guilt over leaving her family, abandoning them and their lifestyle, and after sunrise she would come face-to-face with those feelings.

"You did the right thing, calling me." As her sobs began to calm, Mike let his arms slip away, then shifted in his seat and started the engine. "I'll get you there in a flash. Warp nine."

She sniffed. "What's warp nine?"

"Never mind. It's just my geeky past slipping out."

As they drove west, Sadie plugged her cell phone into the charger that worked off the car battery. "But I must remember to turn it off when I get there," she said. "My cell phone was one of the things that made Adam mad when I lived at home."

He reassured her that they would make it to Halfway before sunrise. "And how long are you planning to stay? Do you need a ride back to the city?"

"I can take a bus. I would like to stay a few days, but maybe they'll kick me out today. I'm not sure I'll be welcomed by everyone."

"You're talking about Adam," he said. "I wish you two could straighten things out."

"A wonderful wish, but it can't come true. Adam is the head of the family. It's his place to steer me toward baptism. He's responsible for me joining the congregation."

"And that's not happening, so Adam's doing a bad job. Is that how the logic goes?"

"Something like that."

Mike gave her a quick look. The lights of the dashboard glowed over the ridges of her swollen lips and high cheekbones. He hated to see her looking so sad and vulnerable.

"Hey, do you want to switch on the radio? Find a good song."

She shook her head. "I've got no mind for music now. I'm worried sick about what's to come at the farm."

"Relax. I told you, we'll be there in plenty of time."

"It's not about being late. This has been eating at my heart since I left the farm. I want to go home, but it will be bittersweet now, knowing I don't belong there. I'll never be a baptized member of the faith. I'll never be truly Amish."

He nodded slowly. "Listen, I know you've been through a lot this summer. You've made some really hard choices, choices a lot of people don't make in their entire lives."

And she had grown. He had seen it in the way she related to Katherine, the way she had decided to teach herself piano, cook for the band, and start a quilt. Even in her budding realization that life issues weren't polarized, black-and-white matters as the Amish ministers preached. Sadie had begun to see that there were many gray areas in life. Room for compromise.

Sadie had stepped out of her culture—a huge step for anyone.

"How could a person not make choices?" she asked. "That would be like turning around at a fork in the road because you can't decide which way to go."

"You're right." He loved her common sense, her wisdom and

fortitude. Who else would scramble through two cities and the Pennsylvania countryside to make it home because of a promise?

Only Sadie.

When he pulled up and cut the engine at the end of the lane to the King farm, the sky was still the pitch blue of night. He checked the digital clock on the dash. "According to that, you've got twenty minutes or so to sunrise."

"Parting at the end of the lane." She looked out the window, toward the farm. "This is just like a rumspringa courtship."

When she leaned close, he pressed a kiss to her lips. A short kiss, with a promise of more to come.

"Thank you. You are a very good Samaritan."

His smile belied the ache in his heart as he watched her hitch her backpack onto one shoulder. Then slowly her form receded and she disappeared into the darkness.

THIRTY-SIX

*A*s Sadie walked down the lane, her old home awakened around her. Cows mooed in the barn and birds began to trill in the trees and bushes. She loved the sensation of dew on the grass, the smell of the haymow and the rough feel of the weathered fence under her fingertips as she said hello to the horses stirring in the paddock.

It would have been a wondrous homecoming, if it weren't for the storm churning inside her. Although she had kept her promise to come home in time for the birthday song, she was returning only as a visitor. Her real life was behind her, with Mike and Katherine and the music that flowed straight from her heart.

A baby rabbit leaped onto the grass of the nearby lawn, then went stiff when it saw Sadie. Frozen in fear.

Sadie paused. "I know how you feel," she whispered to the quivering rabbit. Sadie had run from her safe Amish home to the greener grass of the Englisher world, and though she knew in her heart that God wanted her to be forging her own path far from this Amish community, the thought of the future could still catch her in a panic.

The rabbit eyed her coolly, pounced to the side, then darted down the lane. Probably headed off to nibble some cabbage in Mammi Nell's garden.

"I see that you make choices much faster than I do," she called after the creature, then continued walking down the lane toward the plain white two-story house that was still cloaked in sleep.

When Clive the rooster crowed for all the farm to wake up, she knew it was time to go inside and face her family.

It seemed so simple when the back door opened to her touch. She slipped her shoes off on the mud porch and headed inside.

The wooden stairs were smooth underfoot as she climbed, then paused at the top. The old house seemed small, but still cozy and rich with memories. She stepped lightly toward her old bedroom, her arms aching to hug her sisters.

The creak of a door stopped her. "Sadie?" Mary came toward her, her eyes still bleary from sleep. "You made it!" Her voice was hushed, but full of glee.

"It wasn't easy," Sadie admitted as they exchanged a quick hug.

Then Mary leaned back and studied her, squinting in the moonlight. "Look at you, all grown up. A woman now."

Sadie rolled her eyes. "Gone but a few weeks. I couldn't have changed so much."

"Mmm." Mary pressed a hand to the center of her chest. "Sometimes the change is in here."

She was right. . . . How did Mary have such wisdom when she had never left the farm, never traveled out of Lancaster County?

Sadie longed to talk, but there was no time now. The sun would pop over the hills soon; it was time for the birthday song.

"I'll go get the boys," Mary said. "Why don't you wake Katie?"

In the nursery, Katie was already standing in her crib. "Out!" She held her arms up, then grinned when she recognized Sadie. "Sadie! Sadie home."

With a heartfelt sigh Sadie picked up the toddler and pressed her face to the little girl's smooth cheek, downy hair, and sweet baby scent. "I missed you."

Katie patted her back, then stiffened. "Down!"

"You're right." Sadie lowered her to the floor. "We have to sing the birthday song. It's Leah and Susie's birthday."

"Leah and Susie? Okay. Time to sing the song," Katie said as she toddled down the hall.

They ran into the boys coming from the other direction, and though Adam didn't seem to see Sadie, Jonah clapped her on the shoulder and winked.

She smiled, trying to keep her emotions from brimming over as Gabe nodded and Sam blinked in delight.

When Sadie stepped into the room, Ruthie wore a glum expression, waiting alone in the space between the twin girls' beds. Steeling herself with a breath, Ruthie looked up as the family filed in . . . and she spotted Sadie.

Joy sparked in her eyes as she gasped. "Sadie!"

"Shh!" Sam warned. "We must sing the song first."

Sadie moved close to Ruthie and hugged her from behind as they all surrounded Leah's bed. She always got the song first, since she had been born six minutes before her twin. Her hands on Ruthie's shoulders, Sadie asked, "Are we ready?"

The family seemed to take a breath together, and Sadie began. "Rise and shine and give Gott your glory. Today is Leah's birthday and this is her story. . . ."

Afterward, Sam and the girls congregated in the kitchen, where Mary brewed coffee and doled out pieces of cinnamon buns that she'd made the day before.

"Mind you don't fill up on these," Mary said as she poured Sam a cup of milk. "Leave room for real breakfast after the milking."

Simon, Adam, Jonah, and Gabe were tending to that, much to Sadie's relief. With Adam out in the milking barn, there were no barriers between her and her siblings, who were thrilled to have her home.

Ruthie wiggled onto the daybed between Susie and Sadie, and wrapped herself around Sadie's arm. "I couldn't believe my eyes when I saw you come into the bedroom! I had given up. I thought you'd surely forgotten us."

"I didn't want to break a promise to you," Sadie said. She wouldn't mention the fright she'd had about almost not making it here in time.

"After all this time, I wasn't sure you remembered the promise." Ruthie pressed her head to Sadie's shoulder. "I was afraid we'd never see you again."

"I could never stay away for long." Sadie looked from one to another, so happy to see their smiling faces. "I missed you all, very much."

"And we missed you," Leah said, popping a piece of cinnamon bun into her mouth. "We got your letters. I can't believe you saw the ocean! Is it wondrous beautiful?"

"More than I can say."

"And now that the tour is over, are you home for good?" Ruthie asked, squeezing Sadie's arm. "Say that you're here to stay!"

"Oh, honey girl, I'm sorry to disappoint you, but I have to go back to the city." Sadie braced herself for an argument, but there were only downturned frowns of disappointment.

"I don't want you to go," Ruthie said.

Sam slapped his notepad onto the table. "I don't like the city."

"Lucky for you that you live on a farm," Mary said, trying to keep things positive as she wiped down the counter.

"So many things happened while you were gone," Susie said. "Do you know that we bought ten new milking cows?"

"Really?" Sadie had known they planned for new cows once the milking machines were in, but this was news.

"And lightning struck the Stoltzfus' house and set it on fire," Leah added. "Jonah has been over there, helping them fix it."

As Leah and Susie filled Sadie in on what she had missed in Halfway, Katie crawled into her lap with her dolly.

Then Sam wanted to show her the letters that Leah had taught him. He could write his name and knew the full alphabet. Numbers, too. "Did you know that two plus five is seven?" Sam asked as he showed her how to make a plus sign.

"Arithmetic already? You're growing up before my eyes," Sadie told him.

Sadie felt warmed from head to toe when the family sat around the big table for breakfast. They talked of making hay and canning peaches, and Sadie relaxed in her old spot at the table . . . until she noticed that Adam did not look at her or speak to her. She stared at him, studying his dark, furrowed brow as she wondered if he was still angry at her for leaving.

Quickly, she looked away from him, deciding that it was best to avoid him for now. It wouldn't do to draw out fury at the family table. But as the day went on and she pitched in weeding the garden and cleaning the milkhouse, she was struck by how it hurt to be ignored.

While Sadie was scrubbing the long hallway between the row of milking stalls, Jonah came in wheeling a bale of hay.

"Spic-and-span," he said. "The milk inspector would give you a high rating. Nobody cleans a place the way you do, Sadie."

She took a break to wipe sweat from her forehead. It had been hard work scrubbing everything from the bulk tank to the milk-house walls and windows. "Do you think that's why Adam is letting me stay a few days?"

"I think you're welcome to stay whether you clean or not."

"I'm not so sure." She told him how Adam had been avoiding her.

"Bishop Samuel is mighty concerned about you leaving the way you did. Ya, you're in rumspringa, but no one expects an Amish girl to leave her family like that. There's a lot of disappointment among the church leaders. The bishop expects you to come back to us, the way Adam did. But Adam and I know how bullheaded you can be. You're not going to be baptized, are you?"

She shook her head. "I am sorry for that." Sadie swabbed the floor with a passion. "It was the right thing for me to leave. The Lord in heaven didn't make me to live Plain; I'm sure of that now. But I felt terrible leaving our family. It still tears at me. I need to go, but when I'm away my heart aches from missing all of you."

Jonah left his wheelbarrow and came closer to lean against a stanchion. "Adam has different responsibilities, being head of the family. Me, I'm allowed to say that we all missed you while you were gone. But if you have to go again, just remember this: You'll always be my sister," he told her. "You can travel a thousand miles from home, but you'll always have family here at the farm."

His words were reassuring, but it didn't break down the wall forming between Adam and her. Would he ever look her in the eye again?

That night, the family gathered round an outdoor fire to talk and catch fireflies and enjoy the cooler night air. Ruthie had fallen ill with a fever that afternoon—probably a flu. Mary explained that some folk had complained of a summer fever last Sunday at church. Mary had taken her to an empty room in the Doddy house. Mammi didn't mind tending her, and it was best to keep the germs from spreading to the rest of the family, especially Susie, whose special condition made even the smallest illness a problem.

Adam was also missing, and Sadie wondered what excuse he had used. Was he visiting Remy or working the wood in the little workshop behind the horse barn?

She tried to tell herself that she didn't care, but it wasn't true. She cared about Adam, and she longed to tell him of her adventures in the Englisher world. Wouldn't he be happy to know that she had met someone who suited her perfectly? She glanced over at Sam and Simon chasing fireflies. How she wished Mike could be here to share this with her, to get to know her family this way.

Adam didn't approve of Mike; Sadie knew that. But surely he could reach deep in his heart for some understanding. During his own rumspringa, Adam had left home on a search. Wouldn't he understand that God had called her away, to a different kind of life?

As Leah and Susie begged to hear the birthday song one more time before it was all over, Sadie pushed her thoughts aside and brought herself back to the night with a blanket of stars above and crisp grass beneath her. "One more time," she told the girls. "And then we put the song away for you . . . until next year."

The next morning, Sadie rose early to help with the milking. Working beside Jonah, Simon, and Gabe with the new machinery, the task was quicker than ever, even with the additional cows to milk.

"I think the cows missed you, Sadie," Gabe teased. "Or at least they missed your singing. They're usually not this quiet."

"I like to think they missed my beautiful music," Sadie said.

"But Gert and Meadow are new cows," Simon pointed out. "They never heard you singing before."

They all laughed as they sent the cows out to pasture and went back to the house to wash up for breakfast.

In the kitchen, Mary cut egg casserole into pieces while Leah and Susie, barefoot and sleepy-eyed, set the table.

"I see Mary let you two sleep in this morning," Adam said, coming in from the front room.

"They were sleeping like rocks," Mary said. "It was hard waking them. Not even Clive the rooster made them stir."

"I was up late reading," Leah said as she placed a pitcher of milk on the table.

"I went to bed early," Susie said, focusing on the platter of ham as she crossed the kitchen. "I don't know why I'm so tired."

Sadie noticed that Susie's eyes were shiny as glass, and she moved slowly. Her usual bouncy joy was gone.

"Do you feel all right?" Sadie asked her.

Susie hugged herself, then sat back on the daybed. "I'm hot and cold . . . and my skin hurts all over."

"That's not good at all." Sadie sat beside Susie and touched her cheek. She was burning up.

"She's sick." Sadie's words brought silence to the kitchen. Everyone knew Susie was not able to endure sickness well. With her condition, even a small cold or virus could make her very sick . . . even kill her.

"Do you want to go back to bed?" Sadie asked.

Susie nodded, then collapsed onto the daybed.

It was the middle of the night, but the sound of Susie calling her name rousted Sadie from a dreamless sleep in the sickroom of the Doddy house.

"Yes, Susie . . . I'm here." Sadie slid from the top of the bed and crossed the room to her sister's bedside. "What is it, liewe? Do you want something to drink? Dr. Trueherz says you should drink."

"I'm sorry, Sadie." Her eyes closed, Susie writhed against the mattress. "I'm sorry but I can't sing the song. I can't sing anymore."

She's delirious, Sadie thought. "It's okay. You just rest."

"But I need a drink," Susie whispered.

"Okay. Good." Sadie poured a cup of water from the bedside table and gave it to her. "Here you go."

Susie's eyes opened to slits as Sadie helped her sit up and take a sip. "Denki." Susie sighed as she sank back against the pillow.

Sadie stood over her watching. She was determined to see her sister through this. Ruthie was all better now, but Susie—not so good. Mary and Mammi had helped care for the sick girl during the day, but Sadie had insisted on taking the night shift. She would not leave Susie's side until Susie recovered.

A moan escaped Susie's throat as she rolled to her side and choked, throwing up on the bed. Sadie went to clean it up, but the color of it was so odd. Unnaturally green. Bile.

A shrill warning chilled her blood as she remembered Dr. Trueherz's words: "Call me if she doesn't get better or if she starts throwing up. We can't let her get dehydrated."

"Oh, Susie . . ." Fear ruled Sadie's heartbeat, a cold, dull thud, as she pulled the soiled sheet away and wiped Susie's face with a cool cloth. She had felt sure that Susie would get better with her constant care and God's blessing. . . .

But that wasn't happening.

Dear God, please shine your healing light on her, she prayed as she washed her hands. Back in the sickroom, where Ruthie had stayed but one night and then moved home, Sadie sat on the bed opposite Susie and looked at her silver cell phone. Two bars—enough of a signal. The time said 3:43 A.M. It was the middle of the night, but Susie had gotten worse. She had to call.

Please, let this call go through, she prayed as she waited.

"This is Doc Trueherz," he answered.

"It's Sadie King calling for Susie. I'm sorry to bother you in the middle of the night, but she just threw up." She explained what happened, and the doctor listened and asked a few simple questions.

"Okay, Sadie, I'm glad you called me." His words reminded her of Mike. A helper. He sighed. "I wish we'd gotten her to a hospital yesterday, but that can't be helped right now. The thing is, a virus like this can be very serious for someone whose system is compromised by her GA type I. I don't mean to scare you, but I want you to know what you're up against."

Sadie tried to swallow but her throat was dry and gritty. "I know." Her voice sounded small and distant. "We've been giving her twenty-four-hour care, like you said." Sadie hadn't left her side since she'd collapsed.

"Good. That's good. She really needs an IV, but since she's not in the hospital, we'll have to settle for a spoonful of water every ten minutes that she's awake to keep her from dehydration. Do you think you can do that?"

A spoonful every ten minutes . . .

"Yes."

"And keep an eye on her temperature. If her fever gets any higher . . ."

His words went on but Sadie was picturing a spoonful of water, clear, sweet water, and a giant clock ticking away.

Every ten minutes . . .

She couldn't forget. She couldn't let Susie down.

"Call me again if you need me. Anytime, okay?"

"Okay. Thank you."

She closed the phone and fumbled at the bedside for the silver spoon.

Every ten minutes . . .

Sadie worked the spoon between Susie's dry lips. There . . . that would help her get better soon.

She held the spoon tightly and sat on the opposite bed.

The two of them in this little sickroom seemed a world away from the farm. So isolated. Two beds on an island.

She thought of the long day and night of nursing her sister. Susie's fiery red cheeks, the verhuddelt talk from her fever.

All this sickness . . . so much to clean up, to wipe away the germs.

While Susie had dozed she had scrubbed the floors and walls. She had washed sheets in a tub out back and cooked broth for Susie and Ruthie, though only Ruthie had eaten it.

So much work to do, but if it would heal Susie, she would work. She thought maybe, maybe if she worked harder and got the room spotless, God would have mercy and spare Susie.

If she just worked harder . . . maybe she could make things right.

THIRTY–SEVEN

This is my fault." Sadie's voice was flat, but her stern expression cut right through Mike. Cold eyes and red flares on her cheeks . . . this was not the Sadie he knew.

One look, and Mike knew something was very wrong. He was glad he had driven out here, concerned after a strange phone conversation.

"I brought this on my family," she said as she fiercely scrubbed the banister of the Doddy house with a sponge.

"No, you didn't," Mike argued. "God isn't vengeful. He wouldn't punish you by making your sister sick."

"You don't understand! I broke the rules. I went against the Ordnung, pouring my heart into music and letting people photograph me. And now work is my punishment. I'm working for forgiveness for all of the family."

"Sadie . . ." He touched her wrist, trying to still her hand. "Please, take a break for a minute and talk to me. When was the last time you got some sleep?"

"No, no, I can't sleep. I've got bedding to wash and broth to make."

"How about if I wash the sheets while you lie down?"

"And then who will care for Susie?"

"Susie's fever broke. I just checked on her, and she seems well hydrated. You did a good job taking care of her, but now it's your turn to rest."

She turned back toward the stairs as if someone had called. "A teaspoon every ten minutes." Suddenly she dropped the sponge and ran up the steps.

"Wow." Mike stared after her, unsure of how to handle this. He couldn't force her to go to sleep, but she was freaking out from exhaustion.

"There's no talking to her," came a gravelly voice from behind him.

He turned and saw a short Amish woman. On her face were the creases of time and wisdom. "Are you Sadie's grandmother?" When she nodded, he said, "I'm Mike Trueherz."

"The doctor's son." She moved a little closer. "You'd best go get your father. We've all tried to talk to her, but she's like a log being swept downriver. The fever's got her, too."

Fever. Of course. Mike had assumed it was exhaustion.

"Okay, I'm going to get my father here. Would you please make sure she doesn't leave this house? I'm really worried about her."

She nodded. "I'll keep her here."

When Mike couldn't get cell service at the farm he jumped in his Ford and headed down the road. By the time he got service, he was almost at the clinic on the outskirts of Paradise. He explained the situation to his mother, and she told him to head over and pick up the doctor.

"I'm glad you're doing this," Henry said as Mike cruised back toward Halfway. "I've seen a few cases of this virus, and sometimes the fever hangs on for days. With a patient like Susie, we can't take any chances. After her sister's call last night, I was planning to head over there today."

Mike bit his lower lip, wondering how to break this big picture to his dad. "The thing is, Susie seemed stable when I stopped by there. Hydrated and a normal temp. It's her older sister Sadie I'm worried about. She seems delusional. Probably running a fever, but I didn't check. She's under the impression that she needs to keep working and scrubbing to heal her sister."

"Sounds like a fever. I'll check it out."

Although Mike's eyes were on the road, he could feel his father studying him. "I have to ask you, how did you come upon these cases? You've been so vocal about not going into the medical profession. Have you changed your mind?"

"No, no . . ." Of course his dad would think that. It was time to get honest. "Sadie King, Susie's sister, has become a good friend, and I've been trying to help her navigate between the Amish world and the English."

"Oh, really? Well, I suppose you're an expert on balancing those two worlds, having grown up out here in Amish country."

Mike blinked. His father got it.

"I guess I always suspected that you didn't love living out here. You and your brother grumbled a lot when we moved here from Philly, but I was on a mission, and kids adapt." His father shifted in the seat, turned toward the window. "But you're not a kid anymore. You're old enough to call the shots for your own life. I see that now. You've got your own plans and dreams. I'll find someone to take over the practice here."

Mike shot a quick look at his father's earnest face. He really meant it.

"I can't tell you what a relief it is to hear you say that, Dad."

"Yeah, I know, I put a lot of pressure on you and your brother. Thought I'd dangle the bait, only no one went for it."

"We just can't fill your shoes, Dad," Mike said.

"Yeah, and you want your own pair of shoes."

Both men laughed.

At the King farm, Dr. Trueherz paused in the doorway of the Doddy house, assessing Sadie's quiet panic.

"I'd like to take a look at your sister," he said, stepping forward to press the back of his hand to her cheek. "And then I'm going to take a look at you, okay? Okay. Up we go."

He trudged up the stairs, medical bag in hand.

Mike knew Sadie wanted to follow, but she turned and sat on the bottom step, her purple skirt pooling around her legs.

"What was I going to do?" She pressed her hands to her temples. "Ach. My head hurts so much."

"Have you taken any Tylenol yet?" Mike asked.

"No, no. I have to take care of Susie."

"Not anymore," Dr. Trueherz called as he came down the stairs. "Do you know your sister is sitting up in bed? Susie is doing much better. Her fever is gone, and for that I think we have to thank you, Sadie. You followed my instructions about small sips of water, I see."

Sadie stared up at him, a confused look on her face. "She's okay?"

"She's going to be fine." Henry propped his black bag on the floor and reached inside. He took out a thermometer, which he placed near Sadie's ear. "A hundred and two. You poor kid. You've caught the virus, Sadie."

She pressed her face into one palm. "Are you sure?"

"Positive. You need rest and hydration, just like your sister. Oh, and these will help." He handed her sample packets of fever-reducing medication.

She didn't seem to notice, so Mike took the packets and began to open them. "You need rest, Sadie."

"Absolutely," the doctor agreed. "Rest and liquids. If you start to throw up, try to take a spoonful of water every few minutes."

"I'll stay with her awhile." Mike handed over his car keys. "I'll give you a call if I need a ride."

The doctor nodded, then squatted down to meet Sadie face-to-face. "And one more thing. I studied medicine and anatomy, and I've practiced for twenty-five years. And I am very sure that your actions did not bring on your sister's virus." He straightened. "Rest now. Things will make more sense when you feel better."

Mike helped Sadie to her feet, pleased by his father's ability to reach Sadie. He had always known his father was an astute scientist; he had just never realized he was such a wise man.

THIRTY-EIGHT

*S*adie opened her eyes and looked toward the window. Sunshine streamed in through simple white curtains. What room was this?

She took a deep breath and it came back to her slowly, like the details of a nightmare. The sickroom, in the Doddy house. She had been sick, but she felt better now. Her head felt clear; the fog had lifted.

She sat up and swung her feet down, but the room started spinning. She rolled back onto the bed, surprised by the ache in her muscles. Not completely better yet, but at least her head wasn't a tangle of thoughts and fears anymore.

"You're awake?" Remy came in carrying a bowl with a spoon sticking out. "I brought you rice—Dr. Trueherz's recommendation."

"Denki." Sadie pushed herself up in bed, noticing the strings of her kapp dangling over her dress. She patted her head. Her kapp was off to the side, but her hair was still pinned back. "I wore my clothes to bed?"

Remy nodded. "You did. Mike was taking care of you, and he said you never take your kapp off. And, of course, he wasn't going to get you into a nightgown."

Sadie covered her embarrassed grin with one hand. "Mike put me to bed? Oh, I think I remember that."

"And he stayed to watch over you, all last night. Adam sat with him for a while, and Mammi Nell made dinner for him."

"Adam was here?" Sadie wondered if he'd come over because of concern for her or a worry about how it would look to have an Englisher boy spending the night in the Doddy house.

"Gabe gave Mike a ride to his parents' house this morning, after your fever broke."

Sadie hugged herself as the curtains lifted in the summer breeze. Mike had taken care of her. He was always doing that. The thought of him sitting here in the Doddy house tugged at her heart. And what had Mammi Nell said to him? She supposed Mike had charmed her, the way he did most people.

Remy handed her the bowl of rice. "Eat this. Mammi is making some broth for you."

While Sadie ate, Remy pulled a chair over to her bedside. "Susie and Ruthie are both perfectly fine now, thanks to your attentive nursing skills. Ruthie's working at the market today, and Leah and Susie are out in the stables."

"Thank the Lord." Sadie took a sip of water to get a glob of rice down. "I was so scared for Susie."

"I know. You were trying to handle too much on your own. Mary said you insisted on taking the night watch, but next time, I'm going to butt in sooner." She pressed the back of her hand to Sadie's cheek. "Poor Sadie. This can't be the way you expected to spend your visit. I'm glad you're feeling better now." She arose, smoothing the skirt of her dark purple dress. "I'll bring the broth up when it's done."

"Remy, wait." Sadie rested the bowl on the night table. "Have you talked to Adam about me? He won't talk to me or even look me in the eye."

"We've talked." Remy tugged nervously on one of her kapp strings as she sat down again. "But it would be wrong for me to speak for your brother. You two need to talk."

Sadie shook her head. "He's not going to like what I have to say. I know he wants me to be baptized and join the community, but I can't, Remy. When I think about living Amish forever, I feel trapped. I can't breathe."

"And you need to breathe, dear Sadie." Remy's green eyes held a spark of compassion.

"I love everyone here." The words were thick in Sadie's throat, but she needed to share her feelings with Remy. "But I believe that the Creator gave me this voice so that I could use it in a positive way. I've got to let the love inside me shine. And with Mike's help, I'm finding my way."

"I had a feeling Mike fit into this," Remy said.

"While I was trying to find my voice, I found love. The Big Love, I used to call it."

Remy smiled. "Mike Trueherz seems like a nice guy."

Kind, generous Mike was everyone's hero and helper. He made her feel alive and spontaneous and so special. "I thank God that I found Mike."

"Sadie . . ." Remy cradled Sadie's hands in hers. "This is something you need to tell your brother. Just because he seems distant doesn't mean that he hasn't worried about you since you went away. Talk to Adam."

Sadie nodded. "The only bad part, the downside, is that my path is taking me away from my family. . . ." Her voice caught in her throat over the heartbreak of it, and she took a breath to calm down. "But I believe that is just how God wants it to be."

Remy nodded. She understood.

For a while, the two women held hands, grateful that God had blessed them both in such different ways. Then Sadie gave Remy's hands a squeeze, feeling the thick calluses on Remy's palms. "Your hands . . . you've gotten used to living on a farm."

Remy looked down at both their hands. "I guess I have toughened up. But your hands have gotten softer. Check out these fingers, smooth and strong." Remy smiled. "You have the hands of a musician now."

Sadie held her hands out, thinking of how she had learned to extend her fingers to reach distant keys on the piano. Manual dexterity, Katherine called it. She had learned that it was a good thing to reach out to new lengths.

New places, new faces, new dreams . . . God willing, she would keep reaching out to the big world beyond this farm.

Food and a shower helped Sadie feel steady on her feet again. She pulled back her wet hair, pinned it up and donned a kapp and Amish dress . . . probably for the last time. The clothing wasn't something she favored, but the clean dress had been hanging in her sisters' room, and somehow it seemed right to dress Amish for this last afternoon on the farm.

The screen door slapped shut behind her as she stepped into the humid, still afternoon. The powerful sunshine that nurtured their crops seemed to weigh on her head, and she was grateful for the cooling effect of her damp hair on this hot August day. The horses seemed sluggish as Sadie passed them on the way to the maintenance shed, where Mary had told her she'd find Adam in the small woodshop.

The door creaked as she gave it a push. "Adam?"

There was movement in the shadows. Adam straightened up and put a tool on the workbench, his eyes on her directly for the first time this week.

"I came for a proper good-bye. It's time for me to leave, but I can't go without really talking to you." The coolness of the shed was welcome as she stepped in. "Mike is coming to pick me up. He'll stay for dinner, if it's all right with you."

"He's welcome here. How are you feeling? The fever's gone?"

"Ya." The thought of Adam sitting by her bedside with Mike made her feel the bittersweet tug of the love and care she had known in the safe haven of her family.

She walked past an unfinished hope chest, trying to put her feelings to words. *Say that you forgive me. Say that there's peace between us.* She knew what she wanted him to say, but how could she lead him to the topic when the words had to come from his heart?

"Thank you for allowing me to visit," she said. "Coming home was . . ." She steeled herself against the realization that this wouldn't be her home anymore. "Being here was a blessing. It reminded me of all the wonderful things that will be so hard to leave behind." Good food, clean air . . . the sweet tang of summer clover and the feel of warm earth beneath her feet. All the trappings of the farm that fit her like a familiar old shoe would be sorely missed. So many good things here on the farm, though none of them compared with the love of her brothers and sisters.

"So you're really going," he said.

She nodded, her throat thick with emotion. Her heart ached at the thought of saying good-bye to her family. "Not a day goes by when I don't think of you and Jonah, Mary and Ruthie. I miss joking with Gabe and Simon in the milking barn. Leah and Susie are done with school now, and Sam and Katie have grown so while I was away. I miss you all so much, my heart aches."

"Then why are you leaving?" he asked, his voice so calm it reminded her of their dat's peaceful way.

"Remember how Mamm used to say that sometimes the right path isn't always the easy one? The right path for me leads away from this farm. It's taken me a while to figure it all out, but now I know what I must do. I have a lot of work ahead of me to make myself useful through music, but you know that I've never been afraid of hard work."

"There's plenty of work for you here, Sadie." He put the sanding block aside and rubbed his hands together in a cloud of dust. "I can't let you go without warning you that Englisher ways are very different from ours. That world is not a safe place for an Amish girl."

She put her hands on her hips, strengthened by the truth of her decision. "It wasn't that long ago that you yourself left here for your own rumspringa. Three years you were gone. You saw the problems with the ... the stiff ways of the Amish. No bending of the rules, no exceptions. It's a hard life to follow."

"I did leave here for a different life. But I was disappointed in the Englisher world. Disappointed and lonely. You and me, we are more alike than you think, Sadie. The reason I stayed away so long was not that Englisher girl. It was my craft work."

"Working with wood?" Sadie had never heard these details of Adam's rumspringa. Intrigued, she moved to the workbench and ran her hand over the smooth finish of a narrow piece of wood. What would it become? A chair spindle? The leg of a short table?

"I made furniture by hand, and I was successful with it. The wood ... I was good with it. I had a talent, working with it, finding its grain, figuring out what a piece wanted to be. It was a good life, but it wasn't mine. I didn't care for the town or the people around me, and I was lonely. I was planning to come back even before

Mamm and Dat were killed, but I was stuck in my ways, so proud of my work. The real shame is that Dat didn't know I would return and join the community."

"That always bothered you, didn't it? Thinking that Dat was disappointed with you."

His head tipped down toward the workbench, his voice solemn in the cool shadows of the shed. "Ya, it was a heavy weight to bear."

"But you're wrong if you think that Dat was angry with you. He could never stay mad at any living thing, and he never gave up on you. Mamm and Dat loved all their children, whether near or far, baptized or . . ." Sadie's voice trailed off as her own words sank in. Their parents hadn't loved Adam any less when he had gone away during his rumspringa, and if Mamm and Dat were still alive, their love for Sadie would have burned on, unwavering, like a lantern in the night.

Whether she was living Plain or fancy.

That thought reassured her, but even the approval of her family couldn't protect Sadie from the decisions of the gemeinde. The church leaders could not accept any reason for leaving, and their disapproval of Sadie would turn community opinion against her. If she was allowed to visit in the future, she would be met with scorn and sour faces. Her life here would never be the same.

"Why must my decision to leave here cause such a stir?" she asked, thinking out loud. "I never wanted to burn bridges behind me. I want to come back and visit. I want to be here next spring when the crocuses push up and the tulips bloom . . . and a year from now when Sam starts school. . . ."

Adam shook his head. "You can't walk two roads at the same time, Sadie. If you leave your Amish home, there's no telling if the ministers will allow other visits. And the wedding . . ." He let out his breath in a huff. "Bishop Sam might not let us have you as a guest. That's why you need to be sure of your choice, Sadie. Because you can't drop in and out of your Amish family every time the weather changes."

She stepped up to the workbench, facing her oldest brother. "I'm sure of my decision to go." She pressed a hand to her heart. "I'm so very sure, but it breaks my heart. And knowing that this is the right choice for me doesn't make it any easier to say good-bye. I feel bad about leaving our family."

The image of Susie's pale face came to mind, and she remembered gripping the spoon and pressing it to her sister's dry lips through the long night. "I don't want to bring shame to our family, but in my heart, I know I have to leave here. I can't commit to living Amish forever, and God has blessed me with wondrous things in the world beyond our farm. I'm learning so much about music, Adam. Beautiful music that lifts the soul and gives glory to God."

"So . . . you will make a joyful noise."

She squinted at him, recognizing the quote from the Bible.

"Just not so joyful for the rest of us when you go. There will be a price to pay, Sadie. The church leaders can't tolerate young folks leaving the faith. And as the leader of this family, I have to say that you were born and raised to be Amish. Baptism is the good and proper thing to do."

Her heart sank and she looked away, not wanting to hear a scolding from her older brother. Of course there would be a price to pay. There would be consequences . . . but Sadie had hoped these things would not drive a permanent wedge between Adam and her.

The knot in her throat seemed to block her words from coming out. "I'm sorry," she said, her voice trembling, "but I have to go."

"I was afraid of that. But I'll pray that Gott watches over you."

She lifted her gaze, catching a glimmer in his eyes.

"His eye is on the sparrow," he said.

"And I know he watches me," she finished, blinking back tears. "So you do . . . you understand?"

"Ya, I do. Dat would have understood. He would have kept a light burning for each and every one of us."

Sadie swallowed, and the thick emotion eased from her throat as guilt lifted from her heart. Relief mingled with sorrow as she threw herself against her brother and hugged him hard, her face pressing into the cloth of his shirt.

"Denki, Adam," she said as his arms closed around her reassuringly. Such an impossible choice she'd made! But now, knowing that her brother would always love her, it was just a tiny bit easier to go.

Just a tiny bit.

Dinner was a simple summer picnic set outside at the big, long tables. Sadie had helped Mary boil two dozen eggs and chop as many hot dogs and peppers to prepare a family recipe for egg salad. So delicious on a sandwich with cold pickles! Sadie felt her appetite returning. Remy and Ruthie made coleslaw, potato salad, and a green salad from the vegetables in their very own garden.

As she and Mary worked side by side in the kitchen, singing the songs their mother had taught them to mark their chores, Sadie realized this bond with her sister would remain strong no matter how far apart they lived.

She was delighted to hear Remy joining in on a few songs.

"You've picked up quite a bit while I was gone," she told Remy, who had barely a trace of Englisher left in her.

"I've been trying my best. My Pennsylvania Deutsch has improved, too. I've gotten to the point where Sam and Katie understand what I'm saying. And Aunt Betsy is convinced that the chickens in their coop must be Englisher because they seem to understand me the best."

The girls laughed. As Mary reached over Sadie's shoulder to tuck away the spices, Sadie was hit by a wave of dizziness.

"Poor girl," Mary said, dropping a hand to Sadie's shoulder. "Still shaky on your feet, are you?"

"Just a little," Sadie admitted, pressing the back of one hand to her forehead. "But the fever's gone, and I'm thinking straight now."

"You're welcome to stay until you feel better," Mary said.

"But Mike has to get back for his job at the bakery, and he'll give me a ride." Sadie was touched by her sister's concern, but she was eager to go now. The next part of her life beckoned her down the lane, and she was ready to begin the journey.

As they sliced bread for sandwiches they sang "His Eye Is on the Sparrow," and for the first time since her dat's death there was a smile on Sadie's face as she sang this song. Her dat's love had been endless and unconditional, just like God in heaven. Mamm used to say that Gott always leaves a candle burning in the window so that you can find your way home in the darkest night. Mamm was right; the path had been lit for Sadie.

They were setting food out on the table when Mike's car pulled into the lane. Sadie's eyes swept the landscape—green grass, red barn, blue sky—and her heart lifted at the sight of his familiar car. She had to resist the urge to run to the car and give him a big hug, though her siblings were a step ahead of her. Ruthie, Simon, and Leah were already racing across the grass to greet him.

Placing a pitcher on the table, Sadie was surprised to see a second car following Mike's. The cars pulled in beside the parked buggies and she squinted to see. Dr. Trueherz? Mike had brought his father. Well, there was plenty of food, and the good doctor was always welcome. Besides, she would like to get to know Mike's father better. These past months, she had shared good times with Mike's grandmother, but rarely had she seen his father outside the Paradise clinic.

"I wanted to check up on some of my favorite patients," the doctor said when he and Mike approached the table, his black medical bag in one hand. "We've got to stay on top of Susie's condition, and there's no use in you traveling if you're not well yet."

"I'm feeling much better," Sadie assured him. "But it's kind of you to make the trip."

"And since you're here, you must stay for dinner," Mary added.

Henry's eyes twinkled as he nodded. "I'm happy to combine my visit with some socializing. I understand you and Mike have become good friends."

Sadie felt her face grow warm at the talk of courtship. Dr. Trueherz made it sound light and breezy, as if they were discussing the weather! But Mary turned away to tend to the table, and Mike flashed Sadie an easy smile.

"Yes," Sadie managed to say, "Mike has become a good friend. You know, your son is a fine person. He's a helper."

"Just like his father," Mary said from across the table.

The doctor squinted at Mike for a moment, then clapped him on the back. "I'm proud of the man he's become. Very proud."

"Okay, you're talking about me like I'm not here," Mike said. "That's weird."

Over the laughter Sadie sensed that things had shifted between Mike and his father—all for the best.

A sweet breeze swirled around them as they sat down to a meal—Sadie's last supper with her family for a long time. Mike sat across from her, his father beside him at Adam's right hand, and as they bowed their heads for silent prayer, she thanked the Heavenly Father for bringing her to this place, surrounded by people she loved, even if it was only for one simple meal.

Adam began the conversation by thanking Dr. Trueherz for his visit. There was the usual clatter and murmur as people passed the sandwiches and salads and reached for their lemonade.

"This will be our last meal with sister Sadie," Adam began, his words bringing the table activity to a halt. "She's traveling back to Philadelphia with Mike. Spending the rest of the summer taking care of Katherine Trueherz."

The breath swelled in Sadie's chest as she felt all eyes upon her.

"My mother is looking forward to having you with her," Henry said. "She enjoys your company, and I think she's ready to dismiss the health care workers and regain some of her privacy."

"Sadie's a wonderful good caretaker," Mary said, picking up a fresh radish. "I've trained her well."

"And she's not so bad in the barn, if you've got any cows to milk," Gabe teased.

Everyone laughed, easing the moment.

"But we just got you back," Ruthie said, a trace of sorrow in her voice. "Can't you stay a little longer? I want you to stay with us forever and always."

"I'm afraid not, honey girl." Sadie met Ruthie's eyes, sorry to disappoint her.

"Will you ever come back again?" Simon asked.

"I'll be back to visit." Sadie passed him the relish tray. "Wild horses couldn't keep me away."

He grinned. "Not if you know how to calm a horse."

"You'll come for the weddings?" Leah asked.

Susie clapped a hand against her heart. "You must return in November. The celebration won't be the same without you!"

The weddings . . . "I'll come back for that," she said, catching Adam's stern gaze. "If the bishop allows it."

"You can get around wild horses," Simon said, "but Bishop Samuel? Not so easy."

Sadie smiled at his joke, funny but true.

As talk continued she turned to the ones who planned to marry: Remy, the Englisher who had brought light back to her brother's eyes. Sister Mary, who had been filling her hope chest with quilts since she'd begun courting Five. And brother Adam, who had left to pursue his own dream but returned to take Dat's place at the head of the table, head of the household. In a few months they would be young Amish couples, starting families of their own.

The farm would go on, with a new batch of calves, the milking and planting and harvest. But it would go on without Sadie.

Emotion rose, overwhelming her for a moment. Such an odd mixture of excitement at her new life and sorrow over the end of her childhood here. Holding back tears, she reached under the table for the bag she had stashed there before supper. Her plastic Walmart bag.

"There's something I want to show you." She eased back from the table a bit and pulled the bag into her lap. Colorful squares of fabric emerged as she rolled down the edges.

"Oooh, colors," Katie crooned. "So many colors."

"Ya, bold, beautiful colors. I chose them because they reminded me of the cloth we sew our dresses from. Deep blues and greens and purples." She held up a swatch. "They're squares for a quilt, but they're all a little different. This one is for Simon." She had embroidered his name there—a little rough but readable—along with an appliqué of a horse. The woman in the Walmart had shown her the collection of images, and she had fallen in love with the idea of a family quilt.

"I started the squares to pass the time on tour. There's one for each of my brothers and sisters. And you too, Remy. And Five," she said with a glance at Mary. "I found a big number five to add to his square."

Mary pressed a hand to her mouth. "He'll be glad to know he's in the family."

"And a book for Leah," Ruthie said, reaching over to open a square. "What did you get for mine?"

"A flower reaching for the sun." Sadie squeezed her sister's shoulder. "Because you are a sweet flower and you always find the sunny side of things."

"Oh, that warms my heart." Ruthie pressed against her for a hug.

"And there's a dolly on Katie's, and a car on Remy's to show how she came into our lives."

"Driving off the road in an ice storm." Remy twirled a kapp string around one finger. "It's all part of the story, isn't it?"

"And mine has a heart with a smiley face on it! It's so very cute," Susie exclaimed.

"A heart for good health and a good heart," Sadie explained.

"What's on my patch?" Sam asked.

"You have a chicken, because you're wonderful good at gathering the eggs, and you're the only person who's not afraid of Lumpig."

Sam grinned. "Can I see it?"

"Ya." The chatter was lively as the patches were passed around the table, and Sadie sat back and tried to soak up the joy of being with her family.

"I'm going to sew all the patches into a beautiful quilt," she said. "It will be a way to remember my family when I'm away from you." Her throat grew thick with emotion again until the doctor interrupted.

"A family quilt." Dr. Trueherz nodded. "That's a wonderful idea, Sadie."

"Coming from Sadie, it sure is a surprise." Jonah grinned at her, amused by his patch with a puzzle piece sewn on. "Especially because you always hated quilting. As I remember, you used to say that quilting was slower than watching paint dry."

"Did I say that?" Sadie grinned. "I guess this tells you how boring a tour can be."

"Mine is a house?" Adam scratched his chin.

"Because you're the head of the household," Sadie explained, "and a carpenter, too. At least, a carpenter at heart."

He fingered the patch, a hint of a smile tugging at his lips. "I think your quilt is a very good idea, but unusual."

"It's not an Amish quilt," Sadie said, "not a traditional one."

It will be sort of like me, she thought, taking a welcome breath.

"We all want to see it when it's done," Adam said, handing her the patch.

"Just as we want to see you whenever you can make it back to us," Remy added.

"Promise to visit whenever you can," Susie said.

"And bring books," Leah added.

"I promise." Sadie nodded as she tucked bits of fabric into the bag.

"I don't know what the bishop will decide." Adam's voice revealed his concern. "But we'll weather that storm when it comes. We'll always be your family."

"And we'll always love you," Remy said.

"Oh, I miss you already!" Ruthie threw her arms around Sadie's waist and squeezed tight.

Patting Ruthie's back, Sadie let her eyes sweep the faces of her brothers and sisters, from Mary, blinking back tears, to little Katie, whose brows were knit in awe of the serious moment.

How she loved them, each and every one!

She let her eyes travel over the barn and silo to the gently sloping hills. She fixed her gaze on the birdhouse they had made a few months ago. Everyone had pitched in with the building and painting, and it now stood tall on a spit of grass, sunlight glinting off the roof tiles. "The city suits me well, but I've always felt safe on this farm. Dat made sure it was a safe place for all God's creatures. I didn't realize just how wonderful good my home was until I traveled away from home."

Adam nodded, and she read something new in his dark eyes. Understanding.

"Our farm is still a haven. We keep Gott's peace here. And, Gott willing, it will be a safe place for you to return. Even if it's only for a visit."

The sky was a swirl of pink and purple cottony clouds over the patchwork of fields as Sadie and Mike headed up the lane in his blue Ford.

"Do you want to hear some tunes?" he asked, reaching for the radio.

She held up a hand. "Not just yet." When the car pulled onto the paved road, she turned to face the farm, taking a moment to memorize the familiar peaks of the farmhouse roof, the barns and outbuildings, the silos, and the three buggies lined up in front of the barn. She wanted to remember the home of her childhood exactly as it was.

With a sigh, she shifted in the seat and faced forward, looking toward the future.

"Will you sing with me, Mike? Let's sing in that harmony that's so beautiful."

"Sure. 'Be Thou My Vision'?"

She nodded, took a breath, and began the first song of her new life. Country air blew in through the open windows and their song traveled out over the fields as the car glided down the sloping hill.

Mike shot her a smile as they finished the first verse, and she felt pure joy bubble inside her at the wonderful journey ahead. The home of her youth was behind her now, and she was on a steady path toward the home of her heart.

A heart bursting with love and joy and God's plentiful blessings.

ACKNOWLEDGMENTS

To Dr. Violet Dutcher, who helped me navigate everything from unzufriede to the unspoken rules of Amish culture, I am in awe of your understanding and appreciation of the Amish community. It is only with your help that I'm able to write an authentic representation of Amish life. All that experience and an excellent eye for detail and story—Vi, you are a gem!

You can't find a better editor than Junessa Viloria! Thank you for cheering for my characters and helping me push them to enact stories with drama, humor, and heart. Your compassion comes through in your editing, and I hope it's well-woven throughout this book.

To the wonderful good staff at Random House, including Junessa Viloria, Jane von Mehren, Melissa Possick, Sonya Safro, and Loren Noveck: You have made me feel that this book is in very capable hands. It warms my heart to be on such a talented, bright team.

To my agent Robin Rue, thanks for staying one step ahead. It's great to know that help is only an email away.

And to my family, who have learned to weather the quirks and extremes of having a writer in the house, thanks for sharing the love. And by the way, I haven't had a chance to make dinner tonight. . . .

ROSALIND LAUER grew up in a large family in Maryland and began visiting Lancaster County's Amish community as a child. She attended Wagner College in New York City and worked as an editor for Simon & Schuster and Harlequin Books. She currently lives with her family in Oregon, where she writes in the shade of some towering two-hundred-year-old Douglas fir trees.

Read on for an exciting preview of

A

Simple Autumn

the next Seasons of Lancaster novel
by Rosalind Lauer

ONE

September

A lull covered the congregation like a warm blanket. The preacher had been talking about faith for so long that his voice was now a gentle hum in the back of Jonah's mind.

Now was the time.

Jonah King knew that church wasn't meant for ogling people, but it wasn't often these days that he was under the same roof with Annie Stoltzfus. He turned his head just a few inches, to find her among the women seated on the other side of the barn.

There she was. . . .

Her face was framed by golden hair twisted back and tucked under her kapp. Jonah imagined that her hair would be as soft as corn silk, her skin as smooth as a vat of milk. . . .

Her blue eyes flashed like lightning and he looked away quickly. All it took was one quick look to get hope frolicking in his chest like a playful pup. Ya, he had it bad. Here he was, a grown man, and his heart got to racing at the sight of a girl.

But there had always been something special about Annie. One flicker of her blue eyes and he was reminded of the summer sky and cornflowers smiling up from a green field. The spark of life behind those eyes—the spirit and humor that made people want to be with Annie—that was the thing that pulled him to her time and again.

Of course, he never spoke about it. No one in his family knew that Annie Stoltzfus had hooked him, ever since they were kids playing on the frozen pond.

How many years had he watched her and waited, hoping she'd notice him? They had learned their lessons together in the one-room schoolhouse, and when they were children she'd come to their house countless times to visit with his sister Mary.

And all those years, she only had eyes for Jonah's brother Adam. Ya, Adam had been the name on Annie's lips. She'd baked many a pie for him, and she'd fretted about him when he went away during his rumspringa.

Jonah glanced to his left, where Adam sat with that squinty-eyed look he got when he was thinking. Adam surely had a lot to think about. He was now the head of their family of eleven, a big responsibility for a man so young. Everyone knew Annie had thought she and Adam would be wed by now.

But Adam had chosen to marry someone else, an Englisher girl with a yearning for a loving family and a heart big enough to help him raise the King children here in Halfway. Now that Adam was out of the running, Jonah wondered if Annie would finally see him in a new light. The Bible said that there was a time for every purpose under heaven. Maybe fall was the season that Gott might answer his prayers and plant a seed of love in Annie's heart.

He could always hope—nothing wrong with that.

Jonah turned his attention back to Preacher Dave, who was still talking about the Bible passage "Judge not that ye be not judged."

"Judgment is a chore for the Heavenly Father to take care of," Dave was saying. "It's not our task to look at our neighbor, our brother or sister, and judge them. Isn't that a wonderful thing? One less chore on my list for the day. We must let Gott be the judge. It's not our place to look to the man or woman beside us and decide whether the things they do are right or wrong. . . ."

Jonah straightened on the wooden bench, pressing his hands flat on his thighs. As his palms brushed the coarse broadcloth of his good Sunday trousers he saw the powerful truth in Preacher Dave's sermon. Of course, everyone knew they shouldn't judge their neighbor. It was a lesson taught among the Amish all the time. Jonah took a deep breath, wishing folks could take it to heart and stop passing judgment on him and his brothers and sisters.

The congregation seemed equally restless. Someone coughed. Little Matthew Eicher came toddling toward the men's section, crossing from his mother to his father. A child fussed in the women's section, and in front of him the Zook boys nudged each other.

Everyone's itching to file out of the barn and catch the tail end of summer, Jonah thought as he let his eyes follow the dancing specks of dust glimmering in a shaft of sunlight from the haymow.

It was a fine September morning, one of those days that wasn't sure whether it wanted to hold on to summer's heat or let the trees and barns begin to cool from the breeze sweeping over the hills. The morning had been crisp and cold, but now, with so many people filling the barn, there was enough body heat to bring to mind a summer day.

Rubbing his clean-shaven chin, Jonah frowned as the Zook boys stirred again.

Eli Zook leaned in to his younger brother John and whispered in his ear. John was Jonah's brother Simon's age, nine or so, and Eli had all the vinegar of a boy pushing into the teen years. John shook his head, and his older brother grabbed his upper arm and gave a pinch. That brought a glare from their father, Abe. Young Eli was a bit of a bully; Jonah had seen him put the squeeze on Simon in the past, but the boy's mischief usually went unchecked. Even now, none of the other men sitting nearby was paying him any mind.

The weight of Simon sinking against him told Jonah that the boy was falling asleep. Jonah slid an arm around his brother's shoulders, boosting him up.

Simon's heavy lids lifted.

Can't let the boy doze off during Preacher Dave's sermon, Jonah thought as his younger brother looked up at him with sleepy eyes, then took a deep breath.

Big John Eicher watched from the bench off to the side. And Jonah noticed that Big John wasn't the only one. Other men had their eyes on him and his brothers.

Always watching. And judging? Even though the preacher had hammered away at them not to judge, Jonah felt disapproval heavy on his shoulders.

A cloak of self-consciousness had hung over the King family these past two years. When their parents were killed, people had rallied to give them support. Casseroles and baked goods had appeared on their table and jars of beets and peaches had stocked their pantry. Nearby Amish families had invited the younger children over after school to distract them from their grief and give the older family members like Jonah, Adam, and Mary time to get the household chores done. Neighbors had helped with the spring tilling and planting. The whole community had turned out to raise the new milking barn.

The good folks of Halfway, Amish and Englisher, had been more than generous with their help during the Kings' time of need. But the farm was running smoothly now, better than ever with the new automatic milking equipment and the larger herd. Thanks to Gott, the family no longer needed assistance. Jonah had been relieved when folks were able to start greeting him without the veil of pity over their eyes.

And just when things seemed to settle back to an even pace, Remy McCallister, Adam's Englisher girl, had come along and turned everyone's heads again. And then there was sister Sadie leaving home for her rumspringa, going off and singing with a group of Englisher musicians. He suspected tongues were still wagging over the King family.

Jonah didn't like the extra attention. It was like a splinter stuck under the skin. The skin healed over it, but the dull ache lingered. That was the problem now with his family. So many folks saw the Kings as different from other Amish families, and it wasn't going to change anytime soon, with Adam about to marry an Englisher girl, an aussenseiter. Ya, Remy was working hard to learn their ways, but good and kind though she was, she was still Englisher inside.

As one of the other ministers spoke about the evils of gossip that came from judging others, Jonah spoke a silent prayer in his heart. Gott knew that the Kings were a good, obedient family that followed the Ordnung. If only the people here could see that. "Help them see us with fair and honest eyes."

TWO

After the service, Jonah pitched in with the other men to move the benches from the barn to the tables that had been set up for the light lunch. The weather was holding, so the meal would be taken at tables outside in the sunshine.

"Right over there," one of the older women instructed as Jonah and his brother Gabe toted a long wooden bench. "Over by the beech trees. They're in need of benches over there."

Jonah and Gabe followed her directions, clearing the crowd outside the barn and maneuvering around the rows of parked carriages.

"Just put it over there in the state of Ohio," Gabe said wryly as they traipsed through the grass toward three portable tables on the lawn.

Jonah grinned. His brother wasn't a big talker, but when he spoke his words were pointed. "Not that far," Jonah said. "Just carry it in to Bird-in-Hand." Usually the tables were grouped in one spot, but the layout of the Eichers' yard didn't allow that, especially with the many carriages and buggies parked there today.

When Jonah saw Annie over at one of the tables with his sister Mary, his fingers nearly lost their grip on the bench.

This would be a good chance to talk to her. Some smart comment would be good. Something funny to make her laugh. Annie's laugh made everyone smile.

But what could he say? Talking with girls had never been his strength. He kept quiet, and Annie didn't pay any mind to Gabe and him.

"They've already started packing," Annie said as she set each place with a knife, cup, and saucer. Mary followed her down the table, pouring water into each cup. "They'll be staying with Perry's uncle till they get on their feet. It's an Old Order Amish group in upstate New York."

"Annie, what will you do without your sister?" Mary asked sympathetically.

"And little Mark," Annie added.

From his time spent doing repairs at the Stoltzfus house, Jonah knew Annie was attached to her nephews Mark and Levi. Mark was just a toddler, but Levi was around brother Sam's age—a time when small chores could be turned into play.

"It breaks my heart to see them packing up their little family," Annie said.

Jonah kept his eyes on the bench as he drank in the conversation. So Perry and Sarah Fisher were moving to New York. He'd heard some talk of Perry pursuing an opportunity down in Maryland, but wasn't sure the young family would be willing to pick up and leave Halfway.

"I'm going to miss them so much." Annie's voice was laced with sadness. "But Sarah says I should come join them after they're settled."

A chill curled up Jonah's spine. Would Annie really think of leaving?

"Annie, no!" Mary gave voice to his concern. "Could you just up and leave us in the blink of an eye?"

"It wouldn't be all that soon, and . . ." Annie's voice broke off as she noticed Gabe and Jonah nearby. "Anyway, let's finish up here so we can help Lizbeth with the second shift."

Jonah lowered the bench and straightened. He kept his eyes on the ground, knowing anyone would see his worries in them. Annie couldn't leave Halfway. She wouldn't.

"Come on." Gabe clapped a hand on his back and gave him a shake. "The sooner these tables get set up, the sooner we can eat. And the way I'm feeling, I could tuck away half the church spread."

As he followed Gabe, Jonah turned back to steal a look at Annie. She was talking with Mary again, the two of them close enough for private words. Jonah lifted his straw hat to rake back his dark hair.

A few overheard words from Annie and his heart had clouded over.

Was Annie really going to leave Halfway?

He was plodding back to the barn when he heard someone calling to him.

"Jonah? Jonah King. Come."

He glanced up and saw two bearded men beckoning him from the porch. Uncle Nate stood beside a squat man with black eyeglasses—Jacob Yoder.

Squaring his shoulders, Jonah tamped down his worries and climbed the porch steps. "The sunshine is back," he said, tipping his hat.

"After five days of rain, it's good to know there's still a sun to shine down on us," Nate said with a wry smile.

"But it got a little warm in the barn during the services." Jacob's brown eyes were magnified by his glasses. "I noticed that young Simon was dozing off in there. Everything okay? Is the boy sick?"

"A boy needs his sleep, and we know our Simon has his problems with that," Uncle Nate said. "Is he having the bad dreams again? I remember when he was sleepwalking through the night. That was a terrible thing."

"Night terrors," Jacob said, wanting to set them straight. "That's what Dr. Trueherz says they're called. But the doc thinks they were caused by trauma."

And Simon had been through more than his share of pain. The only witness to their parents' murders, Simon had suffered deeply during those dark days. Many nights the boy had paced the halls with a crazy look in his eyes and panic in his heart.

But not anymore. Many things had been resolved when the police had arrested the man who killed Levi and Esther King. And when the puzzle pieces had fallen into place, Simon settled into an easier peace.

"I don't think Simon has had a nightmare for a long time," Jonah said, glancing over at the paddock where Simon was tossing a football with other boys his age. "And the night terrors ended in the winter."

"Good! That's good to hear." Jacob nodded, his head bobbing on his broad shoulders.

"No more sleepwalking?" Uncle Nate asked.

"No more. I think he's just tired today," Jonah said. "Probably because he's been staying late in the stable with his horse."

Simon had become close with his horse, Shadow, whom he'd been working with all summer. Since school had started, Simon had been worried that he'd have to cut back Shadow's training. "She's a good horse," Simon told Jonah nearly every day in the stables. "A hard worker. It won't be long before she'll be able to pull the plow with the rest of the team.'"

Shadow had come to them as a squeamish loner of a horse, but Dat had seen something in her, and Simon had refused to give up.

Now, with Simon's training, Jonah had no doubt that Shadow would become one of the most valuable horses on the farm.

"I'm counting on you to make sure Simon gets the sleep he needs," Nate told Jonah. Their uncle did his best to look out for the family, Jonah knew that, but he felt himself bristling over the warning. Simon was a good boy.

And Jonah didn't notice anyone asking about why Eli Zook was pinching his brother during the service.

Jacob Yoder turned the talk to Ira and Rose Lapp, members of their church who had attended the service today after being shunned for nearly two months.

"Is the ban over?" Nate asked, touching his beard lightly.

"They were allowed to attend church today," Jacob explained, "but the bishop said they still can't sit at the same table as members come mealtime. Still shunned, until the bishop says otherwise."

Jonah let his eyes skim over the tables near the kitchen door, where the ministers and older members were sitting down to the first shift of lunch. A small table, barely bigger than a sewing table, had been set off to the side near the rose trellis. Not the most desirable spot, with fat bumblebees buzzing over the late blooms. Old Ira Lapp sat there with his wife, Rose. The couple had their heads bowed. In silent thanks for the meal, or bidding the Lord to bring them back into the community?

How miserable it would feel to be shunned. Even as he vowed never to be in such a position of shame, Jonah felt a pang of sympathy for the older couple.

"What was the real story about that car?" Uncle Nate asked.

"It's a Jeep, actually," Jonah offered. "Sitting on the side of the road with a 'for sale' sign in the window now. I pass it every time I take the covered bridge into Paradise." He stopped himself, not wanting to be one of the gossips, even if he had heard murmurings of Ira's story.

"Ira got in a pickle over the automobile. His son Daniel left it behind when he went off during his rumspringa, and Ira just let the car sit behind the barn. Bishop Samuel warned him many times to put it up, but Ira did nothing." Jacob shrugged. "What else could the bishop do but bring on the ban?"

"Mmm." Uncle Nate's lips curled to one side. "There's probably more to that story."

"Cars have tempted many a good man," Nate said. "Didn't you and your brother drive a Ford back in your rumspringa?" he asked, squinting at Jacob.

Jacob's cheeks flushed red above his beard, but he smiled. "That was a very good car. When you pressed the gas, it could really gallop. Remember that, Nate? Faster than any horse I ever knew."

"Fast, but you can't feed a car hay and oats."

The two older men chuckled.

"Those days are far behind us now," Jacob said with a sigh.

Nate nodded. "Ah, but sometimes it seems like yesterday."

Seeing the smile on his uncle's face, Jonah wondered if his own father had ever learned to drive a car. Dat had never spoken of it, but Jonah knew it was something most young men tried.

Even Jonah. He was embarrassed to admit it now, but he had driven the very Jeep that had gotten Ira in trouble. Ira's son Daniel had been a friend, and he'd taught Jonah everything about the vehicle. How many times had they climbed dusty hills and plunged through the low part of the river in that Jeep? He had very clear memories of gripping the plastic stick shift. The pattern of the gears was like a road map in his mind. He'd been a good driver, but he'd known that driving wasn't going to be a part of his life. Jonah had always known that he would never stray from the path of the Amish.

"But time marches on," Jacob said wistfully. "Now we have our own boys in rumspringa. Hard to believe. And you and Betsy have an Englisher girl living with you." He tipped his hat back, squinting at Nate.

"We do. But Remy's living Plain now. She's been going to the classes. Going to get baptized."

"Is she learning the language?"

"She's getting better at it," Nate said.

"The little ones love to teach her words." Remy's arrival had overturned the applecart for his family, but Jonah had to admit, she was trying to fit in.

Jacob pushed his glasses up on his nose. "She seems like a nice girl, but do you think she'll really stay? Some Englishers like to dabble with Amish life, but they never stick with it."

"I think Remy is a special one." Nate's brown eyes scanned the gathering on the lawn.

Jonah followed his uncle's gaze to the girl in the purple dress, her bright copper hair framing the edge of her kapp. She was helping the women serve the meal. For an Englisher, she was a hard worker.

"All I know is that Remy is quick to pitch in, and Betsy likes her sunny outlook," Nate added. "I think she'll stick around."

Jonah nodded in agreement, but Jacob shook his head doubtfully. "You can't make a Jersey into a Holstein."

Uncle Nate laughed. "That's true."

Jonah held his tongue, though he was bothered by the small-mindedness of some people in the congregation. To compare a young girl to a cow?

It was a relief when the older men were called to sit for the meal.

Saved by the lunch bell.